EVERYWHERE THAT
TOMMY GOES

EVERYWHERE THAT TOMMY GOES

Howard K. Pollack

Image by Marlene Piskin; cover design by Marlene Piskin and Natanya Wheeler.

Produced with the assistance of The Stonesong Press
www.stonesong.com

ISBN-13: 9781497524590

To Mom: you inspire me with your relentless passion for books. You radiate a softness and love that is unmatched by anyone I have ever encountered. I am because of you.

To Dad: you are my hero. You are a man of few words who says so much. You have shown me the way with love, understanding, and honesty. If I shine, it is because of your light.

To my brothers: I love you all and regret that I don't say it enough.

To my wife: you are my sounding board and my critic. This story is far better because of you.

To my children: you move me, you are my future, and you make my life worth living.

Thank you all for believing in me.

"All human beings . . . are commingled out of good and evil."
—*Robert Louis Stevenson*

PROLOGUE

The blue glow emanating from the night-light plugged into the wall of Tommy Sullivan's bedroom cast murky shadows across the floor. The bed creaked as Tommy turned and rolled uncomfortably under the covers, wetness dampening his pajamas in the most embarrassing of places for an eight year old. He jumped up midway through the recurring dream that had plagued him for three years. He still didn't quite understand it, but he knew deep down that something very bad had happened when he was born. It had all blown up after his fifth birthday celebration, and the dream always jolted him awake just as his mother screamed, "I want him back."

Tommy reached out for the baby blanket that lay securely by his side. When he couldn't locate it, his heart began to pound against his chest. He sat up and switched on the lamp beside his bed. Light flooded the room. He still couldn't find his security blanket. After a few seconds of panic, he remembered that his mom had said that he would have to go without it for the night because it was being washed.

Tears began to flow. He pulled the covers over his head and started to wail.

But no one came to comfort him.

PART ONE

CHAPTER ONE

I don't know how many punches I've taken, but the metallic taste of warm blood is overwhelming. Dazed, I can still hear them laughing. The bigger guy's laugh is deeper. He's got my arms pinned behind my back, and I feel his hot, stale breath against my ear. The smaller guy snorts a laugh, and every time he hits me, my brain rattles.

I tighten up, waiting for him to belt me again, when another dude comes out of nowhere. Moving like lightning, he blocks the next punch, spins the guy around, and unleashes a barrage of blows that drop the guy cold. The big guy is slow to react, but he soon lunges forward and squares off. The new guy takes a boxing stance, quickly pivots, and connects with a rear-leg round kick to the head. The big guy wobbles for a second, regains his composure, and charges, swinging wildly.

The dude steps aside and absorbs a glancing blow across the chin. He shrugs it off, follows the big guy, and shoves him from behind. Stumbling forward, the big guy regains his balance and turns, but the dude is already waiting for him. He nails him with a throat strike, follows with a leg sweep, and the guy goes down. Then he positions himself on the big guy's chest, all MMA, and starts pummeling his face.

After the first few punches, the big guy is out, but the dude keeps punching away like a madman. I pull him back by the shoulders. He looks up at me—all crazy eyes—almost slugs me, then he starts laughing. After a second, he looks down at the blood on his fists. Then, all casual, he stands up, licks his knuckles, and sticks out his hand.

"Troyer Savage, at your service," he says, as calm as can be.

I look at him sideways, wipe my forearm across my mouth, and hesitantly push out my hand to shake his. "Thanks, dude, but where the hell did you come from?"

He grins, showing the straightest, whitest teeth I've ever seen. "Back at the club, I happened to see you hitting on that punk's girlfriend. Not too smooth, by the way. When he and his buddy followed you outside, I had a feeling you might need some assistance."

"Thanks. Those guys would have killed me if you didn't step in."

"Probably, but lets book before the cops show up." He pulls me by the elbow and starts to run.

I follow him at a quick pace for a few blocks, barely able to keep up. Then he slows to a jog and finally stops in front of a Japanese restaurant. A lighted sign says: SHIKI. He starts laughing again. "Now that was fun, wasn't it?"

Breathing heavily, I bend over, hands on my thighs. Staring down at the sidewalk, I suck wind for a few more seconds. "You call that fun? I think my nose is busted, along with a few ribs. That's not my idea of entertainment."

"Oh, come on, you don't look so bad. Besides, I gave them a lot worse than you took. That should make you feel better."

"Not really," I say, finally catching my breath. "Hey, where'd you learn to fight like that anyway?"

"Forget it. Let's go inside. I feel like sushi." Then, almost as an afterthought, he says, "I'm sorry. I don't even know your name."

"Name's Tommy, Tommy Sullivan . . . and how can you think about eating at a time like this?"

"Because I'm hungry."

"Well I'm sick to my stomach."

Troyer chuckles, "You need to toughen up, Sullivan." He pulls open the door, walks through the place like he owns it, and sits down at a table.

I follow behind and slide onto the seat across from him. "I gotta say, you're blowing my mind here. How can you be so calm?"

"Hey, this is no big deal, just relax."

Seconds later, the waiter appears with the menus. "Good evening, would you care for anything to drink before I take your order?"

Troyer answers quickly. "Bring out a double shot of Patron Silver and a large bottle of Sapporo beer."

I shake my head.

"Very well," he says, nodding as he walks away.

I lean in to Troyer. "No big deal! That was amazing! I've never seen anything like that in my life. Where'd you learn to fight like that?"

He flashes a perfect smile. "Please, that was nothing. I've been training since I was seven years old."

"Seven? Really? Tell me more."

"I'd rather not talk about it."

"Come on, I've never seen anyone kick ass like that. You have to clue me in."

"Trust me, how I became who I am is not as glamorous as you suspect."

"What's that supposed to mean?"

"It means that you shouldn't be so impressed. Necessity is the mother of invention. Sometimes we have no choice. Life directs us and we cannot control it. I am who I am and I do what I do because I wasn't given a choice. While the end result may be different, I'm sure it's the same with you. Go ahead tell me a little about your past and I'll prove it."

"Honestly, I'm probably the most boring, lame-ass loser who ever lived. Do you really think I want to explore that after watching you destroy two guys like they were nothing? Frankly, I'd rather hear about you."

"Maybe later." Troyer grabs my wrist. "Right now there's something else on my mind."

"Huh. Like what?"

"Like, I don't believe in coincidences. From the moment I saw you fumbling at the bar I had this feeling about you. I think fate put us together so I could help to rescue you from being a so-called 'lame-ass loser.'"

I pull my hand away and look at him crossways. "What the fuck are you talking about? All I know is that you just wiped the floor with two guys like it was nothing. That was sick! I still can't believe it, even though I saw with my own eyes. I want to know how you can do that shit."

The waiter interrupts, puts down the shot and pours the beer into a glass. "Are you ready to order?"

Troyer orders a sushi and sashimi combo.

I shake my head "no" again. The waiter nods, and walks away.

Troyer hoists the glass and takes a sip. "Ahh, now that's good. I just love an ice-cold brew after a fight." He puts down the beer and pushes the shot toward me. "Come on, shoot it. You'll feel better."

"I don't know dude, that's a double."

"Don't be such a pussy."

"Hey, I'm no pussy. But I'd sure like to be able to do what you just did."

"You, and every other tough guy wannabe that ever lived."

"Yeah, so, then tell me, where'd you learn to do that shit?"

Troyer smiles, gestures to the shot, then to my mouth. "I'll think about it. In the meantime, show me you're a man and throw that back."

I roll my eyes, hoist the shot, and down it.

Troyer slaps the table hard. "Excellent! You do have balls after all. Now tell me a little bit more about yourself."

My throat burning from the tequila, I push out a breath and force an awkward grin. "I don't get it. Why would you be interested in anything about me? I mean, this is probably the craziest night I ever had."

"Forget that. I saved your life, didn't I?"

"Yeah, you did."

"Okay, so don't you think that entitles me to know a little bit more about you?"

"I suppose. But to be honest with you, my life has been pretty dull, until now."

"Maybe, maybe not. Why not let me be the judge?" Troyer sucks in a deep breath, holds it for a second, and blows it out. "Okay, I can see you won't give up, so I'll go first. Just be prepared. This is no fairy tale." He takes a big swig of beer, puts the glass down, and pushes it away. "It's like this. I grew up in an orphanage. And the kids there were very tough. If you didn't stand up for yourself, you got the shit kicked out of you every day. It was a Catholic place, and one of the priests saw that I was being bullied all the time, so he offered to teach me how to fight.

He acted as if he really cared for me. In fact, I quickly discovered that he had an ulterior motive. Ultimately, I had to make a choice; learn to fight from Father Ryan, and allow him to . . . ," Troyer hesitates, looking up at the ceiling. "Or get beaten up every day."

"You mean he . . ."

"Yes."

"Oh my God!"

"God had nothing to do with it."

"So why couldn't you just tell them what was going on?"

"Them!" Troyer shouts under his breath. "Who the fuck do you think I could have told? Do you really believe the Church would ever listen to a piece of crap like me? Anyway—and I can't believe I'm actually telling you this—it's not the point. Father Ryan taught me basic fighting skills. Then I ran away from the orphanage and took to the streets. I survived on my own for years, doing the dirtiest jobs a kid could ever do. I ran drugs, I fronted for pimps and their whores, I slept in alleys, I ate from garbage pails . . . then fate stepped in. I hooked up with the first guy in my life that ever did right by me. He gave me a job cleaning the locker room and the toilets at a kickboxing gym. In exchange, he gave me lessons, fed me, and let me crash in the storage room. Being in that place night and day, watching all these tough guys beat each other up, was mind-blowing. I decided right away that I had to become an expert, so I could return to the orphanage and kill Father Ryan."

"Holy shit! So what happened? Did you ever go back there?"

Troyer shoots me a wide smile, raises his glass, and takes a long swallow. "Now it's your turn."

...

It's only been a month or so since our first encounter, but I can honestly say that meeting Troyer Savage has been a turning point in my life. He is a very different kind of dude. Not only is he a badass: He's also a chick magnet. I swear he is the ultimate player. He's real good-looking, like some movie star or something, and all the chicks want him. I'm not joking—*all* of them. From the hottest party girls to the darkest Goth chicks, he gets them all. Thick, wavy blond hair, high cheekbones, and a tight build can take you far, but Troyer takes it to the next level. And no, if you think I'm gay, you're dead wrong. Furthest thing from it. I'm just saying.

Anyway, I've been hanging out with him a lot lately, and he's been schooling me on the finer points about picking up women and how to handle myself in a bar. It's been quite a learning experience. I mean, I'm no slouch, but I don't carry it the way he does. I'm just a regular guy. I work at a pizza place and volunteer at an animal shelter. Troyer, though—he's cut from a totally different mold. I'm not ashamed to admit it, but I want to be more like him, so I've been watching him and taking notes. I know he doesn't mind. You see, he's taken me under his wing, and tonight's my next lesson.

Troyer is planning on hooking up with these two hot babes at Club Radical, down on Fourth Street. He told me that if I get there by 10:30, he'll hook me up with this righteous brunette who has a tongue piercing. I think he just wants me to occupy her while he locks it in with her girlfriend. No prob though. I'm game for that, that's for damn sure.

Now this guy moves like nobody else. He's got this swagger when he walks, this drawl when he talks, and a killer smile that chicks just can't resist. And like I said before, I've never met anyone like him. I've got to figure out how he does it and make it my own.

I pull up to the club knowing for sure he's inside with a posse of girls surrounding him, all dripping wet. The place is rocking.

I pass all the dorks lined up trying to get in and walk to the door. This six-and-a-half foot bouncer with a neck the size of my thigh is checking IDs. I slide on up to him. "Tommy Sullivan," I say, because Troyer told me he'd get my name on the list.

"Sullivan, huh?" he says, eyeballing me like I'm from Long Island or something.

"That's right," I say, as tough as I can.

So the jock-head looks at this list he's holding, as if it's the freaking Bible, looks back at me again, and—get this—he steps aside, lifts up the rope, and ushers me past like I'm some big-time celebrity. Just like that, I'm inside one of the hottest clubs in the city.

Some new Lady Gaga shit is pounding in the background while these pasty, eye-shadowed chicks, sporting six-inch stilettos, are standing around and texting. *Texting.* And the dudes, all swervy and ripping outta their shirts—probably juicing on the latest steroids and hanging little pinky-dicks— they're posing and flexing, probably thinking that'll impress the babes.

I look down toward the end of the mirrored bar, where the waitresses drop their orders and pick up their drinks, and Troyer is standing right in the middle of the action, working it. These chicks are the hottest I've ever seen. And if you ask Troyer, that's what brings in all the muscle. Fuckin' guys, all thinking they can get the waitresses and barmaids, so they tip 'em like crazy, all horned up and wearing dumb looks on their faces. Trouble is they've got nothing new to say. Those chicks have already heard every line ten times over. At least that's what Troyer says.

The bar is three-deep, so I squeeze my way between two jerks drinking Buds, who look like they're in the middle of a swillin' contest to see who can swallow a bottle in one damn swig. A crowd of tight-skirted girls is busy yapping it up, trying to look hot and get the attention of the group of guys hovering around.

I slide up next to Troyer. "Hey, Tommy," he says, stepping away from the bar and smiling. He hands me a shot and a brew. "Drink up, then I've got a present for you."

"Thanks dude, but what are you talking about?"

"Just do the shot first."

I toss it back and chase it with a swig of the brew. "Nice."

Troyer reaches into his pocket, pulls out a silver necklace, and hands it to me.

"Very cool. What is it?"

"This, my friend, is the phoenix. It signifies strength and the ability to conquer against all odds. It's for you. If you ever start to question yourself, just hold it between your fingers and repeat over and over again that you are indestructible. Remember, you are only limited by the thoughts in your head. If you think you can do something, you can."

"Wow, man, I'm touched. I can't believe you're actually giving this to me."

"No sweat, it's for good luck, so wear it all the time. It will remind you that even when I'm not by your side, I'll still be with you in spirit."

"Thanks." I fasten it around my neck.

Troyer reaches out and holds it in his palm. "Yessir, Tommy Boy. That is one fine piece." Then he slaps my face playfully. "Okay, now pay attention. You see that babe over there?" He points up the bar to this gorgeous blond bartender, checks his look in the mirror, and gives me a perfect, toothy smile. "She's all mine. Watch me work it, and learn how it's done." He stares right into my eyes and says, "Just keep your distance, you got it?"

He eases his way through the crowd, and they all step aside like he's Moses parting the Red Sea. I follow right behind before the floodwaters fill up and drown me. He stops in front of the babe as she's serving a fat, hairy dude who's wearing a yellow Ed Hardy T-shirt, all that colorful crap on its front. A shirt that probably hasn't seen the laundry in—shit, forever.

Troyer doesn't say a thing. He just turns sideways, puts his left elbow on the bar, and leans in real close. With two fingers, he motions to the knockout. The chick comes right over and leans into him from the other side of the bar. They're almost nose-to-nose. "Patron Silver, luv," rolls off his tongue in—get this—a fuckin' Australian accent.

"You want that chilled?" she asks.

Troyer shakes his head and looks deeply into her eyes. "Where I come from, luv, we take it pure or not at all." He grins again. "To dilute perfection is senseless, don't you agree?"

"Are we talking about drinks?" she asks him, like she really cares.

"I'm talking about everything . . . life, in general, and all it has to offer."

"Interesting analogy," she says, "but way too deep for a place like this." She smiles, turns, and walks down the bar to serve some loudmouth, big-haired Goth chick.

Troyer turns and whispers in my ear, "She'll be back quick. Just watch."

Two minutes later, she's back with his drink. Sliding it across the bar, she says, "Where you from, handsome?"

"Down Under, luv," he answers, in that same bullshit accent. Man, it's smooth, though. I didn't even know he could talk like that.

Grinning, the chick says, "I figured as much." Then she goes, "That'll be twelve bucks, tourist, but the next one is on me."

Troyer turns to me for a second, smiles quick-like, and nods me off, like I should just disappear. Then he turns back to the babe and slides her a hundred-dollar bill. "What makes you think I'm a tourist?"

"Well, aside from the accent—mate," she giggles, "you don't have that phony, tough-guy, New York attitude I see here night after night."

"Truth is, luv, I'm just passing through—visiting my cousin for a spell and don't know my way around here at all. He's working tonight, so I'm on my own."

Now, I'm barely hearing all this, because I move down the bar and act like I don't know him. But I have to say, the dude is smooth. He's got the attention of the hottest bartender in the place in less than two minutes. I definitely have to get me an accent.

I watch him for a while as the chick bounces around serving people, making drinks, and doing the whole bartender thing. But every few minutes, she comes back to him and smiles all sweet and shit. Meanwhile, I keep trying to get his attention. He either flat-out ignores me or gives me these looks like I should take a hike or something. I guess he wants to make her believe he's really a tourist and doesn't know anyone, so I can't blame him. But shit, now I'm gonna miss out on the brunette with the tongue piercing.

Finally, when the chick leaves the bar for a minute, he walks over to me and leans in, mouth to ear. "Sorry, Tommy Boy. I got this thing going on here, and I don't want to mess it up. She thinks I'm from Australia and I don't know anyone. I'm getting her to show me around later on, when she gets off. She's going to cut out at one, just for me." Apparently, I didn't hear their entire conversation. Troyer is always smoother than I even expect him to be. "I'll make it up to you another time, I promise. And hey, look—you can still hang out here. Just don't make like you know me."

"No problem," I say to him, but I don't mean it. This totally sucks. I'm not real good all alone in places like this. I hate feeling like a fly on the wall, just peering at everything and looking desperate. But you know what? I'll tough it out—watch him and learn.

"You sure you're going be okay?" he asks me.

"Yeah, I'm sure. But what about those other chicks you were supposed to meet?"

"Don't sweat it," Troyer says, as he takes out his cell and punches in a number. "I'm going to call them right now and tell them I can't make it out tonight. They'll be cool about it. Women always are."

Maybe they are to him, but not to me.

So he calls the chicks and blows them off. They don't seem to care—at least it sounds like they're cool about it. I mean, Troyer smiles at me and nods the okay, just before the hot bartender chick comes back and he snubs me.

So I back off, disappear into the crowd, and watch him play her for a bit. Then I wander around, find my way to the other bar, and hit the sauce real hard. Later on, I come back for another look. By this time, Troyer's got the babe leaning in on him and smiling so much that she's ignoring the rest of the dudes at the bar. Me, I'm piss-drunk from tequila shots and feeling no pain.

After a time, Troyer nods at her, pulls away from the bar, and heads for the back of the club. Sure enough, within a few seconds, the hottie whispers something in the other bartender's ear and slides out of the bar. I figure now's the time to head out and follow Troyer, so I ease away from my spot and leave through the back door. Troyer doesn't see me as I slip out and hide behind this smelly green dumpster. *I'll just wait and watch what he does.*

A couple minutes later, Troyer walks out with the girl on his arm. I knew it: the dude picked her up just like he said he would. So I follow them, staying far enough behind to see but not close enough to hear what they're saying. It doesn't matter, though: I can figure it all right. He's probably telling her how strange it is coming here from another country and not know-ing anything about the place, and she's probably telling him not to worry, that she'll show him around just fine.

So they walk around for a bit, and he leads her down a dark alley. I guess maybe he's planning on banging her just for a laugh. Anyway, I creep up on them and hide myself against a steel doorway that probably leads into some sleazy peep show dive. I half-expect the door to swing open any second, some drunk-ass lowlife stumbling out while holding a little brown bag that hides a bottle of Colt 45. Whatever, I have to see what Troyer's up to.

They're both arm-in-arm and walking together until they get behind this heap of garbage piled up next to a dumpster—I knew it! They start making out, and he slides his hand along her leg and up her skirt, real smooth and sexy-like. Then—get this—she pulls his hand away and stops kissing him. Two seconds later, she reaches up with both hands and pushes him off at the chest.

Troyer steps backs, tilts his head to the side, and stares at her. Then, before I can blink, he reaches up and slices her throat with a knife. The chick goes down like her legs have been cut off at the knees. No sound, no reaction—she just collapses and dies right there.

Without thinking, I let out a puke-like hurl sound and scream, "Troyer! What the fuck!" Troyer turns around, sporting this blank stare and a distorted smile that creeps me out so bad that I feel like I'm laid out in a snake pit, tied to the ground and three dozen snakes are crawling all over me. I can't move.

"You like that, Tommy Boy?" he asks, still in the Australian accent he pulled out of nowhere.

I just stand there staring at the dead chick with my mouth open wide.

"Say something, mate," Troyer says, turning and looking up at the sky, bellowing out a throaty, psycho laugh. Then he raises the knife skyward and shakes his fist like a goddamn lunatic.

I still can't speak and just fall to my knees hurling up all the chips I ate along with all the tequila I drank. Troyer kneels down, too, and coughs a bit, still howling that sicko laugh.

Finally, he stops ranting. My heart is beating against my chest so hard that it feels like it's going to burst out. It gets real quiet for a time, and then, out of nowhere, Troyer goes, "Okay, Tommy Boy, now we must dispose of the bitch and cover our tracks."

It's weird, because the dude is still talking in that hammed-up Australian lingo. It's like he's a totally different person.

"This is crazy, Troyer," I say, finally finding my voice. "I'm outta here. Don't bring me in on this shit."

"Don't be such a wuss, mate, or I may have to slice you, too," he says, pointing the knife at me. "You're not going anywhere. You and I are going to make this all go away. We're going to take lovey here and make her disappear. Go get your car and bring it around, before someone else shows up. Even a fool can see it already looks like you did this. After all, it's your vomit staining the pavement. And that's all the authorities will need."

I look down at the pile of puke and another wave of nausea comes over me. Frozen in place, I just keep staring.

"Quit screwing around, mate," Troyer yells in a hush. "Get a move on."

I'm drunk and scared shitless, but Troyer's voice brings me back to reality. I shake it off and bolt, like half a dozen MS-13 gang members are on my ass.

Ten minutes later, I pull my car into the alley.

There's no sign of Troyer.

The motherfucker bailed on me.

CHAPTER TWO

I'm totally screwed. My puke is sitting ten feet from a dead girl. If I don't get the body out of here fast, some TV series CSI will catch me like a one-show loser starring in a two-hour premiere.

Moving quickly, I lift her into the trunk of my car but not before getting blood all over my clothes. I slam down the hatch and channel *CSI*. I've got to get rid of the puke, so I grab a pizza box I've got stored in the back seat and use it like a shovel. After tossing it all into the dumpster, I jump back in my car, and haul ass. No one sees me.

As drunk as I am, I know this is wrong, but something inside me has already taken over. Maybe it's because Troyer saved my life, maybe it's because I know how hard it was for him growing up, or maybe it's because I'm scared shit of the dude. Whatever it is, it's too late for second guesses. I just know that I need to get far away from the city before I hide her.

I speed off and drive over the Brooklyn Bridge, leaving the lights of Manhattan behind me. As I cross into Brooklyn, I hear the dead girl calling out: "Troyer, what'dya do to me?" I shiver and open the window to clear my head.

I know she's dead, but I still hear her calling out over and over again: "Troyer, let me go, let me go." I turn up the radio to drown out my imagination while I follow the highway around to the Belt Parkway. The voice is lost within the music and the wind. I keep my pace at 60 miles an hour, which is fast enough to avoid suspicion but not so fast that I attract the attention of some dickhead cop.

With the radio blasting and air rushing through the open window, my mind races. I start to wonder if there really is any DNA in puke. I mean, I probably could have left the girl right there and no one would have been the wiser. As quickly as it comes to me, I shake off the thought. There's no turning back for me now. I've heard it said that you can't un-ring a bell, and now I know what it means. I'm in this thing up to my neck.

I continue through Queens and get on the Southern State Parkway, which takes me to the Meadowbrook Parkway, where I head toward Jones Beach. This brings me onto Ocean Parkway, where I go east. The lights along the road blur together in a haze while my brain jumps from one crazy thought to another. Led by a force beyond my control, I find myself at a desolate spot by Gilgo Beach. I pull over, get out, and take the girl from the trunk. The dim moonlight casts an eerie glow. I can't bring myself to look at her face, so I set her down, grab her by her legs, and drag her a few hundred feet through the brush. Winded, I suck in heavy breaths, and a foul, salty odor materializes on my tongue, which reminds me of the stale smell the ocean sometimes unleashes at low tide. I close my mouth, but the odor penetrates my nostrils. I can't take much more, so I quickly cover her with some dead weed grass and bolt.

The trip back to my house feels like an eternity, but I pull into my driveway less than an hour later. Bellerose is darkly quiet. As I walk through the front door, a faint light in the den focuses my attention on the table beside the armchair, where a half-empty bottle of whiskey sits. Routine Friday evening for dear old Dad. Keeping silent, I head down to the basement bedroom where I live, grab some rags from the laundry room, and head back outside to clean my car. I can't leave any evidence around to link me to all this. Later on, when it gets light, I'll hose her down some more and bleach out the trunk. Bleach cleans away blood real well. Again, I've got to thank *CSI* for that info. I remember one show where the killer used bleach to clean up the blood. He almost got away with it, but they still managed to track him down. They always catch them on TV. But this is real life, and real life doesn't wrap itself up so easily. I pray that, so long as I'm careful, I'll be fine.

I clean the trunk as best I can in the dark. Then, after I'm done, I bag up the rags and my clothes—even gotta give up my Nike sneakers—and jam them under my bed. I'll ditch it all later. Then I take a hot shower, scrub myself raw, and hit the sack. It's almost six AM, and I'm still too wired to sleep. So I switch on the tube and channel surf for a bit, trying hard to lose myself in the never-ending parade of unimportant images.

CHAPTER THREE

I wake up to the sound of my dad stomping around in the kitchen. The smell of frying bacon penetrates my room. It takes me a few seconds to separate dream from reality, but when I look under my bed and see the plastic bag jammed underneath, I realize that last night was not a dream. Bile rises from my stomach and I'm about to puke, so I run into the bathroom and splash water on my face. My head is still foggy from almost no sleep, but I have to finish cleaning my car and get rid of the evidence. I also have to face Dad and act normal, so he doesn't get suspicious.

I take a few breaths and calmly walk upstairs. There he is, standing over the stove in a ratty gray sweatshirt, frying breakfast up like some sweaty diner cook. In one practiced motion, he lifts the pan from the fire, turns, and dumps everything onto a plate. Then he gives me a nasty look.

"Mornin', kiddo," he snarls. "Out damn late last night, weren't ya?"

I swallow hard, as the scene from last night quickly replays itself, and I see myself dragging the bartender through the weed grass.

Dad barks at me, "I said, '*Out damn late last night, weren't ya?*'"

"Uh . . . no, Dad," I say, returning to the present. "You were sleeping. I didn't want to disturb you. I was home by one."

"Bullshit. I didn't fall asleep until well after one."

"Okay, maybe it was one-thirty." Man, he's a ball-breaker. Ever since Mom cut out on us back when I was a kid, he's been a real prick to me—like it was my fault she left. I know it wasn't, though. Dad is just an asshole—drunk all the time, out of work a lot, and just plain mean.

"Did you enjoy yourself?" he asks, with a look of disgust.

"As a matter of fact, I did. I went out with my friends. We grabbed some chow and hit a bar in Manhattan."

"You didn't drink, did you, Shithead?"

"Not really, Dad. Just a couple of beers, that's all." He hates it when I drink. I don't know why, since he drinks every damn night.

"That's good, Tommy," he says, as he sits down with a full plate, leaving nothing for me.

Then he starts shoveling the grub into his mouth as fast as he can. I don't think the old man even chews anymore.

"Listen, Tommy," he says, egg slime dripping down his chin, "I'm going over to the track today—got a line on a good horse in the second race—so make sure you clean this place up before you go anywhere." Then he swings his arm around, backhands me in the thigh, and hollers, "You hear me, Shithead?"

"Yeah, Dad. Quit it! You almost hit me in the nuts!"

"Just don't forget what I said."

I should have figured it'd be a waste of time to even come upstairs. I can't remember the last time he even left a few scraps for me. I head back down, get dressed, and wait until he leaves. Then I grab the bleach and head out to my Honda.

In the bright daylight, I see all the blood I missed earlier, so I hose down my car again and bleach the trunk with this color-safe stuff from the laundry.

Once I'm done, I grab the bag from under my bed, toss it in the trunk, and head out. I drive around for a while, trying to find a good place to ditch the bag. It doesn't take long before I pull into a MacDonald's on Lakeville Road. I drive through and order a Big Mac meal. Then I park next to a dumpster to eat. When I'm done, I toss the bag, and all the evidence in the dumpster. Then I take my baby over to the car wash and run her through, just to make sure I didn't miss anything. In a twisted but funny way, she's never been cleaner.

With all angles covered, I start wondering about Troyer again. He surprised the hell out of me last night. What would make him kill a girl like that? Then again, with his history, who knows? But slicing a girl's throat? I still can't wrap my head around it. And now I'm stuck right in the middle. I never should have moved the body. What was I thinking? I really must have been wasted.

I drive around aimlessly for a while unable to stop reliving last night. Then I start to wonder if anyone has reported the girl missing. I race back home and turn on my computer.

Now I'm not what you would call a computer geek, but I do know that news travels fast on the internet.

Paranoid, I spend the rest of Saturday on line but nothing comes up. By nine PM my head starts pounding so I take some migraine pills and climb into bed.

...

Early Sunday morning a beeping sound beckons me from a dream world where I'd prefer to remain. I stumble to my computer and turn off the alarm. The screen lights up and AOL is still scrolling the latest news. I watch the newsreel for a few seconds and a short article comes up which reports the disappearance of a bartender from Club Radical. No specific details are given. Freaking out, I switch on the TV and stop on a local news channel that's talking about the missing girl.

I turn up the sound as a pretty, dark-haired reporter begins speaking: "In a breaking story, we're live in the Village, outside Club Radical, where, Friday night, a young bartender disappeared before the end of her shift. The local hotspot, which caters to the chic, twenty-something crowd, is a melting pot that attracts tourists and locals, as well as people from Long Island and New Jersey. The police will have their hands full as they try to sort this out. So far, we have learned that the girl's roommate reported her missing when she didn't come home Saturday morning. Additionally, the police have cordoned off an alley nearby, where they have discovered a substantial amount of dried blood on the pavement."

The TV screen flashes to a picture of the girl as the reporter continues: "The missing girl's name is Jamie Houston. She is shown here in a recent picture. If anyone in our viewing area has any information, please call the number at the bottom of the screen."

I get up from my chair and walk over to the TV, totally focused on the photo. Man she is one pretty girl. She's nothing like the heavily made up chick I saw teasing the guys on the other side of the bar at Club Radical. She looks so innocent in that picture I can't believe it's the same girl. But it is. My stomach churns as I envision rats crawling all over her at Gilgo.

In a panic, I return to my computer and refine the search. In seconds the responses tell all. The story is all over the Web.

Not good. I keep surfing and settle on a news site, where I click on the video. An elderly reporter, suited up and sporting a heavily dyed, black moustache, stares into the camera. The site is clearly second-rate, but something inside tells me to continue watching.

"Carson Devlin here, bringing you the latest development in the disappearance of Jamie Houston. Our sources tell us that NYPD detectives have interviewed a number of patrons from the bar who said she was talking to a handsome blond man, dressed in a black button-down shirt. Apparently, the surveillance cameras were under repair and no video was available. However, one of the bartenders told the police that the missing girl cut out before her shift ended so she could meet up with a guy who was in town for a visit. In addition there have been reports of an older model Honda speeding away from the scene at a time that corresponds with the disappearance."

Holy shit . . . I've got to book.

CHAPTER FOUR

By Monday morning, I'm itchier than a flea-bitten mutt waiting in line to get euthanized at the local pound. I don't even bother telling my dad that I'm leaving. I don't think he gives a crap, anyway.

I pack up a duffle, throw it in the back seat, grab a water from the fridge, and head out to Carmela's Pizza to talk to my boss, Mario. It's just after ten AM, and he's the only one in the restaurant.

"Hey, Tomas," he calls out, all off-the-boat Italian. "What you doing here so early? We not even open yet."

"I know, Mario. I just came by to ask you for some time off. I promised this girl I'd take her to visit her mother who's in a hospital down in Florida."

"Ahh, you good boy, Tomas. Take all time you need. You job always here."

"Thanks, Mario. That's great, but I need another favor."

"What you mean, 'favor'?"

"Well, actually I need a little advance pay. I'll be gone for a while."

"Money before work? I don't like do that."

"Come on, Mario. You've known me a long time. I'm good for it."

"Maybe, maybe not. How I be sure you come back and work off?"

I take off the watch my grandma gave me and hold it out. "I tell you what: this is worth at least five hundred dollars. Keep it until I return."

Mario takes it from me and eyeballs it. "Okay, Tomas, you good boy. I give you five hundred dollars." He puts the watch on his wrist and admires it. "I hold until you come back." He pulls out a wad of cash, peels off five crisp bills, and hands them over.

"Thanks, Mario. You're a great boss. I'll see you in a few weeks." I'm not thrilled that I had to give up the watch, but I need a bankroll more than I need to know what time it is right now.

It doesn't take long before I'm on the Verrazano Bridge, heading to Staten Island. I love this bridge. Whenever I cross it, I feel like I'm going on vacation. It goes back to when Mom and Dad used to take me away, after school ended, to celebrate the coming of summer. We'd go down the Jersey Shore, all the way to Cape May, and stay at this old hotel with these tiny rooms that had no TV. The bathrooms were down the hall. It was all they could afford, but it was a real vacation. To me, one whole week bumming around on the beach, eating hot dogs, and diving in the surf was really something special. Back then, Dad even played miniature golf with me. Those were the only times we were a real family.

I figure I'll head down to the Cape, since I know it so well. There are plenty of cheap places to stay this time of year. Not much going on in April. I can get some work at a pizza place or a gas station or something.

A few hours down the Pike, I need a break from driving, so I pull off the highway and find myself in this small town called Seaview, a half hour north of Atlantic City. Just a mile down the main road, I come across a place called The Tide's Inn. I head inside. The place smells like an old fish market on a muggy day with no ice to store the catch. The floorboards by the bar are all rotted and uneven. The top of the bar is slicked over with layers of polyurethane, making it shine like new, even though the rest of the place is so dilapidated it should have been closed down years ago. There's a large, handwritten sign that reads, BATTLE OF THE BANDS TONIGHT 8 PM

This short old man, with a fat, red nose limps down the bar to me. "You eating or drinking sport?" he asks me, all Irish.

"Both if you're serving lunch, mister; a beer if you're not."

"Serving food and drinks all day long here, laddie," he says, grinning like he knows something that I don't. "You plan on staying around a while?"

All of a sudden, a weird, paranoid feeling comes over me, like this bartender knows I stashed a dead girl and he wants me to stick around until the cops show up. It's not possible, but I feel like the old man is reading my mind. He keeps staring at me, and I get this queasy feeling like I should just book. I give him this lame smile and say, "You know what? Just gimme a shot of your best tequila and chase it with a Heineken for now."

"Coming up," he says, as he turns around to get my drinks.

Whew, that was close. What the hell is wrong with me? I'm thinking way too much. This old guy doesn't know anything, but I still feel like I better jet right after I down my drinks. I'll pick up some food later. Shit, I've never been paranoid before, but I think this whole thing is starting to freak me out.

"You with one of the bands?" the old man asks as he pours the Heineken.

"Nah, just passing through."

"Well you sure do look like one of those types we get in here during battle week. You picked a good time to pass through."

I just nod at him and slide him a twenty. I don't want to get into no heavy dio' with this guy. He gets the hint real quick, takes the dough, and walks to the register.

I down my drinks quickly and head back to my car. I get in and turn the key, but she won't start. I twist the key again, but she just keeps cranking and coughing. She won't turn over.

I sit there for a minute, then try once more. Same thing. So I head back to the bartender to see if he knows a mechanic.

"You forget something, laddie?" he asks, wiping down the bar where I was sitting.

"My car won't start. You know any mechanics nearby?"

"Mobil station down the road a piece. They have a few."

"You got a number?"

Fat old Irish reaches under the bar, pulls out a card, and hands it to me.

"Thanks," I say. Then I start getting the chills and feel like I'm being watched—or set up or something.

This is messed up. Something feels very wrong, and I don't like it one bit. I go back outside, pull out my cell, and call the number. I get some hick on the phone who tells me they'll be sending someone over soon and I should just wait. No shit— what else am I going to do?

While I'm standing by the car, a knock comes from the back. Then I hear bizarre laughter. I pull open the trunk, and, get this: It's fuckin Troyer.

CHAPTER FIVE

"Troyer! What the hell, where did you come from? And where the fuck did you go the other night?" He just climbs outta the trunk, grinning wide and laughing all psycho and shit. "Quit it, Troyer. Answer me."

Still laughing, he says, "You have to see the look on your face, mate—like you've seen a ghost."

"Screw you, man! And what's with that bullshit accent?"

"What are you talking about? This is how I've always spoken."

He says it to me like he totally believes it. This dude is unreal.

"Whatever. How the hell did you get in my trunk?"

Troyer grabs me by the shoulders. "I've been with you all along. I slipped in there right before you left home."

"You *what*?" I shout, pulling away from him. Then I take a few steps back, trying to gather my thoughts.

"Don't look so surprised. I saw you preparing to leave town, so I just jumped in."

"So why'd you leave me with the dead girl?"

"Leave you? *You* left *me*. You were gone for almost a half hour. I couldn't just wait there. Besides, the chick was alive when I left her. I checked, and she was breathing. She wasn't cut that deep. She was going to be all right."

"No way!"

"Yes, sir, Tommy Boy. She was still alive."

"Look, man, I'm telling you, she's dead. I dumped her body by the beach."

"Well, we have to go back and get her, mate."

"Are you nuts? I'm not going back there."

"Then this is all on your head, mate. I won't be held responsible for what you've done."

"*Me?* You're the one who slit her throat."

"I did not kill her, Tommy Boy, so if you'll excuse me, I've got to hit the head. Bouncing around in your trunk all morning has left me quite full."

Troyer turns and walks off as casual as can be. I'm totally blown away. I can't believe he actually hid in my trunk like that. Then, just as he disappears inside, a dude in a tow truck pulls up.

"Afternoon," he says as he shimmies out of the cab. Man, this dude is fat, and I don't mean regular fat like some guys. We're talking massive fat. He's got three chins and no neck, and he's wearing these big gray overalls. His nametag reads CHUNKY. No joke.

"What seems to be the trouble, pal?" he asks.

"My car won't start. Not sure what's wrong with her." I do a double take toward the bar, still flipped out about seeing Troyer.

"Lemme check it out."

I refocus as Fatso opens the door, leans in—stretching those overalls to the max—and pulls the hood latch. Then he waddles around to the front of the car and says, "Okay, pal, try and start her up."

I get in the car and turn the key. Same thing, she just keeps coughing and sputtering but doesn't kick in.

"Okay, hold it up," the Chunk-monster shouts from under the hood.

He fiddles around for a few more minutes and says, "Okay, try it now."

I try again—still nothing.

"That's enough," he yells as he comes over, dripping sweat. He pulls a rag from his rear pocket, dabs his forehead, and looks right through me. Wiping his hands, he says, "Got to take it back to the shop, pal, and hook it up to the computer."

"Is this going to take a while?" I ask him, like some dumbass schoolboy who doesn't know shit about cars.

"Not sure, pal, but it'll probably need parts, which means you're stuck here till tomorrow."

"That's just great. I've got no place to stay."

"There's a motel a half mile down the road," he says, pointing with his chubby index finger. "I could drop you there."

"Nah, that's okay. I'll hoof it after I've chowed down, if you know what I mean." And, trust me, he definitely knows what I mean.

"Suit yourself. I'll hook her up and be on my way. The shop is another half mile past the motel." He hands me a card. "Here's my number. You can call later if you want to check on the repair. The name's Chunky."

"I can see that," I say, trying not to smile.

I head back inside for the third time now, and there's the old man wiping down another corner of the bar. No one else has even come in, but he's still wiping the bar. Guess there's not much else to do around here.

"You again, laddie?" he Irishes at me. "They fix your car?"

"Nah, gotta tow her over to the shop and figure it out. Hey, where's the head?"

"Around back, through those doors." He points over to the corner, past the Battle of the Bands sign.

"Okay, be right back."

"Take your time. I'm not going anywhere, and the bands should be rolling in soon."

Any other time, I would have been excited about the entertainment, but right now, I couldn't care less. Anyway, the shitter is out back—I mean, real outside out back. It's a separate little shack set apart from the bar. A stand-alone crapper made from wood. I walk in and find Troyer sitting on the bowl, reading a newspaper, with his pants around his ankles.

"Is that you, Tommy Boy?" he asks me, looking up over the news.

"Quit playing games, Troyer. What's this all about? Why are you following me?"

"Like I said, I had to get out of the city bloody fast, and you're the one with a car. I was simply going to borrow it. When I arrived at your place and saw you toss your luggage in, I assumed you were packing to leave. I figured it would be a rip to surprise you, so I hopped in the trunk and hid."

I shake my head in disbelief. "Did you do something to my car so she won't start?"

"How could I do anything, mate? I was locked in your trunk."

At this point I'm suspicious, but I just don't know.

"So what's up with your car?"

"Don't know," I answer, still flustered. "They had to take it to the station."

"So what now?" he asks me, like I've got a plan.

"I've got no clue, but I'm stuck here for the night. Guess I'll eat, then check into the motel down the road. Later on, I'll call the mechanic. Once the car is fixed, I'm going to the Cape."

"Sounds good, mate. I'll join you. Just let me finish up here."

"I don't know, dude. You've caused me enough trouble. I think we should just go our separate ways."

His pants still around his ankles, Troyer gets up from the toilet and grabs me by the shoulders. "Are you daft? Haven't you realized by now that you need me? What I've taught you these past few weeks is only just the beginning." Then, with a look scarier than Robert De Niro in *Cape Fear*, he says, "This is the next phase of your education, Tommy Boy, and I won't allow you to give up now."

I pull away from him, more freaked-out than I've ever been in my entire life. This dude is seriously out of control. I don't even know what to say.

My eyes still on him, I back up toward the door. Troyer reaches down, pulls up his pants, and follows me outside.

"Hold on, mate. There's no place for you to go, so you might as well just follow my lead. I am truly here to help you."

I keep walking toward the bar, realizing that challenging him now is just not wise. I mean, I can't get away from him, so I better not make him mad. This dude is dangerous, and he could easily kill me. "Whatever," I say, as I open the door to the bar. Troyer doesn't follow me in.

Back inside, old Irish is arranging some glasses near the beer pulls.

"Gimme a burger, fries, and a Heineken." I say, all friendly and shit, because I know the old guy now. He nods, tosses his rag, and heads off to the kitchen.

After eating and downing a few brews, I ditch the dump and head off to the motel. Troyer is waiting for me out front. He follows alongside me as I walk down the road. He stays quiet for ten minutes, before he steps in front of me and flashes that toothy smile of his. "You know, mate, we should go back there tonight and check out the Battle of the Bands. I'm betting quite a few horny young ladies will be in attendance."

"You've got to be kidding me. You really think I want to watch you do your thing again? Then what—you gonna slice up another one?"

"Not sure, Tommy Boy. I suppose you'll just have to wait and see."

"No way, no how, no chance am I doing that."

"We shall see, mate, we shall see."

I get the shivers and start sweating. My body can't seem to make up its mind about being hot or cold, but I'm really starting to shake. Something bad is up with Troyer, and I can't get away from him.

We walk in silence for a while, finally reaching this dingy, wood-shingled building fronted by a yellow neon sign that reads, THE WATERSIDE. The place looks like it came right out of some old-time western movie, except the sign just doesn't fit. A porch runs along the entire front, and three cars are lined up facing the rooms.

We walk in. The place smells like curry. Troyer quietly says to me, "I'll handle this." Then he walks up to this pretty Indian girl sitting behind the counter. He leans in and slides his elbow along the counter, smiling all nice and shit. Fuckin' Troyer, he never passes up a chance to hit on a babe. Now, I'm not exactly sure what nationality she is—I mean she's got that medium dark complexion, she's got jet-black hair, and she's wearing one of those kerchief things on her head—so I figure she must be from India. But anyway, Troyer doesn't care. If they've got legs that end in a Y, he's game.

"Hello, luv," he says, all Australian. "Would you happen to have a room available for tonight?"

The girl smiles back at him. "Well, sir, it is Battle of the Bands week, and we have a lot of reservations."

Troyer turns around and winks at me. "I don't see many cars out front. You must have at least one room available, luv. I've come from very far away, my car's broken down, and I'm stuck for the night. Couldn't you find just one room here in this lovely place?"

Man he's talking sweet, and with that smile of his, there's no way she's refusing.

"Well, sir, I suppose for just one night I might have a room."

In five minutes, he's got the key. I still can't explain why I follow him, but I do. We head down to room 21, which is located around back. Well, at least it will be quiet with no street noise passing by.

As we walk inside, I get smacked in the face with a musty cigarette stench. "Shit, Troyer, this place stinks, and to top it off, I feel one of my nasty headaches coming on." I reach into my pocket, pull out my pills, and drop four—dry. "I've got to rest for a while." I take off my pants and shirt and dive onto one of the beds while I wait for the pills to kick in.

"You do that, mate. I need some fresh air, so I'm going to take a walk. I'll be back in a few."

I'm relieved when Troyer leaves, and part of me hopes he never returns. I stare at the ceiling for a bit before I doze off.

. . .

A car door slams and wakes me up. It's a little past nine PM. Sounds like people are starting to check in for the night. I look around—no sign of Troyer. I get up and turn on the light.

There's blood all over the place. The bed, my undershirt, my hands—everything is soaked.

Shocked, I look in the mirror and see that my face is streaked with blood, too. I bolt toward the bathroom, pull open the door, and find the girl from India laid out in the tub—naked and tied around the ankles. My eyes almost pop out of their sockets, and my mouth opens wide, but no sound comes out. The poor girl's wrists are bound and held up above her head by a rope suspended from the shower spout. Blood is still dripping from dozens of knife wounds all over her body. The bottom of the tub is a pool of red liquid. I drop to my knees, gag, and dry-heave. All at once, my stomach reverses, and I lose my lunch.

About to scream, I catch myself. If anyone hears me, I'm dead.

The whole room starts spinning.

. . .

Some time after midnight, I wake up in the same spot. Nothing's changed. The girl is still as dead as can be, and her blood is still everywhere. Fuckin' Troyer—he's done it to me again.

I pace the room back and forth, passing the mirror and looking, hoping to see someone else on the other side. Troyer, even—that backstabbing, stupid-ass, toothy-grin, murdering motherfucker.

CHAPTER SIX

It isn't until eight AM that I wake up, sunlight bursting through the blinds. No sign of Troyer. I leap out of bed and rush into the bathroom, hanging on a glimmer of hope that maybe this was all a dream. No such luck. The girl is still there drenched in blood. My knees get weak. I fall to the floor and start crying like a baby. I can't stop shaking, and I can't think straight. My heart slams against my chest, and I roll over, curl up into a ball, and wrap my arms around my shins. My mind is spinning out of control, so I stay in the fetal position, praying for my head to clear.

Slowly, reality sinks in and I get up, convinced that the only way to escape this nightmare is to wipe it out of my mind, forget it ever happened, and bolt before the cleaning crew comes around and finds the mess in the bathroom.

After splashing water on my face, I get dressed and scan the room hoping that I haven't left any evidence that can tie me to all this. Then I grab the white undershirt I left drying on the heater and stuff it in my crotch. I did my best to clean it last night, but it still has some faded bloodstains on it. If anyone finds this, I'm dead, so I can't leave it here. Gotta find a good place to ditch it.

Once I'm satisfied that I haven't left anything behind to screw me, I head off to the Mobil station. To buy extra time, I put the DO NOT DISTURB sign on the doorknob, then wipe away my fingerprints with a towel. I leave casually, still sweating bullets. Thank God no one is outside.

I walk for a half hour still trying to clear my head of the horror behind me and knowing that when I get to the shop, I'm going to have to put on an act to avoid suspicion. I keep trying to fill my mind with nonsense thoughts to distract me, and by the time I reach the gas pumps, I'm back in control. After a few deep breaths, I ease my way into the garage bays. Chunky's head is buried in my baby's hood. He's still wearing the same pair of overalls. At least I think they're the same pair—unless the dude's got a rack of 'em back at his crib—which isn't as strange as you think and is a perfect example of the kind of nonsense I have to focus on to distract me.

You see, a while back I watched this story about Albert Einstein. It seems he had a rack of identical shirts and pants all hanging in the closet, so he never had to think about what he was going to wear. I suppose he was too busy thinking about that relativity crap to waste time worrying about what to put on for the day. Maybe Chunky is the same way. He's probably all messed-up thinking about what he's going to eat, that he can't be bothered deciding about what to wear. Anyway, I sneak up and tap him on the back. The dude jumps right out of his skin and almost hits his head.

"Are you crazy, pal?" he yells. "You scared the piss outta me."

"Sorry—I just wanted to see if my car was fixed."

"Can't you see I'm working on it, you idiot?" Then he stares me up and down with this real nasty look.

"Like I said, sorry. Don't get your balls in an uproar."

"Gimme a few more minutes," he says, shaking his head. "I'm almost done putting in the parts. Go wait by the office. And don't creep up on me again!"

I leave the garage and walk around, looking for a place to get rid of my undershirt. I'm not surprised when I find a dumpster out back. Perfect. No one will ever look in there.

I reach in, lift up some greasy old car parts, and stick the shirt underneath. Then I head back to the office and sit down on this bench. I've got some time on my hands and don't want to think about the girl in the bathroom again, so I start thinking about how Chunky jumped when I tapped him, and I start laughing. Lucky no one else is around or they'd think I was nuts or something, just laughing out of nowhere. But you know what? That was pretty funny. I mean, I've never seen someone that big move that fast. In fact, I don't think I've ever seen someone that fat move, period.

A half hour later, Chunky waddles out of the garage. "Come on over and start her up for me."

"About time. You sure she's fixed?"

"I'll bet my lunch on it."

"Could be a big bet."

"Funny, pal—real funny. Just get in and start her up. And make it fast. I've got other cars to work on today."

I get in and turn the key. The engine roars to life. "Yeah, boy, you did it. She's fixed!"

"That'll be a hundred fifty bucks for the car and another twenty for my lunch."

"Hey, I never agreed to that. Besides, twenty bucks is way too much for lunch, even for you."

"All right, then, that'll be a hundred seventy bucks for the car. I'll pay for my own lunch."

"What? You've got to be kidding. That don't seem fair."

"It's fair to me. Now pay up if you want your car back."

"Damn!" I can't believe this porker is hanging me up for the extra dough, but I don't want to make any waves here. I just want to jet. So I reach into my pocket, pull out the cash, and hand it to him.

"Thanks, pal. And next time you're in town . . . don't bother to look me up."

I don't answer. I'm never coming back here anyway. I pop the trunk—to make sure Troyer isn't hiding in there—slam it closed, and take off.

CHAPTER SEVEN

Driving toward the Garden State Parkway, I spot a hitchhiker in the distance. As I close in, I realize its Troyer. Part of me says to keep driving, and part of me says to stop. Don't ask me why, but yeah, I pick him up. He jumps in, flashing that stupid-ass grin of his.

"Good day, mate," he says, pleasant as the morning sun. "How's it hanging?"

"Are you shitting me?" I say, totally blown away. "How could you kill that girl and leave me like that?"

"Pardon me, Tommy Boy: I didn't kill anyone. What are you talking about? If memory serves me correctly, you fell asleep on the bed. When I returned from my walk, I tried to wake you, but you were out cold. I decided to revisit the bar and check out the bands. While I was there, I hooked up with a very sexy lassie and spent the night with her. When I went back to the motel this morning, you didn't answer the door, so I started down the road, hoping to hitch a ride to the Cape."

"That's a load of crap, dude. You're setting me up."

"I'm afraid not, mate," he says, so innocently it makes my skin crawl.

Part of me says I should keep pressing him, and part of me says it's a waste of time. Don't ask me why, but yeah, I reach for the radio and crank up the tunes. But even with the music blasting, I can't stop my mind from racing. How could Troyer do all of this? The dude is out of control.

Troyer closes his eyes, tilts his head back, and goes to sleep. Amazing.

I drive along the highway for an hour or so and try to focus on the music, but my mind keeps replaying the chain of events that brought me here. Over and over, Troyer slices the bartender's throat. Again and again, I drag her through the brush. Then, my waking nightmare pans to a still-frame picture of the girl hanging in the tub. I feel like I'm never going to get away from this insanity. Panic sets in. I get the damn shakes again, and the sweat pours out. My vision blurs, so I pull over right in the middle of bumfuck nowhere. I mean, there's nothing around but wide-open space and some trees way off in the distance. Cars are speeding by every few seconds, echoing that windy, whistling sound they make when you're not moving. But they are.

I don't even look at Troyer as I throw open the car door and get out. I walk through the weeds, trying to clear my head. Then I pull out my junk and take a leak. Guys are damn lucky we're made the way we are. You know, able to drop trou anywhere and let it fly. I finish my business, zip up, and start back. As I look up at the car, I see Troyer leaning against it and waving at me. My head starts pounding, and I get real dizzy. I fall to my knees and puke. That shit's been happening way too much lately.

Still queasy, I reach into my pocket and pop some of my pills before I stumble back to the Honda. Troyer is looking at me kind of funny, but he doesn't say a word. My head is spinning so fast there's no way I can drive, so I climb in the back seat, take a few deep breaths, and . . .

CHAPTER EIGHT

I wake up in the dark, totally disoriented. Get this: I'm still in the back seat, and some chick's lips are wrapped around my cock, giving me the business. Troyer is sitting in the front passenger seat staring at me, flashing a half-assed, toothy smile. I look down at the top of the whore's head pumping up and down, then look back at Troyer.

"What the fuck is this?" I scream. "Where'd she come from?" I can't remember anything after I climbed in this afternoon.

"Come again, mate?" Troyer says with a grin. "I was wondering if you'd ever blow your load and return to reality."

I'm still half in the bag and clueless. "What's going on, Troyer?" I ask. Meanwhile, the chick barely misses a beat, as she keeps pulling on my withering cock.

"Finish up there, Tommy Boy. Then we can talk."

"I don't remember even driving here," I say, shaking my head. Then I grab the whore by the hair and pull her up. "Okay, that's it—party over. Get lost."

The chick gives me a look, opens the door, and bolts.

"Hey, mate, that's not nice. She's just doing the job I hired her for."

"You *hired* her? Why? From where?" I'm so confused that I don't know whether to shit or wind my watch. But before

I can say another word, cop lights flash on behind us. "Shit, Troyer—we're dead."

Troyer smiles and says, "Relax: we can handle it. Just be cool and we'll get through this just fine."

The cop comes over to the car and knocks on my window. I open it, and he looks in.

"Evening. Any reason you're parked here with your lights off?"

"Uh, just taking a break from driving, officer." I say, as calm as I can.

"Izzat so, son? You see, there's some fella been hanging around in the area, dressed up like a hooker, and offering blow jobs for thirty bucks a pop. Wouldn't want you to get suckered," he snickers, "if you know what I mean."

I turn and look at Troyer, who isn't saying a word. Then I get sick to my stomach. "Not to worry, sir. I'm the kind of guy that stays far away from trouble."

"I'll bet you do, son. I'll bet you do. Show me your license and registration."

Troyer gets my paperwork from the glove compartment and hands it to the officer. He looks it up and down before handing it back to me.

"Now, get back in the driver seat and get a move on. No loitering around here. You hear me?"

"Yes, sir."

As I climb into the driver seat, I catch another glimpse of Troyer, who's holding back probably the biggest laugh of his goddamn psycho life.

After the cop gets back in his car, Troyer explodes with this hack-sounding guffaw and slaps me on the shoulder.

"So, how does it feel getting your dick sucked by some dude?" Troyer is coughing and laughing so hard he can't catch his breath.

"That was no dude. I could tell. The cop was just being an asshole."

"I don't know, mate. She was quite tall—and painfully ugly, as well."

I throw the car in gear and hit the gas. "Fuck you, man. I know a chick when I see her."

"It is very dark," Troyer says, still laughing. "I think you've been shafted."

"Forget that. This is not just a joke, you psycho. You're murdering innocent girls. What the fuck is wrong with you? Why did you kill that girl yesterday?"

"Pardon me, mate. As I said before, I didn't kill anyone."

"Bullshit! You can't deny what you did, and I won't let you pin it on me, either."

"Look here, Tommy Boy: Your imagination is getting the better of you. No one has been killed. You're simply not right in the head."

"Please, dude—you're lying, and I'm not buying it. You're setting me up, and I don't like it one bit." I hit the brakes hard and screech to a stop. "It's time for you to get out."

Troyer slaps me hard across my face. "Listen, mate. I'm not setting you up. But if you want me to leave, I'll make it easy. Let me off here, and I'll find my way. I don't need this."

"Whatever," I say lamely, as I turn and stare him down. "I just need to get away from you, so get the fuck out!"

"Suit yourself, my friend. I'm done with you for the time being, but you haven't seen the last of me."

Troyer gets out, and I floor the gas pedal before he even shuts the door.

CHAPTER NINE

Once I find a main road, I realize I'm just outside of Cape May. I know this place called the Chalfonte Hotel. I can crash there until its safe. I stayed there many times when I was a kid. It's very cheap and more like a rooming house than a hotel. "Victorian-looking" is how I recall my mom describing it. Big old porch, tiny rooms, and bathrooms down the hall. It's three stories tall, and there's no elevator. The staircases are all slanted, and they creak when you climb them. I remember they've got these wooden banisters that look like they're at least two hundred years old.

As I turn onto the street, I see it off in the distance, and my stomach begins to churn. I start getting all anxious and jittery as I get closer. It's just like I remember from when I was a kid. Believe it or not, they still have that same damn sign out front that reads, ESTABLISHED IN 1789. I wonder if George Washington ever slept here.

The place is empty as I walk into the office to check in. Some old bag, who also must have been established around 1789, smiles, showing her crooked, yellow teeth.

"May I help you, young man?" she wheezes.

"Yes, ma'am," I say, all sweet and shit. "I need a cheap—uh, an inexpensive room for a week or two."

"Without baths are the least expensive."

"I need a bathroom though, so forget that."

"What about TV?"

"How much extra for the tube?" I ask, because now I'm thinking I may need the TV, too.

"Five dollars a day."

"That'll be fine."

"Credit card, please," she says, holding out her hand.

I hesitate, thinking *CSI* again. Once she runs that card through her machine, I'm registered all over the place.

"I'd rather pay cash, if that's okay."

"Fine, but we still need something for security. And you need to fill out this information card."

"How's a few hundred," I say, as I pull out two hundreds and hand them to her. I fill out the card with a phony name and address.

"Very well, then," she says, taking the dough. Then she hands me the key and points toward the staircase. "Third floor, halfway down the hall."

I turn and head to the stairs. Simple enough, and I didn't even have to use my real name. After I drop my duffle, I hit the sack.

I don't sleep very long, though, on account of this pounding headache that creeps up on me. Another migraine. I pull out my pills, pop a few dry, and turn on the TV. Figure I'll check the news and see if there's anything I should know about.

Sure enough, it's all over the place. Every news channel is talking about it. I settle on *Eyewitness News*. I always thought that was a great name for the news. Like they've seen it with their own eyes. Whoever came up with that must be pretty clever. Anyway, the whole back of the motel is roped off. The camera pans over to some old guy with tears in his eyes. Her father, I guess. Poor bastard.

The camera refocuses on a reporter holding a microphone. "Mallory Hammond reporting from the Waterside Motel, where the police are investigating a gruesome murder. I have with me Sergeant Monty Tanner of the Seaview police force. Sergeant, what can you tell us at this time?"

"Frankly, Mallory, we are only at the beginning stages of our investigation. I am not at liberty to disclose anything at this time, other than to tell the residents of our town to remain indoors, be vigilant, and be mindful that there is a dangerous individual out there. And if anyone has any information about this incident or if anyone sees anything suspicious, please contact our office at the number on your television."

"Sergeant, with all due respect, the people of Seaview really need to know more about what has happened here. Without compromising your investigation, there must be some details that can be released. In fact, any information may help the citizens of our town in their efforts to assist you."

Tanner thinks for a moment before answering. "Very well. What I can say is that a young girl who worked at the Waterside was found murdered in one of the motel rooms. She was discovered dead from multiple stab wounds. The room was rented by someone who paid cash and registered under the phony name Charles Webb. I am warning everyone to stay alert and report anything out of the ordinary."

Nauseous, I turn off the tube, not just because the news is scaring the shit out of me, but also because the light is hurting my eyes. I need silence and total darkness when my head feels like this. I used to think I had a brain tumor or something, so a while back, I had an MRI done. The doctor reviewed it and found nothing, but the damn headaches wouldn't go away. I'm still willing to bet I have this massive tumor that just keeps growing bigger every day.

Lousy doctors—they don't know shit, and you just can't trust them, either. It all goes back to when I was a kid and my mom took me to see this shrink. They said I was a problem child—whatever that means. The damn shrink would ask me all these stupid questions about what was going on in my life, how I felt and what I thought, but he never did tell me what was wrong with me. He'd just keep checking the time, like he was in a rush or something. Then I'd have to leave his office and wait in the waiting room while my mom would go in and talk with him. Every time she came out, she looked flustered, and her hair and makeup were all messed-up. She almost looked like she'd been crying. She never did talk to me about what he said to her regarding my condition—or even if I had a condition. A load a crap them doctors sling for their dough, if you know what I mean. And you know what, Dad never came with us. Mom didn't want him to. In fact, I remember one time he even said he wanted to come, but Mom insisted he stay home, that it would be better for me. Hell, I didn't give a crap either way. Looking back now, I think that damn shrink had the hots for my mom and they weren't just talking about me in his office.

After about an hour the pills kick in so I get up and go out to look for a bar. It's close to midnight and scary quiet as I walk along the storefronts by the shore. This place used to be full of activity way into the night when I was a kid. I guess the season hasn't started yet.

Even so, I find an open bar that's still got some people inside. Not my type, for sure, but at least there's something going on. I hate hanging out at places where there's nobody around. It makes me feel like some kind of loser. This place is a hole, but at least there's music. They've got Springsteen playing low in the background. "Rosalita"—great song. I sure could use a sweet señorita right about now. Not here, though. Just a bunch of old men drowning away their miserable lives with some of the hard stuff. Makes me think of my old man.

The joint smells of stale beer and wet wood, mixed with some god-awful ammonia stink. I don't think anyone besides me even notices. Man, this place is the pits, but it's all I've got right now, so I strut on up to the bar.

"What can I get for ya, kid?" the bartender asks me. He calls me "kid," even though he can't be more than a few years older than me.

"Gimme your best tequila, and chase it with a Heineken." I answer back, deepening my voice.

"Neat?" he asks.

"Absolutely, dude." I figure if I call him "dude," I can bond with him.

"You got it," he says, reaching under the bar and pulling out a beer, like he's probably done a million times before.

"Where's all the action?"

He chuckles. "Action? There's no action here until Thursday night. College kids start coming around at the end of the week, when the live music starts. Fridays and Saturdays are even better."

"Sounds cool. Guess I'm a bit early."

"Definitely. You from New York?"

"Why you say that?"

"Accent, bud. You sound totally Brooklyn."

"Sorry—don't want to disappoint, but I grew up in Vermont." I'm not sure why I lie. I just do. And then I realize I don't even know the names of any towns in Vermont. I hope he doesn't ask me what town I lived in.

He doesn't. Instead, he heads down the bar to get my tequila, so I spin around in the other direction and take a long swig of my brew. Just then, I notice some old guy, three stools over, eyeballing me . . . and it's making me uncomfortable. I pull out my cell, trying to act like I've got something going on. The old man keeps looking me up and down like I must have just killed somebody.

I turn away, then turn back and stare him down. I'm not letting anyone intimidate me.

"You want something, old man?" I ask him.

He turns away, sulking, and acts like he didn't hear me. That takes care of that shit. I'll kick his ass if he doesn't watch himself. What's with him anyway? Looking at me and then ignoring me.

I don't mean to get carried away. I just get fired up sometimes when people look at me for no particular reason. People shouldn't size you up just because you're sitting at a bar getting a drink.

It's kind of strange, because I'm saying and doing things I would have never done a few months ago—for better or worse. And you know what, it's all Troyer's fault. No doubt, that guy has totally fucked with my head.

The bartender comes back with my tequila. I down it in one gulp and order another.

Before I book out of the dump, I finish off three shots and two brews. As I get up to leave, I see Troyer standing by the door.

"What's up, mate?" he asks me, still Aussie.

"Are you fuckin' kidding me? Where did you come from?"

"Been watching you the whole time. You going to let that old fart get away with that attitude? I saw the way he looked at you."

"Screw the old man. You and me got some talking to do."

"Whatever you say. Let's walk."

We leave the bar, cross the street, and start walking along the strip that runs down the beach. It's dark, I'm drunk, and I'm so mixed up I have no clue where to begin.

"Look, Troyer—I don't know what your game is, but everything you've done these past few days is totally fucked-up. Why are you doing this shit to me? I never did anything to hurt you. I thought we were friends. Why did you kill those girls?"

"First of all, you wanker, I didn't kill the bartender. I've actually been trying to protect you all along. The truth is, it was you who slit her throat. Whatever you think you remember is wrong. It's not what really happened."

"Quit screwing with me. I know what you're trying to do, and it won't work."

"Fine—believe what you want. And like I said before, I didn't kill the girl from the motel, either. I never returned to the room after I found you passed out on the bed. Look, I'm your friend, and all I want to do is help. You simply don't realize that there is something wrong with you."

I stop dead in my tracks and push him off at the shoulders. "You're the one who's nuts, Troyer! I just don't understand why you're setting me up."

"Precisely the point. I have no reason to set you up. Think about it. From the first time I met you, all I've done is save your ass. I don't have to remind you that if it wasn't for me, those two goons who attacked you would probably have killed you. I saw something in you that night and decided to take you on as my protégé. Why would I try to hurt you after all that? The truth is, you don't remember the crazy things you do."

"Bullshit! I'm not crazy. You're the one who's messed up. One day you're from New York, the next you're from fuckin' Australia."

"What are you talking about? I've been an Aussie all my life."

"No, you haven't! You only started that shit the night you met the bartender. Stop screwing with me. What about your whole orphanage story and Father Ryan?"

"Orphanage? Father who? You've flipped your bird, mate, I was born and raised in Melbourne."

Man, Troyer is good. So good I'll bet he'd pass a lie detector test.

"Okay, then, how'd you find me here?" I start patting myself down wondering if maybe he's got a bug on me."

"Actually, mate, you're quite predictable and easy to track. More to the point, I've grown quite fond of you, and I feel obligated to try and help you."

"That's a laugh. It seems every time you show up, trouble follows."

"Look, here, if that's the way you feel, I can piss off right now and leave you to deal with this mess all by yourself."

I'm standing on the walkway, a few feet from the beach, shaking my head in total disbelief. It's dark, waves are crashing in the background, and a chill wind is slapping against my back. Even so, I'm dripping sweat. Troyer's got me so messed up I don't know what's real anymore. I step onto the sand and walk toward the water. Troyer stays behind.

My whole world is out of control. I'm actually starting to think that Troyer is telling the truth. Maybe I did kill the girl and I just don't remember. . . . Nah, it can't be. I know myself and I'm just not capable of murder.

I sit down in the sand and stare off toward the ocean. It's hard to see. The moon is hiding behind some clouds. The sounds of the waves settle me. The salty smell in the air brings me back to summer, when I was a kid, hanging out on this very beach. I wish I could go back to those days. Life was easy then. Now everything sucks.

I turn around, and Troyer is leaning against a light post, looking out at me. I wish I could get inside his head.

Inside my head, though, this phrase keeps repeating itself over and over again like some scratched up CD that's stuck in a groove: "Even when I'm not by your side, I'll still be with you in spirit." It makes me wonder.

I get up and walk back to him. The dude is smiling so wide you'd think he was doing a goddamn toothpaste commercial.

"That didn't take long, mate," he says obnoxiously. "So, what have you decided?"

"Look, man, you're too dangerous for me. I'm gonna deal with this on my own. I don't need your help. I just want you out of my life. No offense, but it's time we went our separate ways."

"No worries," he says, still grinning. "I'll be on my way."

Troyer gives me this creepy stare, turns, and walks away. Five seconds later, he turns back to me.

"Just make sure to watch your back, mate."

CHAPTER TEN

The next morning, I wake up at around nine. It takes me a few seconds to adjust. Then I realize where I am, rub the sleep from my eyes, and roll out of bed.

A half hour later, I'm sitting across the street from the beach at this tiny place that makes the best pancakes and sausages I've ever had. Down the block, there's a big commotion. The police have an area roped off not too far from where Troyer and I were hanging out last night. Some very skinny, long-haired dude is coming from that direction. He's wearing a T-shirt that reads, I'M NOT A GYNECOLOGIST, BUT I'LL TAKE A LOOK. I call out to him. "Hey, what's going on over there?"

He stops, looks at me for a second, and points back in the direction of the activity. "You mean over there?" he slurs. "Seems some old drunk had the shit kicked outta him late last night. He's in a coma, with half his skull bashed in."

"Wow, that's scary. Do the cops have any leads?"

"Nothing yet, but they just started the investigation."

I look back at the scene, then at the dude as he walks away. A cold chill runs down my spine, and suddenly, the sausages and pancakes are inedible.

A few minutes go by before I get tapped on the shoulder by this blond lady sporting a tight ponytail. She's wearing a black jacket and pants, and she's got a black leather pouch slung over her right shoulder. She looks totally out of place in Cape May.

"Excuse me," she says, all official. "Are you Thomas Sullivan?"

"Now, how'd you know that?" I shoot back, pouring on the charm.

"I've got a picture of you here in my case."

"Really!" I say, feeling that chill again. "Now, why would you be carrying a picture of me?"

"To be honest, there are some people looking for you back in New York, and I've been sent to find you."

"Looking for me? Why would anyone be looking for me?"

"I think you know that already."

"Sorry, ma'am—I've got no idea. Maybe you're confusing me with someone else?"

"I don't think so, Mr. Sullivan."

"Well, since you seem to know me, perhaps you can tell me who you are."

"Detective Stone—Theresa Stone. Third Precinct, Manhattan."

"Ahh, a chick dick. Why the hell are you looking for me?"

"How about you answer a few questions for me first?"

"Would I need a lawyer for this, Detective?"

"Only if you did something wrong."

"Well, I haven't, so go for it."

"Fine. Where were you last Friday night?"

"Hmm, let's see, Friday night . . . actually, it's hard to remember, but I think I was home all night."

"Are you sure about that? I want you to know we've already done some investigating, and we know that's not true."

"Well, then, if you know already, why bother asking me?"

"For the record, Mr. Sullivan, I need to hear it from you. But let me tell you this: we've already interviewed your father."

"Dad? He's just a drunk. He wouldn't have a clue where I was—and I don't tell him, either."

"Perhaps. But he did say you were out most of the night."

"Like I said, he's just a miserable drunk and was probably passed out on the couch like every other night. He has no idea if I was home or not, so I'm not buying it."

"Okay. You work for Carmela's Pizza as a delivery guy, correct?"

"Yeah—so what of it? I wasn't working Friday night."

"No, but somehow, one of their pizza boxes wound up in a dumpster not too far from where a girl was reported missing that night."

"Ha, that's a laugh. You're looking for me because a pizza box was found in the garbage?"

"Actually, yes. You see, Carmela's is located in Queens, on the other side of the East River and at least fifteen miles from the dumpster. Your boss says the delivery limit at his place is around three miles."

"And you think this pizza box connects me to all of this?"

"You are one of two delivery guys, and the other one has an alibi."

"Whatever—there's a very good explanation as to how that pizza box got in there. Besides, how would that even tie into some girl's disappearance?"

"Perhaps you can tell me that."

"It sounds to me like you actually believe I'm somehow involved, so I'm not going to say another word here."

"Well, then, come back to New York with me and prove that you're innocent."

"I'm sorry, but I always thought it was 'innocent until proven guilty'."

"That's correct . . . but."

". . . But nothing, Are you arresting me?"

"Not at this time."

"Then I'm not going back to New York right now. I'm in the middle of a vacation, and I expect to be here for a few more weeks."

"Is that how you're going to play this, Mr. Sullivan?"

"I'm not playing anything. I've done nothing wrong, and I'm not going to let you ruin my vacation."

"You are within your rights, but I will tell you this: Refusing to come in and talk makes you look that much more suspicious. And with a little more evidence, I will return with an arrest warrant. Until then, we will be watching you. So don't try to run off."

"I'm not running anywhere. But tell me—how'd you find me?"

"That's my secret. If you want answers from me, then you will have to give me some answers first."

"Like I said, I did nothing wrong, and I've got nothing more to say." I get up and start walking away, still pulling off a defiant attitude but knowing it won't last much longer with that softball growing in my gut. When I'm about thirty feet away, I turn around to see what the detective is doing. I catch a glimpse of her taking my water bottle off the table and putting it in her satchel. Shit! She looks up at me, smiles, and walks off.

CHAPTER ELEVEN

An hour or so later, I find myself sitting on a gray metal bench and facing the beach. The waves are rolling up the sand in soapy white splashes, making it look like the ocean is scrubbing the beach clean. My head is pounding, and I can't think straight, so I take four of my migraine pills and swallow them dry. How did the cops find me? I just can't believe this actually is happening. Now I can't even stay here, I've got to keep moving.

I turn around fast to see if anyone is watching me. There's a couple of old folks holding hands and walking barefoot in the sand. Their pant legs are rolled up, and they're smiling at each other like they're in some corny Cialis commercial, so I start looking around for a pair of claw-footed bathtubs. Off in the other direction, a group of little kids is playing in the sand with pails and shovels. Two women, wearing big hats and sunglasses, watch from low-slung beach chairs. I turn toward the shops along the strip and see some guy in a suit standing alone. He's holding one of those color maps that they sell locally. He seems way out of place. He must be following me. I've got to find a way to ditch him fast.

I start walking along the boardwalk, away from the guy, and make like I don't know he's following me. At the next inter-section, I cross the street and start walking past the storefronts until I find just what I'm looking for—a tourist shop that sells all kinds of clothes. I go inside, pick out a pair of colorful board-shorts, a bright T-shirt, and cheap sunglasses. I top it all off with a Quicksilver baseball cap. Then I grab a pair of beach thongs and walk up to the register, like some cornball tourist. I dump it all on the counter.

This cool-looking Goth chick, with a diamond in her nose and steel bracelets on her wrists, smiles at me.

"Is that all, or could I interest you in a surfboard?" she asks.

"Nah, surfing isn't my thing. I'm just fine here on dry land. Water's still too cold this time of year."

"Not so for the hardcores," she says, as she rings up my stuff.

"Well, I'm no hardcore, that's for sure." I start looking at her more closely because something about her looks familiar.

"You could get a wet suit. With one of them, you won't feel the cold."

"Things must be slow around here," I answer, smiling.

"Why do you say that?"

"Only because you're trying to sell me shit I don't need." I laugh.

"Just a little bored, that's all. I mean, it's real nice out today, but the season hasn't actually started yet. There's not much going on."

There's something about her smile that won't let go. "Hey, do I know you?"

"Are you serious? Is that the best line you could come up with?"

"No, really, it's not a line. You look so familiar, I just can't place it. What's your name?"

She cocks her head to the side and stares at me. "Aurora. What's yours?"

"Tommy. I used to come down here every summer when I was a kid."

"Wait a second. I've lived here for most of the last twenty years. I remember a boy named Tommy, too. We played on the beach together. In fact, he was my first kiss. Tommy, is that really you?"

"Well, my first kiss was here in Cape May, but it was with a girl named Alice."

"Holy shit, it is you! I'm Alice, I mean, I used to be— before I changed my name."

"You changed your name? Why?"

"We used to go to Alaska sometimes. My father worked for an oil company. And when he traveled up there he took me with him every so often. He always told me that I was the light of his life. Some nights, we would sit together on the porch watching these crazy, colorful lights flash across the sky. My dad told me that it was the Aurora Borealis and there was nothing better than seeing it live. We truly were lucky enough to witness the phenomenon first hand. He died suddenly one day, and it turned my whole world upside-down."

"And changing your name made you feel better?" I ask, genuinely curious.

"Yes, and it keeps his memory alive inside me."

"Interesting. I'd rather forget about my dad totally."

"That's too bad. Why?"

"I'd rather not get into it right now. But, wow, I can't believe it's really you."

"Me either. So how've you been Tommy? It has to be almost twenty years."

"I know. This is incredible! We have to hang out. What time do you get off?"

"Six tonight." Aurora smiles and puts her hand on my cheek. "This is so bizarre. I still can't believe it's really you. But before we go any further, the total is $99.85."

In the back of my mind I know that I have to leave town as fast as I can, but running into Aurora like this . . . I reach into my pocket and hand her a hundred dollar bill. "I want to see you later, but right now I need a favor."

"A favor?"

"Yeah, would you mind if I change into these clothes and leave through the back?"

"Sounds mysterious. What's the deal?"

"Ah, probably nothing, but I think some guy is following me, and I need to get away from him. And, after I go, if he comes in here asking questions, can you just play dumb?"

"As long as you promise to tell me more about this later. I'm intrigued."

"I promise. Why don't you meet me at the Oyster Bar after you get off work?"

"Sounds good. The changing room is over there." She points toward a curtain hanging in the far corner.

Once inside, I begin to undress. I pull my cell phone from my pants pocket. As I hold it in my hand I start to think, and all at once I realize that the cops must have traced me through my phone. I'm just about to smash it on the floor when a flash of brilliance hits me. If I simply power it down, they can't track me. And I can always switch it back on later and use it to send them off on a wild goose chase. As an added precaution, I take out the battery. Then I change and walk out the back door looking nothing like I did when I first arrived. Aurora smiles at me as she tends to another customer.

I try to remember more about her, but my memory fails me. Even so, she seems like one cool chick. I can't wait to hook up with her. But I have to make sure I'm not being followed first. I walk down a few side streets and come across a garbage pail. I toss in my old clothes and sneakers.

I've got the whole day to blow while I wait to meet up with Aurora, so I head over a few blocks more and go back to the beach. I find a small shop and go inside. I buy a beach chair, some sunscreen, and a book. I set myself up in the sand. Now I look more like a tourist than a tourist, so there's no way I'll be spotted. "Hide in plain sight," they say, whoever they are.

CHAPTER TWELVE

At five, I head back to my room to shower and change. With my cell phone off, I'm confident they can't track me. I still keep watching my back and weave my way through a few side streets just to be sure. I make it back to the Chalfonte, shower and dress, and head off to the Oyster Bar to meet Aurora. I haven't felt this good in a long time. I can't believe how excited I am to see her. There's something about this chick that just seems right.

Still suspicious, I take a detour and walk through a few shops to make sure I'm not being followed. I get to the restaurant just after six. The place hasn't changed much in the last twenty years. The faded wood walls are still covered with the same photos of proud local fishermen displaying their swordfish, shark, and other large catches. I even remember the ancient ship wheel that doubles as the hostess stand. Meshed netting, littered with starfish, hangs from the ceiling. The faint odor of fish is masked by the smell of sautéed garlic and onion.

I grab a stool at the bar, which runs the entire length of the east wall of the restaurant, and turn to face the door. The bartender, a middle-aged, over-dyed redhead with large cans, slaps down a beer coaster in front of me.

"What'll it be, kid?" she asks me in a dry, raspy voice. She smells like she just came back from her last smoking break.

"You got draft Heineken here?"

"Coming up," she says, as she turns and walks down the bar to the beer pulls. She fills a mug, returns, and drops it in front of me. There's quite a bit of dinner activity, and the voices carry and mix into a noisy conversational buzz.

A few sips later, Aurora bounces into the restaurant beaming a bright smile. She looks even better than before.

"I see you started without me," she says, pointing to the beer.

"Just a habit. I can't sit at a bar without something in front of me. You want one?"

"What're you drinking?"

"Heineken draft."

"I'll take a Coors Lite."

I motion to old orange hair and order the Coors.

"Okay, Tommy, I've been wondering all day: what's going on with you, and why do you think you're being followed?"

"Hold on. First, I need to know: did a guy in a suit come into the shop after I left?"

"No. It was a slow day—just the usual tourists . . . and some locals."

"Really? I could swear I was being followed."

"Whatever—just tell me what's going on. I don't normally get involved in all this intrigue. I mean, who comes into my shop, buys all new clothes, asks me out, changes, and runs out the back claiming he's being followed?"

"That'd be me."

"No shit. So what's this all about?"

"I'll tell you, but first, I've got to be sure I can trust you."

"Tommy, we knew each other when we were kids. That has to mean something. And didn't I come here to meet you, even after that bizarre encounter today?"

"I suppose, but this is much bigger than that."

"You promised me."

"Yeah, but this could be dangerous, and maybe even get you into trouble with the cops."

"I was born for trouble, so spill it," Aurora says, all tough chick.

"Okay, I'll give you the short version for now."

"Fine—just get to it."

"All right, gimme a second." I take a deep breath and, before I can change my mind, I just spill it fast. "It's like this. I've got this friend who did some very bad things and left me holding the bag. I was in the wrong place at the wrong time, and the cops suspect that I'm the one who committed the crimes. My friend—and I use the term loosely—has disappeared. What's more, a detective tracked me down this morning. She wanted me to come back to New York to answer questions. They didn't have a warrant for my arrest, so I refused."

"Well, that means they don't have enough evidence to charge you. Maybe you can just tell them about your friend and get out of this mess now."

"It's a little more complicated than that."

"Why? What did he do—rob a bank or something?"

"Worse."

"Drugs?" she asks.

"No—worse."

"Worse? Tell me."

"Murder."

"You mean your friend actually killed someone?"

"More than one."

"No way!" she says, more excited than scared. "So how did you get involved?"

"I witnessed one murder and can't remember the second one. I blacked out and woke up after she was killed. I didn't see the actual murder."

"You have to go to the cops with this."

"I can't. There's more."

"What more, Tommy?"

"Hey, I can't even believe I'm telling you this much."

"I promise I won't tell anyone, but you have to go to the cops."

"It's not so easy. I screwed up and hid the first girl he killed."

"You *what*?" she screams. "How could you be so stupid?"

"I don't know. I got caught up in it. Troyer cut out, and I put the girl in my trunk and drove off."

"Well, you can still go to the cops and tell them. Get a lawyer first. He can make them understand."

"No, you don't get it. It's worse than that. Troyer has been following me. He actually hid in the trunk of my car while I drove down here. When he showed himself, I stupidly let him come with me to the motel, where he killed another girl and left me covered in blood. You can't believe how many times he stabbed her. But I have no proof he did it. And I'm sure the cops will find my DNA all over the place. No one will believe my story. Don't you see? I'm dead."

"I believe you."

"Thanks, Aurora, but I don't think the cops will."

"Then you have to lay low until we can figure this out."

I roll my eyes, smirk, and nod sarcastically. "Duh, that's why I came down here in the first place. But they found me anyway, so what do you suggest?"

"Obviously we have to leave town."

"We? I don't think it's such a great idea for you to get any more involved than you already are."

"I don't think you have a choice. You can't go back to your car or your room, so how do you expect to leave town? I have a car and you can stay with me at my place tonight. We can leave tomorrow morning and no one will ever find you."

"I already went back to my room, but its okay, I figured out that they were tracking me from my cell, so I took out the battery. I don't think they know where I am right now."

"Still, Tommy, I'm sure they'll find your car, so you can't use it to get away. Just stay with me tonight and don't take any more chances. Tomorrow we'll take off in my car."

"You really wanna do this for me?"

"Sure, Tommy. I never forgot my first kiss."

PART TWO

CHAPTER THIRTEEN

Detective Theresa Stone paced in front of her desk. Her partner, Jake Watts, followed her with his eyes.

"You've got to relax, Stone," Watts said, as he gestured for her to sit down. "Take a load off. The results won't be in for a while."

"I know. It's just that everything takes too long around here. I know in my gut that Sullivan is our guy, but, as usual, procedure prevents me from acting on it. While we wait, he might disappear. Even worse, he could kill someone else."

"It's not that I doubt you," Watts said, shaking his head. "But the evidence is all circumstantial." He pulled at the two-day stubble on his chin. "I mean, come on—a pizza box in a garbage dumpster?"

Stone slapped the desk. "That pizza box was nearly fifteen miles from the restaurant. Sullivan does the deliveries; he fits the general description; he leaves the jurisdiction right after Houston disappears—oh, and he came off pretty damn suspicious when I approached him in Cape May."

"Whoa—calm down. I'm not the enemy, but until the DNA comes back, we have nothing—absolutely nothing. So we better expand our investigation; otherwise, if this ever gets to trial, some smart-ass attorney will argue that we focused too soon and failed to consider any other theories or any other suspects."

"Screw the lawyers. I'm telling you the DNA will confirm it; I feel it in my bones. Then we'll have enough to get a search warrant and rip his place apart."

"Yeah, but I'd feel much better if we had a body," Watts said, then, a moment later, wished that his mouth had come equipped with a backspace key. "Uh, let me rephrase that—if we knew what happened to the girl."

"Right—let's not jump the gun. We have to hold out some hope that she's still alive somewhere."

"Of course," Watts said, loosening his too-small necktie. "Although the blood at the scene suggests otherwise." Watts grimaced. "I don't think I'll ever get used to this. No matter how many violent crimes we investigate, I can never wrap my head around the senselessness of it all."

"Wake up, Watts. The world is filled with sickos, psychos, and nut jobs, and trying to make sense of it is a waste of time. You've been doing this a lot longer than I have, and you know it's our job to catch them and get them off the street . . . and make sure they stay off the street. Analyzing why they do it is for the shrinks."

"Precisely why we have to handle this one carefully. Without a body, and with little evidence, we have to be sure. And consider also that we don't want to put the wrong person behind bars."

"True." Stone said. "But I feel this one in my gut."

"Fine—then let's make the case . . . the right way. Solid evidence first, then we arrest him."

"Always reeling me in, aren't you?"

"Just being your partner, Stone. I know you're one of the best out there, and I'm by your side every step of the way, but sometimes even you need a little help from me."

"Gotcha. I wouldn't be where I am today without you, so you just keep on doing what you do."

"And you, too, partner."

"Don't worry—I will."

"Uh-oh." Watts said, doing a double take. "I'm not sure I like that look on your face. What are you doing that you haven't told me about?"

"Nothing for you to worry about."

"Yeah, right."

"Need to know basis, Watts. Just trust me."

CHAPTER FOURTEEN

Stone was asleep at her desk waiting for the results to come in. Watts fielded the call from the lab and made some notes on a pad as he stared at the sleeping detective. Shaking his head, he smiled flatly.

"Stone, wake up. The results are in."

Abruptly lifting her head from the desk, Stone shook off the sleep, rubbed her eyes, and focused. "Okay, then: spill it. What'd they find?"

"Well, it looks like you were right; the DNA is a match."

"I told you." Stone jumped up and shouted. "Let's go pick up the search warrant. We need to do this now."

"Slow down there, partner. It's ten o'clock at night. No judge is going to be available to sign it until tomorrow morning."

"Come on, Watts—who do you think you're talking to? The warrant's already been issued."

"How can that be?"

Stone laughed. "I had the prosecutor's office apply for it this morning, in anticipation of the result. I simply stretched the truth and told them the results were already in. We just have to go and pick it up."

"You're too much. You know procedurally that could pose a problem."

"This is the real world, Watts. We don't have the luxury of time. Evidence tends to disappear if you don't search it out fast enough. Now let's get moving."

Less than an hour later, Stone and Watts pulled up to the Sullivan home in Bellerose, Queens. The neighborhood was quiet. The only light illuminating the area radiated from the porch lights of the row houses that lined the suburban street.

Stone took the lead and rang the doorbell repeatedly until a light clicked on inside the home. The door opened, and a balding, gray-haired man, wearing a stained white undershirt, greeted the two detectives.

"Can I help you?" the old man slurred. His breath, and the stink of his sweat, was of cheap whiskey. "Heyyy," he said, stretching the word into a long wheeze. "Weren't you the cops that came here the other day looking for my son?"

"That would be correct, sir," Watts said as he eyeballed the drunken man.

"I tol' you guys, I ain't seem him for days. What the hell you want from me at this time a night?"

Stone held up the warrant. "We have a search warrant, and we need to search this place."

"Now? You kidding me—this time a night? What're you—some kinda Communists? This is America. You can't just come barging into a man's house in the middle of the night."

"This warrant says we can, Mr. Sullivan," Stone said, firmly. "Move out of the way and let us do our job."

Watts stepped forward and brushed the old man aside. "Where is your son's room? We'll start there."

"I want a lawyer," Sullivan demanded. "You can't do this."

"You're welcome to call a lawyer any time, sir." Stone offered.

"This time a night—you gotta be joking."

"In the meantime, where is Tommy's room?" Watts asked again.

Sullivan pointed to the stairs. "It's down there. Just don't make no mess. I ask that kid a hundred times a day to keep it clean down there, and he does what he's tol'. You hear me?"

The old man trudged off into the living room, opened a cabinet, and took out a bottle of whiskey. He took a long pull from it, walked over to the stairs, and hollered down at the two detectives. "So what kinda trouble is my stupid-ass son involved in that's got you all worked up this late at night?"

Ignoring him, Stone stopped in the doorway, wide-eyed and mouth agape. "Holy crap, would you look at this place? It's immaculate. Everything is so damn neat."

Watts squeezed through the door and opened the closet. "This guy is seriously disturbed. All his clothes are tightly folded and stacked. Even the hangers are evenly spaced apart."

Stone shook her head. "It reminds me of my days in the service." She patted the bed. "Look at these bed sheets: they're sharply wrapped underneath the mattress."

"I'll bet you can bounce a quarter off them." Watts pulled open the dresser drawers and admired the neat rows of socks and underwear. "There's not a speck of dirt here."

"Just our luck," Stone said, as she examined a pair of sneakers that she pulled from under the bed. "Go check out the laundry room. I'll go through the rest of this room."

Watts nodded, left quickly, and began searching the washroom.

Minutes later, he called out to Stone. "There's not much in here. Just a pile of smelly undershirts and clothes, which clearly belong to the old man. No bloody clothes or anything to link this guy to the girl. And no laundry has been done for days. The old man probably has the kid doing it for him, but since he's not around, it's just building up here."

"Sounds about right," Stone said.

"One thing though: there's a container of bleach, mostly empty. And the cap isn't screwed on right."

"Whaddya mean?"

"You know, the threads—they aren't lined up, like someone was in a rush and didn't close it properly. It's also a little out of place. If you think the bedroom is far too neat, you've got to see this. Every container is faced out like they do at the grocery store. The labels are all lined up and facing out, except for the bleach. That label is turned around and almost backward."

"May be nothing, but you never know. Bag it and keep looking." Stone eyeballed the computer on the desk, "Watts, get back in here. He's got a computer."

Watts grinned. "You know, I just love digging into a perp's personal life directly though his computer. Turn it on. Let's see if we can get in."

"I'm way ahead of you, partner. It's already booting up. If we're lucky, he won't have a password; otherwise, we're going to have to bring it in and have one of the geeks look at it."

Watts took his place behind Stone, watching as the icons loaded on the screen.

"Check the word-processing directory."

"I know the drill." Stone said, as she rolled the mouse and double-clicked the Word icon.

She scrolled to the index. "There's only a few files, I'll check the latest one first."

Stone opened it and began to read: *A while back I experienced a life changing event and I haven't been able to stop thinking about it.*

On a scale of one to ten, it was a twelve. Two guys followed me out of a bar, cornered me in an alley, and started kicking the shit out of me. They would have killed me, but this dude showed up out of nowhere and laid them out like it was nothing. He totally saved my life.

I've gotten to know Troyer Savage over the last few months and I have to say he is one very cool dude. We've become friends and he's been teaching me some of his moves. He's taught me a few wicked fighting skills and schooled me on some of the finer points about how to score with chicks. The guy is smooth as silk and tough as nails. Troyer says if I play my cards right, I can be too.

Tonight I'm meeting Troyer at Club Radical.

"Hello!" Watts shouted. "That puts him at the scene."

"That it does."

"Is there anything else?"

"No. That's the end of the file." Stone fingered the keyboard and opened more documents and found nothing of interest. "Dead end with the rest of the files. Sullivan is clearly not a wordsmith."

"Don't sweat it. Now we have evidence tying him directly to Club Radical. Why don't you check the Browser. See what he is into."

"You read my mind." Stone double-clicked the Explorer icon and opened the search history. She drew in a breath and held it as she scrolled down.

"What? What is it? You know I can't read anything without my glasses."

"You're not going to believe this, but most of his latest searches are about Gilgo Beach and the unsolved murder."

Watts gasped as his mind flooded with thoughts about the infamous case. "Holy crap! This can't just be a coincidence."

"Another missing girl, another connection to Gilgo Beach, I'd say we just stumbled onto something big."

"That's putting it mildly. Let's get a team over there right away."

"And we need to pick up Sullivan. Now we've got more than enough for a warrant."

"I'm on it," Watts said, pulling out his cell. "Ross, its Watts. You need to move in on Sullivan now and arrest him."

Ross hesitated before he spoke. "Uh, Detective—I—uh, I lost him and haven't been able to track him down."

"You *what?* How in the world could you lose him?"

"He just slipped away. I'm sorry."

"Well, then why don't you GPS him with his cell phone?"

"I tried that already. He must have wised up and turned it off."

"Great—just great. Look, Ross, this is a serious screw-up. You've got to find him . . . and fast."

"I know. I'm sorry. I'll do what it takes and get back to you."

"Okay, just get him!" Watts turned to Stone. "Can you believe that? He let Sullivan slip away."

CHAPTER FIFTEEN

Sergeant Monty Tanner of the Seaview police force was reexamining the murder scene at the Waterside. The area was still roped-off, but Tanner deftly maneuvered his slender frame and stepped over the police tape. At six-foot-five and weighing less than two hundred pounds, he looked gaunt and ill-equipped to handle the rigors and physical demands of a job that required intimidation to achieve results. But what he lacked in appearance, he made up for in diligence.

Tanner stood by the bathroom door and scanned inside. The body had been removed from the tub, but the area was still covered in blood. He turned as his deputy, Samuel Sung, approached.

"Have you ever seen so much horror in one spot, boss?" Sung asked, in a Chinese affect.

"Can't say as I have, Deputy. This is by far the worst I've seen. Before my time, about eight years ago, there was another one that was pretty awful, too, but not as bad as this. Anyway, we're running down a new lead, and I need you to come with me to question the witness."

"Witness, boss? I thought no one saw what happened?"

"Not here, but Johnny, the old bartender at the Tides Inn, he may have some relevant info for us. I just wanted to take one more look before they clean this place up."

A half hour later, Tanner and Sung arrived at the Tides Inn. Johnny Mulligan was a fixture behind the bar, wiping an imaginary stain from a spot in front of the beer pulls. For fifteen years, Mulligan had been wearing out the wood floors behind the counter, pacing back and forth, serving customers at an often feverish pace, and at other times at a pace so slow you'd wonder if perhaps the entire town was on the wagon. It was the end of a crazy week, with the Battle of the Bands coming to a close in only one day.

"Afternoon, Monty," Mulligan said, as he looked up.

"Howdy, Johnny. How ya been?"

"A bit tired, Sarge. The Battle's been a killer this week."

"Not funny, Johnny."

"Sorry—I didn't mean it that way. It's been so busy this is the first real chance I've had to clean up."

"Place looks fine to me. Why don't you take a break and tell me about the loner that came in here Monday."

"Sure thing," he said, as he began wiping the imaginary stain again. "It's like this: Midday Monday this guy comes in—turns out his car broke down and he's stuck—so I give him Chunky's number at the Mobil down the road. Chunky comes by and picks up the car and the guy has to stay overnight because Chunky needs to get some parts to fix it. I'm pretty sure he stayed at the Waterside that night, so I figured I'd call you. The kid seemed harmless and all, but I've never seen him here before. Anyway, then it got all crowded with kids and Battle week, so I just forgot all about it, until I started thinking about the murder."

"So, Chunky worked on this guy's car?"

"Yup."

"Anything else you remember?"

"Nope."

"All right, then, time to go see Chunky and find out what he knows."

Ten minutes later, Tanner and Sung pulled into the Mobil station. They found Chunky in the back, snacking on a pair of chili dogs, a basket of fries, and a jumbo frosty shake—standard pre-dinner dietary supplement. Chili sauce dripped from his chin. He pulled a greasy hand towel from the pocket of his overalls and wiped his face.

"Hey, guys," Chunky said between chews. "Johnny called and tol' me you were on yer way. What can I do to help?"

"You fix some kid's car Monday?" Tanner asked.

"Yeah, there was this kid from outta town stuck over at the Tides. I hadda tow him and keep his car overnight for some parts. I tol' him to go to the Waterside for the night."

"What can you tell me about the kid?"

"Aww, he was a punk-ass wise guy. Seemed in a rush to get outta here and all pissed off his car couldn't be fixed right away."

"What kind of car?"

"2002 Honda Accord. Silver. New York plates. Got some info inside," Chunky stuffed the last of his first chili dog down his throat and chewed. "Punk said he was just passing through. Could be a killer, though. He looked the part."

"And what does a killer look like, Chunk?"

"Oh, I dunno—shifty eyes, punk-ass attitude, dirty, whatever."

"So what did this kid look like, then?"

"Slim, blond hair, girly features, something in his eyes that looked nasty. A real punk, if ya ask me."

"When did he pick up his car?" asked Sung.

"First thing Tuesday morning. Maybe around ten."

"What else can you tell me about him?" Tanner asked.

"Well, he didn't talk much, but he did sneak up on me while I was working under the hood. Practically scared the crap outta me."

"Then what?" Tanner asked.

"I tol' him I'd be done soon and to wait. So he sat on the bench and waited. I hit him up for some extra dough 'cause I didn't like the way he snuck up on me, but he paid cash and took the car. That was it."

"Anything else?" Sung asked.

"Nah—why? Do you really think this kid coulda done that girl at the Waterside?"

"We're just running down the evidence," Tanner said. "No suspects yet. Just keep it quiet, and if you can think of anything else, let us know."

"Will do," Chunky said, as he lifted the lid off the frosty shake and guzzled.

"One more thing," Tanner said. "You get a license plate?"

"Yeah, 'course. It's on the receipt."

"Great. Can you get that for me?"

"Sure thing." Chunky grabbed a handful of fries, stuffed them in his mouth, and headed toward the office. The two detectives followed behind.

A small stack of repair invoices littered a faded wooden desk. Chunky rifled through it.

"I got it right here," Chunky declared, triumphantly raising a piece of paper above his head.

"Great, Chunk," Tanner said. "Give it to me."

"Do I get some kinda reward?"

"I'll buy you lunch tomorrow."

Deputy Sung was already on the phone and reading off the plate number. He covered the phone and looked up at Tanner.

"I've got New York DMV on the line. They'll have a name and address shortly."

Tanner nodded as Sung pulled out his pad and pen and began to write.

"Okay, boss, the car is registered to a Thomas Sullivan. I've got an address in Bellerose, New York."

"Looks like we're headed to Bellerose, wherever the hell that is," Tanner said, as he turned and walked to the cruiser.

"You really think this guy could be our perp, boss?" Sung asked, following at his heel.

"No idea, Deputy, but it's our first real lead, so we've got to follow it up. In the meantime, get on the computer and see if this guy's got any priors."

"Will do, boss," Sung answered. Sung was a follower, not a leader. He took orders well enough and did what he was told, but beyond that, he was neither an asset nor a liability. When he was first hired, the force had needed to meet some imaginary quota of non-white employees, and Samuel Sung had come along at just the right time. He was hired not for his skills but for his heritage. No other force in central Jersey employed a Chinese, so when the opportunity arose, Seaview jumped on it, with the expectation that it would result in kudos and more state aid. Ultimately, it did neither, but Sung became a fixture on the force and did his level best to prove himself worthy. In Seaview, that wasn't too difficult. DWIs, shoplifting, and domestic disputes were the routine in this jurisdiction. There had been only one other murder in the last eight years—until now.

Sung vacillated between excitement and fear, not knowing if he was possessed of the wherewithal to help solve the crime but thankful for the opportunity to escape the mundane. He took his place on the passenger side of the police cruiser, pulled open the laptop, and punched in a password to access the online database. Tanner took the wheel, and they began the three-hour drive to Bellerose.

"Okay, boss—here it is. Sullivan appears relatively clean. He received a speeding ticket a few years back, but other than that, nothing."

"Does that tell you if he's ever been fingerprinted?"

"Not this record, but I can check elsewhere."

"Good—let me know. And while you're at it, get me directions to Bellerose. I know how to get to the Verrazano Bridge, but after that, I'm lost."

"I'm on it, boss."

That afternoon, Tanner and Sung arrived at the Sullivan home and pulled in the driveway behind an old, blue Nissan Sentra. The door was wide open in the detached garage out back.

Tanner called out, "Hello? Is anyone home?"

There was no answer.

"Mr. Sullivan, are you out here?" Sung yelled loudly.

Still nothing.

"Okay Sammy," Tanner said, pulling his gun and pointing, "you head around back the other way, and I'll move in from here."

Sung nodded, took out his gun, and clicked off the safety. Tanner took a low crouch, moved quickly up to the house, and leaned his back against the brick wall. Inching his way forward, his eyes darting back and forth, Tanner slowly made his way to the garage.

Sung took the other direction, circled the house, and approached from the far side.

Again, Tanner called out, "This is the police! Is anyone out there?"

No answer.

Tanner reached the garage and entered pointing his gun. Sung watched from the far corner of the house. As Tanner disappeared inside, Sung moved closer.

"Sammy, get over here—fast!" Tanner yelled, as he holstered his gun and ran to the back of the garage.

"What is it, boss?"

Sung found Tanner crouched over a body laid out behind a small workbench.

"Is he dead, boss?"

Tanner felt the man's neck. "No, he's got a pulse, and he's still breathing. He also reeks of alcohol."

Sung pointed to the shelf behind Tanner. "Whiskey bottle, almost empty—you see it?"

"Yeah, the old man is piss-drunk. Better call nine-one-one. Let's get an ambulance here."

Tanner found some old rags and bunched them up beneath the man's head while they waited. "This must be the kid's father. Too bad—now we're gonna have to wait to question him."

"Should I check out the house while we're here?" Sung asked.

"We have no warrant. If we find anything, it may screw up the case. I think we better wait until we can do this right. The old man certainly isn't going to be able to hide anything at this point, so whatever is in the house isn't going anywhere. We're also out of our jurisdiction across state lines. I'm not familiar with the procedure, but I think we have to bring in the FBI or at least the local cops."

CHAPTER SIXTEEN

Ten police officers and three dogs gathered at Gilgo Beach, just off Ocean Parkway, to begin the search for Jamie Houston. Detectives Stone and Watts took the lead.

"Okay, people," Stone called out, holding up a stack of papers. "Each one of you, take a map. You're to break up into groups of two and cover the assigned areas that I've designated on each of the maps. Focus on your particular grid and look for signs of drag marks, clothing, blood—anything that looks like it doesn't belong. You all know the drill. And those of you who are using the dogs, I have a pillowcase from the girl's bed. Let's see if the dogs can pick up a scent."

The teams set off in varying directions searching for the young bartender. Curious onlookers began to gather, and the police presence was insufficient to control the growing crowd. Before long, local news reporters also showed up.

Watts pulled Stone aside. "We have to contain this. It's too soon for the media."

"Leave that to me," Stone said as she walked toward the crowd of onlookers standing behind the police tape.

As she reached the edge of the roadway, Stone called out, "Attention: all non-police personnel are directed to leave the area immediately. Anyone without proper credentials will be detained for questioning in five minutes. Any media personnel with proper proof of their status may remain for a very brief press conference."

After the crowd dispersed, Stone addressed the media. "Ladies and gentlemen, please give me your attention and cooperation. I know you're all anxious to find out what we are doing here, but right now I need a little latitude and some discretion from you. All I can say is that we have an unverified lead that we are investigating—nothing more. This is all very premature, and you are wasting your time. Please just give us the time we need to do our jobs, and if there are any developments, we will be sure to transmit the information to you. I will not be fielding any questions right now. Thank you."

Audible shouts and groans rang out from the throng of reporters.

"Can you at least tell us if this has anything to do with the disappearance of Jamie Houston?" one reporter asked.

"At least give us that!" shouted another.

"Yeah—give us *something*," came from a third.

"No comment at this time," Stone answered, as she walked off.

Shortly thereafter, Stone's walkie-talkie crackled. A voice spoke though the static. "Detective Stone?"

"Stone here. What is it?"

"Detective, this is Officer Morgan. We're in grid four, and we've found a body. We don't think its Houston—the body is seriously decomposed—just tattered clothes covering a skeleton. Has to have been here for a year or more. Looks like the skull was smashed, but we need an M.E. to evaluate."

"I'll be there in five minutes. Don't touch anything," Stone said as she turned to Watts.

"Lets roll. This investigation just escalated."

Stone and Watts rushed to the scene and found the partially clad body half-buried in the sand. Watts bent over the remains to focus on the skull. "Check this out, Stone: looks like serious blunt-force trauma here. The M.E. can confirm it, but to me, there's no doubt. Also, no question this isn't Jamie Houston. The body's been here far too long."

"Which begs the question: could this be the body of the girl who disappeared around here last year?"

Watts interrupted, "And could there be even more bodies out here? Maybe this guy is the serial killer they've been looking for."

"This thing just escalated big time."

CHAPTER SEVENTEEN

My head is pounding as I lie wide-awake in bed next to Aurora and stare at the ceiling in her bedroom. We agreed hours ago that sex was off the table until we got to know each other again. I should say she agreed, because if it was my choice, I'd be all over her. But something inside me says this girl is the real deal, and jumping her too soon could blow the whole thing. I mean, she's all onboard backing me, even with the load of shit that's going down. I can't think of anyone else in my life who would be here like this. And she hasn't seen me in twenty years! I look over at her sleeping soundly. I climb out of bed, fumble around in the dark in search of my jeans, and dig into the front pocket. The clock says 3:10, and I need a few of my migraine pills to chill the pain in my head. They are the only things that have ever been able to make me feel better, and they're running out fast. I'm thinking that I have to find a way to get more, but they aren't regular prescription pills, so I'll have to go back to New York—to the clinic—to get a refill.

About three months ago, I joined this experimental trial group that was advertised on the radio. They actually pay you to try out some new drug, and all you have to do is keep track of when you take the pills, whether they work, and if you notice any side effects. Then you report back to them every few weeks for an evaluation. So far, the damn pills have been great. The migraines go away less than an hour after I take them. The prescription calls for two, but I found that four work like magic. Trouble is they run out faster.

Aided by the soft light glowing from the bathroom, I see Aurora curled up in fetal position, her hands folded neatly underneath her face. The corners of her lips are creased up in an innocent smile. Yeah, she's one cool chick.

I sit down in her loveseat and stare at her while I let the pills do their thing. I still can't believe she was actually my first kiss. I kind of, sort of remember, but not really. Anyway, after a time, I get up, walk into the kitchen and open the fridge. The leftover Chinese food catches my eye. I just love cold spare ribs and wonton soup—even better than when you eat them the first time. Makes me think of that dish they call "Twice-Cooked Pork." Some brainiac must have realized that cooking the dish a second time makes it taste better—and there you go: another page full of dishes gets added to the menu. Same shit, just cook it twice. I tell you, Chinese restaurants have more choices on their menus than any other place I know. You could spend a whole year eating every single dish, and I bet you wouldn't eat 'em all. Now, that'd be a study. Forget that Spurlock dude who ate McDonald's for a month to see how bad it would screw him up. I say try and eat every dish on a Chinese menu and see how bad that messes you up.

My head starts feeling better and I get sleepy, so I head back into the bedroom and quietly crawl back in bed next to Aurora. Later on, I'll break the news and tell her that I have to go back to New York to get more migraine medicine.

. . .

I wake up to the smell of bacon and eggs.

Aurora yells, "Breakfast is served."

Aurora is unbelievable; she actually cooked for me. I could get used to this. I'm almost at the kitchen when I realize I've still got the morning wood on, so I stop and readjust before I enter. Wouldn't want her to get the wrong idea.

"How'd you know that's my favorite?"

"I didn't. It's my favorite," she laughs. "I figured if you didn't like it, more for me."

"Too bad—now you've got to share."

"You're lucky I made enough."

"That, I am."

"So how'd you sleep?"

"Actually, I woke up with a migraine in the middle of the night and had to take some of my pills—which reminds me: I'm running low, so I'm gonna have to go back to New York, to refill my prescription."

"Don't you think that'd be dangerous?"

"Actually, I've been thinking about it, and going back to New York is probably the smartest thing to do. The cops would never suspect I'd return now, especially after that detective found me here. If anything, they'd probably think I'd go further south. Anyway, I can't go without my meds. The pain is too much. So I have no choice."

Aurora patted her index finger against her lips, deep in thought. "You know what, I think you're right. That's pretty smart."

"Yeah, but still, you don't have to come if you don't want to."

"But I do, Tommy. I want to help."

"You sure? I mean, what if the cops find you with me? Then you're an accomplice and you could get in big trouble."

"I'm not worried. As long as we take my car they can't track you. So we go to New York and get your meds, then just keep moving north."

"Sounds like a plan."

. . .

We load Aurora's little bag into the trunk of her Mustang and head up to New York, four or five hours away, depending on traffic. And you can always depend on traffic when you hit New York. I mean, as soon as you get over the Verrazano Bridge and onto the Belt Parkway, there's always a damn traffic jam.

Once we make it into Brooklyn, I direct her to the clinic.

"You stay out here, Aurora. I'm going in alone. It shouldn't take long, but you never know; they always ask these lame-ass questions. I know how to duck 'em, though, and get out quickly. I promise I'll be right back."

I head inside, hell-bent on getting in and out in ten minutes. No such luck. First, they make me wait for a half hour. Then the nurse comes out and brings me into a tiny room with one of those doctor beds. I wait there for another fifteen minutes. Finally, the nurse comes back, takes my blood pressure, and needles my arm for a sample. Then she hands me a cup to pee in. This wastes another fifteen minutes before the doctor finally shows up.

"Hey, doc, what's up? Why all the delay, here? I've got to get back to work."

"Just routine, Thomas. I have to ask you a few questions."

"Shoot."

"Okay. First, how are you feeling?"

"Great, doc—never better. Now can we get on with it?"

"Have you had any anxious feelings, any nervousness, sweating, or feelings of excessive heat?"

"Nope—nothing like that."

"Any other things out of the ordinary?"

"Like what, doc? What're you getting at?"

"I can't tell you that, Thomas. The study is objective, meaning that you have to report your feelings. I can't tell you what to expect."

"Gotcha. In that case, no—I'm all good."

"Great—one more thing: these pills were supposed to last three more weeks. Have you been taking them more frequently?"

"Uh, sure, doc. Like you told me when I first started, any time I feel that migraine pain coming on, just take two pills."

"Right, but I also said not more than two at a time or more than four every twelve hours."

"Yeah, I know. No worries—I'm cool. Now can you fill me up and get me outta here?"

"Sure, Thomas—just relax. I'll have another prescription in a few minutes. Just take this survey with you and answer all the questions. Please get it back to me in the next few days. You can mail it in; there's a self-addressed, stamped envelope inside."

He hands me a large envelope.

"Great, doc, and thanks; these pills have really helped. My migraines go away so quickly now it's unbelievable."

"Good to hear that, Thomas. Just keep in touch, and remember: if you feel anything out of the ordinary, you must call me and let me know."

"Gotcha, doc. No prob."

Yeah, the doc is cool but a little too stiff for me. Always writing shit down in that folder of his and nodding or shaking his head. No way am I telling him I take four pills at a time.

He's liable to stop the study and cut me off. Then I'd be miserable with pain. Anyway, the meds can't be bad for you. They stop the pain like nothing else I've ever had.

Five minutes later, I've got another ninety pills. That should last a while. I head back outside and find Aurora dozing off in the front seat.

"Wake up, gorgeous," I say, tapping the driver window.

Aurora jumps up like she's seen a ghost or something. I just laugh.

I walk around to the passenger side and climb in.

"That wasn't funny, Tommy."

"I know. I'm sorry."

"Apology accepted. So where to now?"

"Okay, I've been thinking about it and I've got a great idea. There's this place upstate where I used to go to camp after I stopped going down to Cape May. I know the area real well, and no one would ever think to look there in a million years."

CHAPTER EIGHTEEN

Joe Sullivan was hooked up to monitors in the cardiac care unit of North Shore University Hospital on Community Drive in Manhasset. He was being treated for alcohol poisoning but showed signs of a minor heart attack. He was still in a coma. Officers Tanner and Sung had all but given up waiting to question him when Detectives Stone and Watts walked into the room.

"Gentlemen," Stone said, "I understand that you found this man unconscious, in his garage, yesterday afternoon."

"That would be correct, ma'am," Tanner answered. "And who might you be?"

"I'm Detective Theresa Stone. This is my partner, Detective Jake Watts. We're with the Third, over in Manhattan."

"Good to meet you. We're up from New Jersey, investigating a homicide."

"So we've been told. Can you tell us what this man has to do with your investigation?"

Sung chimed in, "Detective, I'm not sure if you heard the news, but there was a brutal murder in our county a few days ago."

"I wasn't aware until I was informed about what happened at the Sullivan house," Stone answered. "We were just there executing a search warrant the other day."

"Well," Tanner said, "we've uncovered some evidence that suggests that Thomas Sullivan—the son of the man in bed over there—may be involved. We came up to investigate and found the older Sullivan passed out in his garage."

"What can you tell us about this murder?" Watts asked. "We're actually investigating the disappearance of a young bartender last week. And our information has led us to Thomas Sullivan, as well."

"You think this guy might be a serial killer?" Tanner asked.

"That's what our evidence suggests," Watts answered. "And now that we've learned about this other murder . . ."

Stone chimed in. "Can you share some details about your case?"

"Gruesome, to say the least," Sung answered. "A female motel clerk was repeatedly stabbed inside a motel room. She was covered in blood with at least thirty knife wounds all over her body."

"Sounds horrible," Watts said. "And what evidence do you have that suggests that Thomas Sullivan was involved?"

"He was seen in the area. His car broke down, and he had to stay in town the night of the murder. The only motel in the vicinity of the repair shop was the one where the murder took place."

Watts shook his head. "Doesn't sound like much to go on."

"We know, but it's all we have for the moment. We were hoping to find something more at his house. Unfortunately, the old man slowed us down. . . ."

Tanner interrupted. "What can you tell us about your investigation, Detective?"

"Everything we have is preliminary. We're holding back what we've found until we have some more proof. Suffice it to say, we believe we're on the right track, but we need more than what we have to be sure."

"Well, you can certainly tell us. We're on the same side here," Tanner said. "Anything you have may help us, and in turn, we'll help you. Just don't keep anything from us."

"Fine. Why don't you come to the station, where we can give you a full briefing?" Watts said. "Also, please have your people send up whatever info you've got down in Jersey."

CHAPTER NINETEEN

Aurora drives us across the Tappan Zee Bridge as we head upstate to hide out. By ten PM, we reach Port Jervis and stop at this dump motel.

"You really know how to pick 'em, don't you, Tommy?" she says, scrunching up her nose.

"Hey, beggars can't be choosers. We should be safe here, though. I know the area. You see, when I was a kid, I worked a bunch of summers as a junior counselor and a waiter at a camp nearby. This place is a ghost town until summertime."

"If you say so."

"I do. Now go get the room. I'll stay here. It's better if they think you're alone. One thing, though, get a non-smoking one. I hate the smell of cigarettes."

"Ha—what makes you think they even have them here?"

"Nothing. But if they do, get one."

"Gotcha."

Five minutes later, Aurora comes back and shows me a card that apparently replaces a conventional key. "Technology at its finest, even at a shithole like this."

"You can say that again."

We drive to the room, I hang Aurora's bag over my shoulder and we climb the stairs. "I guess we can stay here for a few nights while we figure out what to do."

Aurora slides the card into the door slot. "Yeah, but we shouldn't stay in any one place for too long." She walks through the door, draws a breath and makes a face. "They told me this was a non-smoking room."

"Losers. You think we can change before we get comfortable?"

"No—not wise. That may bring attention to us. You'll just have to deal with it."

"I suppose you're right." I pull her bag off my shoulder and the strap catches on my necklace, snapping the chain. It falls to the floor. "Damn, I really liked that thing." I pick it up and toss it on the night table. I'll fix it later.

Aurora opens the bag and starts taking out her toiletries. "I'm going to take a shower and wash up, okay?"

I look away and start thinking about more than just sleeping. I'm still not sure how she'll react if I make a move, and it's been a while since I've gotten any action, but just being alone with someone as hot as she is makes it very tough to resist. . . . It's too soon, though. Imagining her soaping up in the shower is just about all I can take. I've got to bolt. "I think I'm gonna take a walk and clear my head while I sort things out."

"Are you sure that's wise? Maybe you shouldn't be out in the open."

"Relax. No one would ever think of looking for me up here." *Besides, if I stick around much longer I'll never be able to control myself.*

. . .

My short walk turns into a much longer one, and I lose track of time. It's real peaceful out here. The chill of the night feels good, and the smell of the country air is refreshing as I walk along the side of the road. At least a half hour goes by, and not even a single car passes.

I come up to a large boulder sitting at the edge of the woods. I climb up on it and stretch out, putting my hands behind my head as I stare up at the sky. The stars are really out tonight. I can't remember the last time I looked up at the heavens and even saw any stars at all. Crazy thoughts start banging around inside my head, and my mind begins to race. I hear whispering. It sounds like Troyer calling out to me in that dumb-ass Australian accent.

I look around, but no one's there. No way could the dude follow us up here. No way!

Then I start hearing that bartender girl calling out Troyer's name. I feel like I'm back in my car heading toward Gilgo Beach and she's in the trunk. "Troyer, why'd you do this to me?" she's pleading. "I can't breathe. Please let me out of here."

My chest feels like it's about to explode. I start shaking and sweating, and now *I* can't breathe. I sit up quickly and jerk my head from side to side, expecting somebody to burst out of the woods and shoot me dead on the spot. What the hell is wrong with me?

I climb off the rock, stand up for a second, and a wave of nausea comes over me. *Bam*, just like that, I double over and puke my guts out. I fall to my knees and keep heaving until there's nothing left inside.

I crawl up against the side of the boulder and try to catch my breath. Everything goes black.

. . .

I'm standing right outside the motel room, and I have no idea how I got here.

I slide the card key into the slot, turn the door handle, and step inside. The lights are out, so I flick the switch, expecting to see Aurora tucked in and fast asleep.

The bed is empty, and there's a note on it. I pick it up. Written in large block letters it says:

I HAVE HER NOW MATE. SEE YOU SOON.

CHAPTER TWENTY

The detectives from New York and the officers from New Jersey sat huddled around a conference room table inside Manhattan's third precinct. The far wall was covered with an outline containing a sequence of events, names, arrows, photographs, and circles. It was all written in different colors. A map of Gilgo Beach and the surrounding area was posted beside the outline. A large yellow X marked the spot where the body had been found. An enlarged photo of the crime scene was positioned beside the map, with smaller yellow numbers placed in various locations within the photo.

"Looks like some real fancy police work you got going on there, Detective." Tanner said.

"This is how we do it in New York," said Watts.

Sung rose from his chair, walked over to the wall, and put his face inches from the map. A confused look played across his face. "Care to explain?"

Watts stood, held up what looked like a pen, and clicked. A laser light beamed across the room. Pointing at the wall, he began. "This time sequence tells us approximately when Houston disappeared. We discovered that she left the club after midnight. From there, we go to the time she was reported missing, who reported it, the relationship, etc. As we continue down the line, it shows when and where we discovered the first pieces of evidence, the time it was collected, and what we found . . ."

Sung interrupted. "What's with the picture of the pizza box?"

"That, officer, was our first real clue. It turns out the box was from a pizza place located in Queens, over fifteen miles from the garbage dumpster where we discovered it."

"So how is that a clue?" asked Tanner.

"Houston's blood was found a few feet from the dumpster. And when we checked out the pizza place, it turned out that Thomas Sullivan worked there as a delivery guy. We also found traces of vomit on the box, as well as on the pavement near the blood." Watts pointed to a spot on the photo. "We ran DNA on Sullivan and it matched the vomit, so we know he was at the crime scene."

"So what does this map of the beach have to do with all this?" Tanner asked.

"We found a body over there," Watts pointed again. "But the body isn't Houston's."

"Then how does it tie in?"

Stone chimed in before Watts could answer. "Are you familiar with the Gilgo Beach case from last year?"

Tanner nodded. "Of course. Are you saying this may be connected to that case? Is that a map of Gilgo Beach?"

"We can't be certain that this is all connected," said Stone. "But we suspect so. We found information on Sullivan's computer that prompted us to investigate the beach."

"That is something. So do you have any leads on his whereabouts?" Sung asked.

"Good question," Stone answered. "Our last sighting was down in Cape May. Then we lost him. We've got some good men there and hope to locate him soon."

"That's close to our jurisdiction, Detective," Tanner offered. "I'm sure we can help with that."

"Good. Now that we're all on the same page, why don't the two of you head back to Jersey and head up the search? We'll cover things up here and report back to you. Maybe you'll have better luck finding this guy with local resources."

"Sounds like a plan, Detective," Tanner said. "Just keep us in the loop, and we'll do the same."

"You can count on it," Stone answered, shooting a nod of approval at her partner.

CHAPTER TWENTY-ONE

I run outside in a panic and look around, hoping to see Troyer in the parking lot with Aurora. Yeah, right—who am I kidding? The psycho is long gone, and Aurora is in deep shit. So, knowing I'll regret it later, I pull out my cell, put the battery back in and turn it on. I speed-dial Troyer. No answer, of course, so I power it down and hope that it wasn't on long enough for the cops to zero in on me. Then, out of nowhere, I get nauseous again and start sweating like crazy. The room begins to spin, and my head pounds. When I get like this I just can't function. So I take a couple of migraine pills, turn out the light, and lie down.

CHAPTER TWENTY-TWO

At precisely ten AM the next morning, Detective Stone's cell phone rang.

"Stone here. What ya got for me, Morgan?"

"We've found another body and some blood and drag marks a short distance away."

"Is it Houston?"

"We don't think so," Morgan said. "Too decomposed. Has to have been here for at least six months, probably more. It's female, and there's a belt around her neck. The cause of death appears to be strangulation."

Stone searched the ceiling of the squad room before responding. "Sounds like a different M.O. Is the body clothed?"

"Yes, and she was definitely a pro. Looks like a low-class streetwalker, though. Certainly not a high-priced hooker from the outfit."

"The plot thickens," Stone said, shaking her head as she looked at Watts. "Get her in for an autopsy."

"Already on it," Morgan answered.

"What?" asked Watts, raising his palms and eyebrows in synch.

Stone shook her head and spoke into her cell. "What about the blood and the drag marks?"

Morgan scratched his head, pacing as he spoke. "The dogs led us to a spot one grid over from the hooker's body. We found dried blood, a bracelet, and drag marks. This one could tie in to Houston. There are some washed out bare footprints in the sand. They're small and could be female. Hard to tell, though."

"Anything else?"

"Nothing yet, but there are a few houses up the beach. We're heading out to question the residents."

"Good. We're on our way." Stone pocketed her phone and filled Watts in.

"Two bodies and evidence of a third, all in one area." Watts remarked. "That's way too much coincidence. Sullivan has to be responsible."

"I want to agree, but something doesn't fit. The M.O.s are all different. Blunt-force trauma to the head on one victim, strangulation of another, and we still don't know exactly what happened to Houston."

"Maybe he is experimenting with different methods to see which one he likes best."

"I don't know," said Stone. "But I'm willing to bet there are more bodies out there."

CHAPTER TWENTY-THREE

Aurora returned to consciousness and opened her eyes into a blindfold. Taking a deep breath, she coughed as the sour odor of mold burned her nostrils.

"Hello!" she called out, writhing and twisting her wrists within the ropes that bound her.

A silent emptiness echoed back at her.

"Is anybody out there?" she yelled, more loudly.

Again, nothing.

Shivering, Aurora began to whimper. "Please let me go. I'm cold."

More nothing.

"What do you want from me?"

Deafening silence.

Aurora struggled and rocked the chair she was tied to. "Is that you, Troyer?"

The wind blew and rattled the room.

"Hello!"

CHAPTER TWENTY-FOUR

I wake up fully clothed, lying across the bed at an odd angle. My mouth is filled with cotton, and my head is pounding. I shake off my sleep, slowly remembering that last night Troyer kidnapped Aurora and I'm more fucked than I can ever remember in my entire miserable life.

I don't even know where to begin to try and figure out where Aurora could be. Or what I should do next.

CHAPTER TWENTY-FIVE

Tanner and Sung reached the Cape. A small, unassuming brick building, two blocks from the beach, housed the local police force.

With Sung at his heel, Tanner strode up to the raised counter. A shorter man would have had to look up to speak with the desk officer on duty, but Tanner faced him eye-to-eye.

"Afternoon, Officer . . . Murphy," Tanner said, eyeing his nametag. "I'm looking for your chief. Is he around?"

"If you mean Chief Knox, *she* is."

"Excuse me. I didn't mean to imply anything."

"No problem. Whom shall I say is asking?"

"Tanner—Officer Monty Tanner, and this is my deputy, Sammy Sung. We're down from Seaview investigating a murder. I'm sure you've heard about it."

"Oh, yes, certainly," Murphy said, stepping back from the counter. "I'll tell her you're here."

A minute later, Murphy reappeared. "Follow me."

The men were ushered into Chief Roberta Knox's office.

"Have a seat, gentlemen," she said, in a gravelly, authoritative voice. "I'm told you're here investigating that horrible murder in Seaview."

"That's correct," Tanner answered, sizing up the buxom, gray-haired woman with steel blue eyes.

Knox returned a cold, calculating stare. "What could possibly have led you two down here?"

"Well, Chief, we've been coordinating with detectives from New York who have been investigating a murder up there. Some of the evidence ties into our murder and suggests that the perp was seen in your jurisdiction a few days ago. We've got a lead on his car and figured we'd come down here to look around."

"I see," Knox said, nodding. After a long pause, she continued. "We're a small resort community down here, you know, and we can't have any high-profile, media-circus events scaring our tourists away just before the summer season."

"I understand, Chief. We're not here to raise a ruckus. We'll keep things quiet. We only want to find this guy. His name is Thomas Sullivan, and he owns a silver 2002 Honda Accord, with New York plates."

"And you think he's hiding somewhere around here?"

"We were told that he was seen last Tuesday morning having breakfast at a place called The Nook."

"Then it shouldn't be too difficult to track him down. The season hasn't begun yet, and there are mostly locals around. We can check the inns to see if he took a room. You have a picture?"

"We do," Sung said, pulling a photo from the folder he was carrying. "And here is the license plate number."

"We'll make some copies and circulate them to our officers."

"That would be great, Chief," Tanner said. "Please keep us informed of any developments."

"Acknowledged."

"May I ask you something, Chief?" Tanner asked.

"You may."

"Has there been any criminal activity around here in the past week or so?"

"Out of the ordinary, you mean?"

"Well, that depends on what you consider ordinary."

"Domestic disputes, shoplifting, DWIs, bar fights—that's what we get around here. Certainly no murders."

"Well, how about in the last week or so?"

"Let's see," Knox said, turning her eyes upward. "A local man was beaten up pretty badly a few days ago. He's still in the hospital. It seems he stumbled out of a bar very drunk and was found hours later in a nearby alley."

"Any suspects?"

"None yet."

"Have you questioned the bartender?"

"Not yet, but we'll get around to it."

"I don't mean to intrude," Tanner said, "but that'd be the first place I'd go."

"Don't worry. We're on it," Knox said, sternly.

"Yes, Chief, I'm sure you are. What bar was that?"

"Listen, I said we're on this. I don't want you snooping into our affairs, here."

"I know. I assure you we will be very discreet. We only want to help, and a violent act like you've described may be pertinent."

"Very well," Knox said, reluctantly. "The place is called the Schooner."

"Thank you. So, were there any other incidents worth talking about?"

"A DWI, but we caught the guy. A missing persons report, a shoplift . . ."

Tanner interrupted. "Missing person. What was that all about?" "It's probably nothing. A local girl who works over at the Surf Shop by the beach. Her boss called it in when she didn't show up for work two days in a row, and he couldn't reach her by phone."

"Well, that seems odd," Tanner said.

"Not really. She's one of those girls who dresses in black and has piercings all over the place. You know the type. She's probably strung out on drugs and just sleeping it off."

"Have you checked her home?"

"It only came in a day ago," Knox said. "We're looking into it."

"Okay, then," Tanner said, letting out his breath. "We'll be on our way. Here's my card. Please call me if you come up with anything."

"We will. Just stay clear of trouble while you're here."

"Of course." Tanner rose and walked out, Sung still at his heel.

Once outside, Tanner turned to Sung. "Can you believe that? She's got to be the most disinterested cop I've ever met."

Sung shook his head. "It's almost as if she doesn't want to admit that crimes take place around here."

"Yeah, she's more concerned with keeping things quiet so the tourists don't get turned off by the crime rate."

"So what are we going to do about it?" Sung asked.

"First, we go to the Schooner and talk to the bartender. Then, we go to the Surf Shop. It all may be for nothing, but it's a start."

CHAPTER TWENTY-SIX

A door slammed shut. Aurora awoke.

"Hello. Who's there?"

Troyer slid quietly over to Aurora and stopped directly in front of her. Slowly, he began tapping his foot on the wood floor.

"Is that you Troyer?"

Troyer stopped tapping his foot, allowing silence to fill the air.

"Please untie me, or at least take this blindfold off. I want to see you for who you are."

"You're in no position to make any demands, lovey!"

"So it is you, Troyer. Tommy warned me about you."

"I'll bet he did, love. But you didn't listen. Did you, now?"

"What do you want from me? And why are you doing these things to Tommy?"

"Tommy did this to Tommy!" Troyer shouted. "I'm just along for the ride. There's a lot you don't know about that bloke."

"Like what, you psycho? All I know is you killed two innocent girls and left him to clean up your mess."

"My, my, love, you are bloody bold," Troyer chuckled. "I can see why Tommy fancies you."

"Does this amuse you, asshole?"

"Quite, my dear."

"Good—I'm glad you're having fun. Now why don't you take off this blindfold so I can see who you really are. If you're going to kill me, I think I deserve to see your face."

"Not so fast, love—not so fast. Only Tommy knows what I really look like, and that's the way I intend to keep it."

"So what do you want with me?"

"I don't want a thing from you, love. It's all about Tommy." Troyer's laugh echoed from deep inside. "Haven't you realized that yet?"

"So what do you want with Tommy?"

"In time, lovey—in time." Troyer reached out, grabbed the top of her shirt, and ripped it open.

"Ahh, very nice, but oh-so-unnatural." Troyer thrust his hand inside her shirt and squeezed. "Breasts are such an important part of a woman's sexual identity, and inflating them artificially just sends the wrong message."

Aurora squirmed. "Get your hands off me, you slime!"

"Then again, feistiness turns me on," Troyer said, as his fingers softly painted their way down from Aurora's chest until they reached her jeans. After a moment's hesitation, he abruptly pulled at her waistband, tore open the zipper, and exposed the fine lace beneath. Aurora screeched.

"Relax, bitch. I'm not ready for you yet. I'm just curious to see what Tommy desires."

"Is this the only way you can get a woman, you psycho?"

"Oh, how I love defiance. Please keep going."

"Screw you. I won't even give you the satisfaction."

"Very well, then. Perhaps I can entice you with some food. You must be hungry, my dear."

"I'd never be hungry enough to eat anything from you. Go fuck yourself!"

"Now, now, I have a sandwich for you. Stop talking and open your mouth. I'll feed you."

"Not a chance. I don't want your poison."

"See here, love, if I wanted you dead, you'd be already, so wise up and have a bite. You're going to be here for quite some time."

"I'd rather starve."

"Suit yourself," Troyer said, ramming the sandwich into Aurora's mouth. "Chew on this bitch and swallow it now, or I may have to stick something else in there to force it down."

Aurora gagged and spit out the food.

"Not wise, my dear. That will bring the rats."

"I'd prefer rats over you any day."

"Really. We shall see. I think this may be the perfect time to go. Have fun with the rodents. Perhaps I'll check up on you in a few hours; perhaps I won't. Good day, love."

"Fuck you, asshole!"

CHAPTER TWENTY-SEVEN

The Schooner was moderately crowded when Tanner and Sung entered and walked over to the bar.

"Afternoon, officers. What can I do for you?" the bartender asked, looking at Tanner. "You're in uniform, so you can't be here for drinks."

"You're correct, Mr. . . .?"

"Mike. You can call me Mike."

"Very good, Mike," Tanner said. "We're investigating the incident that took place outside the other night."

"You mean the old man who took a beating?"

"Yes, the old man." Sung said.

"Not much to tell. He was pounding them down for a few hours. I've seen him here a few times before. Keeps to himself, never gave a name."

"He get into it with anyone at the bar that night?" Tanner asked.

"Not that I recall."

"Well, then, do you recall who was in the bar?" Sung asked.

"Sure, a couple of old men and some young guy. It wasn't too busy here."

"The young guy—what do you remember about him?" Tanner asked.

"I don't know—not much. Gimme a minute. I gotta serve some drinks."

Mike headed down the bar, filled an order, and returned.

"Come to think of it, I remember that the guy had a Brooklyn accent, but he told me he was from Vermont, if that helps."

"Was he with anyone?" Tanner asked.

"Nope. The guy was alone the whole time he was here."

"How long would that have been?" Sung asked.

"I dunno—less than an hour."

"What time did he leave?" Tanner asked.

"He came in late, so I'd have to say around midnight."

"When did the old man leave?"

"Maybe a half hour after the guy."

Sung took out a picture of Sullivan and showed it to Mike. "Could this be the guy?"

Mike took the picture in his hand and examined it. "Could be—kinda looks like him, but I can't be a hundred percent."

"Thanks. Take my card," Tanner said. "And if he comes in here again, please call me right away."

"Will do."

CHAPTER TWENTY-EIGHT

I'm sitting on the bed, sweating from places you don't want to know, and watching the local news channel. I'm praying I don't see a report about a girl found dead someplace nearby. Thankfully, the biggest news around is tomorrow's weather. A knock at the door makes me jump. I don't know if I should answer it. Maybe it's the cops. Or maybe it's Aurora. There's no peephole, so I look out the window, but I can't see anyone. I hold my breath and stand in front of the door feeling real stupid. As the knock gets louder, my heart pounds inside my chest.

"Open up, mate. I know you're in there."

Holy shit, its fuckin' Troyer! How does he keep finding me? I pat myself down wondering if maybe he's got some kind of bug on me. It's useless though. I pull open the door and he's standing there with this real toothy grin, looking all proud and shit.

"What did you do with Aurora?"

"I have no idea what you're talking about, mate."

"Don't play that shit with me, asshole. I know you took her. Now whaddya do with her? If you hurt her I'm gonna kill you."

"Ease up, you wanker," Troyer says, waving his hand and smiling like he owns the world or something. "Lovey is fine. A bit tied up right now, but she's just fine."

"Why are you playing me like this?"

"I'm trying to protect you from yourself, Tommy Boy. Don't you see that?"

"Get real. Just tell me where she is and get outta my life. I don't need a psycho like you to look out for me."

"Oh, but you do, mate. With every move you make, you are incriminating yourself more and more, so I'm here to make you stop. I know you're still thinking about going to the police and telling them all about me, but believe me, my friend, if you do that they'll arrest you, and you'll spend the rest of your life in jail."

"Right, and you're here to save me."

"That would be correct."

"Yeah, so what should I do next, then?"

"Well, the first thing you must do is kill Aurora. She's the only one who knows what you've done. And believe me, she will tell if I release her."

"Get the fuck outta here. There's no way I'm killing her."

"It's the only way, mate, and I can't do it for you. You have to commit. You have to cut all ties, and you have to do it right away."

"Not a chance in hell motherfucker!"

"Don't be so sure. When you realize it's either you or her, trust me, mate: you'll see the light."

"Let's just end this now. Take me to her and let her go. We'll be on our way, and you can go crawl into some hole and never come out. I swear I won't go to the cops. I just want all of this to end."

"I'm sorry, but that's not going to happen. Perhaps you need to think about this a bit more. Let's go for a brew and a few shots of tequila."

I look at the dude sideways, in total disbelief. He's got Aurora locked up somewhere and he wants me to kill her, and he actually thinks I want to hang out with him and have some drinks. Where the fuck did this guy come from?

"Come on, mate—lighten up! Things aren't so bad. As long as we stick together, we'll be okay. Forget the girl. She's nothing but trouble."

"You are one messed-up dude. Don't you have a conscience?"

"Get real, Tommy Boy, if you want to survive in this world, you have to think about yourself before anyone else. Conscience has nothing to do with it."

At this point, my blood's boiling. I lose control, take a swing, and hit Troyer right across the chin. His head turns, he takes the blow like it was nothing, and shoots me a punch right in the gut. I drop to my knees, lose my wind, and can't breathe.

Troyer gets on his knees directly in front of me, spits out some blood, and grabs my chin with his thumb and index finger. "Not a wise move, mate. You can't hurt me, but nice try. I think I'll come back later—after you've had some time to think. Meanwhile, I'm going to check on lovey." He loads up, punches me in the face, and knocks me out cold.

CHAPTER TWENTY-NINE

Tanner and Sung located the Surf Shop just down the beach from the Schooner and walked inside. The place radiated tourist. Walls were littered with campy T-Shirts, board shorts, and the like. Cylindrical metal stands overflowing with post cards and knick-knacks cramped the aisles. A middle-aged, balding man, sporting an oversized Quicksilver T-Shirt, stood behind the register.

"Is the manager around?" Tanner asked.

"Stock boy, manager, owner. Harry Gold at your service. I wear all the hats around here, gentlemen. What can I do for you?"

"Were you the one who called in the missing persons report the other day?"

"Yup. That'd be me."

"Care to tell us about it?"

"What's there to tell that I haven't told the other cops who came here yesterday? My cashier girl didn't show up for work for two days. She left me high and dry. I've been working twelve-hour shifts trying to find a replacement. You just can't get reliable help these days."

"What do you think happened to her?" asked Sung.

"Not quite sure. She'd been pretty responsible before, but you never know with girls like that."

"Meaning?" Tanner asked.

"I dunno—a bit bizarre the way she dressed and all. Now, don't get me wrong, it was good for business; that's why I hired her in the first place. The kids find it trendy, but to me, she looked like she should have been working in a morgue. All dark and weird. The black nail polish never sat well with me, either."

"So what made you call in the report?"

"Hell, two days with no calls—that's not like her. She was serious about the job—needed the money, too. So when she didn't show up on day two, I called her at home. The machine picked up, and I left a message telling her that if she didn't get down here right away, she was history. I figured that would light a fire."

"And then what?" Sung asked.

"When I still didn't hear from her I decided to call the police. I knew she had no family, and in some strange way, I felt responsible for her. She was a good kid, whatever she was into, and I started thinking that maybe she was messed-up on drugs. That's what I told the other cops."

"Had you ever seen her on drugs?" asked Tanner.

"No, but looking at her with that diamond in her nose and the dark makeup under her eyes, it seemed to me that she traveled in those circles. You just know it when you see it. You follow me?"

"Uh-huh." Tanner nodded.

"Hey, look: I'm not one to stereotype, but . . . anyway, like I said, she was good for business. She talked it up with the customers, made them feel at home here, and sales were always good when she worked the counter. So I looked past her appearance. Different generation, you know. But it wasn't like her to miss two days in a row without calling."

"What's her name?"

"Aurora. Aurora Storm."

"You know where she lives?"

"Yeah, I've got her address."

"You know what kind of car she drives?" asked Tanner.

"Sure—a black Mustang. Nice car. She was proud of it, too. Parked it real careful, in the back of the lot, so no one would hit it."

"Okay, then, we'll take that address if you don't mind." Tanner said.

"No problem. Wait here. I've got all her info in the office."

Gold rushed off, returned in a few minutes, and handed a sheet of paper to Tanner.

"Much appreciated. Please take my card and call me if you can think of anything else."

"Will do. Good luck. I hope you find her and everything turns out okay."

Sung nodded as they turned and left the shop.

Once outside, Tanner grabbed Sung by the forearm. "Aurora Storm?"

"Interesting name, to say the least. You want me to run it through the system?"

"Do you even have to ask?"

"Uh, sorry, boss."

"Come on. You can check her out in the cruiser while we head over to her place."

Tanner took the wheel. Sung clicked away at the keyboard. First, he mapped her address then he searched her name.

Fifteen minutes later, the men pulled up in front of a small apartment complex.

"We're here, Sammy. You find anything yet?"

"I've got a Facebook page, but the public part is very limited. Not even a picture. I'd say this girl is very careful about keeping her personal life private."

"I don't suppose you have a way to breach and access?" Tanner asked, offering a sarcastic smirk.

"Give me a few minutes."

"I will. But first let's check out her apartment. Maybe we'll find something in there the old-fashioned way."

The two men walked through the complex and located her apartment. Sung knocked on the door. "Hello, police. Is anyone home?"

No answer.

Sung knocked again, more loudly this time. "Hello—is anyone in there? This is the police."

Silence.

"All right, Sammy—just break the lock. She may be inside and helpless."

"Are you sure, boss?"

"Of course—just do it."

Sung stepped back, raised his knee, and threw a straight leg kick into the door. It flung open wide, splitting the wood by the doorjamb.

It was a small apartment—one bedroom, one bathroom, and a tiny kitchen set within the main living area. Opened mail littered the kitchen counter. Cups and dishes were soaking in the sink.

"Looks pretty normal in here—no signs of trouble," Tanner said, leafing through the mail.

"Agreed."

"Hmm . . . 'A. Storm' on all the envelopes. Here's an electric bill. Same deal. No other names on the mail. Guess she lives alone."

Sung moved into the bedroom. "Bed's unmade, both sides turned down, could've been two people sleeping here. Can't be sure, though."

Tanner was in the bathroom. "Two towels hanging over the shower rod. Maybe she had a guest."

Sung pushed the answering machine. It started playing.

"First message," came from an electronic voice. "Aurora, its Harry. You've been gone two days, and I haven't heard from you. I suggest you call and let me know what's going on, or I'm going to have to replace you."

"Surf Shop guy . . . called just like he said."

Tanner nodded. "Yeah—any other messages?"

"Doesn't look like it," Sung answered. "Strange—no friends calling."

"A bit odd, but she could be a loner."

"But Gold said she was a friendly type, drew people in, and boosted sales."

"True—maybe her friends call her cell. These days, most people don't even use their home phones anymore. Let's dig a little deeper. Check the drawers in that desk over there. See if you can find a cell phone bill. If we can get a number, we can call it. Better yet—maybe we can locate it using the cell towers."

"Provided it's powered on, boss. And provided we have a general location."

"I'm well aware, Sammy. Just do what I said."

"Right, boss," Sung answered, as he pulled open the top drawer of the desk and began rifling through it.

Tanner eyeballed the dresser and picked up a photo. "Check this out: here's our girl standing right in front of her car. This should do the trick. We even have a license plate."

"You'd think the local cops would've at least come in here," said Sung. "It doesn't look like they even came through the front door."

"No, it doesn't. Pretty sad police work, if you ask me."

"I guess they'll get around to it."

Tanner chuckled. "Sarcasm from you, Sammy? I never would've thought."

Sung pulled a sheaf of papers from the bottom drawer of the desk. "Here we go, boss: cell phone bills, bank statements, utility bills. It's all here."

"Okay, read me the phone number," Tanner said, pulling his cell from his pocket.

Sung read it out as Tanner punched it into his phone. After four rings, it went into voicemail.

"I should have figured it wasn't going to be that easy."

"Well, boss, we can still try to track it. But what makes you think this girl has any connection to Sullivan?"

"Absolutely nothing."

"So why bother?"

"I don't believe in coincidences, Sammy. And even if she isn't involved with Sullivan, she is still missing. Don't you think that any cop worth his salt would make an effort to investigate? Obviously Knox is too concerned with appearances to do anything."

"I hear you. And with her license plate, we have a good chance of locating her."

"How so?"

"Her car is only a few years old. I can run her info through DMV, get her VIN, and contact Ford. If she has GPS, they should be able to assist us in tracking the vehicle. It works like Lo Jack and GM's OnStar. If we're lucky, we may be able to find her via satellite."

Tanner smiled. "I always knew that some day your tech savvy would come in handy."

CHAPTER THIRTY

Tanner's cell rang as he and Sung left the apartment complex. "Tanner. Who's this?"

"It's Chief Knox. We've located Sullivan's car."

"Great! Where is it?"

"A few blocks from the beach. It's parked by the Chalfonte Hotel. We've got an officer waiting there for you. I'll text you the address."

"Thank you, Chief. We're on our way." Tanner turned to Sung. "They found Sullivan's car. Knox is sending the address—some place called the Chalfonte Hotel."

Sung's eyes widened. "I'll have it before she even sends it to you." Sung tapped the keyboard and entered a new search. "Here it is, boss: make a U-turn and head toward the beach. We're only a few miles away."

Ten minutes later the officers pulled up behind a police cruiser that was parked in front of Sullivan's car. Officer Patrick Gilroy exited his vehicle and met Tanner and Sung as they approached Sullivan's Honda.

"I'm Sergeant Gilroy. Patrick Gilroy. This the vehicle you're looking for?"

"Looks like it," Sung answered. "Any sign of Sullivan?"

"No. The car's cold."

"Did you search inside?" asked Tanner.

"Not yet. It's locked, and I was instructed to wait for you. Chief Knox told me it's your case and to give you full control."

"Much appreciated, Sergeant," Tanner said, escorting Gilroy away from the vehicle. "Thank Chief Knox for us. We'll take it from here."

As Gilroy drove off, Tanner slapped Sung's shoulder. "What are you waiting for, go get the tool."

Every cop car came equipped with all the necessary equipment to open a car in seconds. Contrary to popular belief, car thieves had nothing over the police, especially when it came to breaking and entering. Sung inserted the "Slim Jim" into the gap between the window and the door panel. He pulled upward, released the lock, and opened the door. Tanner half-expected that an alarm would sound, but the decade-old model wasn't so equipped.

Tanner began rummaging through the driver's side while Sung took to the passenger area. After a brief search, Sung stood up outside the car. "Check out what I found under the seat, boss." He held up a knife, still in its sheath.

Tanner rushed around. "Looks like we may have found our man. Bag it fast, and let's move. He must be staying at the Chalfonte. Maybe we can surprise him."

Minutes later, Tanner and Sung entered the Chalfonte Hotel and approached the front desk. An elderly woman, as much a fixture as the worn leather chairs that decorated the ancient lobby, frowned behind thick glasses.

"Oh, dear," the old woman said, shaking. "Is anything wrong?"

"What makes you say that, ma'am?" asked Tanner.

"Well, I can't remember the last time the police came in here, and I've been working the Chalfonte for quite some time."

"Please don't be alarmed. We're just looking for someone, and we think he might be staying here."

Sung took out the picture of Sullivan and handed it to the old woman. "Does he look familiar?"

She looked at the picture, removed her glasses, and let them hang from the band fastened around her neck. She brought the picture up to her eyes, held it inches from her nose, then stretched her arm out and held the picture as far away from her eyes as her arm would allow. Seconds passed as she rubbed her chin with her thumb and index finger. She put her glasses back on looking deep into the photo again. "Room 328."

"Ma'am?" Tanner asked, perplexed.

"That man checked in here a few days ago, paid cash, and took room 328. Isn't that what you wanted to know?"

"Yes, but . . ."

"But nothing, sonny boy. I may be old, but I still have my wits about me. He's paid up through next week."

"Okay . . ." Tanner said. "May we have a key to his room?"

"I could ask you for a warrant, young man. You know that. But truthfully, it really doesn't matter much to me." She handed Tanner a key. "Here you go, but don't you go messing that room. We keep a clean place here."

"Yes, ma'am," Tanner said. "Can you tell me if you remember the last time you saw this man?"

"I haven't seen him since he checked in."

"Thank you. We'll check upstairs."

The men traversed two flights of stairs and found the room. Sung knocked. "Hello, is anyone in there?"

Silence.

Tanner banged the door hard. "This is the police. Open the door."

More silence.

Both men pulled their guns in unison. Tanner inserted the key and threw open door. Sung rushed in first, gun pointed ahead. "All clear, boss."

Tanner ran to the bathroom and looked in. "Clear."

Sung began scanning the room and quickly focused on the floor beside the bed. "Check this out, boss," he said, picking up a pair of board shorts. "Feels brand new."

"He probably bought that locally," Tanner said.

"Could be."

Tanner bent down and looked under the bed. Reaching, he pulled out a pair of thongs. "Look at this: a 'Surf Shop' imprint." At that instant, everything became crystal clear and Tanner just knew. "He's got the girl, Sammy."

Sammy nodded in the way cops do when they agree with the conclusion but don't want to interrupt a superior officer on a roll.

"We have to move fast. Get back on that computer of yours and put out an APB on the girl and her car. Then get started on the GPS search with Ford. We have to get the knife to the lab and have it checked for blood and fingerprints to confirm it, but there's no doubt in my mind, that knife is our murder weapon, and Sullivan is our man." Tanner raced from the room with Sung at his heels.

CHAPTER THIRTY-ONE

Stone returned to the car carrying a large tea and a bag that contained a cherry Danish and a Yoo-hoo.

Watts had just hung up the phone. "You've got that look on your face. What's going on?" Stone slid into the car and handed the bag to Watts.

"Major developments, partner."

"I'm all ears."

"Tanner and Sung located Sullivan's car and found a knife. It's being analyzed by their lab as we speak. Not only that, but they think Sullivan may have kidnapped a girl down in Cape May. They believe he has her car, too. They just emailed me the details." Watts pointed to the computer screen in the cruiser. "I forwarded Sullivan's DNA and his prints for comparison. The analysis will take some time, but Tanner is convinced Sullivan is his perp."

Stone should have been shocked, but she wasn't. She calmly placed the large, Styrofoam cup in the cup holder and began reading the email. "Aurora Storm, black 2011 Mustang. If Sullivan is on the run in this car, he's probably headed as far away from New York as he can get. We better alert the State Police in Pennsylvania, Delaware, and Maryland, along with all the other surrounding states."

"Agreed, but we may have a better way to track the car. Tanner already contacted New Jersey DMV, got the VIN number and is checking with Ford to see if the car has a GPS. If it does, we should be able to pinpoint its location via satellite."

CHAPTER THIRTY-TWO

I come to on the floor of the motel room. Man, that dude packs quite a punch. I race outside, but there's no sign of Troyer. I don't even know how he got here, but he must have stolen a car or something. I run down to the parking lot, get into Aurora's car, and take off. Maybe I can catch him on the road, if he hasn't gone too far.

I drive as fast as I can for ten minutes and don't see anything. No other cars are even on the road. There's nothing but woods for miles. No stores, no gas stations—absolutely nothing, all the way to the highway. I spin a U-turn and head back in the other direction. There's only one road, so if he didn't go toward the highway, he must have gone the other way.

I backtrack past the motel, pedal to the metal, and just keep going. In this direction, the road leads into town. There's a diner, a gas station, and a few bullshit little stores. Further down, there's a church and a crappy old high school. I remember that from when I worked at Camp Lakewood. Yeah, those are some good memories. First time I got laid was at that camp. Counselor named Ellen. Biggest tits I ever saw. The guys all called her "Melons," but I never did. And that's what got me laid . . . I think. The chick always wanted me to feel her up and squeeze those babies. So, late at night, during canteen, we'd meet by this weird-shaped tree that grew out of the ground like a banana. She'd lay up against it and lift up her shirt while I massaged her cans like you can't believe. Man, that was hot. In fact, even now, when I think about it, I still get some wood. Anyway, I'm getting off the subject. I have to find Troyer before he does something bad to Aurora.

I've got to start thinking like Troyer because the dude's always one step ahead of me. The only way to beat this guy is to think what he's thinking about what I'm thinking—before I start thinking about it. That sounds fucked-up, but if you think about it, it makes perfect sense.

Then it hits me like a ton of bricks. I slam on the brakes, pull another U-turn, and head back to the motel, hoping I get there in time.

I pull into the lot, jump out of the car, and race inside the office. There's no one at the counter, so I ring the bell and call out. "Hello."

No one answers.

I call out again. Same shit.

I walk over to the door that leads to the back, and turn the handle. It's unlocked, so I push the door open and walk in. "Hello—is anyone back here? I need some help."

I keep walking until I reach an office. I look in.

Holy shit—I can't believe what I'm seeing. I shake my head and rub my eyes, but she's still there. The front desk girl is stretched out on the floor, her body lifeless and dead as can be.

Troyer, the fuck. He did it to me again.

CHAPTER THIRTY-THREE

Tanner and Sung were greeted by Charise Ray, the senior technician at the modest crime lab used by all the local townships around Seaview. It was not a facility accustomed to the pressure brought on by the serious nature of the crime, but, "Cherry"—aptly nicknamed by her co-workers—was up to the task. Seasoned, capable, and possessed of the darkest skin imaginable, she always wore high-gloss red lipstick and too-tight tops that incited whispers, though no on one had the nerve to publicly raise an issue.

"Okay, Cherry," Tanner began, "what do you have for us?"

Despite her appearance, Cherry was all business. "Well, first of all, that knife has quite a few stories to tell. There are at least four different human blood samples and one canine."

"But the blade looked clean," Sung said.

"As a matter of fact, it was cleaned—very thoroughly. But where the handle meets the blade, blood was caked up underneath, and preserved."

"Any DNA matches?" Tanner asked.

"Yes, there were. This knife was definitely used to stab both the bartender from New York and our girl from the motel. No matches on the other two blood samples, though. I ran them through the system, and neither one came up. As to the canine—well, you can just forget that one."

"So the same perp killed both girls?" Tanner asked.

"Likely, but not one hundred percent," Cherry said.

"What's that supposed to mean?"

"The handle tells a different tale. We found a few different prints, and we even extracted some DNA from what appears to be perspiration. There's also dirt and grease imbedded in the sheath. It's pretty clear that a number of people handled that knife recently."

"Great," Tanner said, deflated. "A good attorney will eat that up."

"No doubt," Cherry agreed.

"Well, did you at least match anything to Sullivan?"

"No match on the DNA. And we only have a partial on the prints so we're still looking, but that'll take a while."

Tanner mulled that over. "I dunno, Sammy—I still like Sullivan for this, but the evidence isn't what I expected."

"Well, boss, you know one of the first things I learned at the academy was to follow the evidence."

"Yeah, yeah, I know: fact before fiction." Tanner looked at Cherry. "Okay, what can you tell us about the dirt and grease?"

"All I can say is that there are trace elements of used motor oil, metal filings, and sawdust."

"Best guess?"

"Hard to say—maybe from an auto repair shop."

"Huh? That makes no sense. Can't you do any better than that?"

"Give me some more time. I'll keep digging. In the meantime, we have to wait for the prints to run through AFIS."

CHAPTER THIRTY-FOUR

The continuing search at Gilgo Beach now involved more than a dozen investigators, some with dogs and some with metal detectors. A helicopter was making measured passes over the area, as well.

Detectives Reese and Morgan stepped off the porch of Victor Constantine's beach house. Moving quickly down the long gravel walk, they pushed their way through the tall stalks of overgrown weed grass until they reached the paved road that led back to Ocean Parkway. Morgan stopped as he caught the reflection of something bright on the ground. He bent down, eyeing a piece of jewelry stuck between the stalks.

"What ya got there?" Reese asked.

"Check this out," Morgan said, sliding a pen through a silver bracelet. "I think this one's identical to the bracelet found near the blood and the drag marks back at the Gilgo Beach scene."

"You have to be kidding. How in the world would that get all the way over here?"

"Not a clue, but the implications are huge."

"No shit," said Reese, gazing back at the tiny bungalow-style house set behind the weed grass.

Morgan's eyes followed Reese's. "You don't think this guy is playing us, do you?"

"I don't know. He seemed legit."

"So how do you explain this bracelet?" asked Morgan.

"Logically, the girl who was wearing it had to have passed through here. Either on her own or aided by someone else."

"Aided or against her will."

"Yeah—or against her will," agreed Reese. "But Constantine is way too old and weak to carry her all the way here. It's over a quarter mile, and you saw the guy."

"I know, but either way that means she could still be alive."

"For better or worse."

Morgan's jaw tightened. "Did you have to say that?"

"Sorry, but I've seen too much on this job to sugarcoat it."

"Enough said. But since we found the bracelet along the road, any house in this direction may hold the answer."

CHAPTER THIRTY-FIVE

Leaving Sung at the station, Tanner sat alone in a booth inside the Pantry Diner, trying to gain some perspective. He studied the menu as if it were the first time he'd ever seen it, though it was as familiar to him as the scar that ran across the four knuckles of his left hand. Suddenly, his cell phone rang. He recognized the number immediately. "Give me something good, Cherry."

"I don't rate the info, Sergeant; I just report it."

"Yeah, yeah, okay. What have you found?"

"Well, I've got an ID on the print."

"Great—who is it?"

"A guy named Charles Gantry. Lives right in Seaview, in fact."

Tanner scratched the back of his neck. "Gantry—that name sounds familiar. What else can you tell me?"

"He's a small-time offender, arrested for assault about seven years ago and pled it down."

"That was before my time. And you say he lives in Seaview?"

"He does."

"I need an address and a photo. Email it to Sammy at the station. I'll be there in ten minutes."

"Will do."

Tanner disconnected the call and dialed Sung. "I'm on my way back. Cherry has an ID on the fingerprints. Check your email."

. . .

Sung had just finished reviewing the arrest record for Charles Gantry when Tanner walked in. "Hey, boss, you're not going to believe this." He handed the rap sheet to Tanner.
"What is it?"

"Look at the picture. That's Chunky. Younger and a hundred pounds lighter, but it's definitely him."

CHAPTER THIRTY-SIX

"We going to arrest him, boss?" Sung asked. "His prints were on the murder weapon. That's probable cause."

"It may be, but this just doesn't make sense. I know this guy, and he doesn't seem the killer type. I think we should search his place before we tip him off."

"Well we do have enough for a warrant."

"We do, so contact the county attorney and get the warrant."

"On it, boss, but the warrant has to specify what we're looking for?"

"Blood, Sammy. Come on: there was massive blood at the scene. If he was there, he would have brought some back with him. We check his clothes, his car, the tow truck . . ."

Sung nodded, continuing, ". . . his shoes, his garbage, his laundry . . ."

"Now you're getting it. And then we bring him in and see what he has to say about the prints."

"Makes sense."

"Yeah, and after you call the county attorney, fire up that computer of yours and start searching for anything about Gantry. As much as I can't believe this, we have to check this out completely."

CHAPTER THIRTY-SEVEN

My nightmare just got worse. And it feels like I'm reliving the scene outside of Club Radical. I've got another dead girl on my hands because of Troyer, and if I don't hide her fast, I'm probably gonna get blamed. Without another thought, I pick her up and carry her out, feeling damn lucky that there's no one around. Even better, there's absolutely no blood, which means no evidence. With the body gone, the cops will have a tough time figuring out what happened to her.

I load her in the trunk and jump in the car, and get this: There's fuckin' Troyer sitting right in the passenger seat, wearing that stupid-ass, toothy grin of his.

"You fucked-up piece of shit!" I scream. "How could you do this again?" I get out and back away.

"I suggest you return to the car and start driving, mate. It won't be long before someone comes around and sees you. Then you'll have a lot of explaining to do."

I shake my head, turn, and scan across the motel from one end to the other, looking to see if anyone's around who may be watching. All is quiet, but my heart's pounding so loud my ears are vibrating.

Troyer shouts at me. "I said get in and let's get out of here now, Tommy Boy! You're starting to piss me off." Then he starts laughing like that cartoon character Woody Woodpecker, "Ha-ha-ha-ha-HA, ha-ha-ha-ha-HA, wooo!"

If I wasn't sure before, I certainly am now: This dude has totally lost it. But at the same time, I feel like I don't have a choice. I can't run from the car and leave the body in the trunk; Troyer's still got Aurora, and I'm screwed. He's totally got me by the balls. So I get back in the car and start driving, not knowing where on God's green earth I'm going.

"Now you're finally wising up, mate," Troyer says, as he pushes my shoulder playfully. "And I know you know this area real well, so take us to a safe place to dump her."

Even though I'm facing straight ahead, I still have one eye on the lunatic. I'm gripping the steering wheel so tight that my knuckles turn white. I grit my teeth and pull my lips back, shaking my head from side to side. "What the fuck is up with you, Troyer? I mean, come on man: You didn't need to kill that girl back there."

"Tsk, tsk, Tommy Boy—you still haven't learned, have you? The more you try to escape me, the closer we become. I know every move you make before you make it. And once again, you are mistaken. I didn't kill this girl; you did. I barely had enough time to traverse the stairs when you came stumbling out of the room. So I hid in a storage closet and watched as you ran to the lobby. You came out a few minutes later, jumped into the car, and drove off. I then went inside, saw no one behind the front desk, searched the back, and found the clerk dead on the floor. I left; you arrived fifteen minutes later; and I climbed into the car and waited for you. Why you killed this girl is a mystery to me."

"Get the fuck outta here. I didn't kill this girl! You did."

"Look, Tommy Boy: I'm beginning to grow weary of your fictional accounts of the events that have transpired over this past week. I truly wish to help you because I believe that deep down you're a swell bloke, but until you take responsibility for what you have done, I won't be able to assist you. Ahh, and then there's Aurora—we mustn't forget lovely Aurora. You were foolish enough to bring her into all this, and now she knows too much, and she must be eliminated."

My head's spinning. I'm dizzy, and I can't think straight.

Troyer opens the glove box, reaches in, and takes out my migraine medicine. He shakes the vial and hands it to me.

"You don't look well, Tommy Boy. Perhaps these might help you to think more clearly."

I take the vial from him, thinking exactly the same thing and wondering how he seems to know my thoughts before I do. Anyway, I shake out four pills and swallow them dry.

"Okay, Troyer," I say, pretty much resigning myself to making my next mistake. "There's a lake just a couple of miles through town. It's secluded, so we'll head over there and hide while we figure out what to do next."

"Now you're talking, Tommy Boy."

"Talking is the last thing I want to do right now."

"Aww, come on, mate. Get over it. Just stick with me and everything will work out fine."

"Like I'm really supposed to believe that."

"Yes, you must," Troyer says, pointing. "Hey, check it out. Let's stop and get something to eat."

I look off to my right as I pass a fifty-year-old railroad car they turned into a diner called The Greasy Spoon. "Now? You must be insane."

"Come on. I'm hungry."

"Not a chance." I say, as I accelerate past it. Suddenly, I'm flooded with old memories. I remember sneaking out of camp with the counselors some nights. We'd hang out, eating these unbelievable desserts they had. Boston cream pie was always my favorite. Man, I wish we could just pull in right now and order up one of those sweet-tasting pies.

"I can see it in your eyes, mate. You want to go in there, so turn around. I'll be right behind you."

"Are you that crazy, Troyer? Or did you forget we have a dead girl in the trunk?" Then, out of nowhere, I start hearing a voice coming from the back. "Help! Let me out of here!"

I look over at Troyer. "You hear that?"

"Hear what? I don't hear a thing, mate. What's with you?"

"Help!"

"*That!* Did you hear it?"

"Come now, Tommy Boy. You're imagining things. I heard nothing."

"Well, I did, and I'm pulling over. Maybe that girl isn't dead."

"Listen, mate: Let's just get some food and forget about what's in the trunk. Then we can go someplace quiet, like that lake you were talking about."

"But what if she's still alive?"

"Then she will be when we get there, Tommy Boy."

"Great, and then what do we do?"

"'We,' mate? You mean 'you' . . . what do *you* do? And the answer to that is quite clear."

CHAPTER THIRTY-EIGHT

Stone and Watts were only a few miles away from Gilgo Beach as she talked on the phone with detective Morgan.

"And you're certain the bracelet is identical to the one found at the scene?"

"I am."

"Any blood where you found the bracelet?" asked Stone.

"Not a drop, but we're backtracking between the original scene and this one."

"Good. What about the neighbors?"

"Nothing yet, but we're continuing to question them."

"Okay. We're almost there."

Stone hung up her cell, and looked across to Watts. "There's a slim chance our bartender may still be alive."

"How so?"

"A matching bracelet was found near some house located over a quarter mile away from the beach scene."

"So . . . you're thinking she just got up and walked away from the beach?"

"I really don't know. But one way or another, that body was moved."

CHAPTER THIRTY-NINE

The dirt road that leads to the lake is overgrown, but still clear enough to drive down. Branches scrape the car as we move forward, but within a half mile, we have to stop.

"I guess this is as far as we can go, Tommy Boy," Troyer says. "The lake can't be much further."

"It's not. This road used to go all the way there, but it looks like no one's been through here in years."

"Good for us, then. Why don't you go get the girl from the trunk? I'll scout ahead and make sure we're alone."

I nod, moving on autopilot, because I really have no idea what I'm doing, and I can't figure out why Troyer's got this power over me. That's right: Even though I know I shouldn't be listening to him, I keep doing what he says.

I pop the trunk, walk around to the back, and lift the girl out, when—get this—she opens her eyes and screams. I drop her, stumble backward, and fall to the ground.

"Troyer, quick!" I yell, but she's already off and running.

I get up and call out to her. "Wait! Don't run! I'm not gonna hurt you!" She ignores me and disappears into the woods.

"Troyer! Troyer! Get over here. She's alive!"

Troyer strolls around to the back of the car and shakes his head. "No worries, mate. She won't get very far. Let her go. She'll run out of steam, and then we'll catch up to her."

CHAPTER FORTY

Sung raced into Tanner's office waiving papers. "Warrant has been issued, boss."

Tanner pushed himself out of his chair and grabbed his coat. "About time. Let's go."

Fifteen minutes later, the men pulled up in front of Gantry's home—a small, one-story, wood-frame house with a detached garage.

"He'll be at work for a few more hours, so let's get to it," Tanner said as he strode up to the front door and twisted the doorknob. "As I figured, it's locked. Let's go around back and see if there's another way in."

The men made their way around to the back of the house, found an unlocked door, and entered the main living area.

"The place looks too small for a big man to live comfortably," Sammy said. "And it smells like wet dog."

"Appetizing, with the empty beer cans decorating that coffee table."

"Gross is more like it. This man is a total slob."

"Okay, Sammy, let's get to it. I'll start in the bedroom. You can start with the garbage."

"Come on, boss. If this is how he lives, I don't want to see what's in his garbage."

"Sorry, but you know how important garbage can be in an investigation, so hold your nose and hop to it."

Tanner moved over to the bedroom as Sammy donned rubber gloves.

...

Fifteen minutes later, Tanner called, "Hey, Sammy. I've been through the drawers and the closets; there's nothing in here. And all I found in the bathroom was a recent issue of *Hustler*. You find anything?"

"Just the usual garbage, boss. I checked the kitchen and living room too. There's nothing here. This looks like a dead end."

Tanner returned to the main room. "Okay, let's check out the garage."

The men made their way out back. The aluminum door squeaked, almost begging for lubrication as it folded its way into the ceiling and disappeared. The men were astonished by what they saw. Pristine would barely be sufficiently descriptive. The room looked as if it had come right out of a *West Coast Customs* episode. All manner of tools and car parts were neatly aligned along the walls. The floor boasted a glossy texture that practically dared an oil spill to attempt to defile it.

"Are you seeing this, boss?"

"That's a '57 Bel Aire!"

"Yeah, but look how clean this place is. It's like night and day compared to the house."

"Downright bizarre. But I've gotta tell you, I'm even more blown away by the car. Check it out: the restoration is magnificent."

"Unreal, boss. This guy has some serious talent."

"Truly amazing. I guess I never really knew this guy after all."

"It seems that way."

"Okay, Sammy, you check out the car, I'll look around the place."

Tanner set about inspecting every shelf, drawer, and toolbox in the garage while Sung rifled through the classic Chevy. Before the end of Chunky's shift at the Mobil station, Tanner and Sung had completed the entire search.

Sung closed the trunk and spread his arms wide. "The restoration is immaculate, boss. Not a suspicious thing in the whole damn car. You find anything?"

"Clean as a whistle. But we still have to question him. Let's go pick him up and bring him down to the station."

Fifteen minutes later, the men arrived at the Mobil and found Chunky half-buried under the hood of an old Ford pickup.

Hearing the men arrive, Chunky stood up, tossed his wrench on the nearby Craftsman toolbox, and pulled a dirty gray rag from his rear pocket.

"Back again, guys?" Chunky asked, wiping his forehead and then his hands.

"Afraid so, Chunk," Tanner said. "And we have a problem."

"Problem? What kinda problem?"

"We're going to have to take you down to the station," said Sung. "We need you to answer some questions for us."

"Didn't I answer all your questions before? And why do I have to go there? Why can't you just ask me here?"

"It's a bit more complicated than that," Tanner answered. "And we have to read you your Rights."

"My Rights! What's this all about? Are you guys arresting me?"

"Yes, we are," said Sung. "You have the right to remain silent. You have the right to an attorney. Anything you say can, and will, be used against you in a court of law. If you cannot afford an attorney, one will be appointed for you."

"Come on, Monty," Chunky said, raising his palms and backing away. "Is this some kinda joke?"

"No joke. We have to do this by the book—for all our sakes. We can't have anyone saying you were given preferential treatment because we know you."

"I still don't understand."

"Do you understand your Rights?" asked Sung.

"Yes. Now will you tell me what this is all about?" Chunky pleaded.

"Do you want an attorney?" asked Sung.

"Do I need one?"

"That's up to you," Sung said.

"No lawyer. Just tell me what you guys want to know."

"I'm sorry, but we still have to take you down," Tanner said. "And we have to put the cuffs on."

"You've gotta be kidding."

"Sorry—standard procedure."

"Well, at least tell me what this is all about."

Tanner looked at Sung, then back at Chunky. "Okay. First, can you tell me if you looked through Sullivan's car?"

"Of course I did. I was all over it. You know I worked on it here."

"Yes, we know," Sung said. "But what about the contents of the car?"

"Contents? Whaddya mean?"

"You know, anything inside the car?"

"I'm sure I looked around it, but I got no idea where you're going with this."

"Okay, Chunk, I'll get to the point." Tanner's tone was official now. "Did you find a knife in Sullivan's car?"

Chunky hesitated, then swallowed hard. "A knife? I . . . uh, let me think, uh . . . no, I don't remember seeing a knife. Why?"

Tanner pursed his lips and looked sideways at Chunky. "Let's just finish this back at the station. In the meantime, you keep thinking about what you may have come across in that car."

. . .

Twenty minutes later, Chunky was led into a holding room routinely used to interrogate suspects. There was no see-through mirror, no cameras, and no recorders. The Seaview budget would never allow for such items.

Tanner took this one alone, sat down in front of Chunky, and folded his hands. "Before we go any further, are you sure you don't want a lawyer?"

Perspiring heavily, his face burning deep red, Chunky shook his head no.

"Okay, then, have you thought any more about what you may have come across in Sullivan's car?"

"Like I said, I can't remember anything in particular."

"Well, perhaps you can explain how your fingerprints were found on the knife that killed Syeda Bakht."

"What? My fingerprints? Are you sure?"

"There's no doubt."

Chunky wiped his forehead with his sleeve. "I don't know, Monty. I mean, I did go through the glove compartment, and I musta moved some stuff around looking for the manual. If it was in there, maybe I accidentally touched it."

"Come on. You can do better than that."

"Look at me: I'm the first to admit I'm a bit overweight and it can be a problem. You know I can't always fit into small cars like that, so sometimes I just feel around for stuff without getting all the way into the car. Like I said, I was looking for the manual, and maybe I touched it. I don't remember, though."

Tanner stared Chunky down, scratched his head, and stood. "We'll see about that, my friend. In the meantime, make yourself comfortable. You're here for the night while we do some checking."

CHAPTER FORTY-ONE

I look crossways at Troyer. "So we're just gonna let her run? What if she goes to the cops?"

"Relax, Tommy Boy. We're miles from civilization. She'll tire soon enough, and then we'll find her."

"Yeah, and then what?"

Troyer points at the tire iron laying inside the trunk. "Do you really need to ask?" he says, bellowing out that perfect, psycho laugh that sounds even crazier with an Australian accent.

"Look, man. There's no need to kill the girl."

"Oh, but there is, Tommy Boy. Pick that up and let's get a move on."

Now, you have to try and understand this, because deep down inside I know it's not right, and I know I shouldn't be listening to anything this lunatic is saying, but at the same time, I feel like I've got no choice. It's like I have to do what he tells me.

"Let's hunt her down like the animal she is," Troyer says, staring all crazy eyes at me. "Then, when we catch her, I'll let you gut her. And after she's dead I promise you I'll take you to Aurora so you can finish her off, as well."

I pick up the tire iron. Part of me wants to swing it right across Troyer's face and destroy him, while another part of me says,

No—don't do it. He's the only one who knows where Aurora is. I know that without Troyer, Aurora's dead. I think Troyer knows that, too, and he's playing with me, trying to see how far I'll go. After all, the dude always seems to know what I'm thinking before I even start thinking it. And with his fighting skills, if we do end up in a confrontation, I'm better off with a weapon in my hands.

Without another word, Troyer turns and starts hop-skipping after the girl. All of a sudden, I get this *Alice in Wonderland* feeling, kind of like I'm about to chase the fuckin' rabbit down the rabbit hole. Anyway—and don't ask me to explain it—I race after him, death-gripping the tire iron.

The woods are thick, but Troyer maintains a feverish pace as we wind our way through the lighter brush, dodging small bushes and fallen trees. As if by instinct, he seems to know which way the girl is going. We continue the hunt, barely slowing, until we're led back to the road. Somehow, she must have found her way out.

Even worse, when we get there, we look up ahead and see her flagging down a passing car. That just about does it for Troyer. He starts jumping up and down and slapping his hands together in this mad-ass, wild way.

"Fuck! Shit! Fuck!" Troyer screams, swinging punches at the sky. "That wasn't part of the plan."

Troyer looks rattled for the first time ever, and I don't know what to make of it. On the one hand I'm kind of relieved, because now she's safe, but on the other hand, she's going straight to the cops.

Troyer stops gyrating, squats down, and wraps his arms around his knees. Breathing heavily, he looks up at me. "Quickly—let's get back to the car. There's not much time." He jumps up and takes off.

It doesn't take me more than a second to turn and follow him. At top speed, we race through the woods, dodging branches and leaping rocks, until we reach the car. I get behind the wheel, start her up, ram her into reverse, and nail the gas pedal. The car jolts backward, and I spin her around, throw her into drive, and book out of there at Mustang speed. We bounce along the dirt path for at least a half mile before reaching the paved road. I turn to Troyer and see the dude rocking back and forth, staring blindly, his eyes almost popping out of his head.

"Okay, Troyer, the shit's gonna unravel real fast now, so let's get Aurora and bolt before that girl tells the cops."

Troyer stops rocking, slowly looks over at me, and smiles from ear to ear. "No worries, mate—just a small setback. We can handle this."

"I don't know about that. Once she gets to the cops . . ."

". . . we'll be long gone, Tommy Boy. Just head for the highway."

"Not until we get Aurora."

"Come on, mate. She's as good as dead, anyhow. Like I told you, she knows too much."

"Look—Aurora comes with us, or I don't go. I swear she's no threat."

Troyer slaps me across the back of my head and laughs. "Oh, you have it bad, Tommy Boy. When will you learn? Chicks are just baggage, and you have to travel light."

"I don't care. Those are my terms." I slam on the brakes and stop short right in the middle of the road. "Aurora comes, or you can get out here and start walking."

"Well, well, aren't you growing a set now, mate?"

I turn and stare Troyer right in the eyes. "Fuck you, man. I'm done!"

Troyer returns my stare and doesn't say a word for what seems like an hour but isn't more than five seconds. Then, out of nowhere, he breaks out that stupid-ass grin of his.

"Okay, Tommy Boy, I'll give you what you want for the time being, but if she becomes a burden, I'll kill her myself."

"Whatever. Just tell me: Where is she?"

Troyer laughs again. "You know exactly where she is, Tommy Boy."

I look at him and squint. "No, I don't, so quit playing games and tell me."

"Camp Lakewood, mate."

CHAPTER FORTY-TWO

Sung stood a few feet away and watched Tanner pacing by his desk. "We know he's lying, boss. I found the knife under the seat."

"I realize that, Sammy. But I still can't believe Chunky did this."

"Can't, or don't want to?"

Tanner frowned, about to protest, despite knowing deep down inside that while he truly liked Chunky, he could no longer ignore the evidence. "You've got me there, Sammy. It's just that I've known him for years and he doesn't seem the type."

"I hear you, boss, but the fact is neither of us really knows that much about him. After all, before today were you ever inside his house, or his garage for that matter? Admit it. You were as surprised as I was when we saw the car."

Tanner mulled that over. "Yeah, I see your point. Maybe I don't know him as well as I thought. But even though, I'm having a hard time digesting all this. I mean, think about it. What's his motive?"

"Point taken. Clearly we need to dig a lot deeper."

Tanner pulled at the skin around his throat. "Of course you're right. We need to know more before going back in there to confront him." Tanner grabbed the car keys off his desk. "Let's go search the Mobil. We can update Stone on the way over."

"At your six, boss."

CHAPTER FORTY-THREE

Stone exited the car at Gilgo Beach, leaving the door open wide. A stiff breeze cut across the meager strip of land that separated the ocean from the bay. Watts shivered, pulling the lapels of his coat together as he chased after her. "Clue me in, partner. I see those wheels turning. Time to share it."

"Sorry, but this one's got me all wound-up. My gut tells me that Sullivan's our perp, but the evidence is all over the place. Think about what the M.E. told us. There is no pattern to the killings. One body shows blunt force trauma to the head. Another was strangled. Yet another was shot in the heart. The bodies found last year also suggest that there must be more than one killer. Factor that in with what Tanner reported about the mechanic, and our connection down in Jersey is severed. The only common element is that all of the vics are young women."

"All this troubles me as well."

Stone stood at the edge of the road looking out toward the frenzy of activity deep within the weed grass. Tall yellow stalks, blowing in the wind, waved back and forth, as if calling, "Here we are, Detective. Come and find us. We've been murdered, and we need your help." Shivering, Stone pulled her sweater sleeves through her jacket and over her wrists. "I know there are more bodies out here, and when we find them we'll have all we need to convict Sullivan."

. . .

Morgan and Reese reached the second home on the bluff less than a half-mile from Gilgo Beach. It was an oddly shaped, one-story structure, erected in the middle of the twentieth century. From an empty driveway, a crushed-shell path led to the front porch. A faded, white swing hung from rusted chains, squeaking as it swayed in the wind. Off to the left, a mobile home, planted on cinder blocks, was clumsily attached via a short breezeway. The entire home was painted red in a crude effort to make the abomination appear seamless. Weeds grew through broken floorboards.

"The place looks deserted," said Reese.

"Could be. Gilgo is like most of the other beach communities. The residents hibernate in winter, close up their homes, and return to thaw them out in the spring." Morgan knocked, then called out, "Hello? Is anyone home?"

Reese wiped the window with his sleeve.

"Can you see anything?" Morgan asked, twisting the doorknob.

"Hard to tell. It's totally dark inside. But my spider sense is tingling. Something tells me we're in the right place."

"Okay, Spiderman, we've been partners long enough for me to know when to defer to your . . . uh . . . insectile instincts." Morgan grinned. "This door is locked. Let's check around for another way in."

Reese drew his gun and pointed it skyward. Morgan followed suit.

Crouching against the wall, the two men slid around to the side of the house and made their way to the breezeway door.

Reese checked the handle and turned back to Morgan. "It's open."

Morgan nodded. Reese pushed through the door.

Once inside, Morgan flicked a light switch that lit up the entire area. They found themselves in a kitchen-living room hybrid with a brick fireplace in the far corner. The refrigerator hummed in the background.

Morgan crinkled his nose. "That's the smell of freshly-burnt wood. Someone's been here recently."

"You see that?" Reese said, pointing to the floor near the bedroom door. "Looks like blood to me."

Morgan bent down to examine. "It definitely looks like blood, but we'll have to test it."

Reese nodded, crossed the room, made his way into the kitchen, and rummaged through the pantry. Opening the refrigerator, he was hit with the rancid odor of spoiled something—extremely spoiled something. "I've got some containers of old Chinese food here, along with a six-pack of Heineken. There's also a half-bottle of tequila chilling in the freezer. Seems like whoever lives here drinks more than they eat."

"Oh, yeah," Morgan answered, "Come on in the bedroom and check this out."

Reese spun and ran to Morgan "What did you find?"

Morgan was examining the dresser top. "Women's jewelry—and one piece, in particular, matches the other two bracelets we found."

"Our vic was here."

"Appears so." Morgan gestured toward the side of the bed. "Over there, more blood droplets. The spatter pattern tells me the blood dripped from a warm body. If the blood was transferred from the perp's shoes, or clothing, it wouldn't have dripped like that; it would have smeared."

Reese blew a heavy sigh and shook his head. "Looks like we've found ourselves another crime scene."

"No shit. Get on the horn and find out who owns this dump."

CHAPTER FORTY-FOUR

Tanner and Sung had been searching the Mobil station for over a half hour.

"I've got nothing so far," Tanner said, exiting the office.

"Same here. Looks like a waste of time."

"We're not done yet. We still have to check the dumpster out back."

"Not the garbage again," Sung said as he followed Tanner.

"When are you going to learn that trash contains a wealth of information?"

Sung groaned as he flipped open the top of the dumpster. "Just about full, boss."

"Lucky sanitation comes only once a week, Sammy," Tanner smiled, "and lucky for me you're the junior officer."

"Oh come on, boss," Sung groaned. "Do you really expect me to climb in there?"

Tanner's smile widened. "Do you really have to ask?"

"Wonderful."

"Come on—it won't be that bad. This is a gas station. Most of the garbage will be metal and grease."

"Yeah, right. I believe you're forgetting about Chunky. He eats more in a day than you or I eat in a week. Remember his house? The leftovers alone could make you sick."

"That's where you're wrong, Sammy," he laughed. "With Chunky, there are no leftovers." Tanner bent over, lowered his arms, and folded his hands together. Motioning to Sung, he said, "Here—let me help you up."

In no time, Sung had cleared through half of the debris, tossing auto parts, boxes, and other garbage out of the container. "I think I found something, boss," he said, waving a white shirt. "Look at this."

Tanner took the faded white undershirt from Sung and examined it. "These blotches have to be blood."

"Yeah, but the shirt is way too small to fit Chunky."

"I agree. Let's get this to the lab right away."

CHAPTER FORTY-FIVE

Still breathing heavily, Chrissy Carbone was helped into the Port Jervis police station by Davis Lester, the Good Samaritan who had probably saved her life.

Davis sat her down and quickly summoned help from the desk sergeant. Within minutes, Captain Rory Parker appeared. He was a burly man who flaunted a take-charge disposition, but to those who really knew him, he was as soft as a teddy bear. He led the girl into an interrogation room.

"Are you feeling well enough to speak with me, Ms. Carbone?" Parker asked in a gentle voice that defied his appearance.

The girl was still shaking and teary eyed. She held a tissue to her nose and nodded.

"Okay, then, please take your time and tell me exactly what happened—and start from the beginning. I understand you were abducted from the Jervis Lodge, where you work."

"Yes," she said, still nodding as she wiped tears from the corners of her eyes. "It all happened so fast. . . . I was working on the computer with my back facing the door—so I didn't see him come in. I had headphones on and didn't even hear the office door open." She breathed a heavy sigh.

"Okay, now just take a deep breath and relax. You're among friends now." Parker's tone was reassuring. "It's safe here. You have nothing to worry about."

The girl whimpered. "I know. It's just such a shock. I still can't believe what happened to me."

"Yes, and you were very lucky, but we want to catch whoever did this to you. Do you think you can help us with some details?"

"I . . . uh . . . I'll try, but I don't really remember much. Whoever it was snuck through the door between the lobby and the front desk. Only employees are allowed back there. I didn't realize anything until he came up and grabbed me from behind." She looked up at the ceiling, rubbed her throat, and began sobbing heavily. After a few moments, she continued. "The next thing I know, I'm in the trunk of a car bouncing around. . . . Oh, my God, it was terrifying." She stood and placed her hand over her heart. "I can't do this anymore. I have to stop. I can't breathe, and it's just so hot in here."

"I'm sorry, miss. I don't want to make this any worse for you, but I have to ask these questions. If you need to take some time, let's take a break." Parker slid a cup of water across the table. "Here—have a sip and relax."

"It's okay. Just give me a minute," she said, rubbing her eyes with the palms of her hands.

Parker stayed silent for a time, stood up, walked beside her, and motioned for her to sit down. He knelt down on his knee and took her hand. "Did you see the man's face?"

She shook her head.

"What's the next thing that you remember?"

Taking a deep breath, she continued. "I remember feeling the car bouncing up and down, so I knew we couldn't be on a regular road. All of a sudden, we stopped, and it got quiet. They turned off the engine, and I was able to hear men's voices talking to each other. Then the trunk opened. I closed my eyes and made believe I was still unconscious. As I was being lifted from the trunk, I screamed. It must have surprised him because he dropped me and fell backward. I jumped up and started running through the woods. I didn't look back. I just ran."

Parker released her hand and stood up. "That was very smart. Now, I know this is hard, but did you happen to get a look at the man when he dropped you?"

"Not really. I mean, it happened so fast." She reached for the water and took a sip.

"What about the car? Is there anything you can remember about it?"

"It was black, if that helps at all, and the trunk had that new car smell." She swallowed more water. "I don't know much about cars, though."

"Do you remember anyone who may have checked into the Lodge with a car like that?"

"Well, we do ask each customer to fill out a registration card, and the card has a place where you put the model, color, and license number. I never check it, though."

"That's all right. We can go through the registration cards later. But first, I want you to try and put yourself back to where you were and try to recall what was going on while you were running away. Did you hear anything?"

The girl's heart raced as she imagined herself back at the scene. "Uh . . . yeah, now that I'm thinking about it, the one guy yelled for me to stop. Then he screamed out to the other guy."

"He did? Okay, good. What did he scream?"

"I'm trying to think, it was uh . . . it was a name . . . yeah, he shouted the other guy's name."

"Very good." Parker urged, "Now, think real hard and try to remember. Was it a common name or a strange name? Was it a short name or a long name?"

"Short, I think, and it started with a T, like Tony or Travis, but different."

"Okay, keep that thought, and let's go back to the man that dropped you. Try to picture him in front of you and consider his size, his clothing, his voice, the color of his hair."

Tears returned in earnest now. "Oh, I just don't know. I was so scared. I think he wasn't that big and not too old. I mean, his voice was kind of young, but not a teenager. Definitely older than that."

"Very good. This will help," Parker said softly. "And I don't mean to put any more pressure on you, but if we took you out to where you were rescued, do you think you could lead us to the car?"

"Oh, I don't think I'm up to that right now." Chrissy started shivering and folded her arms around her body. "I mean, going back in the woods—what if those men are still there?"

"Ms. Carbone . . ."

"Please call me Chrissy."

"Very well, Chrissy. You're safe with us. We'll have plenty of back up—and frankly, I doubt they'll still be there. It's a safe bet they took off right after they realized you were rescued. I just want to examine the scene."

"Still, even if I could find the strength, I don't know if I could find my way back. Like I said, I just ran. I was lucky enough to run in the right direction. I mean, if I ran another way, I may never have found the road, and then I'd be . . ."

Chrissy put her head in her hands and sobbed. "Oh, my God, I don't even want to think about what could have happened to me."

Parker stood in front of Chrissy, leaned over, and placed his hands on her shoulders. "I understand. Believe me—I do." He paused, then looked directly into her eyes. "What if we take a ride to where Mr. Lester picked you up and you just stay in the car and point in the direction you think you came from?" Parker's tone was subtle and almost charming. "Do you think you can do that for me?"

Chrissy stared back at him and nodded as tears welled up in her eyes again.

. . .

A half hour later, Captain Parker and five of his officers arrived at the spot where Chrissy had been found. Sitting next to Parker in the front of the police car, Chrissy forced herself to look out the window.

"Okay, Chrissy," Parker began, "does any of this look familiar to you?"

"Not really, but if this is where I got in the car," she pointed, "I came out of the woods back that way and ran alongside the road for a short time before the car came."

Parker slowly backed up. "Keep looking out the window and tell me if you recognize the spot where you first came out of the woods."

Chrissy put her hand over her mouth and held back tears. "I'll try."

After a few seconds, Parker stopped the car again and gestured. "How about here?"

"I don't know. It could be . . . I can't be sure."

"That's fine. Just one more thing: Did you come straight out of the woods or on an angle?"

"Straight out," Chrissy answered.

Parker nodded and spoke into his radio: "All right, boys, let's start the search right here."

In seconds, officers exited their cruisers and lined up along the road. Parker left Chrissy in his cruiser, took control of the scene, and dispatched his men to comb the area. Then he went off on his own looking for clues. This was routine for him. He was accustomed to inspecting crime scenes in wooded areas, having worked for the DEA as part of a task force that raided forests and cornfields in search of marijuana farms.

His keen eye quickly spotted a trail of broken twigs and crushed brush. Following it twenty yards deeper into the woods, he found a tire iron lying on top of a bed of dead leaves. Donning plastic gloves, Parker bent down and picked it up.

CHAPTER FORTY-SIX

I don't know which one of us is more worked-up. Troyer hasn't said a word the whole ride over to Lakewood. He just keeps staring straight ahead, shaking his head, and humming from way back in his throat. My heart's thumping, and I feel like I'm gonna puke any second. But then, as I turn down the private road that leads into the camp, I get this weird feeling like I'm coming home or something, and a calmness comes over me. I mean, I really did love this camp when I was a kid.

I pull up to the main building and stop.

"Okay, Troyer, where is she?"

Troyer doesn't say anything. He just keeps shaking his head from side to side, all spaced-out and shit.

"I said, where is she?" This time I push his shoulder and yell at him.

He reaches up, refocuses the rear view mirror so we can see each other, and that toothy grin just appears out of nowhere.

"You say something, Tommy Boy? Not quite sure I heard you, mate."

"You heard me, Troyer. We're here, so let's get Aurora and book."

"In due time, my friend—in due time. First, I'm sure you want to explore a bit. You haven't been here in many years, and

I know you must have some fond memories. Isn't there a place or two that is near and dear to your heart?"

"Cut it out, dude. You could give a shit about what I'm feeling."

"Oh, but I do, Tommy Boy, I do. Think of me as a friend who is helping to free you from all those things that hold you back."

I look at Troyer like he's nuts. "Hold me back from what?"

"Releasing your inner demons, mate, of course. And it all starts here."

"So now you're my shrink? Look—I've got no demons. Just bring me to Aurora. I don't have time for your games."

"There's always time, my friend—always. Humor me, and I promise it will lead you to what you seek."

"Fuck you!'"

"Come now, mate. I'm sure you remember telling me all about this place the night we first met." Troyer snickers, holding back a full-blown laugh. "Perhaps you don't recall how much you disclosed to me, considering all the tequila you consumed."

When he says that a light flashes in my head, and I try to think back to the night he saved my life. I remember him telling me about his troubled childhood, but not much after that.

"Ahh, Tommy Boy. I see that spark in your eyes."

"Spark nothing, I have no idea what you're talking about." The fact is I really don't remember what I told him.

"Are you sure you don't remember, Tommy Boy? Think real hard. It will dawn on you."

"What will dawn on me? What the fuck are you talking about?" At this point, I'm so confused, my head spins. Then, in a moment of clarity it hits me. Troyer must have spiked my tequila that night.

Anyway, Troyer just looks into my eyes for a second and tilts his head to the side. Without another word, he turns, struts all robot-like past the main office, and heads up the hill toward the bunks. Of course I follow him.

Troyer picks up the pace, and before long, I find myself standing right in front of the old banana tree, where I gave it up to Ellen that very first time.

CHAPTER FORTY-SEVEN

Stone was still at Gilgo Beach wading through the sand when the call came in from Tanner.

"We found a T-shirt in the dumpster behind the Mobil station. It's got traces of blood on it. We're having it analyzed right now to see if it matches our vic. When we questioned Gantry again he recanted his original story and admitted he took the knife from its sheath. He insists he had nothing to do with the murder, though."

"So why didn't he say that from the beginning?" Stone asked.

"Well, he says that when we questioned him he panicked and started to think he was going to be blamed for the murder, so he just lied."

"What about the T-shirt, Tanner? How does he explain that?"

"It's not his. It wouldn't even fit over his left thigh. Whoever owns it is easily half his size."

"Well, how do you explain his fingerprint being the last one on the knife?"

"Our forensics girl says that it's possible that the last person who touched the knife wore gloves. Gantry is adamant, and I think he's telling the truth. He was just in the wrong place at the wrong time. Also, Gantry says that when he first met Sullivan at the Tides Inn, he was wearing a T-shirt underneath his long-sleeve."

"Understood," said Stone, nodding her head. "I was having a hard time reconciling all this anyway. It makes much more sense that Sullivan is involved with both crimes."

Sung was in front of Tanner holding his cell to his ear with one hand while shaking his other hand in Tanner's face. "Boss, this is important."

"Can't you see I'm busy here?"

"Yes, but we just located Storm's car."

Tanner's eyes bugged out of his head. Speaking into the phone, he said, "Hold on a second, Stone." He covered the mouthpiece and looked back at Sung. "Really? Where?"

"Back in New York, believe it or not."

"You're kidding. I figured he'd be a thousand miles south of here by now. So where exactly is he?"

"A place called Port Jervis."

"Where the hell is that?"

"A few hours north of New York City."

Tanner spoke back into the phone. "Stone, we've got a new development. Storm's car has been located in New York, not too far from the city. We'll get you the specifics, but you need to get up to Port Jervis right away."

CHAPTER FORTY-EIGHT

Stone and Watts cruised west down Ocean Parkway.

"We should contact the local police in Port Jervis," Watts remarked.

"Not yet."

"But they can get to the car much quicker than we can."

"I realize that," Stone said flatly.

"And what if the signal is lost before we get there?"

"I'll take the chance."

"Are you sure that's the right thing to do?"

"It's our case Watts. We have to make the arrest."

"At the risk of losing it?"

"We won't—trust me."

"I always have, but this is serious. How about a compromise?"

"Meaning?"

"Can we at least alert the locals when we get close? Also, we'll need to give them time to set up and cover the escape routes."

"Fair enough. We can call them when we're a few miles away . . . but not before. I want us to be the first ones on the scene."

CHAPTER FORTY-NINE

Troyer is grinning at me as he leans back into the banana tree. The shape of its trunk supports him like a lounge chair and suspends him off his feet. He folds his legs at the ankles and clasps his hands over his waist. "Well, Tommy Boy . . ."

"'Well' what? I don't get this. What are we doing here? We should be outta here already. It's almost dark, and the cops are gonna be after us."

"Too bad, mate. This is more important. It's the key to all your troubles. So think back and tell me what this tree means to you." Troyer starts to pull up his shirt.

I turn away, all grossed-out. "Quit that shit, Troyer! What's wrong with you?" Then my mind starts flashing scenes from years ago, and all of a sudden it's not Troyer lying against the tree; it's Ellen. Her shirt's up over those big tits of hers, and she's calling out to me, "Come on, T, show me what you've got. My body's aching for you to touch it."

I stumble backward and shake my head, but there she is, still waving me over. Now, get this: I'm standing there, and it's like I'm watching some kinda movie or something. There I am, back when I was a kid, and I'm walking over to her. Then I'm on top of her and my hands are all over her tits, squeezing them like water balloons. Back then, I had no idea what I was really supposed to do. Anyway, it doesn't take long before she's grabbing at my crotch. Then I rip open her pants, and the next thing you know, we're both naked and clawing at each other.

That was the first time I had ever even touched a girl down there, and when I did, she was all wet. Then she started squeezing my cock. Anyway, one thing led to another, and I tried sticking it in, and that's when she freaked out. Funny—I don't remember it happening that way. I mean, that was my first time, and it was all good to me. But now, watching it all playing out inside my head, the whole thing's different. Ellen starts crying and screaming and pushing me off of her, but I don't get off. I just keep on thrusting until I explode. Man, that was wild. Then she screeches as loud as I ever heard a chick scream in my life. So I panic and choke her until she shuts up.

I'm seeing myself doing all this back when I was a kid, but it looks like it's all going on right now, and I can't stop the scene from playing out in front of me.

I keep watching and follow myself as I carry her off into the woods and down to the lake, where I take a rowboat out to the middle and drop her in. Then I start recalling this crazy time at the camp where first they couldn't find her and then she comes floating up a couple days later.

Troyer laughs and pulls me back to the present. "Remember now, mate?

"I don't believe it, this can't be. That's not how I remember it at all."

"Sorry, mate, but you needed to know . . . and now you do."

CHAPTER FIFTY

Parker had only been back at the station for twenty minutes when the call came in.

"Captain, this is Detective Jake Watts with the Third Precinct in Manhattan. We're investigating a murder in our jurisdiction, and it's probable that our perp has made his way into your area. We need your help."

Parker's mind raced. "Excuse me, Detective, but we have a situation here, too."

Watts squinted. "Really? What kind of situation?"

"Kidnapping."

"This just happen?"

"Earlier today as a matter of fact."

Watts thought for a moment, "Too many coincidences."

"What do you mean?" asked Parker.

"Well, we've been tracking a suspect, and it looks like he's hiding out in the woods near a place called Camp Lakewood."

"I'm familiar with the camp, Detective. But how do you know he's there?"

"GPS, Captain. We're a few minutes down the road, and we need backup. Can you get some men out there fast and blockade the roads out of town?"

"You have to give me something more to go on, Detective. Of course we want to help, but we have our own problems here, coincidence or not."

Watts looked over at Stone, who nodded approval. "Fine," Watts said, hesitating. Then he proceeded to fill Parker in.

When Watts reached the part about the motel murder, Parker interrupted. "Wait a second, Detective, that coincidence of yours is starting to make sense. Our vic was taken from a local motel, too. She managed to escape, and from what you're telling me, this is no coincidence. It has to be the same guys."

"Okay, then, get some of your men and meet us at the entrance to the camp. We'll be there in ten minutes."

"Roger. We'll have road blocks set up in the vicinity right away."

CHAPTER FIFTY-ONE

I'm staring out over the lake, captivated by the reflection of the sliver of a moon hanging low in the sky. Canoes are tied up along the dock. Troyer is by my side.

"Reality liberates—does it not, my friend?"

My head's spinning, and I'm all creeped out at this point. I still don't believe that what I imagined was real, but I can't think of any other logical explanation for it. On the one hand, my brain is telling me my first sexual experience was magical—and that's the way I thought I remembered it. But on the other hand, this new vision—compliments of Troyer—suggests that I raped and killed the first girl I ever had sex with. Heavy shit I can't digest and still don't believe.

"Look, Troyer: The only reality I know right now is that we have to get Aurora and book. I'll process this shit later. Let's just get her and go."

"Very well, mate. Go get her."

"Where is she?"

"You know where, Tommy Boy. Think about it."

"Stop this shit, Troyer. What the fuck are you talking about?"

"Come now. You mean you don't remember?"

"No, I don't. Really—I don't."

Troyer laughs that psycho laugh again. "All right, I'll give you a hint. The night we first met I asked you about one of your biggest fears as a kid."

When he says that, it hits me like a punch in the gut. I literally stop breathing for a half a minute. Then I turn and run off toward this beat-up old place set in the woods just outside of camp. We were told to stay clear of this place because it was supposedly haunted. Of course, back then, we believed all that scary ghost shit.

The path to the shack is still here and easy to follow, even in the dark.

Just like when I was a kid, I stop five feet from the door and stare. My heart thumps against my chest. The place hasn't changed one bit, and I'm still scared to death to even open the door.

Troyer slaps me across the back of my head. "Go ahead, mate. Open it. The worst is over now."

I turn and look at him.

"Don't be afraid, Tommy Boy," he says to me grinning. "You're all grown-up now. Whatever lurks behind that door can't hurt you."

Still hesitating, I step forward and reach for the knob.

"Go ahead, mate. She's right on the other side. No need to fret about it."

I look back at Troyer, turn the handle, and walk inside.

The room is vacant except for a broken wood chair lying haphazardly on its side, ropes sprawled out around it. An empty dinner plate looks out of place on the floor nearby.

CHAPTER FIFTY-TWO

Parker and his men met Stone and Watts at the entrance to Camp Lakewood.

"The GPS tells us that the car is in here, Captain," Stone said.

"So who are these guys anyway?" asked Parker.

"Guys? We only know about one, and his name is Sullivan—Thomas Sullivan. We've tracked him from Manhattan through New Jersey to Cape May and now up here. We believe he's with a girl named Alice Storm. It's actually her car that we've tracked."

"And you think he's responsible for this crime spree?"

"We believe so," Watts said.

"You don't sound so convinced," Parker said.

"As convinced as we can be at this point, Captain."

"Well, the girl who was kidnapped said there were two men."

"Really?" said Stone. "Are you sure it was two men and not a man and a woman?"

"She heard men's voices."

"I see," said Stone. "But our intel suggests it's a man and a woman. Maybe she didn't hear the voices clearly. After all, she must have been in shock."

"True, she was very scared when I spoke with her. But she was clear that she heard two men speaking when she was locked in the trunk. Maybe they had a girl with them, too. Whatever it is, if they're here we'll find them. I'm very familiar with the camp layout. I can map out a plan of attack."

"Sounds good, Captain. Just keep in mind that we'd like to take them without any violence. We don't want anyone else to get hurt, and if the girl is with them we have to be extra careful." Tanner looked out toward the grounds. "So what can you tell us about this place?"

Parker motioned with his hands as he spoke. "The bunks form a complete circle around the main center of the camp. Picture a clock with boy's camp from one o'clock to five o'clock and girl's camp from seven o'clock to eleven o'clock. The infirmary separates them at twelve o'clock, and the mess hall separates them at six o'clock. Let's send out three groups, all starting at the mess hall. One group will move clockwise from bunk to bunk, one counter-clockwise. You and I will go straight up the middle." Parker looked at Watts, "Detective, why don't you join one of my crews?"

Watts looked at his partner, then back at Parker. "Captain, with all due respect, I think I'm better off on my own, maybe looking for the car or something."

"Fine with me," Parker said, nodding.

CHAPTER FIFTY-THREE

I stand at the doorway staring at the empty room. "What the hell, man? It looks like she escaped."

"What was your first clue, Tommy Boy?"

"We've got to find her."

"No, mate—you've got to find her. Me, I'll be on my way. I've served my purpose."

With that, Troyer turns and runs out the door.

I shout after him, "Troyer! Wait!" But it's useless; he's gone. Ditched me again.

I run outside and look into the woods, but it's totally dark out. With almost no moon, it's hard to see. I've got to find Aurora.

I head back up the hill toward the camp. As I get closer, I see flashlights flickering through the bunk windows. I stop moving and hide behind a tree. *Holy shit, how'd they find us so fast?* My stomach twists up in a knot, and I double over in pain. My heart starts hammering, and my head starts pounding. I need my pills, but they're in the car.

I've got to get out of here fast. I take a breath and try to relax. I can't go back to the car, so the only way out is by the lake. I can grab a canoe and paddle across the lake to Camp Seneca.

The woods are all creepy when it's dark, but I slowly make my way back down the hill toward the water. Then I start thinking about the stories they used to tell at camp about a guy they called the "Pillowcase Killer." Supposedly, this guy wore a pillowcase over his head with two holes cut out for his eyes and one cut out for his nose. There was nothing cut out for his mouth, though, because he couldn't talk. The story was that his tongue had been sliced off in prison. Anyway, this guy would hide out in the woods around the lake, between the two camps, and if you wandered into the forest after dark, he'd grab you and that would be the end. Now that I think about it, after Ellen disappeared, the kids all said it was the Pillowcase Killer. No one was ever allowed in the woods after dark again.

The echo of a screeching bird cuts right through me, and I stop dead in my tracks. My whole body shivers, and the hairs on the back of my neck stand up.

It's chilly out, but I'm sweating something awful.

I get this metallic taste in my mouth and drop to my knees feeling like I'm gonna puke. I kneel there dry-heaving.

After a few minutes, the wave passes. I get up and continue slowly toward the lake. It's almost pitch-black in the woods. The trees are blocking the moonlight, so I'm practically feeling my way from tree to tree, watching every step.

Finally, I break out of the woods, and the glow of the moon shines over the water. I ease over to the boathouse, take a paddle, and make my way over to the boat dock. The canoes are secured with lines tied to cleats. I untie one, climb in, and quietly set off across the lake. I keep close to the shore, near the shadows, because out in the middle, even the dim light from the moon still lights up the water.

CHAPTER FIFTY-FOUR

A shadow darted between two bunks on the boy's side of camp. Stone saw it first. Pointing, she whispered, "Parker, over there. I saw something move."

"Okay, follow me, and stay low."

The pair quickly crossed the open area by the main field and made their way to the bunks. The flimsy cabins were set on cinderblock supports that elevated them above the ground. There was just enough room for an average-sized adult to crawl underneath, though few would have wanted to—for fear of meeting up with a snake, a rat, or some other unpleasant creature.

Reaching the front corner of the middle bunk, Parker put his finger to his lips in a gesture for silence. He motioned for Stone to move to the front of the next bunk while he went around back. The two separated.

Parker crept around to the rear and disappeared into the darkness. Stone slid stealthily, crouching along the wall as she advanced.

The night was eerily still, and little could be heard other than an odd squeak, chirp, or howl. Parker stopped behind the bunk near the edge of the trees and listened. Suddenly, he heard the snap of twigs a few yards into the woods. He cupped his ear with his hand and waited, trying to lock in the direction of the noise.

Again: a snap, further in.

Isolating it, Parker tiptoed toward the sound and squinted. It was so dark he could barely see five feet in front of him, but he didn't want to use his flashlight, afraid it would alert whoever was ahead of him.

The soft crush of footsteps upon dead leaves was barely audible, but Parker heard it again and followed. Cautiously moving closer and closer, his eyes adjusting to the dark, he made out the silhouette of a body hunched over only yards ahead of him.

Covering the distance in seconds, he leapt at the figure and tackled hard.

CHAPTER FIFTY-FIVE

The lake is like a sheet of glass, so I don't want to make any waves. I cut through it silently, forcing the paddle deep and pulling it back in a slow, even motion—the way I learned when I was a kid.

Floating out here, it's so damn peaceful I have to stop and take it all in. So many thoughts and foggy memories keep flashing in front of me, and I finally have the time to process it. I start to drift, stare up at the sky, and force myself back to that night with Ellen. I still can't wrap my head around that shit. For all these years, the only thing I remembered was having sex with her for the first time in my life. And the memory was a good one. I had completely blocked out her being killed or anything else about what had happened at camp after that. Now, it's sort of coming back to me, but more like a dream. I kind of remember the cops searching everywhere for her, all us kids being scared, and lots of moms and dads coming to take their kids out of camp. But even though Troyer made me see it with my own eyes, it still doesn't feel like I did it. I mean, I must've, but it still doesn't seem real.

Now, here I am on this very same lake, chilling in a canoe, and it's so quiet and incredibly beautiful with all the stars sparkling in the sky.

Some crazy shit, man. I just can't figure it.

I start paddling again, slowly making my way closer to Camp Seneca.

CHAPTER FIFTY-SIX

"Get off me, you animal!" Aurora screamed as she wrestled to break free of Parker's grip.

Parker quickly released his hold on her and helped her up. "I'm sorry, miss! I thought you were someone else. I didn't mean you any harm. I'm a police officer."

"Yeah, well, you could have killed me."

"Again, I'm so sorry, but what are you doing out here?"

"I was kidnapped by a lunatic. I just escaped, and I was running for my life when you tackled me."

"Okay, slow down. You're safe now. We've got a lot of backup looking for this guy . . . Thomas Sullivan, right?"

"Tommy! No, no, you've got it all wrong. It's not Tommy . . . it's this guy Troyer—Troyer Savage."

"Who?"

"Troyer Savage. I don't know the guy; I just know his name."

Stone raced over, shining a flashlight. "What's going on here?"

"Stone, you need to hear this," Parker said. "She says a guy named Troyer Savage kidnapped her."

Stone shone the flashlight in Aurora's face. "Troyer Savage! We thought you were abducted by Thomas Sullivan."

"Well, you're wrong," Aurora shouted. "It was a wacko named Troyer Savage."

"Okay calm down. Tell us all about it."

"It's like I said, I was taken by Troyer Savage. Tommy is a friend of mine. He had nothing to do with it."

Stone reached out and took Aurora's hand. "Look: we're only here to help. If you say Tommy isn't our guy and you have information that incriminates Savage, we're good with that. But you have to tell us everything. It's not just this crime we're investigating."

"Believe me: I know, but I need to be sure that you understand that Tommy is innocent."

"I promise we'll consider all the evidence," Stone said. "Just give us something more to go on."

Deep in thought, Aurora hesitated, looked at Parker, then back to Stone. "Okay, it's like this." Aurora took a breath and then began speaking rapidly. "Tommy and I met in Cape May, and he told me about this guy Troyer—supposedly a friend of his. As it turns out, Troyer was hardly his friend. He actually killed some girl up in New York and left Tommy to clean up his mess. Then he followed Tommy down to New Jersey and killed another girl, making it look like Tommy did it. I tried to get Tommy to go to the cops, but he was afraid to. We came up here to hide, while we figured out a way to prove that Tommy was innocent. Somehow Troyer must have tracked us down, and while Tommy was out, Troyer kidnapped me and brought me here. When he left me alone, I escaped." She thumbed at Parker, "Then this guy jumped me, and here we are."

"That's quite a story," said Stone, "but you seem to be handling the situation quite well."

Aurora laughed uncomfortably. "Actually, I am totally freaked-out right now. But I'm not some petrified little schoolgirl. I don't sit around all teary-eyed and helpless. That's not my style. I've gone through a lot of shit in my life, and I can take care of myself. Been on my own for some time and even learned a bit about handling guys. I mean, yeah, I was scared, but deepdown inside, I knew I'd be okay."

"I'm impressed," remarked Stone. "For the record, most victims—men included—would be sobbing and thanking us for saving them and unable to give us any useful information."

"I don't mean to disappoint you," Aurora answered, "but I'm not like most people—*men included*."

"I'm beginning to see that, Aurora, so may I continue?"

"Go right ahead."

"Okay, then, how long have you known Thomas Sullivan?"

Aurora's response was quick. "As I said, we met in Cape May."

"You've known him for less than a week?"

"Not exactly. You see, we actually met a long time ago, when we were kids. But I hadn't seen him in like twenty years. Then, just last week he walked into my store. It took a few minutes until we recognized each other."

"I see. And so even though you haven't seen him in all this time, you're certain he didn't commit these crimes?"

"Hey, I knew him then and I feel like I know him now. I can just tell. Tommy's gentle and honest. And if Tommy did what you're saying he did, why would Troyer kidnap me?"

"I don't know," Stone said, shaking her head. "That's what I aim to find out."

"Well, you better start looking for Troyer," Aurora insisted. "He's the one you should be after."

"Okay, then—help us, here. What does he look like?"

"Umm . . . I don't know. When he kidnapped me, I never saw his face. He brought me here blindfolded and tied me up."

"So you have no idea at all?" Stone asked.

"No idea."

"Well what *can* you tell me about him?"

"He's a psycho with an Australian accent. Tommy says its phony, but it sounded legit to me."

"Did Tommy ever describe Troyer to you?" Parker interjected.

"He did say that Troyer was very good-looking, smooth with women, and could easily star in a toothpaste commercial."

"Okay, that's a good start," Parker said. "How long ago were you kidnapped?"

"I don't actually recall being abducted. I remember Tommy leaving last night while I was taking a shower. The rest is hazy. I think I fell asleep on the bed. The next thing I remember was waking up blindfolded and tied to a chair. I called out for a while, but no one answered. Then, hours later, the door opened, and Troyer spoke to me for the first time. He ripped at my clothes, grabbed me between the legs, and tried to stuff a sandwich down my throat. He seemed amused when I defied him, but then he just took off. That was at least four or five hours before I escaped. It took me that long to free myself, but I was finally able to. Once I got loose, I bolted right out the door."

Stone chimed in. "Can you take us back to where you were being held?"

Aurora pointed down the hill and away from the bunks. "There's a beat-up old cabin down there. It won't be hard to find. I'll show you."

Parker radioed back to each group one by one and asked for a status report. The response was unanimous: all was quiet.

Stone called Watts on her cell. "Anything to report, partner?"

"Yes and no. I found the car, but no sign of Sullivan. I'm just hiding behind a tree and watching."

"That's good, but I want to fill you in on a new development. We've found the girl."

"Aurora Storm?"

"Yes, and she's alone. Her story is she was with Sullivan, but she was abducted by Troyer Savage."

"Troyer Savage," Watts said, alarmed. "You mean the guy Sullivan wrote about in his computer."

"That's right."

"Wow—that's something."

"No doubt. Anyway, keep your eyes open and call me with any news. We're headed back to where the girl was being held."

"Will do."

Aided by flashlight, Aurora led Parker and Stone down the hill. As they approached, light radiated from an open doorway.

"I didn't leave that door open," Aurora said.

"Are you sure?" asked Stone.

"Positive."

With that, Stone and Parker drew their guns in unison and eased toward the entrance.

Moving cautiously as he reached the door, Parker took the lead and looked inside. "All clear."

The cabin was exactly as Aurora had left it less than a half hour before. Stone and Parker did a quick search.

"Nothing here to go on, Parker. I think we should be out there looking for our perp, whoever he is."

"Agreed," said Parker. "Let's move."

Leaving the shack behind, they began walking up the hill, back toward the camp, when Parker stopped in his tracks and turned around. "Hold on a minute. There's another place we're forgetting about. I know this camp, and there's a whole section we haven't covered."

"And that would be?" Stone asked.

"The waterfront. It's not too far from here, and I think we should check it out."

"Okay, but what about the girl?"

"There's no time. She'll have to come with us."

"I'm okay," Aurora said. "I can handle myself."

"Looks like we don't have much choice," Stone said. "Just stay close behind."

Locating a path, the three made their way to the boat dock. As the clouds cleared past the moon, dim light reflected off the water, providing sufficient illumination to see without a flashlight.

The floating dock shook and gave way as Parker stepped onto it. Made of hardened plastic, it was durable and light, but weight and movement caused it to react much more than a typical wooden dock. With all three on it, the dock rocked even more.

Canoes were tied up along one side, and three mini catamarans were fastened along the other. A few rowboats were positioned between the catamarans.

Parker stepped along to the end of the dock as softly as his large frame would allow.

"Check this out, Detective." Parker said, pointing his flashlight at a free line anchored to a cleat. "The last spot is empty. I'm guessing a canoe was taken from here."

"To go where?" asked Stone.

"There are a few spots on the lake where you could land a boat and get out without too much trouble. The closest would be Camp Seneca. It's the only other camp on the lake. It's also the easiest way to get back to the road. In all other directions, there are deep woods for miles and no way out, especially on a dark night like this."

"How long would it take to get there?"

"By water, I'd say less than a half hour."

"That doesn't give us much time," said Stone. "Can you radio your men and get a group over there?"

Parker pulled the radio from his hip. "I was just thinking the same thing."

CHAPTER FIFTY-SEVEN

As I approach Camp Seneca, clouds are passing in front of the moon. It's so damn dark I can't make out the shoreline, so I don't know exactly where I am. I was here a bunch of times when I was a kid, doing raids and shit, and I know the layout. Seneca is big, much bigger than Lakewood, but once I'm on land, as long as I stay on the paths, I should be okay. Right now, all I have to do is locate the docks.

I wait a bit until the clouds clear out. Then the light comes back, and I can just about see my way clear to the shore. It looks like they haven't set up for summer yet; there are no rowboats or canoes. The dock is empty, so I coast in, use the paddle to pull me over, and grab the first cleat I can. You've got to be careful getting out of these canoes, though. One wrong move, they tip, and you get dumped into the water. I remember that from camp. I must have fallen in at least a half-dozen times, before I got the hang of these contraptions. One thing I learned for sure: don't ever stand up in one.

Anyway, I kind of roll-slide and pull myself out, while holding onto the cleat. Smooth as silk, I don't get wet at all.

There's no line to tie the thing up, so I just let it go and watch as it slowly floats away. I know the general direction where the road is, but I still have to climb the hill and make my way through the camp. Seneca isn't set up like Lakewood, though. The boy's camp is far away from the girl's camp and set into the woods, close to the lake. You have to go all the way through the boy's side, past the basketball courts, over another hill, and past the pool before you reach the girl's camp. I guess they were real worried that the boys would sneak over to the girls in the middle of the night, so they kept them totally separated. There is almost no way you can get from one side to the other without being seen. Lakewood is just the opposite. All you have to do is go out the back of the bunk, head into the woods, and circle around and you're at the girl's bunks in no time.

As I walk off the dock, and onto dry land, more hazy memories begin flashing inside my head. I start remembering times me and some of the other guys raided Seneca and scared the crap out of the kids here. One time, we came over with a Molotov cocktail and accidentally started a fire by the basketball courts. We were only planning to drop the thing in a garbage can, but someone saw us and one of the guys just threw it as we ran. It landed near the wooden bleachers, and they caught fire. We got out without getting caught, but everyone at Seneca suspected it was guys from Lakewood. They just never found out which guys.

Yeah, and the Seneca kids raided us, too. But it was easier for them because of how Lakewood was set up. It was no problem getting in and wandering around the camp without anyone knowing.

But all that stopped after Ellen got killed. No one would dare go back in the woods at night after that.

CHAPTER FIFTY-EIGHT

With their lights off, two patrol cars rolled into the gravel lot at Camp Seneca. Soundlessly, five men exited the vehicles. A sixth man stayed back to cover the road.

Sergeant Fess Scottler had the command. "All right, boys, flashlights off, fan out, and let's move down toward the waterfront. Best to stay off the path and keep to the woods. I figure this guy has no idea we're onto him, so he'll probably take the easiest way up from the docks and walk right up the road. I know this place well. He has to pass by the basketball courts, so if we don't run into him before, we'll take our positions over there and just wait for him. I want two men on each side of the path doing a military roll out as we proceed down the hill. I'll follow fifty yards behind and shore up the rear."

In silent acknowledgment, the men spread out and advanced through the woods, leaving the walkway empty and inviting.

The trees along the path provided good cover, while the sounds of the forest masked their movements. In synchronized fashion, one officer held his position as the next pushed forward. Once in place, the next one rolled out, moved past, and advanced further. Both groups continued this pattern on opposite sides of the path, always staying at least ten yards deep into the woods. Scottler maintained his distance fifty yards back.

The men were only halfway down the hill when the moon disappeared and a thunderstorm erupted. Suddenly, rain exploded from the clouds, and the wind picked up. In no time, the rain began blowing sideways, drenching the entire team. Puddles of water appeared from nowhere, further slowing their progress.

CHAPTER FIFTY-NINE

As I'm making my way up the dirt path toward the basket-ball courts, the sky goes black, and it starts to pour. Right out of nowhere, the clouds open up like somebody just turned on a faucet full-force. That's the way it is around here. One minute, everything's all calm and quiet; the next, it's storm-ing like a hurricane. I remember times like this when I was a kid and we'd be hanging out at the canteen when the first sounds of thunder rumbled in. We'd run like maniacs, laugh-ing and hollering all the way back to the bunks, trying to reach them before the downpour. Usually, we couldn't make it, but we really didn't care. And by the time we did get inside, we were as drenched as if we'd jumped in the pool with our clothes on. Then we'd strip down, dry off, and put on these soft yellow and green Camp Lakewood sweatshirts and shorts and gather around the windows, waiting for the lightning flashes while we counted the seconds until the thunder boomed. Those were some good times, and I had totally forgotten about them until now. Funny how just being up here like this is bringing back all these memories.

The rain is whipping at me and stinging my eyes. I'm get-ting soaked, and I can barely see. Moving up the path, I raise my forearm and hold it across my forehead to keep the rain from my eyes. It doesn't help much, so after I pass the courts, I head into the woods, hoping the trees will block some of the rain.

I try to keep going, but I have to stop because it's almost pitch-black, the clouds are blocking the moon and the trees are making it even darker. I can't see more than five feet in front of me. I stand there, looking around while trying to get my bearings, when, out of nowhere, I hear footsteps splashing up ahead. I still can't see shit, but my heart starts pounding like it knows something that I don't. I crouch down behind this tree, hold a deep breath, and try to concentrate. The rain is slapping against the leaves and making a racket, but it's got a pattern to it, so I block it out and focus. There it is again—movement in the woods up ahead.

Either someone's out here or a big-ass animal is nearby. My first thought is that it's a deer, but you can never be too careful because there are bears around here, too, so I figure I better just stay put.

It doesn't take long before the sounds come right up to me. I actually sense people moving around before I see them. Then, in a flash, a shadow passes and stops. Seconds later, another one rolls past and keeps going. Now, get this: these guys are literally five feet away from me, and they walk right by like I don't even exist!

I hold my breath and actually hear my heart hammering inside my chest. I try to calm down and keep watching as the shadows disappear in the direction of the basketball courts. Suddenly, lightning flashes; the whole forest lights up; and I see two guys making their way further down the hill. Seconds later, the ground shakes from a thunder blast.

This is not good at all. I've got to get out of here real fast, but I can't move until those guys are far enough away that they can't hear me. I wait another minute or two before I turn and head up the hill.

I make it another twenty feet before I get slammed to the ground and lose my wind.

CHAPTER SIXTY

They fingerprint me then handcuff me to a chair inside this room with one of those mirrors. I'm not stupid; that's a two-way. No doubt there's a bunch of cops standing on the other side, just staring at me. What do they think—I'm a moron or something? Anyway, no one comes in to talk to me so I just sit there waiting. I know what they're doing, keeping me here all by myself, thinking it'll drive me nuts and make me want to confess to something I didn't do. Well, the hell with them. I'm not saying shit. As soon as someone walks through that door, I'm asking for a lawyer.

A half hour goes by, maybe more—no one comes to talk to me. Where the hell are they? Why don't they come in here and talk to me?

Another half hour or so goes by, and still nothing. Now I'm starting to get real pissed off. They can't do this to me. I've got rights!

So you know what I do? I start screaming at the top of my lungs. "Help! I can't breathe—help!" Then I try to stand up, and the chair comes with me because I'm handcuffed behind it. I start banging it on the floor, and I fall over sideways. Two seconds later, a cop comes racing through the door.

"Easy now, son," this big old cop says to me as he lifts me up and sets me right.

"You can't do this to me!" I shout. "I got my rights. I want a lawyer."

"Yes, you do have rights, and you are entitled to a lawyer, but we also have procedures here, and all this takes time. So you'll just have to wait until we process you. In the meantime, I'm Captain Parker, and you are a guest at my facility. I expect my guests to act accordingly, so try to control your outbursts."

"A guest. Is this how you treat your guests?" I pull at my handcuffs.

"Procedure, I'm sorry. We're still gathering our information, and until we have a complete story, we have to keep you this way."

"Hey, man, you've got nothing on me. This is bull."

"Well, Mr. Sullivan, that's not exactly true. We've got a lot on you, and the evidence is mounting as we speak." The cop steps around to the other side of the table and sits down across from me.

"Evidence? What kind of evidence?"

"Sorry son, you've invoked your right to counsel, we can't talk to you unless you agree to talk to us without your lawyer being present."

"So get me a lawyer then."

"Okay, I'll contact legal aid, but before I do I want you to know that I'd be willing to tell you what we've found if you give me something in return."

"And what would that be?"

"Tell me about your friend Troyer Savage first."

That takes me by surprise. "You know about Troyer?"

"Yes. And we also know about the bartender from Manhattan and the girl from the motel in New Jersey. Oh, and by the way, we also have your friend Aurora Storm in custody."

When he says that, it just blows me away. I do my best not to show it. "Well then you have to know that Troyer is the one who did all of this, not me. It's all because of him that I'm even sitting here in the first place. The guy has gotten me into so much shit in the last couple of weeks you wouldn't believe it. Just ask Aurora. She'll back me up."

"Well, then, why don't you tell me all about him."

I eyeball Parker and squint at him. I think he's playing me and trying to get me to talk without a lawyer. "If I clue you in about Troyer, what's in it for me?"

"Well, son, you have the right to remain silent, and you are entitled to a lawyer, and anything you say can and will be used against you. But if Troyer is the culprit, then you shouldn't have anything to worry about."

"I don't know, man; this sure doesn't feel right. I watch *CSI*, and every time they talk, they get screwed royally."

"Look: Why don't you start at the beginning and tell us all you know about Troyer? Don't say anything about yourself, and you should be fine. And you know what, if Troyer is our man and you help us to capture him and put him away, I'm sure I can get the DA to drop our charges against you."

"You could do that?"

"I could."

Now, this cop doesn't seem like any cop I've seen on TV, and he really sounds like he can help me. I think for a minute, and then I say, "Okay, if you tell me what kind of evidence you're talking about, I'll tell you what I know about Troyer."

"Sorry, Tom, but it doesn't work that way. You have to give me something first; then I'll tell you what I know."

At this point, I'm really conflicted. I mean, I really want to tell this cop about Troyer, but I 'm afraid that if I do, somehow it's going to be used against me. After all, that's how those *CSI* shows always go—and I'm a lot smarter than that. "This shit is way too much for me. I know I've done nothing wrong, so I'm just gonna wait until I talk to a lawyer."

Parker looks back at the two-way mirror, then looks back at me. "You know what, Tom, maybe we can compromise a bit here. I'll give you some information and then you tell me about Troyer? You can always call a lawyer after that."

I tilt my head sideways and look into his eyes. They say the eyes tell all, so I figure maybe I can see something that'll help me make a decision . . . but they don't. I can't read anything other than a cold-steel, dark-eyed stare. I swallow hard and nod. "Fair enough, tell me what you've got."

Parker turns and looks at the mirror. Then he stands and begins pacing on the other side of the table. "Okay, Tom, the victim tells us that while she was working at the front desk at the Port Jervis Lodge, you grabbed her from behind and choked her. She blacked out, and when she came to, she found herself inside the trunk of a car. Minutes later, the car stopped and you pulled her from the trunk. She screamed, you dropped her, and she fled. A motorist picked her up by the roadside and upon investigation we discovered a tire iron in the vicinity. We ran it for prints. I'm sure you already know that the prints are yours. We've got you dead-on for attempted murder and kidnapping."

With that, my entire body goes limp, and I just collapse into myself. I can't look weak or guilty, though, so I think fast and quickly force myself to sit straight up and act like it's no big deal. "I can explain that. When I packed the car, back in Cape May, the tire iron was lying in the trunk, so I picked it up and moved it. I'm sure that's how my prints got on it."

Parker looks at me crossways and says, "That's the story you're sticking with?"

"It's the truth. Troyer is setting me up."

"Okay, Tom—fine. So tell me about him. Who is this guy, and why do you think he's setting you up?"

"That's not an easy question."

"Why is that?"

"It's like this: I met him a couple of months ago when he saved my ass outside this bar in Brooklyn. But with all of the shit that's come down these last few days, I'm starting to think we must have known each other before. I get this feeling that he's been planning this for a while and for some strange reason he's trying to set me up. Otherwise, why he would be doing all this to me?"

"I see what you mean. Go on."

Parker gives me this sympathetic look, and I proceed to tell him the short version of everything from the night Troyer pulled that MMA shit, to the night he sliced the bartender's throat, to kidnapping Aurora and then leading me to her and running away when he saw that she had escaped. I don't say anything about the Indian girl from the motel, even though Parker seems to know all about it.

Parker just keeps writing shit on this pad in front of him while looking up at me every few seconds. Finally, he puts his pen down and pushes the pad away. "Okay, Tom, I get what you're saying, and I promise we will investigate all this. Meanwhile, we're still searching Camp Lakewood. So far, there's been no sign of Troyer Savage. And, if he was there, as you say, we will eventually find him."

"I hope so, because he's the key to all of this. I'm an innocent victim."

"We'll see, Tom. But procedure requires me to put you in a lineup. If you're telling the truth you have nothing to worry about. If not, and if the motel clerk identifies you, charges will be filed. And if we can't find your friend Troyer, you will probably be extradited to New York City to be charged in connection with the disappearance of the bartender. After that, you will also have to face charges in Seaview."

"A lineup? For what? I had nothing to do with any of the crimes you're talking about. Can't you just tell them what I've said and let me go?"

"I'm sorry, but things don't work that way."

"Well, I'm not going into any sort of lineup right now. My head feels like it's been crushed in a vice. I need my migraine pills. I'm really getting nauseous."

"I can get you some aspirin."

"No, that won't help. These are prescription, and the only ones that help."

"Well, where can I find them?"

"In the glove box of Aurora's car."

"Fine, I'll get someone to check out your story. Meanwhile, you just sit tight."

Parker gets up and walks out, leaving me all alone again.

CHAPTER SIXTY-ONE

Stone and Watts witnessed the entire interrogation from the other side of the two-way mirror, watching as Parker exited and came into the viewing room.

"What do you two make of all that?" Parker asked.

Watts answered first. "Well, Captain it's quite a story . . . if you believe it."

"Sounds like you don't."

"Actually, I'm leaning against," Watts said, "but still open to the theory."

Stone interjected. "I'm not convinced, either. My guess is the two of them are in this together."

"I'm with you, partner, but if we press him now, he could shut down, and then we may never find out what happened to Jamie Houston. Even worse, the way Sullivan tells the story, a jury may still want answers to the Troyer angle. And you know that a defense attorney will distract them with all of that. Collaring an accomplice is good, but landing the actual assailant is what it's all about. I think Sullivan can lead us to Savage, but more than anything, we need to find Jamie Houston . . . alive or dead. And Sullivan is the key to that."

Stone nodded and directed her attention to Parker. "No disrespect intended, Captain, but I have a lot more questions to ask Mr. Sullivan. I think we should let him stew for a while though . . . he seems like the type that will crack if left alone. Then I want to have a go at him."

"No problem, Detective," Parker said, "but until you do, what is your position on getting him his medicine?"

Stone's voice had an edge now. "Use it as leverage, of course. Meanwhile we'll just wait. The DNA from the blood spatter Morgan collected at the home on Gilgo should be back soon, and if it matches our vic, we're one step closer to solving this."

"Perhaps, Detective. In the meantime let's hope my men track down Savage."

"I never like to rely on hope," Stone said, "but it's better than nothing. Anyway, where are you with the lineup?"

. . .

A half hour later, a local drunk, two officers, and Sullivan were paraded into a room separated by a two way mirror.

"Does anyone look familiar, Chrissy?" Parker asked.

Visibly uncomfortable, Chrissy spent a few minutes examining each man, one by one.

After a time, she shook her head and spoke. "I'm sorry, Captain. I just can't tell. None of these men look familiar. I wish I could help, but I can't. I never got a good look at him. I just jumped up and ran as soon as I hit the ground. I had no time to look at anything or anyone. I'm so sorry."

"That's okay, Chrissy. We understand. We just wanted to make sure."

"Well, which one of them do you think it is?" Chrissy asked.

"I'm sorry, but we can't say. It would compromise our investigation."

CHAPTER SIXTY-TWO

Sitting across the table from Aurora Storm, Stone examined the label on the vial she had found in the glove compartment of the Mustang. "Do you know anything about these pills, Ms. Storm?"

"Like what?"

"Oh, I don't know, like the label is clearly not from a regular pharmacy, and the date on it is from two days ago? Which means you had to be with him when he filled this."

"As a matter of fact, I was. So what of it?"

"As I said, the label is not from a pharmacy. It is direct from some laboratory or something, and it says 'Experimental' on it. So I was wondering if you could shed some light."

"Well, Tommy told me that he gets terrible migraine headaches sometimes, and that he's been taking these pills as part of a study he signed up for a few months ago. He said the pills are the only thing that has ever worked to stop the pain."

"Is that all?" asked Stone.

"Pretty much."

"Fine, that will do for now, but I'd like you to remain here while I make some calls. Can you do that for me?"

"To tell you the truth, I have no place else to go. And until you release Tommy, I really don't want to leave anyway." Aurora stood up. "Two questions, though."

"Yes."

"First, do I really have to stay in this room? Don't you have some place more comfortable? I feel like a prisoner here. And second, when can I see Tommy? I really want to talk to him."

Stone turned and looked toward the mirror. "Well, Ms. Storm, I'll inquire with the Captain about a more comfortable place for you. As to your friend, however, he's off-limits. You will not be permitted to speak with him. I'm sorry."

"I don't understand. Why can't I talk to him? That makes no sense."

"Procedure, Ms., and unless you're his lawyer, that's all I can say." Stone rose from her chair and headed out the door. "Now, if you'll excuse me, I will look into your accommodations."

Stone, Watts, and Parker gathered inside the viewing room.

"I'll leave her accommodations up to you, Captain," Stone said, shaking the vial of pills. "But before I agree to give any of these to Sullivan, I'd like to speak with the doctor who prescribed them. Can you set us up with a quiet place to work and make some calls?"

Parker led them to an office, ushered them in, and closed the door behind them.

Once alone, Watts prodded Stone. "Where you going with this, partner?"

"Not sure, but I have a hunch. I need to talk to the doctor, though."

"What makes you think he'll talk to you? You know doctors. He'll claim doctor-patient privilege and clam up . . . especially over the phone. The only chance we have is in person, with a threat that we'll upset his study if he doesn't answer our questions."

Stone had her back to Watts and stared out the window. "We don't have time to go back and talk to him in person, so I'm hoping we can pressure him by phone." Stone slid into the desk chair, opened the vial, and spilled its contents on the desktop. One by one, she counted every pill as she placed it back into the vial.

Drowning in curiosity, Watts plunged into the seat opposite the desk. "What are you doing?"

"No time to explain," Stone answered, reaching for the phone. "You'll understand in a minute."

The phone rang at the Center for Migraine Pain Management. Stone exchanged pleasantries with the receptionist and eventually made contact with Dr. Baruch Diamond.

The phone was on speaker. "Dr. Diamond, this is Detective Theresa Stone. I'm with the Third Precinct in Manhattan, and I have a delicate situation that I need to speak with you about."

The doctor put down the chart he was reading and refocused. "Excuse me—did you say you are a detective?"

"Yes, Doctor, I did. And as I said, I'm with the Third Precinct in Manhattan."

Dr. Diamond was a professional with thirty years of experience and countless degrees to his credit. "Well, how do I know that you are who you say you are?"

"Fair question. You can certainly call the Third and inquire, but before you do, give me a minute of your time and perhaps that won't be necessary."

"Very well, Detective. You have my attention. Please proceed."

"Okay, this concerns a patient of yours. . . ."

The doctor interrupted, "I'm sure you're aware of privilege, Detective."

"I am, but hear me out."

"At this point, all I intend to do is listen. Go on, Detective."

"Understood. This is about Thomas Sullivan." Stone was examining the pill vial as she spoke. "We know he's a patient of yours and that he's involved in one of your migraine studies."

The doctor rose from his desk, walked to his office door, and closed it. "You've got my attention."

"Thank you," Stone said, casting a glance at Watts. "As I said, this is regarding Thomas Sullivan. We have him in custody, and he's a suspect in a number of serious crimes, including kidnapping and homicide."

"That's horrible, Detective. I never would have imagined. . . ."

"Yes, Doctor. I don't doubt that, but it's true. In any event, Mr. Sullivan has been complaining of a severe headache, and he's asked for his pills . . . which is why I tracked you down."

"I'm listening."

"Well, my first concern is whether I should give him his medication."

"Okay, Detective. At the risk of breaking privilege, is there any reason why you feel you shouldn't give him his medication?"

"As a matter of fact, there is. You see, I've counted out the number of pills he's taken since the prescription was refilled two days ago."

"Your point?"

"Based upon the instructions on the label, it appears that he may have taken quite a few more pills than directed. The label says 'Contents: ninety pills,' and the dosage says 'Two every twelve hours.'"

"And?" Dr. Diamond said, growing impatient.

"There's only seventy pills here, Doctor. Which means he's overdosing big-time."

Alarmed, the doctor quickly changed his tone. "I see."

"My question to you, then: Have any of your patients experienced side effects from the administration of large doses of the drug?"

Dr. Diamond thought for a moment and sat down in his chair before answering. "Now we're treading on thin ice. You see, this is a very important study. I've been working on this for quite some time. I have a lot invested here, both in time and money. And if this drug continues to perform as our initial results indicate, we may be on the verge of a breakthrough. If you're suggesting that a large dose may be responsible for causing someone to engage in violent criminal activity, I would have to say no, and then I would have to end this conversation right here."

"I'm not suggesting anything, Doctor; I'm just trying to gather some information. As I said before, there may be a life at stake. I simply want to know whether, in the course of your study, any of your patients have exhibited behaviors that seem . . . uh . . . let's say . . . violent or erratic."

"No, Detective. I assure you that we have not observed reactions like that. Our study focuses on the type of pain the patient is suffering, the frequency, the medications they tried in the past, and the success of those efforts."

"Still, Doctor," Stone continued, "you prescribed a certain dosage based upon something. Why limit it to two pills every twelve hours?"

"The dosage varies among our test subjects. That is part of our study. Some are given more, some less, in an effort to determine the most adequate dosage."

"Okay, then, let's talk in generalities. Of the subjects who have been given higher doses, have you seen any indications of abnormal or aggressive behavior?"

"I'm sorry, but disclosing our findings at this stage is premature." Dr. Diamond was pacing now and becoming concerned that perhaps a critical angle of inquiry may have been overlooked in the study.

"You're being evasive, Doctor, and that won't help either of us." Stone hardened her tone. "You must know that given sufficient time we'll get a court order and compel you to disclose the information we seek, and that may completely undermine your study. If you work with us, we'll keep things quiet and let you continue your research. We certainly don't want to ruin legitimate efforts to find a cure for migraines."

"Sounds like you're strong-arming me, Detective."

"No, just giving you the facts as I see them."

Dr. Diamond swallowed. "You're putting me in quite a predicament here. I don't want to compromise a patient's confidentiality, but at the same time, you have no idea of the magnitude of this study." He picked up a wire-stick figure of a doctor that had been collecting dust on his desk for the past fifteen years. On the base was an inscription that read, "World's Greatest Doctor." It had been made by his son when he was nine years old. Diamond began to wonder if he would regret the next thing he said. "Detective, what I *can* tell you is that I have not seen results in any of our test subjects so far that would indicate a propensity toward violence or other abnormal manifestations."

"I get it. One more question and I'll let you go for now. As relates to Thomas Sullivan, can you tell me if any of his results have caught your attention?"

"Answering that question puts us on a slippery slope, Detective. I have to be careful about privilege, you know, but I do want to help, so I will say this off the record. Sullivan has responded well to the therapy, and the drug seems to be working for him. When I last saw him, he thanked me and said no other medicine had ever stopped the pain like this one."

"Fair enough. So would it be your recommendation to give him the pills he's been asking for?"

"That depends. First, I would ask him when he took his last dose. If it was more than twelve hours ago, it should be safe to give him two, but monitor his behavior and let me know if you notice anything strange."

"Okay, Doctor. I'll be in touch."

Dr. Diamond hung up the phone, immediately pulled open the file cabinet behind his desk, and thumbed through it. In seconds, he found the file he had been looking for, ripped it open, and madly flipped through the pages. Reading from the notes: "Patient number forty-one reports a series of blackouts during which he cannot account for his time or his actions." Turning back to the first page, he focused on the dosage—four pills every six hours. More concerned, he went back to the file cabinet, pulled out another file, and read the patient's report: "Patient number seventy-seven reports that he woke up in his car with no memory of how he got there. Hours were unaccounted for and the last thing he remembered was lying in bed with an agonizing headache." Dr. Diamond checked the dosage—four pills every four hours.

The doctor stuffed the files back in the cabinet and slammed the drawer shut. He knew there were others, but at that moment, he didn't have the stomach to continue.

CHAPTER SIXTY-THREE

I look up as the door to the room opens, and in walks the cop from Cape May.

"Remember me, Mr. Sullivan?" she asks, with this smart-ass grin.

"How could I forget?"

"I told you we'd be seeing each other again."

"Yeah, so what of it?"

"You're in quite a bit of trouble here, Thomas. I wouldn't be so nonchalant if I were you."

"Look, I'm not being that. I'm just in a lot of pain right now. My head is killing me. I asked that other cop to get me my pills from the car. I hope you have them because otherwise I'm gonna say you cops are torturing me. Speaking of which, aren't you supposed to be getting me a lawyer or something?"

"A lawyer is being arranged, and I have your pills, as well. I just need to ask you a few questions first."

"I already answered the questions. Isn't that enough for you? I mean, come on. My head feels like someone hit me with a baseball bat. I can't even think straight."

"I'll make this quick, then. When was the last time you took these pills?"

"What difference does it make? Just give me four. Then, when my headache goes away, I may feel like talking again."

"I'm afraid I can't do that just yet. It would be improper. You see, the dosage on the bottle says two every twelve hours, and I wouldn't want to be responsible for an overdose."

"Come on. I haven't taken any pills since yesterday, and two don't work; I need four. I always take four."

"As long as you agree to answer my questions when you're feeling better."

She has me by the short hairs and my head's killing me, so at this point, I'll say anything. "All right, gimme my meds and let me rest for a bit. Then I'll answer your questions."

"Very well, Thomas." She shakes the pills out of the bottle and places them in my mouth.

I swallow them dry. "Any chance you can take off these handcuffs?" I ask, pulling at them.

"Not at this time. I'll be back in forty-five minutes. Meanwhile, get some rest."

"Yeah, right. You got a pillow?"

"I'll see what I can do."

. . .

I wake up to the sound of the door opening. In walks Detective Stone.

"Are you ready to talk, Thomas?" she asks, all sweet and shit.

"I suppose."

"Okay, let's start with the night Jamie Houston disappeared. You told Captain Parker that you witnessed Troyer Savage cut her throat. I want you to know we also have your computer, and we know you've spent quite a bit of time researching sites related to the Gilgo Beach case. We've also found a number of bodies there too."

"So what? I just happen to be interested in all that. I'm a big *CSI* fan and that case got up my curiosity. Especially because it's so local."

"I don't think you understand, Thomas. We are no longer just looking at you with regard to the disappearance of Jamie Houston, you are now a suspect in connection with the other bodies discovered there."

"But I didn't do anything."

"That's not what the evidence is telling us. Oh, I forgot to mention that the police in Seaview found a soiled white undershirt of yours in the dumpster behind the Mobil station where your car was repaired. There's blood on it that matches the girl who was murdered in your room at the motel. It's time to come clean and admit what you've done. Save us the trouble of a trial and the embarrassment it will cause you."

My heart's racing, and my mouth goes dry. "Hey, this is crazy, I didn't do any of this. It's all a huge mistake. I don't know anything about bodies at Gilgo Beach. All I can say is that Troyer Savage is the one responsible for the bartender and the girl at the motel."

"Well, if that's true, then you need to help us find him. Until then, you're our prime suspect. The fact is, everything points directly to you, and the evidence is overwhelming. Oh, and we haven't even gotten to the latest crime. Kidnapping the motel clerk from the Jervis Lodge was not your smartest move."

"That wasn't me either. I told Parker that before."

"Come on, Thomas. You lifted her out of the trunk and dropped her. She also heard you call out Troyer's name. She can identify your voice. We're putting together a voice lineup right now. In a few minutes you'll be brought in to be identified."

It takes some acting, but I say, "Fine. You do that. I'm not worried. There's no way she'll be able to identify me."

"If you say so, Thomas," she laughs, "but I'm not finished yet. We found Aurora Storm at Camp Lakewood. We also know that you took a canoe from Lakewood and paddled across to Seneca, where we caught you."

"You found Aurora! Is she okay?"

"She's fine, Thomas. But it makes me wonder: What were you doing at Camp Lakewood?"

"Like I told the other cop, Troyer kidnapped Aurora to stop me from ratting him out. I convinced him that I wouldn't, so he agreed to let her go. He took me to Lakewood to get her, and when we got to the shack, we saw that she escaped. Troyer freaked out and took off. I started looking for her, but when I saw lights flickering in the bunks, I got scared. I panicked and ran."

"Well, if you didn't do anything wrong, why did you run?"

"Are you kidding me? You just rattled off enough shit to bury me for the rest of my life. The only way I'm getting out of this predicament is if you can find Troyer. You've got to help me. I swear I'm not responsible for any of this. Troyer is framing me. You've got to believe me."

"I'm not saying I don't, Thomas, so help us catch him. Where do you think he'd go?"

"I haven't got a clue. The dude ran off like a bat outta hell when he saw that Aurora escaped from the shack. He has to be somewhere nearby the camp."

"For your sake, I hope you're right. We have a lot of men searching the area, and Captain Parker just dispatched another six officers to join in. If he's out there, we will find him."

CHAPTER SIXTY-FOUR

After leaving Sullivan, Stone joined Watts and Parker in the viewing room.

"First you give him four pills, Stone," Watts yelled, incredulously. "Then you continue to question him without his lawyer. What are you trying to do?"

"Cut me some slack. He's in handcuffs; he can't do anything. And he waived his rights. We have it all on tape."

"Yeah, but what if he strokes out?"

"Come on. They're only headache pills. That won't happen."

Watts looked Stone in the eyes. "And you know we can't back any of the crap you said about the murder in Seaview or the Carbone girl."

"We know that," Stone answered, "but he doesn't."

"Your partner's right," Parker said. "That bluff won't hold up after Sullivan gets his lawyer."

"I realize that, so delay his counsel for now. There's no reason why we need to provide him with an attorney at this late hour."

Parker placed both hands behind his head and squeezed his neck uncomfortably. "Detective, I can only do this for so long. I run a clean precinct, and the law is the law. Where are you going with all this?"

"I need some time. I want to observe him for the next few hours and see what the pills do." Watts pulled Parker aside. "Captain, we understand your position. Just give us until morning. You've got to trust her instincts. She's one of the best cops I've ever worked with."

Parker thought briefly, then turned back to Stone. "You have until morning. After that, I have to give him his lawyer."

Watts sat with Stone in the viewing room for three hours and watched as Sullivan alternated between consciousness and sleep, sometimes staring directly into the mirror. Finally, Stone rose and made her way into the interrogation room.

...

I'm really spacing out and thinking about Ellen, Troyer, and the banana tree when Stone storms into the room and breaks my concentration.

"How are you feeling, Thomas?" she asks me, like she's trying to be my friend or something.

"I'm all good," I say, even though I'm real foggy and I just want to get my head back to the banana tree, because I'm starting to think that I actually didn't kill Ellen and maybe I was watching someone else do it.

"I just wanted to let you know that I've received some additional information. It seems that the trunk of your car was cleaned with bleach very recently. What's more, traces of blood have been found and the blood matches Jamie Houston's DNA. There's no doubt she was in the trunk of your car."

"I have no idea what you're talking about."

"Come now, Thomas: you don't really think you're dealing with amateurs. We searched your house, and we found a container of color-safe bleach in your laundry room."

"So, I'm sure a lot of people have bleach in their laundry."

"Perhaps, but the chemical composition matches, and the container we found was close to empty."

"So what does that prove?"

"Please, Thomas, admit it. You and Troyer have been in this together since the beginning. What did you do with Jamie Houston? Is she still alive? I promise if you can lead us to her, and she's still alive, things may go a lot better for you."

"That's crazy. I didn't do any of this, Troyer did."

"It's clear to me that you're lying. You see, new evidence found at Gilgo Beach suggests that Jamie Houston may still be alive. You see, her blood was found inside a home near the beach. I'll say it one more time, talk now and tell us what you did with her."

I almost gag. Then I start thinking about the voice calling out for Troyer as I drove to Gilgo that night. "I've told you everything. As I said, I've got no idea about the girl. If I did, I'd tell you. I'm done here. You tricked me. I've probably said too much already. I'm not gonna say another word until you get me a lawyer."

CHAPTER SIXTY-FIVE

The next morning, Watts made a call to Tanner in Seaview. "Just checking in. Have the tests come back on the undershirt?"

"They have, and unfortunately, the blood was too degraded to make an analysis. However, the DNA we collected from perspiration at the armpits matches the DNA your lab sent to us on Sullivan. There's no doubt at this end."

"As we suspected," Watts said. "But without a blood match, all we have is a discarded undershirt, and that's not enough."

"I realize that, Detective. We are continuing to investigate."

"I'm letting you know, Tanner: We've questioned Sullivan, and he insists that Troyer Savage is framing him for everything."

"Have you come up with anything on Savage?"

"Not yet. So far, he's a mystery. Nothing has come up in any of our databases."

"I'll check down here, too, and let you know if we find anything."

Watts hung up the phone and moved over to Stone, who was fast asleep on the couch. He shook her by the shoulder.

"Wake up, partner. Latest report: still no sign of Troyer Savage."

Stone stirred, sat up, and rubbed her eyes. "What time is it?"

"Eight thirty."

"You let me sleep that long?" she said, bolting toward the door. "Follow me. I have to see what Sullivan is up to."

Watts followed her with his eyes, jumped up, and fell in behind. "Okay, but I have some other news. I spoke to Tanner a few minutes ago."

"Fill me in," Stone said, as she headed around the corner.

Seconds later, the two entered the viewing room. Stone positioned herself inches from the mirror and stared at Sullivan as he slept in his chair, head on the pillow and snoring loudly.

"Peaceful enough," Watts remarked.

"So it would seem."

"What were you expecting?"

"Oh, I don't know," Stone said, deflated. "Maybe I was hoping he'd be bouncing off the walls or at least foaming at the mouth."

"Well, he is handcuffed, you know."

"Yeah, but he could have knocked over the chair like he did earlier. I mean, even finding him laid out on the floor would have been better than this."

"So, Stone, you really believe those pills have something to do with all this?"

"I had a hunch, but he looks too calm."

"He does," Watts said. "And there isn't much time left. Parker's going to bring in a public defender at ten AM."

"That doesn't give us much time."

"For what, partner? I don't like the look in your eyes."

"No time to fill you in. Just stay here and watch. Better yet, turn your back and don't watch. You may not want to see what I'm about to do."

"Oh, no, I don't like the sound of this," Watts said. "But before you go, you should know that Tanner advised me that the blood on the undershirt was too degraded. The sweat in the armpits is Sullivan's though."

"Understood," Stone answered as she ran out the door and reappeared seconds later in the interrogation room.

Moving over to Sullivan, she slammed the desk hard with both palms. Sullivan jumped awake.

"Good morning, Thomas. I didn't mean to scare you, but I wanted to let you know that I spoke with your doctor. You need to start on a more consistent therapy." Stone placed four pills on the table in front of him.

. . .

It takes me a couple of seconds to focus before I realize where I am and who is talking to me. "Really? "What's that for? I don't have a headache right now, what's the point?"

"Preventative medicine."

"Uh . . . I don't know. I mean, I guess. He is my doctor, so why not?"

Stone picks up the pills, drops them in my mouth, and offers me a cup of water. I shake my head and swallow 'em dry, as usual. "You know, I'm really hungry. I haven't eaten since early yesterday. Can I get some breakfast? And while you're at it, can you do something about these cuffs? My hands are going numb, and my wrists are hurting real bad."

"I tell you what, Thomas. I'll switch the cuffs to your ankles and get you a plate of eggs, but you have to answer a few more questions."

"Just get these cuffs off and bring me my eggs!" I shout. Stone is one tough cop, but I can't let her get over on me.

She steps around the table and looks right through me. "Okay, Thomas, I'll cut you a break," she says, as she takes a key from her belt, moves behind me, and unlocks my cuffs. For a second, my hands are free and I get this urge to turn around and slam my fists in her back before she puts the cuffs around my ankles. Then I realize that some other cops are probably watching us through the two-way. She locks me in and walks out the door.

. . .

Stone returned to the viewing room, and Watts confronted her.

"I don't like where this is heading. It is one thing to lie to a suspect to try to get a confession out of him, but playing around with drugs that you don't know anything about is pushing things beyond the boundaries. None of this will ever be admissible in court, and if his lawyer finds out, it could undermine our whole case. Forget the fact that we don't know what these pills could do to him at such a high dosage."

"I understand your concern. Just bear with me on this. I need to see if the pills set him off. Besides, the doctor said that he had other patients in the study who were prescribed a much larger dosage and there were no bad reactions, so how bad could it be?"

Watts shook his head. "I don't know, partner, I think you're playing with fire here."

"Let's just get him some breakfast while the pills kick in. Then I can get back with him and push some more."

CHAPTER SIXTY-SIX

Parker fielded the call from Scottler, who was still on the scene outside of Camp Lakewood.

"Captain, we've got some new intel."

"Go on, Fess."

"Well, sir, we weren't able to find anything at the camp, so when dawn broke, we refocused our efforts at the road and pulled over every car that passed by. A few minutes ago, we spoke with a motorist who was traveling into town. He told us that a mile or so back in the other direction, he happened to pass a car heading toward the Interstate. He said that the driver had just pulled over to pick up a hitchhiker who was running up to the car. It struck him as odd because he travels to work on that road every day and he couldn't remember the last time he ever saw someone hitchhiking there, let alone so early in the morning."

"Were you able to get a description of the hitchhiker?" Parker asked.

"Just that he had blond hair and wore a dark jacket."

"What about the car that picked him up?"

"Sketchy, Captain. The witness wasn't fully focused. He thinks it was a silver SUV. Best guess, Nissan or Toyota."

"And you say it was headed toward the highway?"

"Correct, sir," Scottler said.

"Have you checked with our man at the Interstate roadblock?"

"Sorry, sir, but when you ordered our guys over to Seneca, we had to pull him to cover the search back at the camp."

"Are you saying you left the road unattended, Fess?"

"Sorry, sir, but we figured that our perp was on foot, so a roadblock was unnecessary."

"Apparently, you figured wrong," Parker yelled. "You damn well better get some men out to the highway. I'll put out a BOLO on every car that even remotely fits the description."

"Excuse me, sir, but that description fits about fifty percent of the vehicles on the road."

"Then you better get started right away," Parker said, disgusted.

"As you wish, Captain, but do you really think this hitch-hiker could be our man?"

"Use your head, Fess. There are no homes anywhere near that area. The only places nearby are Lakewood and Seneca, and both camps are deserted until summertime. We're more than a month away from that, so who else would even be around there?"

From the sound of Parker's voice, Scottler figured he had just dropped two notches on the promotion list. He turned and called out, "Yo, Coop, Stewart—get your asses over here."

Brad Cooper was a good cop with seven years under his belt. Eddie Stewart was still green. Both responded instantaneously and in seconds stood before Scottler. "Each of you, grab a cruiser and hit the Interstate in opposite directions. I need you to look for a silver SUV with two men in the front seat. The passenger has blond hair and may be wearing a dark jacket. Get a move on; we've got a lot of ground to cover and not much time. I'll have a roadblock put in place about five miles up the highway in both directions. Let's not allow this guy to escape."

"Roger," Cooper said, as he raced off.

Stewart turned and followed shouting, "On it, sir," as he ran.

...

After hanging up with Scottler, Parker pulled out his radio, called in the BOLO, and coordinated the roadblocks along the highway. Satisfied he had all bases covered, he grabbed his cell and called Stone.

"Detective, we've had some developments here. I need you to ask Sullivan what Troyer Savage was wearing last night."

"Will do, Captain," Stone answered, "but clue me in. What's going on?"

"We've got a possible ID. It seems someone may have picked him up about a mile down the road from Lakewood. We have a basic description, and I want to see if it fits."

"Okay, I'll get back to you shortly," Stone said, still watching Sullivan through the two-way mirror. "I'm going back in, partner. If the lawyer shows up, keep him busy."

"I'll try, but what was that call about?" Watts asked.

"It seems they may have spotted Savage, and they need some details to ID him."

...

Stone flies into the room and sits down. I look up at her. "So where's my breakfast?"

"On its way, but can you tell me something first."

"What now? I already told you I want my lawyer."

"Yes you did, but this is harmless. I was wondering if you could tell me what Troyer Savage was wearing the last time you saw him."

"You're joking."

"No, not at all," she says, all serious. "This could be very important."

"Well, that's easy. He's got this dark blue suede jacket that he wears all the time. It happens to be very cool. He let me try it on once, and it looked great. Fit me perfectly, too. He was wearing a pair of very faded jeans that rocked. The dude always dresses fine."

. . .

Cooper was flying down the road toward the Interstate with Stewart following in the cruiser behind when he caught sight of a body lying a few yards off the side of the road. He slammed the brakes so hard the anti-locks kicked in and vibrated the car to a halt. Stewart almost rear-ended him, jammed on his brakes, and screeched to a stop inches behind.

Cooper jumped out of his cruiser and bolted over to the body. Bending over, he checked the neck for a pulse. No response. The body was still warm, though. Stewart exited his vehicle and ran over to the scene.

"He's dead, Eddie. Looks like his neck's been broken." Cooper pointed. "You see that?"

Stewart moved closer and bent over the body, focusing on the awkward position of the head. "Looks like a clean break. Definitely a powerful guy who knows what he's doing."

Cooper checked the dead man's pockets. "No ID, Eddie. I'll call it in and get an ambulance. We need to move now. There's nothing more we can do here, and the longer we wait, the more time this guy has to escape." He took a picture of the man with his cell phone. "We've got to hit the highway now. Get back in your car and let's roll. I'll call Parker and fill him in."

"Roger, Coop," Stewart answered, as both men raced to their cars and took off.

Once on the road, Cooper called Parker. "Captain, we just found a body by the roadside. Looks like the perp broke his neck and threw him out of the vehicle. Update the BOLO; there's only one guy driving the vehicle, and he's dangerous. We need a crew here fast to secure the scene. We're about a mile away from the Interstate. The body is lying a few yards off the west side of the road. We're proceeding to the highway."

"Did you ID the vic?" Parker asked.

"No wallet or cell, sir. But he's about five-ten, mid-thirties, slight build, goatee, and jet black hair cut short. He's dressed in a suit and tie, so he's obviously white collar. I'm sending a picture to your cell right now."

"Got ya. I'll handle it at this end, Coop. We'll circulate the picture. Maybe someone will recognize him. With a name, DMV should be able to give us a plate number and a make and model of his SUV."

CHAPTER SIXTY-SEVEN

Detective Reese was reviewing the blood results from the summerhouse at Gilgo. He looked up from his computer. "Morgan, you need to see this."

Morgan placed his hand over the mouthpiece. "Gimme a minute, here. I'm running down the ownership of that house."

"No problem. I just wanted to tell you that the blood we collected on the floor of that place matches our vic. It's definitely Jamie Houston. Odds are she was still alive when she entered that house."

Morgan nodded, gave Reese the thumbs up, and spoke into the phone. "Yes, sir, so you're saying that the property is held in a trust? Can you give me the name of the trust and the contact info for the trustee?" Morgan held the phone in the crook of his neck and began writing notes on the pad in front of him. Finally, he hung up.

"Well, Reese, I have some info about the owner of the property but no natural person's name. It seems the property is held in a trust and it has been for the last ten years. The Savitch Family Trust is the deed owner. The trust document is confidential, so they can't tell us who the trustee is. There's no mortgage on the property, the taxes are current, and the tax bills go to a P.O. Box in Montana. The property's worth at least six hundred thousand dollars, so it's clear we're dealing with some relatively wealthy people.

"That name mean anything to you?"

"Not at all," Morgan answered. "I think we better call Stone with all this and update her, though."

"I'll do it now," Reese said, sliding his cell from his belt and speed dialing his boss.

"Stone here. What's up, Reese?"

"Got a quick update. The blood we collected at the summerhouse is Houston's. She was definitely alive, at least when she first entered the place. We also have some info on the owner. Seems like the property has been held in a trust for the last ten years. The place is owned free and clear, and the taxes are all paid up."

"Any info on the trust?" Stone asked, still watching Sullivan through the mirror in the viewing room.

"Yeah, it's called the Savitch Family Trust. There's a P.O. Box address in Montana."

"Say again, Reese?" Stone said, alarmed. "Did you say the Savage Family Trust?"

"Savitch, boss. S-A-V-I-T-C-H."

"Interesting. Very interesting." Stone's eyes widened anxiously as she caught Watts' eye. "Listen, Reese: I have to check something out. Keep digging and call me with any new info." Hanging up the phone, she grabbed Watts by the wrist. "You're not going to believe this, but the house at Gilgo is owned by an entity called the Savitch Family Trust. Spelled S-A-V-I-T-C-H."

"No shit!"

. . .

Attorney Harold Levy showed up and was ushered into the viewing room. Stone had been pacing, waiting for Sullivan to finish his breakfast so she could continue her interview. She was taken by surprise.

"Good morning, ma'am," Levy said in a whiny voice as he stretched his hand out to greet her. "My name is Harold Levy. I'm with Legal Aid, and I have been assigned the Sullivan case."

Stone kept her hand by her side, declining the invitation as she examined the short, emaciated figure with greasy hair.

Levy was a young lawyer only three years out of school who had returned to his hometown with a head still filled with idealistic beliefs about the purity and perfection of the legal system. Possessed of a near-photographic memory, he had breezed through law school and could have worked at any of the most prestigious firms in Manhattan. However, he felt his calling was to defend the less fortunate, and he thrived at a challenge. If the case was unwinnable, he wanted it.

Levy looked at Sullivan through the two-way mirror, looked back at Detective Stone, and asked, "Have you questioned my client without the benefit of counsel?"

"He was advised of his rights, Counselor. Whatever he may have said was disclosed with full knowledge that he had the right to remain silent."

"You haven't answered my question, Detective, so I'll repeat it. Have you questioned my client without the benefit of counsel?" What Levy lacked in appearance, he made up for with zeal and intellect.

Stone paused and considered Levy with her eyes. "We spoke, Counselor."

"About what?"

"Perhaps you can ask him, Mr. Levy. I'll take you in to see him and leave you two alone to talk."

"Very well, and I expect that you will give us complete privacy. I do not wish to meet with him in the interrogation room where you can watch and listen. Please set us up in an area where I can be assured of privacy."

"You're a suspicious young man, aren't you?"

"I have reason to be, Detective, so if you don't mind . . ."

"Okay, give me a minute." Stone said, as she exited the viewing room.

. . .

They move me into some office and cuff my ankles again. I'm sitting there waiting in the room when in walks this skinny dude wearing a ratty blue suit that hasn't been pressed in I don't know how long.

"Good morning, Mr. Sullivan. My name is Harold Levy, and I have been appointed your attorney by the good people of the City of Port Jervis. Anything you say to me is privileged, and I am here to help you."

"Excuse me, but are you a real lawyer? I mean, you look like a kid fresh outta college."

"I assure you, sir," the dude says to me, "I am eminently qualified to handle your defense. Please don't let my appearance mislead you."

Eminently? Did he really say that? What the hell does that mean? "I don't know, man. You don't have that lawyer look. How do I know you aren't just some young punk they gave me to help them send me to jail for the rest of my life?"

"Well, sir, that would be a violation of your Constitutional rights. All I can do is ask you to trust me. I have a very successful track record as a public defender, and if you are willing to put your trust in me, I will do everything in my power to see that you are afforded the best defense possible."

"How can I be sure of that?"

"One can never be certain of anything, sir, but perhaps if you allow me to talk with you for a time, I can make you feel more comfortable and secure about my abilities."

He keeps using all these fancy words, and even though he doesn't look like a big-time lawyer, he sure does sound smart, so I guess I should give him a chance. After all, I'm not paying for this anyway, so what do I have to lose?" I eyeball him for a bit, and he just sits there with his hands folded in front of him. "All right, what the hell. Maybe you're just the one I need to get me out of this mess. Where do we start?"

"Okay, Mr. Sullivan . . ."

"Call me Tommy."

"Very well, Tommy, let's start at the beginning. I've read the reports, and it seems you are being investigated for the disappearance of a bartender in Manhattan, murdering a motel clerk in New Jersey, and kidnapping a motel clerk up here in Port Jervis. Not to mention they are putting together a case against you for the bodies they've found at Gilgo Beach."

"Yeah, well, it's all lies. I told them that Troyer did all that and he's trying to frame me."

"I understand, so let's start with the first accusation. Tell me what happened at Club Radical."

So I tell this lawyer everything that happened from the time I walked into the bar in the Village all the way to when the cops nabbed me in the woods at Seneca. But when I tell him the story, I don't tell him that I was the one who dumped the bartender at Gilgo that night. The dude just sits there looking at me. "Aren't you going to take notes or something?"

"Well, Tommy, to be honest with you, I have a near-perfect memory, and anything I hear or read is immediately committed to my mind and can be reiterated word for word."

"Really? You're not shittin' me about that?"

"I assure you, Tommy, I am not."

"That's pretty cool, man. I've never met anyone like that."

"It has its advantages."

"So what do you think?"

"I'm not finished yet. I'd like to talk to you about everything that happened after you were arrested. This is just as important as the events leading up to your capture, if not more so."

"What do you mean?"

"Well, for instance, did the police read you your rights? And if so, when? Did they pressure you to talk after reading you your rights? Did they withhold food or water? Did they promise you leniency if you talked? Did they hurt you? Did they do anything that made you uncomfortable?"

"That's a lot of shit to think about. I mean, yeah, they did do some of that. They kind of read me my rights. I mean, Parker said I had the right to remain silent and all that other stuff they say on TV, but he didn't actually say to me that he was reading me my rights. Anyway, I clammed up at first, but I was hungry, and they had me handcuffed to a chair with my arms pulled behind my back. My hands got numb, and my wrists hurt like hell. I had this massive headache, and they wouldn't give me my migraine pills unless I talked first. Oh, and they also told me that they talked to my doctor."

"Okay, Tommy, slow down. Let's focus on the pills. Tell me about them."

"Oh, it's no big deal. You see, I signed up for this headache study a few months back . . . to earn some extra dough and maybe get cured of these nasty migraines I get. The doc there put me on this experimental medicine to help cure my headaches. All I had to do was take the pills, answer the doctor's questions, and fill out some forms. Then they'd pay me a grand a month just to be a part of the study. It's been great; I get the dough, and my headaches have gone away. Honestly, though, I have to take more pills than the doctor prescribes, but you know what? They work like a charm."

"Did they give you the pills?"

"Not right away. Detective Stone said she would if I answered some questions. And my head was pounding so hard I really had no choice. I mean, I felt like I was gonna die."

"Go on."

"I told her if she gave me the pills, I'd talk. So she did."

"What did you tell her?"

"Everything I just told you."

Levy looked angry. "What happened after that?"

"This morning, she returned and said she spoke to my doctor, who recommended that I take four pills every four hours as preventative medicine, so I did. That was two hours ago."

"And how are you feeling now?"

"Actually, I haven't felt better."

"That's great, Tommy. I think I have enough information for the time being. Let me process this and talk to the detectives, and I'll get back to you shortly."

"You sure? I mean, whatever you wanna know, I'll spill it."

"I'm sure."

"Before you go, can you do me one favor?"

"If I can help, I will."

HOWARD K. POLLACK

"I want to talk to Aurora. She must be flipping out by now."

"I'll see what I can do, but that may be difficult."

"Why?"

"She's a witness, and the prosecutor's office will be concerned about alteration of testimony if you two talk."

"Hey, that's not right."

"As I said, I'll see what I can do, but don't keep your hopes up."

"Well, can you talk to her and give her a message for me?"

"Certainly," he says as he gets up to leave. "What do you want me to tell her?"

"Tell her I'm innocent and that when all this is straightened out, I'll make it up to her."

The lawyer nods at me as he walks out the door.

CHAPTER SIXTY-EIGHT

Levy stormed out of the room in search of Detective Stone. He interrupted her huddled in an office talking with Watts.

"Well, Detectives, in a half-hour interview I believe I've uncovered enough irregularities in the treatment of my client to secure his immediate release." Levy's tone was obnoxiously arrogant.

Stone laughed. "Yeah, right, Counselor. How about looking at the evidence? Are you forgetting that we have blood and DNA that places him at the scene of two murders? Not to mention, we also have the knife and computer evidence that ties your client to Gilgo Beach."

"If you say so, ma'am, but first I'd like to interview Chrissy Carbone. I suspect her testimony, or lack thereof, will be sufficient to exculpate my client from any liability for the local kidnapping."

"Actually, Counselor, you'll be doing us a favor. If he's released up here, he'll be arrested and extradited to New York City to face charges there. So if you want, you can follow us back to New York City and pick up his defense in our jurisdiction."

"That's fine with me, Detective. One step at a time. First, I'll get him out of this mess; then, I'll clear him of your allegations in New York City. I've heard his story, and it is very convincing. A jury will eat this up. He's quite the sympathetic character, you know. And by the way, I'm curious, what have you uncovered about this Troyer Savage? You have an obligation to do all you can to locate him and determine his culpability. If you don't do a detailed investigation, I intend to bring that up at trial. It seems to me that he is the culprit here, not Mr. Sullivan, so you best start doing your homework."

"Don't tell me my job, you pompous little man. I've been here before. Just do your job. I'll see you in court."

"You most assuredly will. In the meantime, my client is off-limits. You are not to have any further communication with him. Do you understand?"

Stone walked out of the room without responding.

. . .

Levy drove out to the Jervis Lodge to interview Chrissy Carbone. It took him only ten minutes before he was convinced that there was no possible way she could identify Thomas Sullivan as her abductor. Armed with that information, he placed a call to the Port Jervis County attorney's office and spoke with his "frenemy" county prosecutor Alexander Codster.

"So when do you intend to arraign Thomas Sullivan?" Levy asked. "Your twenty-four hours are ticking away."

"I'm aware of that, Harold. We've decided to turn him over to the New York City Police rather than pursing our case here for the time being."

"That's fine with me, I guess you found out I've just finished interviewing Chrissy Carbone, and she cannot identify my client."

"Look, Harold, I've already spoken with Parker and the New York detectives. Just because Carbone can't identify him now doesn't mean we won't be able to build a case with other evidence. In the meantime, Sullivan won't be going free. The New York City cops have more than enough to hold him on the other charges."

"I understand, and I'll deal with them next."

Codster was surprised. "You're actually going to keep the case and follow this guy to Manhattan?"

"It's who I am, Alex, and right now my caseload is very thin. This case is just what I need. In fact, there's quite a bit here that is piquing my interest."

Codster laughed. "The more power to you, Harold. Good luck in the Big Apple."

CHAPTER SIXTY-NINE

After a two-hour drive back to New York City, Sullivan was escorted into a holding cell while arrangements were made for an arraignment on the charges in connection with Jamie Houston's disappearance.

Levy followed close behind and found his way to the Third Precinct to talk with Detective Stone once again.

"The arraignment is scheduled for tomorrow afternoon, Mr. Levy. Perhaps we can come to some terms before then."

"Oh, so now you want to be friends? I recall a different tone only a few hours ago."

"Look, perhaps we got off on the wrong foot. My ultimate goal here is to locate Jamie Houston. We have evidence that suggests she may still be alive, and if your client has information that can help us to locate her, we may consider reducing the charges."

"That's mighty generous of you, Detective, but before I even go back to my client with this, I'd like to know what evidence you have regarding her status."

"Well, Mr. Levy, if you give me some assurances, I may be able to disclose some of what I know."

"I'm sorry, Detective, but please understand you aren't dealing with a novice, here. You have to disclose all your evidence on my demand, anyway, so don't play games with me. Either tell me what you've got or don't waste my time."

"Counselor, there may be a life at stake here, and it's my job to try to save it."

"I understand, but I have ethical responsibilities that I take very seriously, too. So work with me, and I will do what I can to try and help."

"All right, Counselor. I want you to understand the urgency of this matter and hope that you will consider what we're dealing with."

"I'm all ears, Detective. Enlighten me."

"Okay, it's like this: When we first investigated the disappearance of Jamie Houston, we believed she was dead. We now have evidence to the contrary; and if this is the case, we need to locate her before it's too late."

"Go on," Levy said.

"As you know, her throat was cut when she was abducted. Your client has already told us he witnessed the attack. You also know that we found evidence in Sullivan's computer that ties him to Club Radical on the night in question, and that his browser history is filled with searches about the Gilgo Beach murder mystery. Based upon that we initiated a full scale search of the area. That search led us to a house nearby. What you don't know is that we found blood spatter inside the house, and the DNA matches Jamie Houston. The spatter pattern suggests that the blood came from a live person. If Sullivan has any information about this and can help us find Jamie Houston, that will go a long way toward making a deal, especially if she's found alive."

"I understand, Detective. Give me some time with my client and I will see what I can do."

Stone led Levy to a holding cell where Sullivan was being kept. When they arrived, they found Sullivan on the floor, unconscious, and foaming at the mouth.

CHAPTER SEVENTY

I wake up handcuffed to a bed with a thing in my arm and a tube up my nose. My lawyer and that detective are standing off in the distance staring at me.

Levy comes over and sits down next to me.

"Where am I? What's going on?"

"Take it easy, Tommy. You're in the prison infirmary. We found you unconscious on the floor of your cell."

"That's messed up. After the cops took me from Port Jervis, the last thing I remember is being led to a jail cell and sitting down on the bed. Then a massive headache hit me like a sledgehammer."

"Really. So how are you feeling now?"

"Okay, I guess, except for not knowing what just happened."

"Has this occurred before?"

I think for a second before I decide to tell him the real truth. "Honestly, it's been going on for a while."

"What do you mean by 'a while'?"

"Geez, I dunno—a couple of months."

"Did you tell your doctor about this?"

"You mean Diamond? No way. If I did he probably would have thrown me out of the study. And those pills are the only things that help me with my headaches. Not to mention I'd lose the dough."

Levy lightened his tone. "Tommy, has it ever crossed your mind that perhaps the pills could be responsible for your blackouts?"

"Please. They're just headache pills. And they've always made me feel better."

"How long have you been a part of this study?"

"Three months maybe."

"I don't know, Tommy. It seems pretty clear to me that the pills are the cause of your blackouts . . . and who knows what else. I'm going to need to talk to your doctor. But before I do, I need to ask you a few questions about the night the bartender disappeared."

"Hey, look: I already told you what I know."

"Yes, but is there anything you haven't told me? Detective Stone thinks the girl may still be alive. Her blood was found in a house near Gilgo Beach. Do you know anything about that?"

I start thinking about that night again and how I heard that girl's voice calling out Troyer's name from the trunk. I thought I was just hearing things, but maybe I wasn't. Maybe she was alive. I mean, that's what Troyer said too. "Okay, I guess I better tell you this. After Troyer slit her throat, he convinced me to get my car so we could take her out of the alley. I know it was stupid, but I got my car, and when I returned, Troyer was gone. I panicked, put her in the trunk, and took her to Gilgo Beach. While I was driving there, I thought I might have heard her calling out for Troyer, but when I pulled her out of the trunk, she looked totally dead. I dragged her into the weed grass and took off."

"What made you take her to Gilgo Beach?"

"I dunno. I guess I figured that since the cops had already searched there after that girl disappeared last year, it would be the last place anyone would look. I know all about that story. You see, I've been following it ever since it first came out in the news. To me it was like real life *CSI* but as close to home as it could ever get. I mean, holy shit, right here on Long Island!"

"And you know nothing about a beach house nearby, or any of the other bodies that have been found?"

"Nothing at all. I swear."

"Very well, then, just one more thing. Your file says that the police questioned your father and served him with a warrant, which is how they obtained your computer. I would really like to speak with him as well."

"Be my guest. He's probably at the house drunk though, so I don't know how much help he'll be."

CHAPTER SEVENTY-ONE

Levy exited the infirmary and approached Stone.

"Sorry, Detective. It's not that he is refusing to cooperate; he simply doesn't know anything."

"That is most unfortunate, Mr. Levy, because without more, we have no choice but to charge him with murder."

"Once again, let me remind you that you are not dealing with a rookie. You do not have a body, and you've already told me that the evidence you've developed indicates blood from a live person. Clearly, there is insufficient evidence for a murder charge at this time."

"Is that how you intend to play this, Counselor?"

"I honestly want to help, but I have to represent my client ethically and zealously. So without more, this is what I have to do. Trust me: I intend to conduct my own investigation, and I would like to begin by speaking with Tommy's doctor and with his father.

Stone took a pause. "You may have a problem with the father. The last I heard, he was in a coma and being cared for at a hospital on Long Island. It seems he was found unconscious by officers from New Jersey who were looking to question him about his son. He was diagnosed with acute alcohol poisoning."

"What is his present condition?" Levy asked.

"I don't know, but give me a minute and I will give you the location of the hospital and you can visit him. But where are you going with this?"

Levy didn't try to hide his smile. "That, Detective, is privileged. And while we're at it, I would like to see my client's meds and I need the address of his doctor too."

Stone became visibly uncomfortable but tried to hide it. "Sorry, Counselor, but for the time being, the meds are evidence."

"Fine. I'll just have to get the information I need from his doctor. In the meantime, I'll take those addresses now."

. . .

Levy made an afternoon appointment with Tommy's doctor and headed out to the hospital first. An hour later, he arrived at North Shore University Hospital in Nassau County and made his way to Joseph Sullivan's room.

"Good afternoon, Mr. Sullivan," Levy said, stretching out his hand.

"Who the hell are you?" Sullivan asked, still focused on the TV screen fastened high on the wall.

Levy pulled his hand back. "My name is Harold Levy. I'm your son's attorney . . . I was told you were in a coma."

"Do I look like I'm in a coma, kid?"

"Uh . . . no, sir, and it's good to see that."

"Lawyer, huh? What the hell's going on with Tommy, anyway? He hasn't even been here to see me."

"Frankly, sir, I don't believe he knows you are here. He's been having a bit of his own troubles, which is why I came to see you."

"I suppose that's got something to do with all the cops that've been coming by the house lately?"

"It does."

"Well, where is he now?"

"He's being held at the Third Precinct in Manhattan."

"Just great. What'd he do?"

"Sir, it's not necessarily what he did; it's what he's accused of doing, and I'm investigating to see what I can do to help." Levy treaded lightly. "Are you feeling up to answering some questions for me?"

"That depends, kid. How do I know you're really his lawyer?"

"I'm a public defender from Port Jervis." Levy reached into his breast pocket, pulled out a card, and handed it to Sullivan. "Your son was first picked up in my jurisdiction on a kidnapping offense. He has since been extradited to Manhattan to answer charges locally. I told him I would continue to handle his case because I think I can help."

"Well, the kid's not too bright, but he's no criminal, either; so what can I do to help?"

"Good—I'm glad you want to assist. Do you know much about the drugs he's taking?"

"Drugs? He don't do drugs!"

"I'm sorry. I meant to say medication. Are you aware he's been involved in an experimental study and he's taking medication for his migraine headaches?"

"I don't know nothing about no study. I do know that he's always had these bad headaches ever since he was a kid, but that's it. We don't talk much these days. I work, he works, we don't see much of each other. He comes and goes as he pleases. Sometimes I don't see him for days at a time."

"What about his friends? Would you recognize any names if I told you them?"

"Probably not. No one comes around, and like I said, we don't do a lot of talking."

"Let me try, anyway. Does the name Troyer Savage mean anything to you?"

Sullivan rubbed his chin with his thumb and index finger while rolling his eyes upward. "I can't be sure." He shook his head, still thinking. "No, I'd remember a name like that."

"Excuse me, sir, but you hesitated for a moment."

"It's nothing, I was just trying to remember the names of some of his friends, but he's not one of them."

"Okay, then, what can you tell me about his past? You said Tommy's had these headaches ever since he was a kid. Do you remember when they first started?"

"Ever since I can remember—even before my wife ran out on us."

"I'm sorry, but I have to ask: When was that?"

"Ah, it's no problem. She's been gone for over fifteen years already. Tommy was around ten or eleven, and he'd been having the headaches for years by then. She used to take him to the doctor for that and for other stuff."

"What you mean by other stuff?"

"Hey, we're going way back now. Best I can remember my wife thought he was a difficult kid, always getting into trouble and not doing good in school. I said it was a phase, but she never listened to me."

"Would I be getting too personal if I asked why she left?"

"Hell, so much time's passed, I don't really give a shit anymore."

"Yes, sir, but it may help in building a defense for Tommy."

"You think so?"

"I do, so please tell me everything. If he had a troubled childhood, I could use that."

"Troubled ain't the word," Sullivan said with regret. "How 'bout dysfunctional. And it's been eating me up inside ever since he was born. Believe me: I've had a lot of time to think about the mistakes we made back then."

"I'm sorry. I don't understand."

"I don't know why I'm telling you this, but maybe it's because I'm lying here in a hospital half-dead." Sullivan reached for his stomach in obvious pain. "I mean, I've been drinking myself to death just trying to forget for so long."

"That's okay, sir. Sometimes it's good just to let these things out."

"Yeah, right," Sullivan said as he reached for the TV remote and clicked it off. "Back when Tommy was born, we didn't have much money. I mean, we were excited about having a kid and all, but we were young and not totally prepared. Anyway, toward the end of her pregnancy, we found out that my wife was having twins. We knew we could barely afford one kid, but two—there was just no way. So this doctor suggested to us that we could put up one for adoption and get paid for it. We thought about it and figured the extra money would help us with raising the other, and so we just went for it."

"I understand." Levy said, compassionately.

"No, I don't think you do. You see, we sold our son, and we actually had to look at both of them and choose one. That was hard enough. But what we did to Tommy after that was probably worse."

"Go on."

"Well, we felt so guilty all the time while we were raising Tommy, and we started blaming each other and fighting all the time. It took its toll on my wife; she started taking drugs and drinking, and I started drinking, too. I'm sure it's why she left us. Then, a year or so later, after a night of drinking, I finally told Tommy about his twin brother. I didn't have the heart to tell him we actually sold his brother, though, so I told him he died at birth instead."

"Wow, that's quite a story. How did Tommy take it?"

"He was young, so it didn't seem to affect him, but now, looking back, it destroyed my marriage, so who knows what it really did to Tommy?"

"May I make an observation, sir?" Levy asked.

Sullivan nodded.

"From what you've told me, it appears that Tommy's troubles started at a young age. Children are very perceptive, so it makes sense that he would have been affected by the guilt you two carried around—and certainly the fighting, drinking, and drugs."

"Believe me: I've thought about that, too. But there's more. Ever since my wife left us, I've been a shithead. I started drinking more and more and never even got involved with Tommy's schooling or raising him. I just worked, came home, drank, passed out, and did it all over again the next day. Tommy practically raised himself, and I still came down hard on him. I mean, I'd yell at him for every little thing. I'd force him to clean the house, do the laundry, and do the shopping. If that wasn't bad enough, I'd take out my bad days on him all the time."

"Sounds like you have quite a few regrets, sir," Levy said.

"Yeah, well, lying here these past few days has really started making me think about what I've done with my life, ya know?

I haven't had a drink in all this time, and I'm actually starting to think more clearly than I have in a long time."

"That's a good thing, sir. Perhaps you and Tommy need to reconnect."

"That's an understatement. At this point, I doubt he'd even be concerned enough to visit me. And if he did, I wouldn't even know what to say to him."

"A suggestion, sir: If you do get the opportunity, why not tell him some of what you told me? Perhaps it may not be the time to tell him everything about his brother, but if you open up about your regrets, he may respond."

"I dunno. Anyways, this ain't as important as getting him out of jail. Do you really think you can help him?"

"I do." Levy said as he got up to leave. "And what you've told me will be very instrumental."

"That's good. Hey, can you do me a favor and tell Tommy I asked about him and that I'll come and see him when they let me outta here?"

"Of course. I have one more question, though."

"Go ahead."

"Did you or your wife have any contact with your other son or the people who adopted him after you gave him up?"

Sullivan shifted uncomfortably in his bed, looked away from Levy, and shook his head. "No."

"Very well. Get some rest. I may need to talk with you again."

CHAPTER SEVENTY-TWO

Levy made his way to the Center for Migraine Pain Management in Brooklyn and was led into the office of Dr. Baruch Diamond. It was an impressive room decorated with professional aesthetic care. Scholarly books lined one wall; a large window behind the desk overlooked a courtyard. The side wall, covered with degrees, was fronted by a mahogany credenza that displayed professional accolades and family photographs.

Dr. Diamond looked up from a report he was reading and offered a warm smile. "I'm told you represent Thomas Sullivan."

"Yes, Doctor. My name is Harold Levy, and I'm a public defender with the City of Port Jervis."

"A long way from home, young man."

"It is, sir, but circumstances warrant my appearance locally."

"I see. So what can I do for you?"

"Well, Doctor, first let me give you this." Levy handed him a document. "It's an authorization form. As you can see, it is signed by my client and notarized. It gives you full permission to discuss everything about Thomas Sullivan's treatment here. Understand, you are not waiving privilege by speaking with me. I, too, am bound by an equally important privilege, so everything we talk about will remain confidential. I am in need of complete candor, though, sir, if I am to properly and effectively represent my client."

"I understand. However, you need to understand things from my perspective, as well. As I told the detective I spoke with on the phone the other day, this is a very important study we are conducting here. Beyond the privacy concerns of Mr. Sullivan, we have privacy concerns of a much larger dimension. There are over one hundred and fifty subjects whose privacy I am obligated to protect, as well as that of the study itself."

"It is not my intention to upset or undermine your study," Levy said. "I simply need information about Mr. Sullivan."

"Yes, but as far as questions relate to the effects of the medicine and comparisons to other test subjects . . ."

Levy interrupted. "I assure you, Doctor, I am only interested in helping my client. Everything you say will remain between us. I fully appreciate doctor-patient privilege."

"Fair enough. Ask your questions, and I will answer them to the best of my ability, taking into account that if I believe something is outside the scope, I will reserve my right not to answer."

"Very well, Doctor. To begin with, can you tell me generally about the study and how you came to meet Thomas Sullivan?"

"The study is quite simple. My colleagues and I have been working with a private drug research group, and we have developed what we believe is a breakthrough formula that can cure even the most severe migraine headaches in less than an hour. We have been testing the drug for almost three years, on a variety of subjects, as part of the FDA approval process. We have reached the stage of the trials where we are testing those patients who are chronic and experience severe symptoms on a regular basis. Thomas Sullivan is one of them."

"How did you find him?" Levy asked.

"Actually, he found us. The Center advertised for subjects on the radio and in print. He responded and filled out a questionnaire. After reviewing his history, we selected him for an in-person interview, found him to be a good candidate, and took him into the study. That was almost three months ago."

"And how has he been responding?" Levy asked. "I assume you have regular examinations and written reports?"

"He has been doing very well. And yes, of course we have regular exams and written reports. Those, I'm afraid, are confidential and cannot be inspected or released."

"I respect that, Doctor, but what if I told you that Mr. Sullivan has been experiencing blackouts?"

The doctor looked directly into Levy's eyes. "I'm sorry, but I find that hard to believe. Mr. Sullivan has never said anything like that to me at all. In fact, he was here to refill his prescription only a few days ago, and I spoke with him at length. He never mentioned anything about blackouts. Thomas was ecstatic about the performance of the medicine. He reported to me that he has never felt better."

"Well, Doctor, did you ever consider that he may have had ulterior motives in reporting his results to you?"

Dr. Diamond was perplexed. "I'm not sure I understand."

"Think about it. He is being paid a substantial amount of money. Additionally, if the pills are working but have certain side effects, he may not have wanted you to know for fear of being dropped from the study. After all, he'd lose the money and the medicine. Perhaps to him the side effects may be worth it."

"Point taken, Mr. Levy, but that is out of my control. We emphasize the importance of reporting all side effects and stress this over and over again. All of our patients sign an agreement acknowledging this. Moreover, the failure to disclose side effects is grounds for termination from the study. You must understand that, to a large extent, we have to rely on the individual's own common sense and desire to protect their health at all costs."

"I see. Let me ask you this, then. Have any of your other subjects reported experiencing blackouts while taking the drug?"

Dr. Diamond rolled his chair away from the desk, stood up, and walked over to the credenza. "Now we're heading into dangerous territory, Mr. Levy." The doctor picked up a family photo from a ski trip taken five years before. Staring at it, he said, "Once I start talking about the results of other patients, I not only compromise their privacy, but I also compromise my study. Until the trials are over, and we have analyzed all results over the full term of the study, any evaluation is premature."

"I'm sorry, Doctor, but you're over-complicating my question. I am not asking for names or an evaluation. I simply want to know if, over the course of your study, anyone has reported blacking out. Not only is my client's health at risk, but perhaps there is more to this than simply blackouts. And let me remind you: there are felonies under investigation."

"I understand, and I apologize. I wish I could help you more."

"Doctor, I don't think you fully realize where this can go. You see, if we learn independently of any serious side effects of this drug, and if you failed to either report them or stop the study when you learned of such effects, you may be held criminally liable. You could lose your license to practice medicine, and you could end up in jail. The study will be the least of your troubles."

"Please don't threaten me, young man. I am aware of the consequences."

"Then perhaps you may want to reconsider, because I have a client who was found unconscious in his cell and foaming at the mouth, with no recollection of how any of it happened. Moreover, he advised me that it wasn't his first episode."

"That just isn't possible, especially at the dosage he's been prescribed."

"Excuse me, Doctor, but my client told me that you increased his dosage the other day and put him on four pills every four hours as preventative medicine."

"What? That's ridiculous. I would never have done such a thing. Did he actually tell you that?"

"He told me that you gave those instructions to Detective Stone when she spoke with you."

Dr. Diamond was incensed. "That conversation never took place. In fact, it was just the opposite. When the detective asked me if she should give Thomas his medicine, I told her to first make sure he hadn't taken any pills in the last twelve hours and then to administer two pills—and only two pills."

Levy's eyes widened. "Well, then, someone is lying . . . and I have a good idea who it is. Tell me, Doctor, is it possible that an overdose such as that could cause a blackout?"

"All I will say, Counselor, is that anything is possible."

"Thank you, sir. That will have to do for now. I need to prepare for the arraignment tomorrow. And this one will be quite interesting, to say the least."

CHAPTER SEVENTY-THREE

The New York County Supreme Court was an architecturally impressive building standing ominously on Center Street in lower Manhattan. Marble columns had greeted counsel and criminal alike for many decades, while the courtrooms echoed with the history of mobsters, murderers, and con artists who had met the firm hand of justice throughout the twentieth century and into the twenty-first.

Judge Norman Fairgrieve brought his courtroom to order for the call of a late afternoon calendar. The only case scheduled was the Thomas Sullivan matter. Sullivan sat at a table beside his attorney, Harold Levy. Prosecutor Joyce Galub sat at another, flanked by Detective Theresa Stone on one side and Detective Jake Watts on the other.

Judge Fairgrieve's clerk proceeded. "Good afternoon. This will be a special call of the calendar. We have one case on for arraignment: the matter of the People versus Thomas Sullivan, docket number 02364/13." He looked over to the prosecutor's table. "Ms. Galub, are you ready to proceed?"

"I am, sir," she answered, standing as she spoke.

"Very well, then," Judge Fairgrieve interjected, looking over to Harold Levy. "We have a series of felony offenses, here. Mr. Sullivan is being charged with assault, kidnapping, aiding and abetting, attempted murder, conspiracy, and conspiracy to commit murder. . . ."

"Excuse me, Your Honor," Levy said, interrupting as he stood. "We waive a public reading and plead not guilty."

"I beg your pardon, Counselor," Judge Fairgrieve said firmly. "But you are in my courtroom now and I do not appreciate being interrupted."

"My apologies, Your Honor. I simply wanted to save the Court's time with my waiver."

"Very well, Counselor. Please introduce yourself. I haven't seen you in my courtroom before."

"I am a public defender with the City of Port Jervis. I'm here on special assignment, as this case originated in my jurisdiction."

"I see, young man, and since you have never appeared before me, I will overlook your . . . inadvertence, but the next time you interrupt me while I am speaking will be your last."

"Once again, Your Honor, I am very sorry. It was not my intention to disrespect the Court or these proceedings."

"Understood, Counselor. I will accept your client's plea, and now I would like to hear what the People have to say regarding bail." Fairgrieve turned to the prosecutor. "Ms. Galub, what is your position?"

Galub cleared her throat. "Yes, Your Honor, these offenses all stem from a brutal assault on an innocent woman who is still missing. The accused has shown no remorse. He was tracked down while in hiding. He is a flight risk with little ties to the community and has refused to cooperate to assist in locating the victim. There is also some suspicion that he may be connected to the Gilgo Beach murder from last year. He should be held without bail."

"Thank you, Ms. Galub. Now you, Counselor," the Judge said, focusing on Harold Levy. "Your turn."

Levy walked out from behind the table. "Thank you, Your Honor. I would request the defendant be released on a minimum bail. Contrary to Counsel's rendition of the facts of this matter, Mr. Sullivan denies any involvement in the current matter. He has indicated to me that he is merely a witness who has no idea where the perpetrator is. He is desirous of helping the police to locate both the victim and the perpetrator, but his information is limited. He insists he is being framed. As to the Gilgo Beach incidents, my client denies this entirely. And further, the People haven't a shred of evidence to connect Mr. Sullivan at all, it is sheer speculation and grandstanding by the prosecution in an attempt to misdirect the court and refocus the issues."

Galub interjected. "Your Honor, the evidence in this matter is overwhelming. We have blood DNA from Mr. Sullivan's car that matches our victim. There is compelling evidence he was involved in a murder in New Jersey. He has already admitted involvement in this matter, as an accomplice at the very least, although we believe he is directly responsible. In addition, evidence discovered in the defendant's computer suggests direct involvement in the murders at Gilgo Beach."

"Excuse me, Your Honor," Levy said, "but any evidence the People have obtained through questioning my client and while searching his home is inadmissible, and I intend to make a motion in that regard as soon as we finish here. Detectives continued to question my client under duress after he was Mirandized." Levy raised his voice. "Food and water were withheld, his prescribed medicine was withheld, and he was lied to, threatened, and subsequently over-medicated by the detective sitting right next to Ms. Galub."

Judge Fairgrieve banged his gavel. "Enough, Mr. Levy! This is an arraignment, not a hearing, and these are serious allegations. You better have some solid evidence of this if you intend to proceed in my courtroom."

"Yes, Your Honor, I understand. But this is all relevant to the prosecutor's no-bail demand. And I have firsthand knowledge about the allegations I am making here with respect to over-medication. I am seriously concerned about leaving Mr. Sullivan under the control of the very people who would use his own medication to violate his rights, while putting him at serious medical risk."

"Very well, Counselor. I will give you some latitude here. Please tell me about this, and it better be good."

"Objection, Your Honor," Galub shouted as she rose from her seat. "This is the first the People are hearing of this, and I'd like an opportunity to discuss this with the detectives."

"I'm sure you do, Ms. Galub, but I'd like to hear this right now. There's no jury, and no prejudice, so we will simply go off the record while I hear what Counsel has to say."

"Thank you, Judge," Levy said. "May I continue?"

"Off the record now," Judge Fairgrieve said to the court reporter. Then he looked back at Levy. "Yes, please proceed."

"Your Honor, when I first arrived at the Third Precinct, I had a brief conversation with Detective Stone. Subsequently, she brought me to the cell where my client was being held. We found him unconscious and foaming at the mouth. He was rushed to the infirmary, and when he awakened a few hours later, I had the opportunity to question him. He informed me that he was in severe pain and begged Detective Stone for his pills. Apparently, Detective Stone withheld his prescribed medication and then used it to elicit information. He also told me that Detective Stone then gave him additional higher doses of his medication on the advice of Mr. Sullivan's physician. As it turns out, I had occasion to meet with my client's physician yesterday afternoon, and he completely denied giving Detective Stone such advice. In fact, he told her to first make sure Mr. Sullivan hadn't taken any pills in the last twelve hours and then to administer only two pills in the next twelve hours. Instead, Detective Stone gave him four pills, and then only six hours later, she gave him another four pills, even though he didn't have the need for them. The end result: Mr. Sullivan blacked out, could not remember what happened to him, and wound up in the infirmary."

Judge Fairgrieve turned to the Prosecutor's table. "Detective Stone, what do you have to say about this?"

Stone stood up. "This is ludicrous, Your Honor. The Defendant is making this up."

Sullivan jumped up and shouted. "That's a lie. She totally said that and put the pills right into my mouth. . . ."

The judge banged his gavel. "Quiet, Mr. Sullivan! You're out of order! Counsel, restrain your client from any further outbursts."

Levy grabbed Sullivan by the wrist, pulled him down, and whispered in his ear. "Calm down and allow me to handle this. You don't want to upset the judge."

Judge Fairgrieve continued. "Go ahead, Detective. Finish what you were saying."

"Yes, Your Honor. It is true that Mr. Sullivan asked for his pills. I didn't want to administer them until after I spoke with his doctor, so I made the call, received his advice, and gave Mr. Sullivan two pills. He asked me for more, but I refused. That's it—plain and simple. This is a ploy Mr. Sullivan and his counsel have concocted to discredit our investigation. I believe Mr. Sullivan has psychiatric problems and needs to be evaluated. We cannot allow someone like him to roam the streets."

Levy stood up. "May I respond, Your Honor?"

"Please do."

"I have no problem with a psychological evaluation. In fact, under the circumstances, I am reserving my right to plead a defense of mental impairment. With the little information I have gathered about the medication Mr. Sullivan has been taking, I have serious concerns about his mental capacity over these past few months. The pills we have been discussing are part of an experimental study being conducted by a private research group. The drug has not been approved yet by the FDA, and it seems to have a direct effect on the brain. Additionally, I am now asking the Court to order the People to turn over a few of these pills so I can have them analyzed. This is a material aspect of my intended defense, and I will be unable to proceed further without such an analysis."

The judge turned to the prosecutor's table. "Counsel?"

"Your Honor, these proceedings are going far beyond the scope of an arraignment, and I would once again request a recess to further investigate."

"I appreciate the People's position, Ms. Galub, so let's do this: I've heard enough about the side issues for now. I'm prepared to wrap up the arraignment." The Judge turned to the court reporter. "Back on the record, please." Then he turned to the defendant's table. "Mr. Sullivan, please rise."

Sullivan and Levy stood and faced the bench.

Judge Fairgrieve continued. "The Court sets bail at five-hundred thousand dollars. Further, I want an immediate evaluation of the defendant's mental condition by a psychiatrist to be chosen by the People. The defendant may engage his own experts as the law provides. Lastly, the People will deliver four of the defendant's pills to Mr. Levy immediately. I suggest that the People do their own analysis of these pills, as well. I would like a report before the next scheduled court date, which will be in two weeks. Until that time, no further pills shall be administered to the defendant."

Sullivan grabbed Levy's arm. "But I need those pills. Without them, my headaches get so bad I can't even think straight."

"I'm sorry, Tommy, but the judge is right, and I'm worried about what they might be doing to you. Also, if I'm ever going to mount a defense based on these pills, I can't be asking the judge to allow you to have them."

"But the pills aren't doing anything to me. You know this is all because of Troyer. He's the one responsible."

"Tommy, we can talk about this later. I still have a lot of investigating to do, and in cases like this, we have to keep all our options open. I can't give up a mental incapacity defense under these circumstances. Just trust me. I know what I'm doing. Go back to your cell, don't talk with anyone, and if your headaches return, ask for an over-the-counter migraine medication for the time being. I will make sure they have some available."

"So where you going now?"

"I need to do some digging, and I'm going to ask a psychiatrist friend of mine from Port Jervis to come down here and meet with you. I'm also going to send some of your pills up there to a lab I know for analysis. I've got a lot to do. Oh, and by the way, I met with your father. I'm sure you didn't know this, but he is in the hospital. He suffered alcohol poisoning last week and was in a coma for a few days. He's doing okay now, though."

"Dear ol' Dad. Like I could give a shit, the drunk bastard."

"Actually, Tommy, he was concerned about you and asked that I tell you he intends to come and see you when they let him out of the hospital."

"Really? That doesn't sound like him."

"All I can say is he appeared remorseful about a lot of things that happened between you two over the years."

"Yeah, right. Why, all of a sudden?"

"If you ask me, I think almost dying had a lot to do with it. Perhaps it made him reflect on how his life has gone. You may want to give him another chance."

"Not in this lifetime."

CHAPTER SEVENTY-FOUR

Parker looked up from his desk as Scottler entered his office. "What have you got for me, Fess?"

"We're at a dead end, Captain. It's been hours and the road-blocks have turned up nothing. We've been patrolling the roads in and out of town and questioning everyone we can."

"So this guy just disappeared into thin air?"

"I don't know. Maybe he made it through before we set up the roadblocks."

"Not good news."

"Yeah, I know. But I've got another idea, Captain. We should get in touch with Gordy at Camp Lakewood."

"What for?"

"Well, something doesn't add up."

"Go on."

"Think about it. The waterfront was completely set up for summer, yet no one was around. That doesn't happen by itself, so who did it, and when? Better yet, where is he?"

"Very good point, Fess. Make the call and find out."

Fess located the contact information and called Gordy Branson, the owner of Camp Lakewood. They had known each other for a long time, and while you couldn't quite say they were friends, their paths had crossed in friendly encounters over the years.

"Gordy, it's Fess over at Port Jervis Police. Seems we've had an incident at your camp, and I need some information."

"What do you mean 'an incident'? What happened? Has anyone been hurt?"

"Calm down, Gordy. Let me explain."

"Okay, but you've got me worried. What's going on?" He pulled a cigarette from the pack of Newports that lay on his desk, placed it between his lips, struck a match and drew in deeply.

"Well, it seems that you've had some trespassers on your property, and they were using it to harbor a kidnap victim."

Gordy coughed out a smoky breath. "Holy shit!"

"Take it easy. We've recovered the victim, and she's okay. We've also arrested someone in connection with all this, but we still have some loose ends."

Still wheezing, he managed to say, "Thank God." Then he sucked in another breath, swallowed hard, and jammed the cigarette into the ashtray, reminding himself of his vow to quit the habit. "So how can I help?"

"Okay. I need to know if you've got anyone working at the camp right now. The waterfront has already been set up and all the boats are tied up and ready for the season."

"Yeah, that's right. We hired a new maintenance guy this year. We're getting started early. You see, we're introducing an advanced water program that will require interviewing and testing potential candidates. In fact, my brother and I are headed up at the end of the week to start the process."

"So you have someone at the camp right now?" Fess asked.

"I'm not sure if he's there as we speak. His job was to get the waterfront ready before the weekend. If he's finished, he may have already left. I haven't spoken with him, so I don't know."

"How well do you know him?"

"Not that well. I only met him once."

"And that was enough to hire him?"

"Sure, Fess. He's just a local handyman, and he doesn't work with the kids, so we don't do a full background check." He eyeballed the cigarette still smoldering in the ashtray.

"I see. Can you at least describe him for me? What's his name? What does he look like? How old is he? Where does he live?"

"Hold on. Gimme a second to open his file, I've got it in the computer." Gordy sat down and palmed the mouse that sat on his desk. "I met him at the end of last summer and don't remember all that off the top of my head."

"Fine, just hurry up. This is urgent. We're trying to piece this all together, and if your handyman was there, he may have seen something."

"Of course, anything I can do to help." Gordy fingered the keyboard. "It's loading now . . . Ahh, okay—here it is. His name is Bart Randolph. He's thirty-one, five-ten, has long blond hair, and lives in Greenville."

"Greenville. That's only a couple of miles from here. Give me his address."

"No problem, Fess. Four twenty-three Dover Road."

CHAPTER SEVENTY-FIVE

I've never been in a jail cell before all this shit, and it really blows. The mattress sucks, and the toilet is out in the open. I can't believe I have to crap right here where people can see.

I'm bored as hell sitting on the bed, so my mind starts racing. But you know what, the thing I least expect to be thinking about is what I can't stop thinking about. That's right: my dad. The prick—what the hell is he thinking telling my lawyer that he wants to see me? Where does he get off? The old man never wanted to talk to me before. And like I could give a shit that he's in the hospital and almost died. Probably should have, the bastard.

So what'd Levy say? Dad started thinking about his life and where he screwed up. Well, I've got a clue. The thing I remember most about the old man is his ratty gray sweatshirt and a bottle of whiskey in his hand. Yeah, every night after Mom cut out, he'd be laid out on the couch slugging down the shit without even pouring it in a glass. Right from the bottle, man, every damn night. Didn't give a crap about what I was up to. I mean, there were times when I'd just go out back with my pals, a case a beer, and a bag a weed. For hours, we'd hang out there and just get wasted. Every now and then, we'd look in the window to see what he was up to. Most of the time, he was passed out, piss-drunk, with no clue what we were up to.

Back then, we thought it was cool because everyone else's folks never let us get away with shit like that. But at my house, it was always a party. Then I start thinking about my mom for like the first time in years. I don't remember much because she cut out when I was around ten. Who knows—maybe that's what screwed me up? I mean, it sure did do a number on dear old dad. One thing I do remember, though, she was tough. There's no way we could have gotten away with drinking and smoking in the yard if she was there. She would have taken a strap to all of us, and if any of my friend's folks went up on her, she probably would have smacked them around, too. Yeah, she was mean and always messed-up on something. You know, booze, pills, coke. That's what Dad said, anyway. Whatever. I haven't thought about any of that shit for a long time. And now Dad wants to reminisce? Screw him.

CHAPTER SEVENTY-SIX

Scottler pulled into Randolph's driveway, an unpaved dirt and gravel road that led to a small one-story house in desperate need of paint. Off to the side, partially obscured by tall weeds, lay the rusty carcass of an ancient and indeterminate-model pickup. Before Scottler had even reached the front door, an elderly woman pulled it open, blocking the doorway. "Can I help you, Officer?" she asked in a creaky voice.

"I hope so, ma'am. I'm looking for Bart Randolph. I understand he lives here."

"Well, he ain't home. Haven't seen him in a few days."

"But he does live here?" Scottler asked.

"Some of the time. This is my place, and he's my grandson, but he's got a girl over in Port Jervis whose place he stays at a lot." She looked Scottler up and down suspiciously, then gazed out toward his cruiser. "He do something wrong?"

"Not that I know of. I just have some questions for him. Do you know if he was working over at Camp Lakewood this week?"

"Said something about it before he left."

"And when would that have been, ma'am?"

"Maybe three days ago, his girl picked him up."

"He doesn't drive?"

"Truck's in the shop."

"Can you tell me his girlfriend's name and where she lives?"

"Maryanne from Port Jervis is all I know."

"Would you mind if I had a look around in his room, ma'am?"

"I thought you said he ain't done nothing wrong."

"Yes, but I still need to talk to him. And perhaps there is something in his room that may tell me more about his girl-friend and where I can find her."

"Sorry, but I don't feel comfortable letting you in, so I'll do the looking. You just wait outside."

"Fine. I just need an address."

The old woman closed the door, locked it, and shuffled off to her grandson's room. Opening the door, she said, "All right, mister. Why are the police here looking for you, and why don't you want me to tell them you're home?"

Randolph sat up in bed. "You've got it all wrong, Grams. I just don't like cops. The other day I had a fight with that skinny, black guy Frankie over at the shop. He wouldn't give me my truck back until I paid him, so I pushed him down and threatened to bust up the place. That's probably what it's all about."

"Wonderful." The old woman glared at her grandson with a look that defied her age and could still elicit fear. "When are you gonna get your act together? I'm telling you, Bart, I've had it up to here. This is the last time I'm covering for you. Now stay in your room while I get rid of him."

"Thanks, Grams."

She waited a few minutes, then opened the door. "I looked through all his stuff and didn't find anything, Officer."

"I see, ma'am," Scottler said, handing her his card. "Please take this and have your grandson call me when he returns."

"Sure, but it may be a while. I don't keep tabs on him."

"Thank you." Scottler began walking away, then turned back, almost as an afterthought. "One more thing, though. Does he have a cell phone? Maybe I could call him?"

"He used to, but he couldn't pay the bill, so they shut it off last month."

"Very well, then. Just have him call when he gets back."

CHAPTER SEVENTY-SEVEN

Two days go by, during which I suffer through a couple of minor episodes. The over-the-counter Excedrin Migraine pills help a little, but not like my real meds. I'm just glad that I haven't had a full-blown attack. Anyway, I'm lying on the bed, bored out of my mind, and wondering what the hell is going to happen next, when this tough-looking, spike-haired cop pulls me out of my cell and brings me into an interrogation room. He cuffs my ankles and leaves me alone without saying a word. I sit there for a while, and then this chubby old lady walks through the door. "Good afternoon, Mr. Sullivan," she says to me, smiling like my grandma. "I'm here to help with your defense, Harold Levy sent me to speak with you. My name is Dr. Sinead O'Reilly."

"Well, where is he? I haven't seen him in two days."

"He's working on your case. He told me to tell you that he's following up some leads and in the process of drafting a motion to suppress evidence. He wants me to evaluate you, and if I am to help, you must be completely honest with me about everything. Understand that whatever you say will be kept confidential."

"Whatever. I told him I'm not crazy, but if this will help . . ."

"Mr. Levy believes it will, but before I begin, you should know that I have read your file and I have been fully briefed. I have also reviewed a report about the active ingredients contained in the experimental medication you've been taking."

"Yeah, well, speaking of that, my head's been killing me, and I sure could use a dose of that stuff right about now."

"I'm sorry, Thomas, but I don't think that's a good idea. In fact, after the research I've done, I believe that the drug is causing more problems for you than you know."

"What do you mean?"

She gives me a sympathetic look. "Thomas, before I draw any conclusions, I really need to ask you some questions. Can we start with that?"

"I guess so."

"Good, I understand you've been in this study for about three months. When did you start experiencing these headaches?"

"A long time ago. They actually started when I was a kid."

"Really? Did your parents know?"

"Yeah."

"Did they do anything about it?"

"My mom used to take me to this doctor."

"What kind of doctor?"

"He was a shrink."

"And did he help you?"

"Nah, he was a stiff. I'd just go every couple of weeks and talk to him, but nothing ever came of it. After a few months, my mom just stopped taking me."

"Did he prescribe medication for you?"

"Yeah, I think so. I mean, I remember my mom used to give me a pill every morning for a while."

"Did it help with the headaches?"

"Sometimes. But to be honest with you, I really don't remember too much about my life when I was a kid."

"Okay, Thomas, I'm going to go in a different direction, here. How would you feel if I were to hypnotize you and see if we can jog your memory?"

"Hypnotize me? Can you really do that?"

"Yes, if you're willing."

I nod my head. "I suppose so." Of course, I really don't think Granny can actually hypnotize me. I never believed that stuff for a second, but what the hell? Let her try.

"Good. I'll be right back."

She gets up, leaves the room, and returns a few minutes later with the spike-haired cop. They move us into a room with a couch where I lie down. Then she tells me to close my eyes and begins talking to me in a whisper. Before long, I start feeling real sleepy.

. . .

"Okay, Thomas, you should be completely relaxed now," said Dr. O'Reilly. "I want you to think back to when you were a little boy, just playing and having fun. Can you recall a time like that?"

Tommy was stretched out comfortably on the couch with his eyes closed. A childlike grin played across his face. "Yeah, I remember."

"Good—very good," Dr. O'Reilly said, her voice soft and soothing. "Now, can you tell me where you are?"

"On the beach playing in the sand." Tommy answered, in a much younger voice.

"That's great, Tommy. How old are you?"

"Six or seven. I'm not really sure."

"Who is with you?"

"This kid I know from down here."

"Down where, Tommy?"

"The Cape. We're at the Cape for the week now that school's over."

"Very nice. Where are your parents?"

"They're sitting on a blanket watching us build a sandcastle."

"Wonderful. Tell me more."

"We're digging a moat around the castle to catch the water when it comes up the beach. Dad says that as the tide comes in the water will fill it. We just have to wait. It doesn't take long though, and first the moat fills up, then a few minutes later a big wave crashes in and wrecks the castle. We get soaked and race up the beach laughing."

"Sounds like great fun, Tommy. I'm glad you remember that. Now let's move on. Can you recall another time you were enjoying yourself like that?"

Tommy giggles. "I'm playing miniature golf, and I just got a hole-in-one."

"Where are you, Tommy?"

"At the Cape again."

"How old are you now?"

"Maybe eight?"

"Okay, go on."

"Dad's with me, clapping and laughing louder than ever. He picks me up and puts me on his shoulders, and we're dancing around celebrating the hole-in-one. Mom's watching us from the bench, and she's cracking up."

"What a great time, Tommy."

"Yeah, it is. I always have a blast here, but it never lasts. Once the week is over, things just go back to normal."

"What do you mean?"

Tommy squirmed and began scratching his forearm. "Well . . . back at home, Mom and Dad are not the same. They always fight with each other and scream at me. Even when I don't do anything wrong."

"Well, let's explore that further. I want you to go back to a different time—and this may be a little harder—because I want you to think about when things were really bad and you were very sad. Can you do that for me?"

Tommy began to frown, and his face took on a pained expression. "No, don't hit me, Mom. I didn't mean for that to happen."

"What did you do, Tommy? Tell me."

"It was Louie's idea, I swear." Tommy started crying.

"I believe you, Tommy. What was Louie's idea?"

"We have this firecracker—and there's this stray dog by my house, and Louie says it would be fun to feed it to the dog. So I go inside my house and get a piece of cheese, and I wrap it around the firecracker." Tommy was shaking his head from side to side.

"It's okay Tommy. Relax. Just keep going."

"Louie is holding onto the dog, and I light the firecracker and put the cheese in front of the dog." Still in a trance, Tommy shivered. "Oh, no—he grabs it out of my hand. Boom! It explodes right in his mouth."

"Then what happens, Tommy?"

"Louie takes off just as Mom runs out of the house." Tommy's speech became urgent. "She's yelling at me something awful."

"Go on, Tommy, don't stop now."

"Okay, now she's screaming: 'You little bastard, what's wrong with you? How could you do that to a poor, defenseless animal?'"

"I'm right here, Tommy. Let it all out."

"I'm standing there crying and staring at the blood all over the dog's muzzle. Mom is on her knees, holding the dog and crying. She looks up at me and says, 'I should have chosen your brother, you nasty son of a bitch.'"

"What does that mean?"

"I've got no idea. I don't even have a brother." Tommy starts pressing his palms into his temples and rolling his head.

"Okay, Tommy, calm down. You have to relax."

"I can't. It's my head. It's pounding so hard I can't stand it. Make it stop. Please make it stop!"

Dr. O'Reilly got up, walked behind Tommy, and placed her hands on top of his. She spoke slowly in a hushed voice. "Close your eyes, Tommy. Focus your mind on the sounds of the ocean. Listen to the waves rolling up the beach, and hear the seagulls cawing. I know you can do it. Everything will be fine. Your headache is going away. The pain is easing." Gently, she removed Tommy's hands from his head and placed them softly in his lap. Standing behind him, she began rubbing the sides of his head and continued to whisper, "Feel the sand under your feet and the sun at your back. All is good, Tommy. Relax, and take a deep breath."

In seconds, Tommy's demeanor changed, his body slumped, and he let out a sigh that seemed to expel some demon from deep within, a suppressed evil that must have been plaguing him since childhood.

"How are you feeling now, Tommy?" she asked, returning to her seat.

Tommy's breathing steadied, and the color returned to his face. "Much better now."

"No more headache?" the doctor asked.

"All gone."

"Fantastic, Tommy. You're doing great. Let's move forward. Why don't you take us to something you remember after that?"

Tommy started to quiver and hugged himself. His breathing became fitful, and his face turned red.

Concerned, Dr. O'Reilly asked, "What is it, Tommy? What's happening?"

Tommy went on, speaking in a voice from the past. "Mommy, where are you. Where'd you go?"

Dr. O'Reilly interjected again. "Tommy, answer me. What's going on?"

"She's gone. Her clothes are gone, and Dad is screaming, calling her names, and using nasty curses. Now he's in the hall holding a bottle of whiskey, and he keeps drinking from it and yelling like mad, 'Jenny, where'd you go, bitch? You can't cut out on me now—not like this!'"

"Keep going, I want to hear it all."

Tommy is bawling. "I'm in my room, hiding in the closet. Dad is storming up the stairs and calling out my name, 'Tommy, where the fuck are you?' He pulls open the closet door and grabs me by the shirt. 'You did this, you little prick, didn't you? It's your fault she ran off. I hope you're happy now.' He throws me on the bed, rips off his belt, and starts whacking me with it over and over again. I'm screaming and crying and trying to pull the covers over me, but he keeps whacking away, so I get up, run down the stairs, and bolt out the door."

His eyes still closed, Tommy's body contorts, writhing until he rolls off the couch. Dr. O'Reilly rushes to his side and cradles him. "Everything is okay, Tommy. Just calm down, you're safe here. We're going to make this all go away. I'm going to count to three and snap my fingers, and when I do, you're going to wake up and you won't remember any of this. You'll just feel refreshed and alive and better than you have in a very long time. One, your breathing is getting slower . . . two, you're feeling so much better . . . and three, you're feeling great." *Snap!*

Tommy's eyes flickered, and he came awake. Confused, he searched Dr. O'Reilly's face. "When do we start?"

CHAPTER SEVENTY-EIGHT

Dr. O'Reilly phoned Levy immediately upon leaving the police station.

"Harold, I've done a preliminary, and I can tell you right now that there's a lot going on with this young man."

"Well, don't keep me in suspense. What have you got for me?"

"I need to see him again very soon, but from what I've learned so far, he's deeply troubled, and it goes all the way back to when he was a little boy. Definitely a dysfunctional upbringing, which clearly has had a major impact on him."

"Go on. I need details."

"Okay, I was able to hypnotize him—quite easily, I must say—and I brought him back to childhood. Almost immediately, he remembered two very significant incidents from his past. This is important because the simple fact that he picked out these memories first means that they probably have been plaguing his subconscious for some time, while his conscious mind has no memory of the occurrences."

Levy shifted the phone from his left ear to his right. "What kind of memories?"

Dr. O'Reilly breathed a heavy sigh before continuing. "All right. First, he recalled a few happy times in his life. Then, I directed him to go back to some bad times, and he told me a story about an evil thing he did as a child. It seems he and another boy fed a firecracker to a dog. As horrible as that was, what happened next may have been even more traumatic."

"Don't stop now."

"Well, his mother caught him, and apparently she was so incensed that she actually told him that she wished she would have chosen his brother instead."

"Really!"

"Yes, and so I asked him if he knew what his mother meant by that. He responded that he did not. Honestly, though, I have my doubts. I mean, you did tell me that his father told him about his twin brother; so perhaps he may have known before his father ever told him. Maybe he was living with the knowledge all his life and never acknowledged or accepted it, and it just festered in his subconscious. It would explain a lot of things."

"I'm trying to process this, Doctor, but what you're saying doesn't make sense. How can he know something but at the same time not know it?"

"The brain is a very powerful and mysterious organ. You would be amazed at what it is capable of. Sometimes it will suppress very painful memories as a defense mechanism in an effort to protect its host, but at the same time, the very information that has been buried grows like a cancer until it takes over the mind and causes all sorts of psychological problems."

"But his father didn't tell him about his twin until after his mother left. And when he did tell him, he lied and said that his twin died at birth."

"As I said, perhaps he found out much earlier but never fully acknowledged it. We just don't know."

Levy thought for a moment. "I see. Is there more?"

"Quite a bit. The night his mother left, his father got very drunk and took it out on Thomas. He blamed him and beat him with a strap until he ran away. I imagine things were never the same between them after that."

"Yes, well, Tommy alluded to that when I questioned him. And his father also told me as much. It must have been very traumatic."

"That's not all," Dr. O'Reilly said. "I received the report from the lab. You know those pills he's been taking? Well, the chemical compounds that make up the drug contain a mixture of MDMA, the main ingredient found in Ecstasy, Ritalin, Imitrex, and another compound that the lab has not yet isolated. The combination can be deadly at high doses, and from the research I've read, it could induce delusions and paranoia, among other psychological disorders."

"Unbelievable! So do you think that the doctor running the study is aware of all this?"

"I would say there is no doubt, Counselor."

"How can they get away with this?"

Dr. O'Reilly let out a morbid laugh. "You're the lawyer, Harold. It's people like you who help keep the FDA at bay while this goes on."

"Right, Doctor, but its people like you who come up with these studies in the first place."

"True, but all under the guise of improving the human condition."

"Don't kid yourself, Doctor. It's more about money—big money."

"I can't argue with that, Harold, but this debate won't help Thomas. And if I am to help at all, I need to hypnotize him again and dig deeper. I'm sure there's quite a bit more to learn. At this point, I believe his fragile mental state, coupled with the interaction of the drug, is having a significant effect on this young man. Obviously, he should never take another one of those pills again."

"Understood. And I'll get you back in to see him very shortly. In the meantime, I intend to pay Dr. Diamond another visit."

CHAPTER SEVENTY-NINE

Detective Morgan interrupted Stone as she sat at her desk poring over the Sullivan file.

"We've hit another wall," Morgan said. "The owner of the P.O. Box in Montana is untraceable. Apparently, the box was established by a law firm on behalf of the trust, and all mail is forwarded to the lawyers. Of course, they don't have much to say. All we could get out of them is that a bank account was established at the time the trust was created, and as the bills come in, they pay them from the account. Off the record, I was told that there is sufficient money in the account to pay all the bills for taxes, insurance, utilities, maintenance, and upkeep for the next twenty-five years or so. They have had no contact with anyone regarding the property since the trust was created."

"Just great," Stone said, frustrated. "I guess all we can do is stake out the property and see if anyone shows up."

"We've had it under surveillance since we discovered the blood."

"Good—just make sure the team stays out of sight. We don't want to scare anyone off, should they desire to return."

"I've got a man inside the house and another hidden in the weed grass nearby," said Morgan. "We've removed all vehicles from the site and stopped the search of Gilgo for the time being."

"Sounds like you're on top of it, Detective. Keep me posted."

CHAPTER EIGHTY

Dr. Diamond greeted Harold Levy in a sitting area near the entrance to the Center for Migraine Pain Management.

"What can I do for you now, Counselor?" Dr. Diamond asked coldly as he sat down across from Levy. "I thought we concluded our business the other day."

"Unfortunately, Doctor, our business may have only just begun."

"What do you mean by that?"

"Well, Doctor, to begin with, I've done some research on your so-called 'wonder drug.' In fact, I've had it analyzed by a laboratory, and the results are quite astonishing."

"Enlighten me, Counselor."

Levy continued. "As I'm sure you know, the chemical compounds in your drug contain some very dangerous substances. I'm told that the combination of ingredients can be extremely hazardous and may even lead to psychotic breaks."

"Excuse me, Mr. Levy, but I am well aware of the ingredients. However, the actual quantity of those chemicals in the drug is minimal, and it would take a high dose for a patient to experience even a slight reaction of that kind. We have been testing this formula for over three years now and we know quite well what reactions to expect from our subjects."

"Let's not be so naive. You have been prescribing large numbers of pills to your study subjects and leaving it solely up to them to decide how many to take at one time. Just because you advise them to take a certain dosage doesn't mean they will adhere to your instructions."

"Look, Counselor, I'm not going to entertain any further dialogue on the subject. Why don't you tell me what you want?"

"Very well, Doctor. I'll be frank. My client is presently incarcerated on some very serious charges. It is my belief that he is suffering from the effects of overdosing on your experimental pills. I am considering a mental incapacity defense, and I may need you to testify on his behalf and educate the prosecutor and the judge regarding the effects of overdosing on these pills. I suspect that you are in possession of reports on a number of subjects in your study who may have suffered adverse reactions and psychotic episodes."

Dr. Diamond stood up, furious. "Mr. Levy, I will not let you undermine a study that we have worked so hard on for a very long time. We are on the verge of a breakthrough, and forcing me to go public with any information about this now could jeopardize everything."

"Then I suggest you cooperate with me on a smaller scale, and perhaps we won't necessarily have to go public with this. My immediate concern is to help my client."

"What is it you're suggesting, Mr. Levy?"

"Very simple, Doctor. I would like to retain you to act as an expert witness on behalf of Mr. Sullivan. I will need to put you on my list as an expert for any witnesses who may be called to testify during the trial about the connection between overdosing on the chemical compounds contained in your drug and psychotic episodes. If we can establish that Mr. Sullivan was not in control of his mental faculties, I may be able to negotiate a plea where he is placed in a psychiatric hospital and monitored until they conclude he is not mentally incapacitated. Then I can secure his release. If we approach it in that fashion, you may not have to testify in open court but rather just report this to the prosecutor."

"I don't know, Counselor. This sounds to me like a double-edged sword. I think I'm going to need to speak with our attorneys before I agree to anything or even talk to you any further."

"I understand, Doctor, but I suspect that once you've presented the options to your attorneys, they will advise you that this is the lesser of two evils. It could get quite messy if you are subpoenaed by me—or even worse, by the People of the State of New York. You see, if you agree to act as an expert witness, they will have no reason to subpoena you, and that, in and of itself, will keep things calm around here."

Dr. Diamond nodded. "I see, and I will consider it, but as I said, it is time for me to discuss this with our attorneys. Good day."

"Very well. But do it quickly."

CHAPTER EIGHTY-ONE

Detectives Stone and Watts sat across the table from lab analyst Dr. Rita Thornwood.

Stone began. "So tell me, Doctor: What's the story with this drug?"

Thornwood focused her eyes on the report in her hands as she spoke. "Well, Detective, we don't have a complete analysis, but we have some significant information. The drug contains a number of very familiar active ingredients, including MDMA—methylphenidate hydrochloride—which is the active ingredient in Ritalin and Sumatriptan. There is another compound we are still analyzing, but what we know already is certainly troubling."

"Can you explain that, Doctor?" Watts asked.

"Taken alone, any one of these compounds can have adverse effects on a person. Combined as they are in this formula and administered at high doses, well . . ." Thornwood shook her head and made eye contact with Stone for a brief second before returning her gaze to the report. "At high doses, one could experience a variety of psychological disorders."

"Such as . . ." Watts prodded.

Thornwood put down the report. "Such as anything from simple confusion and nausea to blackouts, memory loss, violence, delusions, and even serious personality disorders."

Stone interrupted. "Excuse me, but what do you mean by 'personality disorders'?"

"Paranoia, schizophrenia . . ."

Perplexed, Stone looked to Watts, then back to Thornwood. "So you're saying the drug could make him crazy?"

"We don't like to use the term crazy, but at high doses, it could have serious implications. Just keep in mind that everyone has a different tolerance."

Stone took a deep breath and began pacing.

Watts followed her with his eyes. "So this guy could get off with an insanity defense?"

"Screw the pills," Stone answered. "He's not getting away with this."

CHAPTER EIGHTY-TWO

"This time, I would like to observe your session, Dr. O'Reilly." Levy said as they waited for Sullivan to be brought from his cell.

"No problem, Harold, but please understand that any outside intervention may upset him and could be very damaging. Tommy needs to trust me completely to let himself go. So the only way you can do it is if the police are willing to bring a couch into the interrogation room for us. That way, you can observe through the two-way mirror."

"Fine—I will make the arrangements. I just want to speak with him for a few minutes before you start, if that's okay?"

"Actually, I'd prefer that you not cloud his mind with anything right now. I really want him to be able to focus on the past, and I need him to be calm and composed if I am to hypnotize him successfully."

"Okay, Doctor. Just one more thing: I'd like to record the session."

"Not a problem, Counselor."

Levy made the arrangements, and a couch was set up in the interrogation room. Minutes later, Thomas Sullivan was brought in handcuffed.

. . .

Doc Granny is sitting in a chair when the cop brings me through the door.

"How are you, Tommy?" she asks, with a big old smile.

"Hey, Doc. What's up?"

She looks at the officer who brought me in. "Could you please remove his cuffs? He's no threat to me."

"If you're sure, ma'am," the cop answers, "but I'll be right outside, so just holler if you need me." What does he think? Like I'm really going to kill her or something.

"Thanks, Doc. Those cuffs really hurt," I say, rubbing my wrists as I sit down on the couch. "So what do you want from me?"

"Well, Tommy, I wanted to continue where we left off the other day. I think we made some real progress, so I'd like to hypnotize you again."

"I dunno—I don't remember a thing about it. But for the first time I can remember, my headache disappeared without any pills." And I'm being totally honest with her. I really did feel better after the last session, but I couldn't remember anything. In fact, I still don't believe she even hypnotized me.

"That's great, Tommy. I'm glad to hear it. Now let's begin."

"Go for it."

. . .

"Are you feeling relaxed now, Tommy?" Dr. O'Reilly asked gently.

His eyes were closed. "Yeah—warm all over."

"Perfect. Just let your mind wander." The doctor continued her soft tone. "Try to think back to when you were a teenager and you were enjoying yourself. Can you do that for me?"

Tommy's eyelids began to flicker, his eyes moving rapidly underneath. Slowly, a smile appeared on his face. "Ahh . . . the air is so fresh up here, and the smell of cut grass is awesome."

"Where are you, Tommy?"

"At the camp," Tommy answered in a teenage voice. "Summer is here."

"What camp? Tell me all about it."

Tommy laughed. "Lakewood, and there's Big Bob. Man, I haven't seen him since last year."

"Who's Big Bob?"

"Oh, he's my best friend at camp—met him last summer. He works in the kitchen. He's a couple years older than me and built like a brick shithouse. The dude lifts weights all the time, and he's funny as hell. Tells the best jokes ever. He's always making me laugh."

"So what's going on, Tommy?"

"I run over to him, and he's got this big grin on his face. He hugs me real hard. 'How you doing, Tommy?' he asks me. Then he lets go and throws some light jabs at my gut, but he doesn't actually hit me. He's just kidding around."

"Sounds like you like him, Tommy," Dr. O'Reilly whispered. "Go on. Tell me more."

"Yeah, he's a great guy. We hung out a lot last summer, but he lives in Florida, so I never got to see him after camp."

"It's nice that you guys became friends and could pick it up after an entire year."

"I know, but that's BB . . . Yeah, BB—everyone at camp used to call him that for short, and he liked it, so one day last year, he carved those initials into the side of the banana tree by the sports field." Tommy's body language changed suddenly, and the color left his face.

EVERYWHERE THAT TOMMY GOES

"What is it, Tommy? What just happened? You look upset."

"Nothing—never mind," Tommy said, agitated. "I don't wanna talk about it."

"That's okay. We don't have to talk about it if you don't want to, but I promise you'll feel much better if you do."

He shook his head, struggling within himself. "I'm scared. BB's gone. They took him to the hospital. I think he's dead."

"That's terrible. I'm so sorry, but you have to let it out."

Tommy began to cry, wincing as he spoke. "I'm leaning on the banana tree watching the baseball game. BB's pitching. The batter takes a swing, and the ball comes flying back and hits him right in the chest. He goes down. All the counselors run over to him and start pushing on his chest. Then they give him mouth-to-mouth. There's so many people around, but I swear it's never been so quiet. Then, like ten minutes later, an ambulance shows up and takes him away. The whole time I'm staring like it's not real, and as hard as I try, I can't get myself to move away from the tree. The damn tree—why does everything have to happen around that stupid tree?"

"What do you mean, Tommy? What is it about the tree?"

Visibly disturbed, Tommy's body shifted as he screamed, "No, don't do that! Leave her alone!"

Startled, Dr. O'Reilly jumped back.

Tommy sat upright, his eyes still closed.

"What is it, Tommy? What's going on now?"

His breathing quickened. "It's real late at night and no one's around. He's got Ellen pressed up against the banana tree. They're both naked."

"Who, Tommy? Who is she with?"

"I dunno."

"Okay, what are they doing?"

"He's on top of her, and she's crying. I wanna go over and help, but I can't move or even speak. It's like I'm paralyzed or something."

"I understand—just go on. Tell me what's happening now."

"He's getting off of her, and she's crying real loud, so he puts his hands around her throat. Oh, no, he's choking her, and I still can't move. Then, all of a sudden, she stops crying, and he lets go. She slides off the tree and falls to the ground. I think she's dead. A few seconds go by, and he puts his clothes on, grabs her clothes, tosses her over his shoulder, and carries her off. Finally, my legs start to work again. I follow him down to the waterfront. He throws her into a rowboat, gets in, and rows out to the middle of the lake. I'm so scared I can barely catch my breath. I run away like some chickenshit and sneak back into my bunk. I crawl under the covers real quietly, shivering like mad."

"That's awful, Tommy. Did you tell anyone?"

"No—I was too scared." Tommy whimpered.

"And you don't know who did this?"

"No! I swear I've got no idea."

"Okay, Tommy, it's not your fault, don't worry about this any more. It's only a bad dream." The doctor stands, moves behind Tommy, and gently massages his shoulders. "Now, I want you to take a deep breath and let it out slowly. As you breathe, the smell of freshly-cut grass is filling up inside you, and you can almost taste it." Her voice was silk-soft. "It's warm, the sun is shining, and everything feels good."

Tommy sighed, his body loosened, and he slumped over on the couch.

"You're feeling much better—aren't you, Tommy?"

"Much better," Tommy smiled. "It smells like summer."

"Good. I want you to jump forward a bit," her voice now mellifluous. "You're no longer a boy. You're a man, and you've made a new friend—Troyer Savage—and I need you to tell me all about him."

Tommy's body stiffened. "Troyer! He's no friend. I hate that lunatic."

"I'm sorry, Tommy. I didn't mean to upset you. Tell me, why do you hate him?"

"He's a total scumbag—that's why."

"What did he do to you?"

"You see, the guy acted like he wanted to be my friend. We started hanging out a lot. One night, he goes psycho on me and kills this bartender, and leaves me to clean up the mess. Then, only a few days later, he kills another girl and does it to me again."

"He sounds like a deranged individual. How did you get involved with him?"

"Shit, it don't matter. The dude's just bad news, and he's ruining my life."

"Please, I really want to know all about him."

Tommy became irritated. "Why do you care about him so much? He's just a crazy prick!"

"It's you I care about, Tommy. I truly want to help. But the only way I can do that is if you tell me more about Troyer Savage. Please settle down and take another deep breath. Fill your lungs with the smell of fresh-cut grass again, and when you've relaxed, we can talk about him some more." Dr. O'Reilly looked up at the two-way mirror knowing that even though she couldn't see him, Levy was watching.

Tommy inhaled deeply, trying to regain his composure.

Dr. O'Reilly took a pause, waiting for a sign that Tommy had calmed down, before she spoke again. "Okay, let's go back to Troyer. I want you to be specific now, so try as hard as you can to get past your anger and tell me everything you can about him."

Covering his ears with his hands, Tommy began to speak. "I thought he was so cool, the way he acted around people—especially girls. I mean, the dude was legend. I watched him pick up chicks all the time like it was nothing. 'Hunting the fox while still in its den' is the way he described it. And he was teaching me. Then, one night, I'm watching the dude while he picks up some hot bartender." Suddenly, Tommy's voice and demeanor changed. "Hello, love, I'm from Down Under, just visiting for a spell, don't know much about New York. Can you help me out?"

"That's a wonderful accent, Tommy," Dr. O'Reilly said lightly, though she was clearly surprised by what she had just heard.

"You wanted to know about Troyer, so I'm telling you. You see, when I first met him he didn't have an accent, but the night he killed the bartender he started talking to her like that. At the time I was impressed, but ever since then he hasn't stopped talking that way. His new story is that he grew up in Australia. But I know that's not true."

"How do you know that?" she asked, looking up at the mirror and wondering if Levy had picked up on what just happened.

"Because when we first met, he told me he was raised in an orphanage. He also told me he ran away from there because a priest was abusing him. For many years after that, he lived on the streets."

"That is quite a story, Tommy. But how do you know he didn't just make all that up?"

"I never really thought about it. I simply assumed it was true. Why would anybody make up something like that?"

"I really couldn't tell you. Hopefully, together we can get to the bottom of this. For now, I think you should get some rest."

Dr. O'Reilly talked Tommy down and brought him out of the trance, leaving him with no memory of what had just transpired.

CHAPTER EIGHTY-THREE

"Quite a session, there," Levy said as Dr. O'Reilly entered the observation room.

"To say the least, Counselor. As you can see, this young man is deeply troubled."

"He's got quite the story. What do you make of it?"

"Tommy certainly has been traumatized—numerous times—which may explain his current manifestations. After observing the change in his body language as he adopted the Australian accent, my sense is that he may be suffering from DID."

"DID? What the hell is that?"

"Come on: you mean to tell me you haven't heard about the latest and greatest psychological re-definition of the modern era?"

"No, Doctor, I haven't. Please enlighten me."

"Well, DID stands for Dissociative Identity Disorder. It's the modern-day equivalent of Sybil. Remember that story?"

"What—like multiple personalities?" Levy asked.

"Precisely. The old definition of Multiple Personality Disorder is now known as Dissociative Identity Disorder. And I think Tommy may be a classic case."

"You can't be serious."

"I never joke about my work, Harold. You know that."

"It's just that this is so bizarre."

"That it is. And I must caution you, that this is only a preliminary diagnosis. I could be wrong. Tommy did give me a very credible answer as to why he mimicked Troyer Savage."

"Yes, but you also said that his body language changed."

"I did, and that is the only reason why I even suspect DID. I need more evidence, though, before I can make a real diagnosis."

"What kind of evidence?" asked Levy.

"After he's had some time to relax, I have to hypnotize him again and see if I can draw out the Troyer Savage personality."

"Sounds logical. I' m sure I can arrange it in the next day or two. In the meantime, please prepare a written report of your findings." Levy put his finger to his lips and thought for a moment. "I've got an idea, and I think Aurora Storm may be able to help us with your diagnosis. She's the only one who has spent time with both Troyer and Tommy. Perhaps she can shed some light."

CHAPTER EIGHTY-FOUR

The Port Jervis police finally released Aurora's car from evidence, and she made her way to New York City to visit Tommy. Levy reached her on her cell while she was still in transit, and the two arranged to meet when she arrived.

An hour later, the two met in the lobby bar of the Marriott Hotel in lower Manhattan.

"I'm glad we could finally get together and talk, Ms. Storm," Levy said, extending his hand.

"Please, call me Aurora," she said, reaching out to greet him.

"Very well, Aurora. Would you care for a drink while we talk?"

"Absolutely. I'll take a Coors Lite."

Levy motioned for a waiter. "Absolut Cranberry and a Coors Lite, please." Turning to Aurora, he began. "Okay, as you know, I'm Tommy's attorney, and I would like to ask you some questions . . ."

Aurora interrupted. "Wait—before you do, how is Tommy?"

"He's fine for now, and he asked me to give you a message. He wanted me to tell you that he said he's innocent and that he's sorry he brought you into this mess, and when he works everything out, he will make it up to you."

Aurora smiled. "When can I see him?"

"Soon. But first, we need to talk, so if you please . . ."

"Fine. What do you want to know?"

The waiter returned with their drinks and set them down.

"Thank you," Levy said, turning to Aurora. "How long have you known Tommy?"

"We knew each other as kids, but I hadn't seen him for twenty years before he walked into my shop in Cape May," Aurora took a sip of her beer.

"Can you tell me about that and how you two ended up in Port Jervis?"

"Well, Tommy came in and bought a bunch of clothes. It took us a few minutes before we realized that we knew each other, but once we did, some of the old feelings came back. Coincidently, he was my first kiss. Anyway, he told me that he was being followed. He bought some new clothes to change his appearance, put them on, and left out the back door. We hooked up again when I got off work, and he told me this wild story about some guy he knew who killed two girls and framed Tommy. I looked into his eyes and believed him right away. I'm very good at reading people, you know, and Tommy's no killer."

"You mean to say that you just jumped right in and took up the cause of a possible murderer? Someone you barely knew at all, and hadn't seen in twenty years, knowing the police were looking for him?"

"When you put it that way, it sounds crazy, but it really wasn't like that at all. You met Tommy, so you know. He couldn't be a killer."

"Honestly, Aurora, I think you may soon find out it's a lot more complicated than that. But let's continue. What can you tell me about Troyer Savage?"

"Only what Tommy told me about him. He's a nutcase and he's the killer. I'm sure you know that he kidnapped me, tied me up, and left me in a shack in the woods."

"Yes, I am aware," Levy answered. "Please tell me more about it. How did it happen?"

"I'm not exactly sure how he first got to me. You see, the last thing I remember, Tommy walked out of the room while I was taking a shower. I was so tired I must have fallen asleep on the bed. When I woke up, I was blindfolded and tied to a chair. I yelled out, and no one answered. At that point, I figured it had to be Troyer, considering everything Tommy told me about him."

"I see. So what happened next?"

"A few hours later, I heard the door open, and Troyer came in."

"How did you know it was Troyer if you were blindfolded, and you had never met him before?"

"It was the way he talked. Tommy told me he was faking an Australian accent. Who else could it have been?"

"That's a good question," Levy said. "Forgetting the accent, did his voice sound familiar?"

"What do you mean? I don't understand."

"The pitch, the tone, the sound of his voice, was there any familiarity to it?"

"Not that I could tell."

"Okay, then, do you recall what he said?"

"He said a bunch of stuff about Tommy and that he didn't want anything from me—just Tommy. It was like he had this vendetta against him and just wanted to do anything he could to screw with Tommy. He ripped open my shirt and grabbed at my crotch. Then he tried to stuff a sandwich down my throat. I spit it back at him, and he seemed to enjoy that. When I talked back to him and didn't act scared, he took off."

"Do you think you would recognize his voice if you heard it again?"

"I suppose so."

"Do you mind if we try something? I have a recording here, and I'm going to play a segment for you. Listen closely and tell me if it sounds like Troyer."

"Okay, sure."

Levy had already set up the recording to play at precisely the point where Tommy had mimicked Troyer. He switched it on. "Hello, love, I'm from Down Under, just visiting for a spell, don't know much about New York. Can you help me out?"

"Well, Aurora, does that sound like Troyer?"

Aurora tilted her head, frowned, and looked up. "No, I don't think so. I mean, I can't say for sure, but from what I recall, it sounds different. I will say this, it does sound like an Australian or English voice, but you know those foreign accents—they're hard to tell apart. Troyer did call me 'love,' though. I remember that for sure. But don't they all say that?"

"So you don't believe its Troyer's voice?" Levy asked.

"It's so hard to say. I thought I would recognize it right away, but when I heard your recording, it confused me. That one sounds a little fake. I don't know—the recording is too fuzzy. And like I said, guys that talk with those accents all sound the same to me." Aurora thought for a moment. "Hey, do they have Troyer in custody? Is that his voice?"

"No, Troyer is not in custody, and we aren't sure if it's his voice. I'm just testing a theory."

"Well, then, what else do you want to know?" Aurora asked.

"When you were with Tommy, did he ever act oddly or say anything that would suggest he was not well?"

"He isn't crazy, if that's what you're getting at, Mr. Levy. And he isn't sick. Although he is taking some pills for migraine headaches. I'm sure he told you that we had to stop at some clinic to refill his prescription."

"He told you about the study?"

"Yes, he did."

"Were you with him when he actually took the pills?" Levy asked.

"As a matter of fact, I was—a number of times."

"Did you ever notice any peculiar behavior after he took the pills?"

"Not at all. But he did tell me that they were the only things that ever seemed to stop the pain in his head."

"I see. Did you happen to notice how many pills he would take at one time and how often he would take them?"

"I'm sorry, but I never really paid attention." A confused look played across her face. "I don't understand. What does that have to do with this case?"

"Honestly, Aurora, I'm just exploring ideas. It's my job to look at all the angles and see what works best when mounting a defense."

"Yeah, but he didn't do any of this. Isn't that good enough?"

"I'm afraid not. There is substantial evidence that suggests he may be responsible."

"Troyer is framing him. Don't you see that?"

"I'm investigating that, too."

"Well, you better keep digging," Aurora said firmly. "So if there's nothing else, can you arrange for me to see Tommy?"

CHAPTER EIGHTY-FIVE

Judge Fairgrieve's clerk called the Court to order. "The next case on today's motion calendar is The People versus Sullivan. This is defendant's motion. Counsel, please proceed."

Levy stood. "Good morning, Your Honor. Harold Levy for the defendant Thomas Sullivan. You have my papers on this motion to suppress. As I've stated therein, the detectives who arrested my client engaged in improper behavior and violated his rights. The evidence will show that after Mr. Sullivan asked for counsel, they continued to question him. They withheld food and water, they withheld necessary prescription medication, and they lied to him in an effort to compel him to talk. I am asking the Court to suppress all the statements Mr. Sullivan made from the point he was arrested and all of the evidence obtained by the People from those statements. The fruit of the poisonous tree, Your Honor. The law is clear: The People cannot use any of the evidence obtained from Mr. Sullivan after he was arrested. My papers detail everything, and I ask the Court to consider all the arguments contained therein."

"Very well, Counselor," Judge Fairgrieve said. "Now I'd like to hear from the People."

Galub rose. "Your Honor, the evidence will show that Mr. Sullivan knowingly waived his right to have counsel present and voluntarily spoke with the detectives. We have videotape of the interrogation, and it has been submitted as part of our responsive papers. Additionally, the bulk of evidence we have amassed was obtained without any assistance from Mr. Sullivan. We have blood DNA found in the trunk of Mr. Sullivan's car that matches our victim. We collected evidence at the scene that points to Sullivan. A pizza box found nearby comes from the restaurant where Mr. Sullivan works. That restaurant is located in Queens, almost fifteen miles away. We also have Sullivan's DNA. We had a valid warrant and collected his DNA legally. So even without Mr. Sullivan's statements, we have sufficient evidence to make our case."

Levy interjected. "Your Honor, the Prosecution makes a number of bold statements, but in reality, they lack substance. The pizza box that the People call evidence was found in a garbage dumpster located in the alley where they found the victim's blood. There is a very logical explanation for this. My client works at the restaurant. He brought some pizza with him and ate it on his way to the club that night. He does not deny being at the club. He does not deny drinking a bit too much and vomiting into the pizza box. He does not deny throwing the pizza box in the dumpster. None of these acts are illegal, none of these acts are suspect, and none of these acts are sufficient to obtain a warrant to search Mr. Sullivan's home. Just because he threw some garbage into a dumpster in the alley where the victim's blood was found is insufficient to justify the issuance of a warrant. Moreover, this begs the question: Did the police run down all the other people who disposed of their garbage in that dumpster? If not, then their investigation is woefully inadequate, highly suspect, and entirely prejudicial. Lacking any real evidence, a search warrant should never have been issued, and the police should never have been allowed into my client's home. Therefore, the DNA obtained from the illegal search of his home cannot be used to identify him. Furthermore, the search of my client's vehicle was likewise illegal. In fact, the blood evidence allegedly extracted from the trunk of my client's car was obtained by the police in New Jersey. I have yet to see any warrant issued by a court in New Jersey authorizing such a search. Without a warrant and without probable cause to search the vehicle, the New Jersey police conducted an illegal search. Therefore, any evidence they obtained and forwarded to the New York police is likewise inadmissible. Clearly, all evidence obtained at my client's home and in his vehicle must be suppressed. Without this evidence, the People have nothing upon which to hold my client. I would ask that all the evidence obtained in this case be suppressed and, upon suppression, that the case be dismissed."

"Do you have a rebuttal, Ms. Galub?" Judge Fairgrieve asked.

"Yes, Your Honor. First, I refer the Court to the videotape of Mr. Sullivan's confession. From it, you will see clearly that he was under no duress and freely spoke to the detectives after he was Mirandized—and after he acknowledged that he wanted to speak without counsel present. At the very least, Mr. Sullivan's statements, standing on their own, are sufficient to charge him as an accessory. Given the time, however, the People intend to establish that the defendant is actually the perpetrator. Additionally, with respect to the defendant's claim of an illegal search by the police in New Jersey, we have been advised that the vehicle was parked illegally, it was unlocked, and an over-whelming smell of bleach emanated from the trunk. The offic-ers had sufficient probable cause and were justified in searching the vehicle. Moreover, the initial DNA was extracted from a water bottle I secured on a table outside a restaurant where the defendant was sitting."

Judge Fairgrieve stood up. "Thank you, Counselors. I've heard enough. I will reserve decision and read your papers. You can expect my decision within the week. In the meantime, the defendant will remain in police custody."

CHAPTER EIGHTY-SIX

Stone cornered Galub outside the Courtroom. "That didn't go so well in there, Counselor, did it?"

"Fairgrieve is a good judge," Galub said. "He'll see past the smokescreen."

"And what if he doesn't and dismisses the case?"

"Look, Detective: I wasn't dealt a great hand, here. Levy had some valid arguments about procedures. We have to hope the judge focuses on the videotape. It's our best chance."

"Still, Counselor, I have a bad feeling."

"Well, we have a few days before the judge renders his decision. That gives you a little time to come up with evidence that I can use. If you do, I'll bring it to court."

"If not, Counselor?"

"If not, then we may want to consider a plea and dispose of this whole mess."

"A plea? Do you really think that worm Levy would consider a plea? My guess is he's feeling real good about his case right now."

"You can thank the Jersey cops for that," Galub said. "A warrant would have made all the difference here."

"Well, that doesn't bode well for their case, either."

"Very true, Detective. When they charge Sullivan for the motel murder, Levy will use the same tactics down there. Unless they get a good judge, the search will be suppressed and Sullivan will walk."

"So what kind of plea are you thinking about?"

"I'd offer him eight to ten years but settle for something less."

"You know the public will go nuts," Stone said. "And that girl's family will never let this go. Even worse, we have no idea what happened to her. I mean, she may still be alive somewhere, and we're going to let this guy plead out?"

"We could always take our chances and wait for a ruling. If we lose, we can still bring charges again with new evidence."

"It's a crap shoot either way, but I'd feel better about a plea if we could only locate Jamie Houston."

"I'm in total agreement, Detective. I'll have another conversation with Levy and feel him out. In the meantime, try and dig up some dirt."

"Will do, Counselor."

CHAPTER EIGHTY-SEVEN

Galub and Levy faced off in the conference room at the District Attorney's office in lower Manhattan.

"We need to coordinate the examination by our psychiatrist, Mr. Levy."

"I've got no problem with that, Ms. Galub. I'm confident that your expert will confirm that I have a sound basis for a defense of lack of criminal responsibility by reason of mental disease or defect. In fact, Mr. Sullivan's fragile mental state coupled with the interaction of the pills he's been taking has had serious effects on his mental faculties. If I don't prevail on my suppression motion—and I strongly believe that I will—there is no doubt in my mind that my defense will be successful. You may want to consider saving us all the trouble and just settle for committing him to a psychiatric hospital, where he can be further evaluated. Thereafter, at such time as it is determined that he is no longer of diminished capacity, he can be released."

"Please, Counselor, do you actually think we're going to just let him walk? What you're suggesting is basically a six-month ticket to freedom."

"Ms. Galub, with the evaluation I have from a well-regarded expert in the field, there is little doubt. My client suffered from delusions brought on by the drug he was taking."

"Really, Mr. Levy? Do you actually think I'm going to believe this fiction?"

"This is hardly fiction. I witnessed a very enlightening session my client had with Dr. Sinead O'Reilly, the psychiatrist I retained as my expert. In fact, I recorded it." Levy took a pause and looked away from Galub before he continued. "Procedurally, you know I don't have to provide you with this at such an early stage of the case—but eventually I will be required to—so after due consideration, I have decided to allow you and your psychiatrist to listen to it now. I believe it will help you to understand what we are dealing with—and perhaps convince you that in the interests of justice, this case should be pled out."

"Please, Counselor, spare me the dramatics and give me a hint. Where are you going with all this?"

"Well, Ms. Galub, what would you say if I told you that I believe that Troyer Savage does not exist?"

"I would say that I have no idea what you're talking about."

"As I suspected. You don't even have a clue what is really going on here."

"I don't know what you mean, Mr. Levy. Would you care to explain?"

"Have you ever heard of DID, Ms. Galub?"

"Are you referring to Dissociative Identity Disorder?"

"Yes I am."

Shocked, Galub said, "Where are you going with this, Mr. Levy?"

"The writing is on the wall, Ms. Galub. Listen to the tape and you'll see."

"So you're saying that this recording of yours will substantiate your claim?"

"I believe so," Levy said, handing her the recording. "Just keep an open mind when you play this back."

"I must say, Counselor, you know how to throw a curve."

. . .

Two hours later, Dr. Elliot Gabay joined Galub in the conference room at the office of the New York County District Attorney. "Good afternoon, Dr. Gabay," Galub said, "I just finished listening to a very interesting recording, and I need you to hear this. I know my partner has already briefed you on the case. I just want to make sure that you have also read the file."

"I have, Ms. Galub," Dr. Gabay said, with a slight Middle Eastern accent. "I am completely up to speed and anxiously await the presentation." The crisp pronunciation of his words conflicted with his Mediterranean features and heavily pock-marked skin.

Galub switched on the recording and let it play without interruption.

Thirty minutes later, the recording ended.

Gabay cleared his throat. "Quite intriguing."

"Please elaborate, Doctor. I have my own thoughts, but first, I'd like to hear your analysis."

"Very well. Just understand that without visually seeing this man and speaking with him, I can only offer preliminary observations. There is insufficient information to make a diagnosis."

"Understood," said Galub.

"It seems evident that Mr. Sullivan has suffered a number of traumatic events in his past and that these events occurred during his formative years. I point this out because when an emotional incident takes place at a young age, it has a much more profound effect on the mental development of the subject. Having said that: I also note that this individual was quite easily hypnotized and very responsive to suggestion. When asked to recall bad memories, he immediately focused on particularly horrific events, which indicate that these memories have been hiding close to the surface."

"Are you suggesting that his conscious mind does not recall what happened?" Galub asked.

"Most likely. And taking this further, I would say these memories have been repressed because they are too painful to think about. The mind has defenses just as the rest of the body does. However, in cases like this, the repressed memory still haunts. Sometimes, it may lay dormant for the subject's entire lifetime and never have an impact. Other times, a trigger can set it off, create havoc in the mind, and cause all manner of psychotic behavior."

Galub interjected. "Do you think that the migraine drug has triggered all this?"

"That's a good point, Ms. Galub. The chemical compounds found in those pills can be dangerous. Any of the substances alone, and certainly combined, could cause problems. Despite all the research that has been done on these drugs, we still don't know precisely what harm they can do though. In fact, different subjects have experienced a wide variety of side effects from the same medications."

"More to the point, Doctor," Galub prodded, "is there any evidence that would suggest that such a combination of ingredients could bring about Dissociative Identity Disorder?"

"If you're asking me if I think that this research group may have created a potion in the fashion of Dr. Jekyll and Mr. Hyde,

I would be highly suspect. That is pure fiction. In all my years of practice, I haven't come across such a thing. Truthfully, though, with all the advances in modern drug development, I cannot rule it out. More research is needed, and the fastest way to do this would be to review the files at The Center for Migraine Pain Management. Of course, I must also conduct my own examination of Mr. Sullivan before I draw any conclusions."

"Well, Doctor, examining Sullivan is no problem, but getting access to the files at the Center may be next to impossible. I'm sure they have a battery of attorneys at their disposal, and doctor-patient privilege will pretty much stop us in our tracks. Unless we can find a way to establish probable cause for criminal activity, no judge in this jurisdiction will sign a subpoena giving us access to privileged medical information."

PART THREE

CHAPTER EIGHTY-EIGHT

Some fat-ass guard takes me from my cell and brings me down to an interrogation room, where my lawyer is waiting for me.

"How are you, Tommy?" he asks me, acting like he really gives a shit.

"Fantastic, dude," I answer, all sarcastic. "I mean, how would you feel being locked in a six-by-eight cell with a toilet standing right next to your bed? Yeah, 'bed'—now that's a laugh. The damn mattress has to be over thirty years old. Who knows what kind of bugs are crawling around inside of it? I haven't slept much these last few days. You've got to get me outta here."

"That's what I came to talk to you about, Tommy. I've got a plan, but I need your permission before I take it much further."

He sounds real serious, and he's talking near a whisper, so I've got to hear this. "Go on."

"Okay, Tommy, I'm going to be frank. Some of what I say may offend you, but I want you to know I'm saying this for your own good. Yesterday, when you were under hypnosis, I was observing through the two-way mirror. After your session ended, I met with Dr. O'Reilly, and we talked about it."

"Honestly, I can't remember any of it."

"I know, Tommy; she said you wouldn't. But the fact is a lot came out, and, well, this is difficult for me to say, so I'm just going to say it. It appears that you've suffered quite a few traumatic events while you were growing up, and you've suppressed them. We now suspect that the drug you've been taking has caused these bad memories to resurface. We also believe that in an effort to deal with the pain of these memories, your mind has created an alter ego."

"What the hell does that mean?"

"Well, it's like this, Tommy: I want you consider the possibility that Troyer Savage doesn't actually exist . . ."

I open my mouth like I'm going to say something, but he holds up his hand and looks directly into my eyes.

"Before you interrupt me, Tommy, hear me out. We think the drug is responsible for causing your mind to create Troyer Savage."

"Wait a second. Are you trying to say that Troyer's not real and I just made him up? No fuckin' way, man. The dude is as real as you are. I've seen him with my own eyes. I've talked to him. I've watched him kill a chick. I've hit him, and he's hit me. You can't be serious!"

"Tommy, I know this is hard to digest. Even I'm not fully clear on how this can be, but Dr. O'Reilly is. And she's an expert in the field. The fact is: It's not your fault and we can use it to help your case."

At this point, I'm starting to get pissed-off because Levy's talking wild shit that makes no sense, and I'm starting to think he's the crazy one—or maybe that shrink is. I get up, walk over to the mirror, and stare deep into it. "Is anyone watching us?"

"No, that would be a violation of your rights. We are all alone, I assure you."

"Still, this is totally messed up. You're never going to convince me that Troyer doesn't exist. I don't care what that shrink says!"

"Calm down, Tommy. Don't work yourself up."

"Are you serious? How do I calm down when you're telling me I made up a whole other person? That's impossible. How do you explain all the shit I've seen him do? And what about Aurora? Who kidnapped her, then? She'll tell you it was Troyer. She knows."

"It's like this, Tommy: You switch and become Troyer and do all these things and don't remember. But in some way, your mind sees Troyer doing these things as a separate person—when, in actuality, you're watching yourself do these things as Troyer."

"Get the fuck outta here. There's just no way." I start pacing back and forth and looking at my reflection in the mirror. "I don't even look like the dude." I stick my nose right up against the mirror and just stand there staring cross-eyed at myself looking for Troyer. And you know what? I don't see anything but me. This lawyer is whacked out. I turn around and look right at him. "Sorry, man, but I'm not buying one bit of this."

"I understand this is difficult, Tommy, but whether you believe it or not doesn't matter. You see, I may have enough evidence to convince the prosecutor that this is true. And if I am able to, I can use this to plead you to a much lesser charge, maybe even get you committed to a psychiatric hospital instead of jail."

"What? You want me to go to a loony bin? Who am I supposed to be—Jack Nicholson in *One Flew over the Cuckoo's Nest?*"

"It would be a hospital, Tommy, with much better accommodations than a prison cell . . . and with a good possibility that you could get out in six months or so. I think that the pills have done this to you, so when their effects have completely worn off, the doctors at the hospital will have no choice but to declare you fit for release. You will never see the inside of a prison cell, and you could be free in as little as six months."

"But I'd have to act like I'm crazy?"

"No, just agree to allow me to plead that you are—or were—suffering from a mental disease or defect and therefore not responsible for your actions."

"So do you think that I did all the shit that Troyer did?"

"I'm not saying anything like that, Tommy. I don't know if you did, and apparently you don't, either, and that is exactly what the defense is all about."

"Hey, man, I'm so confused right now. None of this makes any sense. But there's one thing I know, and that is I'm not crazy, and I don't want anyone else thinking I'm crazy— especially Aurora. If she finds out about this shit, she'll take off and I'll never see her again."

"Frankly, Tommy, if you go to trial with all the evidence they have against you and I'm not able to present an insanity defense, you'll never see her again, anyway. And if they connect you to the other crimes at Gilgo Beach, you're facing life in prison. And don't even get me started on the charges in New Jersey. On the other hand, if I can plead this out up here, while they have no real evidence of any connection to the other bodies found at Gilgo Beach, I'll have a lot more leverage in New Jersey. You'll be much better off. Which would you prefer—spending the rest of your life in jail or being diagnosed as temporarily insane because of side effects from an experimental drug?"

"But what about Troyer? He's the one who's responsible. Shouldn't they be looking for him?"

"Tommy, forget about Troyer for the time being and focus on you. If you don't want to believe that Troyer is a figment of your imagination, so be it. But for purposes of this case, just accept the possibility, and let me try and work out a plea. The terms will provide for mandatory incarceration in a psychiatric hospital until they are convinced that you are sane. Once they are convinced, they must release you. That could be in as little as six months."

"It sounds all good, but what if they try to say I really *am* crazy? They could keep me there forever."

"Trust me, Tommy: I believe this is the best thing for you."

CHAPTER EIGHTY-NINE

I'm back in my cell and still thinking about what my lawyer has just told me. At first, I can't even sit down because I'm so wired. I pace back and forth like a madman while I try to sort through all of the shit that's just been fed to me. I keep coming back to the mirror to stare at myself. It's fucked up though, because the damn mirror has this crack right through it, so when I look at myself, my face is all distorted and messed up.

I try to picture me being Troyer or Troyer being me, and I just can't see it. There's no way I could ever do the things they say I've done. And no matter what that Granny Shrink says, I don't believe what they're saying about Troyer and me. From where I'm standing, Troyer is as real a dude as any other dude I've ever met. I mean, I touched him and I talked to him, I even picked up chicks with him. How could he not be real?

I lie down on this poor excuse for a bed and focus on a spiderweb spun out in the corner of the ceiling. There's a spider creeping slowly toward a fly caught in it. I kind of feel just like that fly. I mean, here I am, stuck in some crappy jail cell, waiting to get eaten alive, and there's nothing I can do about it.

The spider finally reaches the fly, and that's about when I fall asleep.

...

I wake up to the sound of the steel bars sliding open. That same fat-ass guard is calling out my name. The first thing I look at is the spiderweb, and you know what? The fly's gone, and so is the spider, but the web is still there waiting for its next victim.

"Let's go, Sullivan," the round mound says. "You've got a visitor."

"A visitor? Who?"

"I got no idea, punk. Some girl with a nose ring."

"Aurora!" I jump up from the bed.

"Whatever. You just better get a move on. We only allow twenty minutes for a visit."

"Sure, sure—I'm good. Let's go."

The guard takes me to this booth where I can only talk to Aurora on a phone, through a glass barrier. She looks so fine but worried as hell. I sit down and pick up the phone.

"Hey, gorgeous—so good to see you," I force a smile.

"Hi, Tommy. How are you?" she looks real concerned.

"I'm okay . . . Sorry I brought you into all of my shit, though."

"That's okay, Tommy. I know you didn't do what they say. I talked to your lawyer yesterday and I told him so."

"Really—what did he say?"

"Not much, Tommy. He asked me some questions about you and Troyer, but he said he couldn't really tell me anything more because of attorney-client privilege."

"I see. Well, it's pretty fucked-up, if you really wanna know."

"Is there anything I can do to help?"

I have to think for a second because if I tell her what they said about me and Troyer being one and the same, she might think I'm nuts and just run for the hills. But she also may be the only one who can honestly tell me that I'm not crazy and that Troyer is a real person. I mean, the dude kidnapped her, so she's got to know for sure.

"Tommy, are you okay? You're scaring me staring off into space like that."

"Oh, uh, sorry. I was just trying to see if there was a way you could help, and I think maybe you can."

"That's good. Tell me what I can do."

"Hey, I want to, but this isn't easy."

"Please. I'm on your side."

"Okay, okay, but you've got to be totally honest with me."

"Of course. Just clue me in."

"All right, it's like this: My lawyer had a shrink evaluate me. And get this, she hypnotized me—I think—because I really don't remember. Anyway, he told me that while I was under hypnosis, I said some things that made them think that Troyer doesn't really exist. They actually think that I'm Troyer."

Aurora's eyeballs practically jump out of her head. "What? That's ridiculous. Where do they come off saying that?"

"I know. I mean, I think its nuts, too, but my lawyer says if he can convince the prosecutor, he may be able to plead temporary insanity. He says that the pills I've been taking are responsible, and that it's not my fault."

"I don't know, Tommy. That's just too crazy. Like, why would you kidnap me and tie me up in some shack? It doesn't make sense."

"That's what I'm saying. But he says it was Troyer that did all that shit—not me."

"But if you're Troyer, it still means that you did it."

"I don't get it either, but what am I supposed to do? He says it's a lawyer tactic and that even if I don't really believe it, it doesn't matter, and that not believing it is just part of the whole defense."

"That's totally bizarre, Tommy."

"So tell me, then, do you think I'm nuts? Do you think I'm Troyer and I did all the shit they're saying?"

"Honestly, Tommy, there's just no way. You could never do what they say you've done. I'm certain of it. During the time I was tied up in the shack with Troyer, I could feel his evil, and you're not capable of that."

"Are you sure? I mean, I was beginning to think that maybe I really am crazy."

"You're not, Tommy. I believe we all have an inner soul that we're born with. We are who we are. People don't change. You are a good guy, with a good heart."

"Wow—I'm so glad you feel that way. But here's the bottom line: Levy says that if I let him say I lost my mind, and that the pills made me create Troyer, he can make a deal where I get sent to some mental hospital for a while instead of jail. Then, when they see I'm not a nut job, they have to let me go. He thinks that if the effects of the pills haven't worn off already, they should soon enough, and I'll go back to normal. Then they'll have to release me. He says that could be in, like, six months. Otherwise, if I take my chances at trial and lose, I'll spend the rest of my life in jail."

"So what's the problem, then?" Aurora gives me a look like if I don't take the deal I really must be nuts.

"I don't want anyone thinking I'm crazy. That's what."

"Tommy, it's the lesser of two evils. Let your lawyer work the system. You can't take a chance with a trial. Make a deal, and I promise I'll wait for you."

"Would you, really?"

"Absolutely. I believe in fate, and there's no doubt in my mind that you walked into my shop that day for a reason."

Right then, the guard comes over and taps her on the shoulder. "Time's up, miss."

CHAPTER NINETY

As I walk back to my cell, it hits me out of nowhere. My legs become rubber and I miss a step. The guard grabs me by the elbow. "Cut it out, Sullivan." He pulls me up and starts to drag me.

"Hold on a second. I'm dizzy. Something's happening to me. I can't see straight."

"Quit screwing around, wise guy."

"I'm not. This is real. I can tell that a massive headache is coming on. You've got to get me my medicine."

"Go fuck yourself, kid." he says with a laugh as he pushes me into the cell like I'm some sort of criminal.

It doesn't take long—maybe ten minutes after he shuts me in—when the pain comes on full-force and I feel like my head's being squeezed in a vise. I lie down and cover my face with the pillow trying to block out the light. I can't stop the noise, though, and every little sound is like an explosion inside my brain. I roll off the bed, drop to my knees, and puke. For the first time, I'm not going to complain about the toilet being right next to the bed. I hurl my insides out, sweating and choking until finally this young guard comes up to the bars.

"You feeling okay, buddy?" he asks me.

I turn around. "Do I look like I'm okay, dude?" Slime drips from my chin.

"You want me to get you a doctor?"

I figure if I say no, he'll just leave me here, but if I say yes, maybe he'll take me to a hospital like they do on *CSI* and I can get some meds and a normal bed. "Actually, my head's gonna explode any second. I feel like I'm dying." I cough extra-hard and make this disgusting choke/hack/vomit sound that even scares the piss out of me.

This guy has to be new at the job and real green because he actually looks worried. "Hold on, buddy," he says. "I'll get some help." Then he rushes off.

Two minutes later, a couple of guys in white outfits come by with a stretcher. They open my cell and spread me out on the floor. Of course, I play it up much worse than I really am, hoping they'll take me out of here for a while. And guess what? They do. Five minutes later, I'm in this ambulance handcuffed and strapped to a stretcher. They put a mask over my nose and mouth and stick a needle in my arm. Then they pull out the needle and connect me to a plastic tube attached to a bag of liquid hanging from a clip above my head. I start to feel all light-headed and shit and . . .

. . .

I wake up on a soft, clean bed handcuffed to a metal rail. I'm in the hospital and I'm all alone in the room. There's a thin plastic tube hooked into my arm, attached to the usual bag of shit, feeding some kind of medicine into me. I feel a lot better.

I look around, locate the TV remote, and click it on. I run the channels until, lo and behold, I find a *CSI* show. I stop and watch for a minute or so before I realize it's a repeat. But you know what? I really don't care. I settle in and relax for the first time in a while. Yeah, I'm styling now.

A couple hours later, my lawyer shows up with Aurora tagging along. She rushes over to my side and reaches for my hand.

"How are you, Tommy?" she asks, all red-eyed and frowning.

"I'm okay, gorgeous. Don't worry. This place is much better than a jail cell."

Levy is standing at the foot of the bed, and he gets right down to business. "Do you remember what happened, Tommy?" he asks, staring at me like my answer will solve world hunger or something.

"Yeah, I remember. I finished talking to Aurora, and they took me back to my cell. All of a sudden, I started feeling sick. So I asked the guard for some pills. He blew me off and threw me into the cell. My head pounded so bad, I threw up and started choking. Some other guard came by, and they took me away in an ambulance."

"Do you remember anything else, Tommy? Because based upon the time frame, about three hours went by from the time Aurora left you and when the guard found you heaving by the toilet. He also says that he passed by your cell a few times and you were sleeping in bed and talking to yourself. From what you're saying, all this happened right after Aurora left you early this afternoon."

"I don't know. The way I remember it, I started feeling sick right after we finished talking, and I was only in my cell for, like, ten or fifteen minutes before I threw up in the toilet." I look over at Aurora, and we lock eyes.

"Are you sure, Tommy?" she asks me.

"Definitely." I say to both of them, as a chill comes over me. I pull the covers up under my chin and start to wonder. "Is it possible that I blacked out? I mean, I haven't had any of those pills in days."

Levy walks around to the other side of my bed. "It sounds like you had another episode, Tommy. The report I looked at clearly shows a time lapse of at least three hours."

"Well, that's messed-up because only a few minutes went by. Are you sure the cops aren't trying to screw with me?"

"I don't think so, Tommy. They would have nothing to gain. In fact, it only helps to make our case."

Aurora squeezes my hand tight, and I squeeze back. "Oh, yeah, so what was I saying, then?"

"The report says it was gibberish. The guard couldn't make out anything intelligible."

"Whatever. So what if I fell asleep and don't remember? Big deal. The question is, what do we do from here?"

"That's up to you, Tommy," Levy says, looking at Aurora. "I need your permission to proceed along the lines you and I discussed earlier. And you need to make that decision fast, before the judge rules on my motion. You see, if he rules against us and allows the evidence in, we won't stand a chance at trial and the DA won't be willing to make a deal anymore. We will have lost our leverage. Our only hope is to try and plead out now, while the prosecutor is still fearful that the judge may grant my motion. Understand that while I made some good arguments, the videotape of your confession is quite damaging, and the judge may very well allow it into evidence. If he does, a jury will convict you."

I turn back to Aurora. "You still think I should do this?"

She nods and squeezes my hand again.

I look back at Levy. "Okay, do your thing."

CHAPTER NINETY-ONE

The next morning, Levy headed over to Center Street and caught up with D.A. Galub in the main rotunda on the first floor of the New York County Supreme Court building.

Galub caught his eye as he approached, and she stuck her palm out, signaling him to keep his distance while she finished up a conversation with another lawyer. Levy scanned the area, found an empty bench nearby, and sat down.

The hustle and bustle of the courthouse amazed Levy, who was much more accustomed to the small, laid-back Supreme Court in Sullivan County. He marveled at the line of regular people waiting to pass through the metal detectors. It reminded him of airport security. All in all, it did not intimidate him, and once again, he looked forward to the opportunity to appear before the court in such a grand and storied building.

Galub finished her discussion and sat down beside Levy. "Well, Counselor, this is quite unexpected."

"Frankly, Ms. Galub, I didn't plan to be here, either, but perhaps you haven't heard."

"Heard what?"

"Yesterday afternoon, my client was rushed to the hospital after suffering an episode in his jail cell."

Galub was genuinely surprised. "I'm sorry, Counselor. I had no idea. How is he?"

"He's fine for the time being, but it seems he had another blackout and cannot account for over three hours of time. In any event, that's only a part of the reason why I came here to see you. I also wanted to follow up on our conversation from the other day and get your take on the recording. I assume you've had enough time to review it with your expert and come to a conclusion."

"Actually, Counselor, after discussing the case with our psychiatrist, as well as with my boss, we have decided that we cannot make a decision on a plea until after our psychiatrist has had his own session with Mr. Sullivan. Dr. Gabay was planning on meeting with him this afternoon. Is he well enough to be evaluated at the hospital?"

"Yes, I believe so. It is imperative that we resolve this case and get my client the help he needs at a psychiatric hospital."

"Still pushing for that, Counselor?" Galub asked, condescendingly.

"It's the right thing to do, and you know it. You heard the recording. What do you think?"

"What I think, Mr. Levy, is that your client is a sick individual. Sure, he may have suffered some trauma in his life— we all have—but that's no excuse for what he's done. As I said before, he needs to come clean about the whereabouts of Jamie Houston, and open up about his involvement in the other bodies found at Gilgo Beach."

"Come on. You know he has no idea about any of this. I'm sure your expert explained DID to you. The two personalities are separate and distinct. In fact, they are, for all intents and purposes, two independent people. The experimental drug he's been taking has done quite a number on him. And if it comes out on the record that Detective Stone intentionally and reck-lessly administered an overdose, not only will it further under-mine an already weak case, but it will put her in very hot water. I am in the process of preparing a motion to obtain the vide-otape of the entire time my client was held in that interrogation room. And if there are any gaps . . ."

"You are free to make all the motions you want. I'm not convinced that Sullivan and Savage are one and the same. It's too Hollywood for me. All I can say is I will leave open room for the possibility, pending an examination by my expert. Until then, I won't even consider a plea."

"Fair enough, Ms. Galub. My client will be made available this afternoon."

CHAPTER NINETY-TWO

I'm kind of liking it at this hospital, I must say. The bed's real comfortable, and the TV works great. They come and feed me three times a day, and there's no one around to bug me. All I've got to do is keep acting like I'm sick and I can probably milk this for a few more days.

I just finish watching another episode of *CSI: Miami* when I look out the glass door and see my lawyer talking it up with the DA and some foreign-looking dude with really bad skin. I'll bet he had the worst case of zits as a kid and probably spent a couple hours a day squeezing in front of a mirror.

My lawyer walks in alone. "How are you feeling, Tommy?"

"I could be better, especially if I was sitting on a beach in the Caribbean drinking a Corona."

"Well, at least you still have your sense of humor," he says, smiling. Then he leans in and gets real serious. "Listen, this is of vital importance. The gentleman outside is a psychiatrist who works for the District Attorney's office. He has come here this afternoon to meet with you and evaluate you to determine your state of mind. His report will be the deciding factor as to whether the DA will consider the plea. Cooperate and just be yourself. He will be interviewing you alone; neither I nor the DA will be watching, or listening. You will be completely on your own."

"Am I supposed to act crazy or something?"

"Tommy, I am not allowed to tell you what to say or how to act. It is all in your hands. All I can say is be honest. Just remember, he is not allowed to ask you any questions about the crimes you are charged with and you are not to discuss anything about any of that. He can only ask you about you." He waves at them, and Crater Face comes in by himself.

"Tommy, this is Dr. Gabay. He is going to talk with you for a while. I'll be back later."

Levy walks out and leaves me alone with this guy. I have to say, I'm not feeling real comfortable around him. His face totally creeps me out.

"Good afternoon, Thomas. As your lawyer told you, my name is Dr. Gabay. I am a psychiatrist, and I work for the District Attorney's office. How are you feeling today?"

"Actually, Doc, I feel pretty lousy. I've been throwing up since yesterday, my head feels like it's been stepped on, and I'm handcuffed to a hospital bed. Not to mention I've been in a jail cell for the last bunch of days, everyone thinks I'm nuts, and I may spend the rest of my life in prison for shit I didn't do."

"Yes, well, that is quite a lot for any one person to handle. I sympathize with what you are going through. You see, I have counseled quite a few individuals who have found themselves overwhelmed by circumstances, so I know how difficult it can be."

"You're not shitting, Doc. So what do you want from me?"

"Okay, Thomas, I'm very curious about the study you became involved in. Can you tell me how all that came about?"

"Sure, that's easy. It's like this: I've been getting these nasty headaches ever since I was a kid. Anyway, one day, I hear this commercial on the radio where they're looking for people who suffer from bad headaches. The radio said I could get paid for being a part of some study, so I took down the number and called. I went there a couple a times for interviews, and they eventually signed me up. Do you know they're actually paying me a thousand bucks a month to take these pills? And all I've got to do is answer some questions, fill out some forms, and let them examine me. The best part of it is that the pills really work. My headaches go away every time, and I've been feeling great. The thing is, though, that when I started, two pills were enough, but after a month or so, I had to take more to stop the pain. It's all good, though. I just doubled the dosage, and now my headaches disappear within an hour every time."

"That's great, Thomas, but did you ever tell the doctors at the study that you were taking double the dosage?"

"Nah, you kidding? If I did, they'd probably drop me from the program—and there goes the dough . . . and the medicine."

"I see. Well, didn't you worry that maybe taking more pills could hurt you?"

"Like I said, Doc, they took away my headaches. They weren't hurting me. They were helping me."

"Yes, but I understand that you began experiencing black-outs and that you started losing track of time."

"Uh, yeah . . . sort of, but really, all that was happening was that I'd fall asleep and wake up a few hours later and not remember what happened. So, big deal if the pills put me to sleep. They sell sleeping pills at the drugstore every day."

"Yes, they do. So let's change the subject. What can you tell me about Troyer Savage?"

As soon as Crater Face mentions that name, I go nuts. "Troyer's the biggest dick I ever met! I don't want to talk about him."

"I'm sorry, Thomas. I didn't realize you had such strong feelings about him. What did he do to make you feel this way?"

I'm boiling now. "Like I said, I don't want to talk about that guy. He's the reason I'm in this shit in the first place."

"Take it easy, Thomas. I didn't mean to alarm you. But please understand that we have to talk about Troyer, precisely because of his involvement in your problems."

"Look, Doc, that guy is nothing but bad news. He's a fuckin' nightmare that follows me around and pops up outta nowhere just to screw with me."

"When did you meet him?"

"I dunno—a couple of months ago."

"Before or after you joined the study?"

I close my eyes for a second because I have to think about it. Then it hits me. "You know what, Doc? It was definitely after. I remember because I went to the Pain Center in Brooklyn to get my first refill. When I came out of the clinic, I felt a headache coming on, so I swallowed a few pills and stopped off for a brew. That's when I met him for the first time."

"Okay, tell me about it."

"Well, actually, it was real intense, and he probably saved my life. I made the mistake of trying to strike up a conversation with some girl at this bar. Her boyfriend got all pissed off, grabbed me by the neck, and told me to fuck off. I wasn't paying attention as he and his buddy followed me when I left the place. They cornered me, pulled me into an alley, and started beating the crap outta me. Then Troyer shows up from nowhere, unleashes this amazing MMA shit, and levels both guys like he's Jean-Claude Van Damme or something. He practically kills one of the guys. But in the heat of the moment, I guess he did what was necessary. Anyway, he was so smooth and cool, I knew right then that I wanted to get to know him."

"I see," Doc Pock says, sitting up in his chair like someone has just stuck a stick up his ass. "How often did you see him after that?"

"Hey, look. Let's get real, here. I know what's going on. Everyone thinks that Troyer's not real and that I'm just making him up. My lawyer and that other shrink say the pills from the study have fried my brain. Isn't that what you want to know, too?"

"In fact it is, Thomas. That, as well as a few other things. So tell me, then: Do you believe Troyer is a real person?"

I stop and think for a second. "That's a trick question, Doc, because if I say he's real, while everyone else says he's not, then I have to be crazy. And if I say he's just someone my brain made up, then I'm also crazy. See? I lose either way."

"Well, Thomas, we never like to use the word 'crazy,' but I understand your dilemma. Still, I want to know what you truly believe. It will help me with my diagnosis. So rather than giving me an answer based upon your fear of what I might think, just answer from your heart."

I reach for the cup of water and take a sip, like I'm thinking this through, but I already know what I have to say. "Actually, Doc, I'm not sure anymore. Until my lawyer told me what came out while I was hypnotized, Troyer was as real to me as you are. Now, after thinking about everything that's happened these past few weeks, maybe he's not so real, after all. I mean, the dude always seems to show up outta nowhere, and he seems to know what I'm thinking before I do. I just don't understand how he could be inside my head without me knowing about it. And if he is there, why hasn't he come out since I've been in jail? And how do you explain the MMA shit he can do? I don't have those skills."

"All good points, Thomas. This type of disorder is very mysterious, and we still don't have all the answers. Which leads me to my next question. Looking back, did Troyer usually appear soon after you took your pills?

"Geez, I never really thought about it. The truth is, though, in the past couple of weeks, I've been taking my pills almost every day. That's because my headaches are coming on more frequently."

"Well, then, have you been seeing a lot more of Troyer recently?"

"I suppose so, except since I've been in jail."

"Okay, I'd like to go in a different direction for a moment. Let me ask you this: When you picture Troyer in your mind, compared to the way you see yourself in the mirror, do you see a similarity in features?"

"No way. I mean, I hate to admit it, but he's a much better-looking guy than me. He's got perfect teeth and a perfect smile. Here, check this out." I flash a goofy smile at him. "My teeth are crooked, and I can't smile like Troyer does. That's his trademark."

"Interesting," he says, as he pulls out his pen and starts writing a whole bunch of shit in his pad. "Please give me a minute."

"Sure thing, Doc. I've got all day."

A few minutes later, he gets up and starts pacing at the foot of my bed. "Thomas, can you tell me about some of your fondest childhood memories?"

"I'm not sure what you mean. Like, what am I supposed to remember?"

"Oh, I don't really know for sure, I'm just curious if you can recall things from when you were a young boy."

"Well, to tell you the truth, I always had a hard time with that kind of stuff. It's weird because I remember that my folks took me to the Cape when I was a kid, but I can't remember details—even though I went down there for years. I know I made friends there, too, but I can't picture what they look like or even remember their names. Although I have to say that walking around Lakewood and Seneca brought back memories I didn't even know I had. It's messed up because even though I started remembering bits and pieces of my life back then, they still don't feel like they happened to me. It's almost like I'm watching a movie of someone else. It just doesn't seem real."

"I'm sure that must be very frustrating, Thomas. But I've heard enough for now, and you must be growing tired of all this anyway, so why don't you get some rest? Perhaps we'll have a chance to chat at a later date."

"Okay by me, Doc." I say, as he turns and walks out the door like he just won a Nobel Prize.

Crater Face may be smart, but so am I. I think I fooled him real good.

CHAPTER NINETY-THREE

Dr. Gabay had followed through on his promise to meet with D.A. Galub immediately after the session to discuss the Sullivan case, so when he appeared outside her office, she quickly hung up the phone and ushered him in.

"Thank you for coming right over, Doctor. I'm anxious to hear what you have to say."

"I figured you would be, so I won't waste any time. Just understand: I am basing my analysis on the reports your office has given me, the recording we listened to the other day, and finally my interview today. Stated plainly, I believe Thomas Sullivan shows many of the classic signs of Dissociative Identity Disorder. Of course, I can't say this to a certainty unless he was to switch identities in my presence. However, the symptoms he does display are telling. He suffered major trauma as a boy, having to deal with a dysfunctional family, an abusive father, and a mother who abandoned him. He witnessed a murder and the death of a friend. He experiences severe headaches, has blackouts, and can't account for significant periods of time in his life. His memory of important past events are foggy to nonexistent. Under hypnosis, he referred to Troyer as someone to be emulated. He lapsed into an accent, which we suspect is Troyer. And last, while he cannot summon up or fully understand how

Troyer can exist inside his head, he appears to have come around to believe that Troyer is a figment of his imagination." Gabay stopped and took a breath, waiting for a rebuttal.

"Can you bring this home for me so I can use this in court, Doctor?"

"I can, but you may not like what I have to say."

"Just tell it to me straight."

"Very well. Sullivan, as he appears now, is hardly a killer. Rather, he presents as a confused and frightened individual who has no idea how, or why, this is all happening to him. I suspect it is no coincidence that Troyer appeared in Sullivan's life sometime after he began taking excessive amounts of the experimental drug.

"Well, Doctor, that doesn't bode well for my case. It sounds to me like you believe he is suffering from a mental defect or disorder."

"Is—or was."

"I think I know where you're going with this, and I'm not happy about it. So let me ask you this, then. Is he sane now and able to assist in his own defense? If not, we can't bring him to trial, even if we want to. Alternatively, if he is currently fit for trial, was he competent at the time he committed the offenses he's been charged with?"

"The fact is, Ms. Galub, Sullivan appears competent now, but with respect to the crimes, he believes he did not commit them. He is convinced they were committed by Troyer Savage, and he is still trying to digest the possibility that he is Troyer Savage. I suspect that if you subjected him to a lie detector test, he would pass."

"So what are my chances at trial?"

"If I had to testify—and I don't believe you would want me to—I would have to say that if Thomas Sullivan committed these crimes, he did so while suffering from a mental defect or disorder."

"So what is your recommendation?"

"In my opinion, the man should not be let out on the street at this time. We just don't know the extent of his psychosis. He may seem competent now, but we cannot predict what may happen in a few days or weeks. It is quite possible that he may relapse and switch to Troyer Savage again and kill someone."

"That worries me, as well."

"I think he should be placed in a psychiatric hospital for an extended period where he can be monitored and evaluated."

"How long a time would you suggest, Doctor?"

"I think he should be evaluated for a mandatory minimum of six months. Thereafter, it should be left up to the doctors to determine if he is fit to be released. I know of a place where one of the doctors utilizes a novel type of hypnotherapy, during which he administers a mixture of sodium pentothal and some other wonder drug as part of the hypnotic process. He has been able to achieve remarkable results quickly by delving deep into a patient's mind. We can give him our entire file for review, recording and all. He'll know exactly what to do."

"Sounds very intriguing," Galub said. "Do you think he could help to bring Troyer out and maybe learn where Jamie Houston is?"

"A distinct possibility. His success rate has been nothing short of astonishing. I have to advise you, though, he is quite a character and very unorthodox. And his methodology is reminiscent of the bygone era of the early sixties where experimental therapies ran largely uncontrolled and flew under the radar of Constitutional protections."

"Actually, Doctor, I'm only interested in results, and if we have to plead this one out and get Sullivan to this doctor in order to locate Jamie Houston, I don't care if the doctor worked at a Nazi concentration camp and his last name is Mengele."

CHAPTER NINETY-FOUR

Later that evening, DA Galub sat at the bar at Chauncey's Pub in downtown Manhattan waiting for Harold Levy. She'd already downed two Grey Goose martinis in an effort to dull the pain of her impending surrender. It wasn't like her to cave so quickly, but her caseload was taxing, and her boss had given her the okay. There was no sense taking this case to trial and spending a million dollars when a successful outcome was highly doubtful.

Levy slithered in, his rumpled suit sliding off his stooped shoulders. "Good evening, Ms. Galub. I take it your psychiatrist has issued his report."

"He has, Counselor."

"Well, would you care to enlighten me with his conclusions?" Levy was boldly pompous.

"Look, *Harold*, his findings are privileged attorney work product, and for the time being, they will remain as such."

"You do know, *Joyce*, that if it comes down to trial, his entire report is discoverable and you must provide it to me."

"I am aware of the law," Galub said, slurring her speech as the martinis kicked in. "But that is unimportant right now. Let me cut to the chase."

"Please . . ."

"I'm prepared to offer a plea . . . with certain conditions and exceptions."

"Go on."

"If we allow your client to plead out due to a mental defect or disorder, he must agree to be remanded to a psychiatric hospital for a minimum period of one year where he will be treated and evaluated. After that time, it will be entirely up to the hospital board to determine if, or when, he is fit to be released. Further, while under their care and treatment, he must cooperate, he must agree to be hypnotized, and he must agree to be medicated if it is determined medically necessary. Additionally, he must do everything in his power to assist in locating the whereabouts of Jamie Houston. He must also agree to never take another one of those experimental pills again. As to the exceptions, we are not in a position to include a disposition of any potential charges in connection with the other bodies found at Gilgo Beach. Investigation of those charges by the local police will continue."

"You've put quite a few conditions on a plea that ordinarily would simply require an evaluation of his present mental state. You know that if a current evaluation of my client determines that he is sane, he could walk out of the courthouse a free man tomorrow."

"Perhaps, Counselor," Galub said, summoning all her remaining bravado, "but those are my terms. My expert is more than ready to testify that we cannot be sure of Mr. Sullivan's present mental state. It is entirely possible that he could lapse into Troyer Savage at any time and go on a killing spree. So it's either mandatory admission to a psychiatric hospital or no deal."

"Okay, if you bring it down to a six-month minimum, rather than one year, I will sell it to my client."

"Fair enough, Mr. Levy—provided all my other terms are agreeable."

CHAPTER NINETY-FIVE

The court thing goes by real quick, and before I know it, I'm in some van being carted away to the loony bin. My lawyer says I'm going to be stuck there for at least six months while I prove that I'm not crazy. He also says I've got to cooperate and help find out what happened to the bartender. The fact is, I have no clue.

Anyway, I've got these handcuffs on, and I'm strapped into the seat in back, but I can still see out the window. Looks like they're taking me upstate somewhere because I'm crossing the Hudson River and going over the Tappan Zee Bridge. At least I'm out of the city.

About a half hour later, we pull in some place, and they back the van into a garage. These two muscle-bound goons unload me, each one takes an arm, and they lead me down a hall.

"I guess they've got a gym here—huh, boys?" I say, because neither of them says a word, and I can't stand the silence.

"Close your mouth, wise-ass," the dude on my left says as he vise-grips my bicep.

"Hey, man, that hurts. Go easy on me. I'm just trying to be friendly."

They bring me to a door, where some guard is watching from a booth. He pushes a button, and the door swings open.

"Sophisticated security you got going on here," I shouldn't have said, because now the goon on my right punches me in the gut, and I lose my wind. They drag me, wheezing and choking, finally take off my cuffs, and toss me into a room. The door slams, and I hear a bolt click. I guess I'm locked in.

Welcome to my nightmare.

After I catch my breath, I look around. Good—no toilet. Better, I've got a window. So what if it's got bars on it?

There's another bed in here, which means I've probably got me a roomie. I hope he's not too crazy. I mean, if the dude is balls-off-the-wall whacked-out, I may not make it the full six months.

I lie down on the bed and try to relax. I feel a headache coming on. I hope getting meds around here won't be as hard as it was back in that jail cell.

Anyway, I must have dozed off because the next thing I know, some sloppy-ass punk with a beard is pulling at my arm.

"That's my bed, cocksucker," he says, trying to sound tough. "If you don't move, I *may* have to snap your neck."

I look at the dude. He can't be serious. I mean, the guy's trying to hide his bald head with a comb over. He's about five-feet-two and all roly-poly. I could totally stomp him.

"You kidding me, psycho?" I say, like I'm Rambo or some-body. "If you don't back off, I'll snap *your* neck. You're fuckin' with the wrong guy." I stand up and eyeball the shrimp, but before I can move, he unloads and pops me right in the gut. Surprise—I lose my wind again. Twice in one day just isn't good. I drop to my knees coughing, and the munchkin breaks out in this high-pitched laugh. Then he starts dancing around the room with his hands in the air like he's Floyd Mayweather and just scored a knockout. It takes me a few seconds before I can breathe again, but as soon as I do, I get up, fly right over to Junior, and clock him on the side of the head. He goes down like a sack of potatoes. For a second, I think he's actually dead. Then he slowly starts rolling around and tries to get up, but he wobbles and falls down again. Man, that's some funny shit. I've seen that happen to boxers before, after they been knocked out and they try to stand up, but they can't. Totally embarrassing. I actually feel bad for the squirt, but you know what? He hit me first. Anyway, after a minute or so, I help him onto the bed. He sits down, stroking his jaw.

"You okay, man?" I ask him. "I didn't mean to hit you so hard. It's just you hit me first, and that pissed me off. I don't take that shit from no one."

"I'll be okay. It was probably my fault, anyway. That's one of my problems. I'm a hothead, and I don't think before I do things. Let's call it even and start over."

"Fine by me, dude. And you can have your bed. I couldn't care less where I sleep."

Tiny looks at me sideways, still rubbing his jaw. "So what are you in for?"

"Long story—not really something I'm in the mood to talk about."

"Okay, maybe some other time. For now, though, you're going to need to learn a few things if you want to survive around here."

CHAPTER NINETY-SIX

It's only been two days since my lawyer got me out of this mess . . . sort of. I mean, being locked in a nuthouse with a bunch of psychos and lunatics is no picnic. Out of the frying pan and into the fire, they say. Not only that, but they still suspect I had something to do with all the shit that went down at Gilgo Beach—which is ridiculous. And the charges are still pending against me in New Jersey. Supposedly, Levy's going to file some legal shit that should get the case down there dismissed, though. Apparently, the cops in Jersey fucked up and violated my rights, so whatever evidence they found can't be used against me. Isn't it great how the law doesn't give a crap whether someone did or didn't do something? They're more concerned about how you found out about it.

Anyway, it's been kind of interesting here. Aside from my roomie, Curtis, who's as wormy as they come, they've got this one real skinny dude with long, greasy hair. He walks around talking to himself and swatting imaginary flies that seem to be hovering around him all the time. He keeps saying that God is angry because we've forsaken him and that we should be prepared for Armageddon— whatever the hell that is. The dude thinks that any day now a giant asteroid is going to crash down and destroy the world. He's trying to get all the whackos here to pray, but no one pays attention.

Then there's this spaced-out girl who doesn't talk at all. She can't be more than twenty-one. She probably could be hot if she just took a shower, washed her hair, and maybe put on a tight pair of jeans. She just sits by the window and draws pictures of scenery—but not scenery like you would think. I mean, yesterday, she drew this tree with a trunk that looked like bones and branches that looked like fingers. Not only that, but the leaves looked like eyeballs, ears, and noses. She drew a pair of lips in the sky, which I figure was the sun. Weird shit, man. And when I went over to look at what she was doing, she got up and ran away. The chick just left me there staring at the picture. I will say this, though, as fucked-up as it was, I couldn't stop looking at it. Everything in the picture looked real. The details were dead-on. The noses looked perfect, and the ears did, too. This chick sure can draw. Problem is, she draws some psycho shit. I guess that's why she's here.

I'm minding my own business when two orderlies come over to me.

"Time for you to meet Dr. Freud. Please follow us," the taller one says.

Freud? They've got to be kidding me.

They bring me into this room, put me in a chair, and wrap leather straps around my wrists. I can't move, so I sit there waiting for a few minutes. Then some freaky-looking old guy in a wheelchair rolls in. This dude has to be at least a hundred years old. What's left of his hair is sticking out so far sideways, I'll bet he hasn't brushed it in a month. He looks at me with one eyeball while the other eyeball is staring at the wall to my left.

"Mr. Sullivan, I presume," croaks outta this guy like a fart from a frog.

This dude is so scary-looking I'm afraid to answer, so I just look away.

"Something wrong, Mr. Sullivan?" he croaks again.

"Uh . . . I'm just not feeling too good right now."

"That will change shortly," he says, as he rolls up next to me and pulls a needle from a pouch in his lap. Then he grabs my forearm, wipes it with an alcohol pad, and sticks me.

"A little stab will do ya," I say, channeling Nicholson's Randall Patrick McMurphy.

"Truth serum" is the last words he says.

. . .

"How are you feeling now, Tommy?" Dr. Freud asked, the frog in his voice now a soft whisper.

"Never better, man," Tommy answered as if in a dream.

"Then it's time to begin. And I promise if you help me understand a few things, you'll feel even better."

Tommy smiled. "Whatever you say."

"I want you to go back to when you were a little boy and tell me the first thing that comes to mind."

Tommy took a deep breath. "The beach—we always go to the beach."

"Are you at the beach now, Tommy?" asked Freud.

"Yeah, I'm walking in the sand with Mom and Dad. We're at the Cape for the very first time."

"Wonderful, Tommy. How old are you?"

"I'm gonna be five years old this week," Tommy answered, with the energy of a young boy. "And this trip is my birthday present."

"What a nice gift. Please take me to your favorite part of the trip."

Tommy began to giggle. "Throw me as high as you can, Daddy."

"You're doing great, Tommy. Tell me more."

"We're in the ocean, and Dad's tossing me up over the waves as they come in. Mom is standing just outta the water hollering—'Be careful, Joe! He's too young for that.' Dad yells back, 'Relax, honey. He can handle it. My son ain't no wimp.' I'm bouncing with the waves, and Dad grabs me with one hand and rolls me onto his shoulders. I climb up with one foot on each side of his head while he holds my hands. Then I stand straight up and dive into the water again. I'm having a super time."

"I'm happy to hear that, Tommy. Is anyone else with you?"

"No, just Mom and Dad."

"You don't have any brothers or sisters?"

Tommy frowned. "No, just me. I wish I did, though. I mean, I always wanted a brother, but Mom and Dad did a bad thing."

"What do you mean, Tommy?"

"They shouldn'ta done it. It was a mistake."

"What was a mistake, Tommy?"

"I hear them talking downstairs. I'm at the top of the steps, I can't sleep. Mom's crying and saying to Dad that it was wrong and she wants him back."

"Wants who back, Tommy?"

"I don't know his name. Mom says she wants Dad to talk to the doctor who arranged it and to get him back. Dad says it's impossible; five years is too much time. She says she doesn't care. She wants him back."

"Wants who back, Tommy?" Freud insisted. "Please tell me."

"My twin brother. They gave him away when we were born. I heard them talking about it the night we got back from my birthday at the Cape."

"Did you tell them you overheard their conversation?"

"No, not ever—even after Dad lied to me when I got older and told me that my brother died when I was born."

"Why didn't you tell him, then?"

"I don't know. I think maybe I didn't remember it or something, but now I do."

"Yes. You do, Tommy, and together we're going to try and remember a lot of things from your past."

"Like what?" Tommy asked, his eyes still closed.

"Like your friend Troyer, for instance. I know you don't like to talk about him, but I'm very curious. Do you think I could meet him?"

"Well, I don't know about that."

"Why is that, Tommy? It should be very easy for you to introduce us."

"I would if I could, but I don't know where he is. He took off when we were back at Camp Lakewood, and I haven't seen him since."

"Really, Tommy? I thought he was always with you."

"No, I don't think so, and I would know."

"You know you can't lie to me, Tommy," Freud says, in a soft yet stern voice. "It's not possible."

Tommy shook his head. "I'm not lying. I really don't know where he is. I'd tell you if I did."

"Come now, Tommy. We both know he's right there inside of you. Just call to him and he'll come out."

"That's craaazy, man," Tommy slurred. "He can't hear me. I'm sure he's long-gone and probably out of the country by now."

"Very well, Tommy. We'll come back to Troyer a bit later. Perhaps while we wait for him, you can tell me what happened to the bartender, Jamie Houston."

Tommy's face turned red, and he began to cry. "I wish I knew, really." He began to quiver. "I left her in the tall weed grass by Gilgo Beach."

"Well, maybe Troyer knows. Perhaps you could ask him for me."

"Like I said before, I don't know where he is, so how can I ask him?" Tommy was inconsolable and whimpering like a baby.

"Now, now, Tommy—crying isn't going to help. You need to relax and calm down." Freud paused and looked up at the camera lens that was filming them. "In fact, maybe we'll take a short break." He spun around in his wheelchair. "I'll be back in a few minutes, and when I return, I expect you to be dry-eyed and ready to talk with me again."

Freud left the room and met up with Detectives Stone and Watts, who were watching the session from another room.

"Is something wrong, Doctor?" Stone asked. "I'm confused. You told us that this wonder drug of yours would enable you to dig deep inside his mind and that he wouldn't be able to lie to you."

"Yes, Detective, that is what the drug is supposed to do. Quite honestly, I'm not really sure why Mr. Sullivan is reacting this way. Perhaps Troyer is so deep down inside of him he really doesn't believe he is real. I need to go deeper to access him."

"Well, then, why did you stop?" Watts asked.

"It's his first session, and I didn't give him a very strong dose of my serum. I could give him another dose by injection, but I think I'd rather end this session early as a precautionary measure. Next time, I'll hook him up to an IV drip, where I can control the dosage during administration. That will help me to dig deeper inside his mind."

"When do you think you can do that, Doctor?" Stone asked. "We're still hoping that he has some information about the girl that may help us to locate her."

"I understand, but I have to be careful. Too much of this drug all at once may be very harmful to Mr. Sullivan. Especially given his history with the experimental drug he's been taking. I'm sure it is still in his system, and I don't know what type of reaction to expect. We could be playing with fire here, and if we push too hard and he switches to Troyer, anything could happen, including the possibility that we could lose Tommy altogether."

"So how long, then?" asked Stone.

"Give me a day or so to get back to you. Right now, I think it's best to return him to his room and let him rest. He'll come out of it in less than an hour. Later on, I'll see how he's feeling and let you know when I think it is safe to try again."

CHAPTER NINETY-SEVEN

I wake up with a massive headache but not like my usual ones. This one is all the way behind my head, and it runs down my neck and into my back. I look over at the other bed, and Curtis isn't there. The last thing I remember is being strapped to a chair, and some strange-looking doctor, in a wheelchair, is sticking me with a needle. I get up, walk over to the door, and try the knob. It's open, so I push through and head down the hall to the lounge. I'm betting Curtis must still be in the lounge with all the other fruitcakes.

I walk into the lounge, and there they are: all the whackos just sitting around doing all their nut job shit. They couldn't care less that I just came through the door . . . except for Curtis, who runs up to me and almost knocks me over.

"Where you been, Tommy?" he asks me, trying to hug me like we've been best friends since the war. "I was worried about you."

"Hey, back off Curtis," I say, pushing him off. "They had me in with some Loony Tunes doctor who looks like that dude from the Science Channel."

"That would be Dr. Freud. Everyone says he looks like Stephen Hawking. He's the head doctor and senior psychiatrist here. Did he inject you with anything?"

"Yeah—why?"

Curtis groaned. "Uh-oh. That can't be good."

CHAPTER NINETY-EIGHT

It's been about four weeks now since I first checked into this shithole they call a hospital. I've gotten used to all the nut jobs, fruitcakes, and whackos and—if you want my opinion—I'd say the staff here is just as crazy as the patients. In fact, I think everyone here is off-the-wall loony.

I've had so many sessions with Doc Cyclops I've lost count. At least half the time he hooks me up to this IV drip he calls "Enlightenment" and I have no recollection of anything we talk about during those sessions. One thing I will say, though: I still can't look the dude in the eye, and I do mean eye—as in one eye—because his other one won't stop rolling around long enough for anyone to look at it. In fact, I don't think that sucker even works. Anyway, even though I don't remember what we talk about when they hook me up to the IV, during the regular sessions I remember everything. He's been telling me that when I'm under the drip, he goes deep inside my mind trying to bring Troyer out, but so far it hasn't worked. He thinks Troyer knows where the bartender is, and he wants me to help access Troyer from inside my head. From the way he talks, I'm actually starting to believe my migraine medicine messed up my brain and that Troyer is really just a figment of my imagination. Cyclops thinks that the reason he can't bring Troyer out of me is because I stopped taking the pills.

Aurora's come to visit a bunch of times, and I've talked to her about it, but she thinks it's impossible and that they're just trying to brainwash me. The fact is, I'm so twisted up right now I haven't got a clue.

A couple days ago, I told Aurora to go back home to Cape May for the start of the summer season. Not that I really want her to leave me here alone, but I don't think it's fair. She's got a life, too. For whatever its worth, she said she'd wait for me and check back from time to time. I told her I wouldn't forget about her, either, and that as soon as they let me out of this joint, I'd be on my way down to the Cape.

Wouldn't you know it? Dear ole Dad never has come around to see me. I knew he was just blowing smoke at my lawyer. Speaking of Levy, he actually got the whole case dismissed down in Jersey, too. I've got to say, that guy is good. Although he did tell me to be careful, because they could always reopen the case with other evidence if something new turned up.

The detectives from Manhattan also stopped coming around after the first couple weeks, when they realized that Cyclops couldn't get Troyer to come out of me. I guess they finally gave up hope of ever finding out where the bartender ended up. Too bad—I really wish I could have helped them with that shit, but I honestly haven't got a clue what happened to her after I dumped her at Gilgo Beach.

Anyway, I'm sitting here in the lounge watching TV and just chilling. Some new guy they just brought in the other day is sitting a couple chairs over. He's watching TV, but I don't think he's seeing it. He's got that thousand-yard stare going on, and drool is dripping down his chin.

Some orderly walks in through the double doors, grooving to his iPod. He takes the plugs out of his ears and comes over to me. "Hey, Sullivan, you got a visitor. Follow me." He turns around, sticks the plugs back in his ears, and swerves off.

I get up and chase after him. Halfway down the hall, I catch up and tap him on the shoulder. He turns around looking all annoyed, and takes the earplugs out again.

"What is it, Sullivan?"

"Uh, I just wanna know who's here to visit. I wasn't expecting anyone, and Aurora's gone back to the Cape."

"Hey, man, I don't know who it is. The guy just said he's family."

My heart starts pounding because I figure it has to be my dad, and I've got no clue what to say to him. In fact, I'm not even sure I want to see the prick.

When we reach the door to the visitor's room, I look through the small glass window. I can't believe my eyes, so I rub them and look again, and get this: he's still there. Fuckin' Troyer.

EPILOGUE

Seven months, four days, and ten hours is a long time to be cooped up in a place like Haverstraw Psychiatric Hospital. It's nothing short of amazing that I'm walking out of here a free man today. Aurora should be here to pick me up soon. I look out the window at a fresh blanket of snow on the ground, with still more coming down. The trees are covered, and so are the cars in the lot. I never really appreciated the calm and beauty of a winter snowstorm, but being here with nothing much to do all day has given me the time to think about that shit. Get this: I even took up reading books and writing in this journal Dr. Freud gave me. He said it would help me to keep track of stuff. I have to say, he's an okay dude, that Freud—even though it's still tough to look him in the eye. Yeah, Cyclops never gave up on me. He still calls me his pet project and says that "Enlightenment" never worked better on any other patient. He said it was touch-and-go for the first month or so, but he was finally able to break through and get deep down inside my head.

I'm pretty much cured now; I just have to stay on this medicine he prescribed. And as long as I do, I'll never hear from Troyer again. Yeah, that's right. As it turns out, Troyer was just a figment of my imagination. He never existed at all. Doc says I made him up, partly because I wanted the twin brother my parents sold when I was born, and partly because of all the other bad shit that happened to me while I was growing up. The experimental drug just triggered something inside my head and brought Troyer out. Wacky shit, if you ask me.

I also found out that I never actually had sex with Ellen at the banana tree, and I didn't strangle her, either. The Pillowcase Killer was real, and I actually witnessed him rape and murder Ellen. Believe it or not, he was some dirt-bag mountain man who lived in a shack in the woods about a mile from the camp. They caught him the year after I stopped going to Lakewood.

I recently learned that my father died of a massive heart attack a few days after they released him from the hospital. I suppose I can let myself believe that he really intended to come to see me, like Levy said, but knowing Dad, I could never imagine him showing up to visit me. Still, when I think about him, I get all teary and emotional. I just don't understand why I even give a shit about him, but I do.

On another note, a few months ago, Jamie Houston turned up alive. Turns out her throat wasn't cut nearly as deep as I thought, so she got up and walked to some house on the beach, where she recovered. Then she took off. Apparently she was very unhappy with her life and she decided to use the opportunity to disappear for a while. She finally came back and told everyone what had really happened.

Even better, they still haven't found any real evidence connecting me to the other shit that happened at Gilgo Beach either.

Anyway, I feel great. My headaches are gone, and I've got my whole life ahead of me. I'm not sure what I'm going to do, but I'm thinking that maybe I'll become a writer and tell my story.

. . .

Days before Sullivan was to be released, Jamie Houston tracked down Detective Stone. She came with only one thought in mind—revenge. Houston had been plotting for months. Time and again, she rehearsed the scene in her head, and now she was ready.

She explained to Stone that she needed closure, and she wanted an opportunity to confront Sullivan before he was set free.

Stone arranged the trip to coincide with Sullivan's release, and they drove to Haverstraw in the midst of a winter snowstorm.

Exiting the car, Houston checked her pocket one last time to confirm that the switchblade was still there. She gripped the handle, and it felt good. It was at the ready, and when Sullivan appeared in front of her, she intended to slice his pretty face to ribbons.

Her mind was clear. She wasn't crazy. She knew exactly what needed to be done. From her perspective, it was a rational thought, and she felt completely justified.

Dr. Freud met them at reception and escorted them to the visitor's lounge.

"Ms. Houston," Freud began, "I've made wonderful progress with Thomas, and while I think this is a good test for him before he is released, I am asking you to please refrain from provoking him. Can you do that for me?"

"Absolutely, Doctor. I simply want to look him in the eyes. I need closure. My psychiatrist said that the best way to overcome my fear is to confront it. I am through feeling like a victim."

"Wise advice, Ms. Houston. Just try to understand that the man you will see today has changed. Mentally, he is not the same person who attacked you. Also, keep in mind that I haven't told him you are here, so this will come as a big shock. He won't be ready."

"He may not be, but I am."

Within minutes, the door to the visitor's lounge opened, and an orderly ushered Sullivan in. He immediately recognized both Stone and Houston. Surprised and confused, he locked eyes with the young bartender. Her gaze was cold steel.

Houston slowly pulled the blade from her pocket while searching deep into his eyes. She stepped forward, still glaring. Seconds passed like minutes before she turned to Stone and asked, "Who the hell is that?"

36086653R00234

Made in the USA
Lexington, KY
06 October 2014